CW01636540

PATH OF THE SAVIOUR

SEMITA SALVATORIS

BOOK ONE OF THE GAIA TRILOGY

Published by Symbiotic Press

Paperback ISBN: 978-1-7394704-0-1
eBook ISBN: 978-1-7394704-1-8

Produced in United Kingdom.

PATH OF THE SAVIOUR

SEMITA SALVATORIS

BOOK ONE OF THE GAIA TRILOGY

D.R.ELLIS

PROLOGUE

Sanctum
Dreadnoque
Deathspire Valley

Dominating and suppressing large black mountains flanked the small band of bedraggled warriors as they crept along the mountain pass. The sun was cowering behind the thick opaque blanket of night sky, not even the moon dared shine too bright. The tips of the towering subjugating rocks either side of the small military troupe were shrouded in grey clouds full of promise for rain and misery. The ground was still wet from the previous assault by the elements and the boots of the soldiers were soaked through, their footsteps squelching in protest with each forward movement; they were voicing the unspoken grievances of the boot wearers into the dark and treacherous terrain. The news of the loss of the battle they were sent to win would not go down well with their leader, however, to *not* report the result would be just as risky when the information finally reached their master. The most forward member of their group came to a sudden halt. Those following, with their heads bowed in submission, collided into one another.

"Why've you stopped?" snarled one of the hooded members towards the back. "Keep going before the rain returns."

His protest was met with a sequence of groans of agreement.

"I don't wanna go any further into this hellhole," the male leader replied, spitting on the floor to reinforce his point.

"You think *we* do?" asked another. This time the voice was that of a woman, one of the three that made up their eight-person team. She marched forwards and smashed through the arm of the previous leader, almost knocking the fatigued and beaten soldier to the floor. The retinue continued on their way and almost immediately the originally threatening clouds began their barrage. The rain fell in stair rods, battering the already downhearted walkers. There was no cover between the mountains so they had no choice but to walk headlong into the wet abyss before them.

It wasn't much longer before one of the group collapsed to the floor in a coughing fit. His allies watched idly as a woman near the back crouched to help. The little care she could offer was unable to stop the convulsing warrior as he coughed up blood until lying still in a pool of bloodied water. The woman closed the deceased man's eyes and motioned the others to continue their journey. This wasn't the first they had lost to the damp and the cold.

The group wished to travel as fast as they could but the low morale and poor physical state of the travellers meant they could only trudge through the mountain pass. All were soaked through to their skins, armour becoming heavy and many were beginning to stumble before having to grit their teeth and pull themselves to their feet again. "I'm not going any further!" one of the fallen men for the fifth time shouted when he finally regained his feet. "Why should we always be the ones to march up and down Sanctum, going from region to region, doing *her* dirty work when she's so powerful herself? I'm done. *She* can do it herself; if she wants access to this 'other world' so much then she can damn well–" The man was stopped mid-rant by a hand round his throat. The aggressor squeezed until the indignant warrior's face became purple, then he released his grip. The release didn't signal the end of the violence, however. When the colour returned to the face of the soldier and he had finished wheezing, the attacker came again. This time he lifted the man by his arms and threw him into the mountainside. The others were trying to pull him away from his prey now, but the eyes of the aggressor were flaming with hate and malice; he easily brushed aside those trying to stop him. The boots of the man throwing his comrade around like a rag doll were thundering against the ground sending up water with each heavy step. He grabbed his quarry and bashed his head against the hard, cold rock. The target's cranium caved in like a crushed watermelon and his eyes bloodied from the impact. The deathly blow was not enough for the enraged brute who continued to smash the head of his opponent off the jagged stones until it was pulp-like in his huge hands. The lifeless body was left twitching on the floor, blood seeping from his mortal wounds mixing with the rain as it fell.

"Does anyone else have an issue with our mission?" the huge man growled to all those staring at the destruction before them. The silent reply was a resounding 'No' from those asked. The huge man wiped his bloody hands on his armour and picked off a coarse black hair that was stuck to his palm with bodily fluids.

The company arrived at their destination a short while later, the pace having somewhat quickened after the vicious assault – no one wishing to risk getting on the monstrosity's bad side. Despite being the end of their horror-fuelled journey the mood of the group didn't improve. Their terminus was Deathspire, the base of their ruler. The tower was carved from the mountain and stretched three hundred metres into the dark night sky, the top not visible from the ground in such torrid conditions, thinning to a needlepoint at its apex. A sculptured body impaled through the abdomen sat atop the mighty tower. The length of the structure was covered in sharp jagged rocks that made it impossible to climb without becoming impaled or dying a death by a thousand cuts. The three men and three women left of their force were faced with great iron doors at the entrance to the tower. The doors were inlaid with serpentine shapes and a large metallic snake head protruded from each of the doors. Water slowly dripped from the exposed fangs of the snakes looking venom-like from the beasts' mouths as if to warn of the dangers of entering. Nevertheless, they hadn't come this far to turn back now and so they used their combined strength to push one of the giant doors open and begin their ascent. The door squealed and moaned as a final warning to those about to enter, but the warriors paid it no mind. They were faced with a giant spiral staircase lined with torches in the wall; it was the final obstacle before coming face to face with their master. Their legs were already weary from the long walk and so the staircase was a huge ask, however, no one complained in fear of what the brute in their company may do. Some steps were cracked despite the building not being very old and many torches had extinguished leaving large parts of the climb in complete darkness. The tower had many different levels, each with even more locked doors; a shriek emanating from behind each one. The scream was sometimes that of a woman, high-pitched and shrill and other times a man, low and torturous. Different sounds and pleas but always a scream. They were crawling rather than walking by the time they reached the peak of the building and their whole bodies ached from head to toe. The six of them were unaware of what they were about to face, none had been permitted to see the leader of their faction before; normally messages were to be passed on to war chiefs. The brute led the way with the others following close behind. He led them through the first open door they had come across in the tower, the brightest place they had seen since entering the cursed region of Dreadnoque. The light reflected from the room's many torches and made the group's eyes squint as they entered. When they finally adjusted to the brightness they saw a figure sitting cross-legged on the floor in the centre of the room. The door slammed behind them then they heard the bolt slide across, sealing them in. One of the women turned to look but there was no one there. The door had been locked from the outside. When she turned again to face the figure, she saw that it had risen to a standing position. A sudden violent gust of wind plunged the room into absolute darkness. Shivering, she pulled her clothing tight to her body as she realised the warmth of the room fled with the light. The drenched attire only served to increase the shivering, however, and the drips from her nose marked the beginnings of a likely terminal chill. A voice came from the darkness: demonic, feminine, full of hate and dripping with a thirst for power.

"You've failed in your mission again." The statement echoed around the stone room.

One of the men began to reply with, "They have it too well-guarded, there's no–"

"SILENCE!" came the order from the shadow. "I've lost patience with your futile attempts." Then the door could be heard unlocking again before suddenly crashing open.

"Screamers!" cried one of the women as she went to draw her weapon. The action to protect herself was not quick enough, however, as the weary woman was crashed to the floor under the force of her charging opponent. Her throat was ripped out with blade-like claws and her final shriek filled the chamber. The others leapt into action. They managed to draw their weapons despite their fear and hacked at the assaulting forces. When they felled one of the evil creatures it screamed as it died. They couldn't see the number of their foe through the darkness but for every one they killed it seemed to be replaced by two more screeching and howling enemies. The brute was leading the defence, his great two-handed claymore sword sweeping backwards and forwards, wiping out the approaching evil. He was calling to his comrades, they replied how their defence was progressing but after a short time they were not responding to his calls and screamers were closing in from all angles. The brute's claymore was ripped from his hands and he felt his arm get cut by one of the blades from the dark. He fell to his knees but still managed to break the neck of another opponent that charged him. The cuts were becoming more frequent now as the screamers found gaps in his armour and buried him under the sheer volume of their numbers. He was not going to give in that easily. He exploded outwards and sent the smaller enemies flying away from him. He used the moment's respite to try to find his claymore but was unable to locate it in the dark. Nevertheless, he did find a corpse of one of the screamers. Fumbling in the blackness he situated the hand tipped with the sharp blade-like claw at the end and tried to rip it from the beast's arm. There was a crack as the wrist bone snapped off under the brute's superhuman strength. Wielding the fiendish hand, he used the blade to cut his way through a further eight approaching screamers desperate for his blood. The carnage was immense and the brute was beginning to tire and become overwhelmed when the voice returned.

"Stop," he thought he heard it whisper, the soft voice somehow cutting through the blood-curdling cries of the beasts. Suddenly the screamers that had pinned him down and were moments ago trying to kill him jumped up and retreated into the night. The light returned to the room and the figure with the demonic voice was above him. "You're still useful," she said with a slight reptilian hiss. "What's your name?"

The brute struggled to his feet and looked upon his master for the first time. A robe draped her body to hide her features. "Gregorius," he snarled, unimpressed she had tried to kill him. He wasn't stupid enough to try to attack, though; he knew even he was no match for her.

"Well Gregorius, it's time you returned to the war, I think."

He could see a smile under the hood. A killer smile full of pointy snake-like teeth.

"Take these," she motioned to the remaining screamers whom he had not killed. "They won't try to hurt you now. Go cause some pain to the rebels."

Rather reluctantly, Gregorius took the screamers and left the room to undertake his mission. He would have been killed there and then if he refused.

When the brute left, the robed figure signalled her war chiefs to reveal themselves from the shadows. Out of the wings emerged a huge man that would have made the large Gregorius look small. His master had previously tried to bind him to a bear, enabling him to transform between the two, but the magic failed leaving him extremely hairy arms and brute strength. The brown-skinned man wore a white turban covered in bloodstains and a dirty vest which left his hairy arms exposed. The man wielded a long cleaver the size of a sword. Beside him scuttled a small woman with a shaved head. She was slight of build and walked slightly bent over. Despite the difference in appearance and size, the woman was no less deadly, as many had found out to their peril.

"Butcher. Amazon. Thanks for coming," the cloaked female said as means of introduction.

The small woman with the shaved head bowed down and said, "It's an honour to be in your presence, master."

"Rise, Amazon, I think of you more as a friend than a subject." Again, her pointy-toothed smile protruded from her hood. "I've invited you both here today in the hope I can finally open up a rift between our world and theirs for you to start the retrieval of the artefacts."

Butcher scoffed, "Another one of these… The only way to reach the other world is through Magellan Castle. You know that, why waste your time?"

"Because you can't get access to the castle! Every time you try you *fail*." Her hood slipped from her head through her anger and revealed her dark green eyes and long black hair. Her skin was becoming scaly, and the beginnings of a tattoo could be seen on her neck of a snake which coiled round her back and abdomen. She used to be beautiful but magic and power had led her down a path that brought her to her looks now. She calmed herself and continued: "I'll use Gaia to create the portal. I won't be able to hold it open for long so you two must be ready to enter with no questions asked. I'm sending these with you."

Fifty screamers hobbled into the room and sat breathing heavily, awaiting command.

"Your primary objective is retrieval of the artefacts, however, there are those loyal to Tombstone out there, they just don't know it yet. Find them and convince them of their allegiance."

Butcher cracked his fingers together and smiled alongside Amazon at the violence associated with their brand of convincing.

"Butcher is to take test subjects; I want to see if I can create the same bestial humanoids on their world as I've managed here. When you have them ready, I'll know, then I'll attempt the transformation across worlds. Keep record of my progress."

Butcher grunted in agreement, he never was one for data collection, more debt collection.

"Finally, Amazon, when you've convinced some of the pathetic vermin to join our cause ensure they start spreading the word of my coming. I want them to have an army of their own when I get there."

Once convinced her war chiefs understood their mission, she pulled out what appeared to be a glowing rock from her robe and closed her eyes, beginning to mutter an incantation. The rock glowed and her eyes shot open. They were no longer green but completely black.

A searing bright light made Butcher and Amazon shield their faces whilst the screamers lived up to their name. Butcher braved a look at great risk to his vision. "Unbelievable," he growled in his deep, gruff voice. The portal was open.

"Quick! You know your mission," demanded the sorceress, her voice higher pitched and more pained than normal.

Without further instruction, Amazon leapt through the portal and Butcher followed with the screamers in tow. The last screamer didn't make it before the vortex closed, the body having been separated from the legs and the beast's disjointed parts dropped to the ground with a thud.

The conjuror collapsed in an exhausted pile on the floor. She would be unable to open it for so long again, but if her plan was executed correctly, she wouldn't have to. Whilst looking at the legs of the unlucky screamer beside her, a grin played across her exhausted face, then the smile became a small chuckle before erupting into a full murderous laugh. "I've done it! The downfall of Earth begins today."

CHAPTER 1

Earth
England
East Anglia

George awoke with a thumping headache worsened by the tangy sweet smell of a dragon's blood incense stick filling his room. An invasive ray of morning sunlight penetrating through his dragon design curtains fell across his left eye drilling deep into his skull. George gave the curtain a sharp tug to gain some respite from the light, but the damage was already done. Awake and remembering the night before, he stumbled from bed and pulled on some maroon-coloured jeans with a small rip in the left knee. The chosen t-shirt for the day was black with the words 'Legend since 1995' printed in white. The headache was undoubtedly due to the dangerously low drinks' prices at the local Wetherspoons, however, the toxins emitted from the smoking incense stick were sure to worsen the ache. George's mum loved to light the sticks each morning despite being regularly reminded that they not only further aggravated his headaches but also actively degraded her son's respiratory system. The last memory from the night before was finishing a fifth tequila shot celebrating the start of the bank holiday weekend. He remembered preaching to his best mate, Jacob, that tequila was like water after going on holiday to Mexico for the second time. Still slightly dazed, George proceeded with the rest of the morning's routine: showering, cleaning his teeth and finishing off two crumpets covered with a generous layer of chocolate spread. Once finished, George had one last check in the mirror to ensure he was ready for the day. His six foot frame and full head of fiery ginger hair looked back at him pitifully. Same as every morning – no muscle had grown overnight which was a daily let-down. George ambled downstairs and turned the radio on to listen to the morning news. The same boring drivel as every other day spilled from the monotonous voice reporting trouble in some far away country and the government's mishaps and mistakes. The drought in Malaysia was in its eighteenth month, livestock was either dead or dying and watercourses had dried up. Experts were claiming Earth had reached 'tipping point' at which the planet could no longer recover from its climate crisis. The only other standout headline was that a sword had been stolen from the History of the Caribbean Exhibition at some museum in London. It was an irrelevant piece of information for George to know but he still took note in case he had to head to London any time soon and needed to know there was a deranged psycho on the streets wielding a sword.

Better check the mail. There were three letters and a parcel through the large gold-lined letterbox in the oak door. The first, a standard letter from Barclays Bank informing about the latest Barclaycard deals; the next two were for George's parents and the parcel was a unique-looking package that didn't brand any name on the front. The absence of name was more than made up for by the weight. He almost dropped it to begin with, implying it was likely another juicer to replace the most frequently broken appliance in the house. The letter from the bank was filed away and the other two left for the boy's parents to deal with, along with the parcel.

What's the time? 8.46 am. No, not again. For the third time in a week George was leaving late for football practise; *Presley's going to kill me.* A sudden rush ensued as George struggled to slip on his shoes that were still tied in a double knot from their previous use. His father was always telling him to untie them and place them back on the shoe rack neatly, however, he seldom bothered. George had just locked the door and begun his short walk to the training pitch when he realised he had forgotten his boots. Cursing under his breath, he ran home and fumbled with the keys to the back door, dropping them several times in his haste before eventually opening the house. Dashing through the narrow confines of the small house, George almost broke his neck as the cat drifted round the corner at the exact same time and became entangled in his feet. Nevertheless, he only stumbled and quickly took the stairs to his room two at a time, smashing through his door he had left ajar for the cat to sunbathe on his bed. He grabbed his boot bag and spun ballerina-like back out of the room and down the stairs. Upon entering the kitchen, he collided with a ball of fluff returning to its seat in the lounge; George tripped again but caught himself on the work surface. Finally, happy he had all he required, he exited his house, locked the door and tried the handle to make sure it was impenetrable. Despite the cat almost killing him twice in the last minute he would hate to return to find they have a local pet thief in the area. No longer time to walk, George sprinted as fast as he could across the few housing blocks to reach his training area. There were some workers on one of the streets he crossed who didn't pass up the opportunity this time to shout 'Run, fat boy, run!' in that mean bantering way men enjoy so much. He wouldn't have had time to formulate a suitable response anyway, their words were nothing compared to what Presley would do to him if he was any later to practise. By the time he reached the training ground George was dripping with sweat and proceedings were already underway.

"Oh Mr Keen, how good of you to join us!" boomed Presley. The coach was middle-aged with a shaved head and wrinkles covering his forehead. He stood at around six foot six and had biceps like two great anacondas hanging from his shoulders. "If only you were as keen as your name suggests. Get changed into your kit and go over to Jacob, he'll fill you in with the training you've missed so far."

George hated the way Presley used his second name in a mocking fashion but let it slide as coming to blows with the mountain of a man had never merited any success in the past. Nonetheless, there was nothing he hated more than his own stupidity. *I've forgotten my kit*, he realised. Turning a similar shade to his jeans, he dragged his feet to Presley to admit his error. The big, bald leviathan-like man was smirking at him already; he always seemed to anticipate George's mistakes before he even made them.

"You'll find some pink shorts in the kit bag and a top you can wear in there as well." There was malice in the way he said it, ensuring it was loud enough so his friends heard and laughed at his misfortune. There was pink on the top of the bag, so George didn't have to rummage around to find the shorts. He removed his jeans to put on the kit just as a van drove past. A wolf whistle came from the vehicle and, as George looked up, he turned the colour of the shorts he was pulling on. Once the shorts were on he had to find a top to wear; unfortunately there wasn't a top on the surface of the bag where the shorts had been so he had to hold his nose and rummage around for a shirt to wear. Despite pinching his nose, the smell of stale sweat was overwhelming and some of the shorts he was moving to look for the shirt were even sticky. *Why so many shorts?* wondered George. It wasn't until he got to the bottom of the bag and pulled out a solitary white shirt that he realised the bag was rigged to be a maze of smelly foul shorts before reaching a single shirt. As if that wasn't bad enough, the only shirt available was defaced with the badge of Tottenham Hotspur. George shook his head in disbelief and turned to protest to Presley, but he would clearly have not received any sympathy. Whilst George was busy, Presley had gathered everyone around to watch his reaction upon pulling the Spurs shirt from the bag. There was a gale of laughter and George himself couldn't help but chuckle at the plan. Presley gave him a nod of approval at the way he took the prank, acknowledging that a year or so ago the whole situation would have turned ugly as George would have stomped off or refused to join in. George slipped on the shirt and instantly felt dirtier for it. Presley told everyone what the next training drill was, and they all dispersed in their groups to practise it. As George jogged past Presley, the coach gave him a slap on the back and bellowed, "Good man!"

The training drill was a passing one, they had to pass the ball to their partner with their left foot then their right foot alternatively to practise using both feet; it was one of the more boring drills, but still sometimes posed a problem for those who were heavily single-footed. George's partner was his best mate Jacob, and he wasted no time in bringing up the night before.

"How's the head?" joked Jacob. "I'm feeling a bit on the rough side, but I guess your sixty percent Mexican blood can handle it a little better than me?"

Laughing, George replied, "Maybe I overestimated just how much a couple of trips to Mexico can boost one's ability to drink tequila, granted."

Jacob was of similar height to George at five foot ten inches, but differed in hair colour which was black and had a more suitable amount of muscle for a twenty-one-year-old. After a few training exercises and laps around the pitch everyone was ready for a game with the exception of Andy who inevitably pulled a muscle during the warm-up and had to sit out like the past six weeks. Presley sorted the teams and George was happy to discover he was team blue along with Jacob and undoubtedly the best of the bunch, Lincoln, an academy player for the local professional team.

The game kicked off fast with the red team immediately looking dangerous when a high ball over the top found their small pacey striker – it looked a certain goal – stopped only by a brilliant bit of covering from Lincoln who instantly set the blue team back on the counter. Jacob was in possession when a hefty challenge brought him to the ground; shooting straight back to his feet he was immediately in his opponent's face screaming obscenities and shoving him backwards.

George rushed to his friend and tried to pull him away but the opposition player pushed him too. George fell to the floor and stayed there. "Relax, mate, I don't want to fight."

"That doesn't surprise me," the opponent bullied.

Jacob stepped back between them but Presley reached the scuffle before the situation escalated any further and pushed the two boys apart, denying the potential scrap. Both players involved in the incident escaped with a yellow card before Presley turned to George with a sigh and a shake of the head. "Get to your feet!" he ordered.

George was designated free kick-taker and was well known for his prowess from set pieces. It took a lot of bottle to stand over a dead ball whilst the rest of the players and onlookers watched in anticipation, yet George was always keen to try.

"You're blocking my view… Left... left..!" screamed the opposition goalkeeper, arranging his wall in front of him. George took a short run up and pinged the ball into the six-yard box, it swerved in the air and looked to be going over every head when a towering header at the back post put the ball back in the mixer. A short goalmouth scramble ensued as the ball bounced up, down, left and right, legs swinging at it from all angles. Finally the ball was cleared, however, only as far as Lincoln who, with a series of stepovers, went around two players. A hard shove from behind that would have knocked anyone off the ball only served to drive Lincoln on harder and faster. Chopping and changing, Lincoln then went past another two of team red's helpless players and with a final skill of his he flicked the ball over the head of one last player before connecting sweetly on his left foot for a volley that rocketed straight into the top corner. The keeper dived but didn't stand a chance. When he looked up there were the downhearted faces of his team and a topless Lincoln being chased by several boys in blue looking possessed with love and awe. Jacob made a special effort to confront the guy who fouled him earlier and gloated tastelessly until Presley pulled him aside and gave him some stern words. The game didn't offer much after that with both teams being well matched, the only real talking point being a possible penalty for the red team in the dying minutes. Nonetheless, George felt that his last-ditch attempt tackle from behind was perfectly well timed; had the striker not been in the way there would have been no contact and the ball would be cleared fairly. Presley blew the whistle to signal the end of the match and the game ended one nil to George's side. Before letting everyone go, the trainer called them over and gave his observations on what he had seen.

"Great work today, gents. I love to see a bit of fire in your bellies but sometimes we need to turn that furnace down a bit, lads, hey?" he directed his final words at Jacob and the player he almost tussled with. "Lincoln, you were superb as always, but overall a great effort from the lot of you. Mr Keen, let's just focus on arriving on time, then we can work on your poor footwork… Dismissed!"

After saying goodbye to everyone and worshipping the football god, Lincoln, George and Jacob decided that with such nice weather it was never too early to start drinking. The sun had been beating down during the entire match and the temperature must have been around twenty-five degrees Celsius. "Perfect pint drinking weather," declared Jacob on the walk to the pub. "You know, Presley said he was going to skin you alive and use your hide to create a new bag for the footballs," he chuckled.

George turned white, a threat like that would normally be null and void. No one could possibly do that to another human, however, with Presley he wasn't so sure it *was* a joke.

"You know, he's always had it out for me since day one," moaned George. Day one was a very long time ago as Presley had been coaching George since the little ginger child first learnt about the beautiful game. George began reminiscing. "Remember that time I scored my first goal and was beside myself? I was only a kid, buzzing off my nut and that bald oaf put me down with his comments that if there was a goalkeeper it never would have beaten him."

Remembering the moment, Jacob was smiling and nodding to himself and then burst out laughing again as he could recall another episode of bullying from Presley. "Hey, remember when you hadn't scored all season and Presley told you that if you screwed up again he'd put you on the goal line and let everyone kick a ball at you?" questioned Jacob.

"I still wake with a pain each morning." George replied while grimacing and rubbing his backside. "I still don't see how it's fair to punish a centre back for not scoring. I stopped loads going in at our end that season." He was not finding the memory half as funny as Jacob clearly had. Thinking back had reopened a can of worms for George; he turned on Jacob suddenly. "You didn't *have* to finish off my shot in the last game that year. It had plenty of power on it already and was destined for the top corner. All you did when you deflected it into the other corner was earn me that punishment."

Jacob merely laughed again and, without showing even a morsel of guilt, admitted that in stealing that goal Presley gave him fifty pounds of his own money for ensuring George's punishment. Jacob didn't expect George to react so aggressively as the memory must have taken place around ten years ago, but, in seeing his best mate was clearly not amused he decreed, "I'll buy the drinks today, mate, as an apology. I still stand by my theory that you're his favourite, though. He's only trying to push you, wanting the best for his star player." George accepted the apology pints but in no way accepted he was Presley's star player.

"Oh no, it's One-eye Pete," noticed Jacob. One-eye Pete was the park ranger who passed out drunk most days on a bench in the park. He picked up the nickname by the way that, whenever he shouted at passers-by, he always left one eye closed whilst the others pupil grew and shrank with increasing vigour.

"If we're quiet we might be able to sneak past him," suggested George. They crept as slowly and silently as possible, but as they drew level with the drunk one of his eyes shot open and he began cursing and yelling at the two of them. They sprinted past to avoid the confrontation and let Pete's insults fade into the distance. Once safely out of range of the taunts they slowed back to a walk.

The talking and short run had made the journey to the pub seem like nothing, without even realising they had passed through the woodland and crossed the farmer's field, coming out opposite their destination. George and Jacob looked to each other and mirrored one another's cheesy grin. "Nothing brings happiness like the sight of the Purple Giant," allowed Jacob.

"No, especially when *you're* buying the drinks!" George retorted. They entered their regular brewhouse together and were met with the overwhelming smell of battered fish and chips. The usual cronies were in their normal seats, most of them almost as old as the building itself. When George and his friend reached the bar, they were not surprised that Betty asked them both for ID.

"I'm still born in the year I was born in last night, Betty," joked George.

"Yeah, and the same as it was the day before and the day before that and, oh, hang on, every day before for the last three years since we've been old enough to drink," added Jacob cheekily. They knew they had been coming here for the odd drink long before they were legally old enough. George glanced back over to the table of elderly men. *Thanks, Jerry*, George thought to himself.

Betty returned their IDs and gave her usual response: "'Think twenty-five', that's the law; until you two baby-faced boys grow up some more and get some hair on your chins, I'll be checking your age. Now, what can I get you, anyway?" she cackled.

"Two Peronis, please," requested Jacob. "Oh wait, you don't want a shot of tequila to refresh yourself do you, George?" The sign language he received was a clear 'No'. Again, he wasn't surprised to see that Betty already had the Peroni ready – they had been ordering the same for the last three years after all. Jacob paid, took the drinks and turned to find George had disappeared. *Must've gone outside,* he supposed. He began walking to the door leading to the beer garden and had to put on a quick sprint to acknowledge Jerry holding it open for him. Jacob saw his mate instantly in the crowded beer garden, the bright red hair a dead giveaway. As he placed the drinks down, he informed George that he saw Jerry leaving.

"Probably returning to his wife for lunch," suggested George.

"Why doesn't he stay here?" inquired Jacob. "We all know Betty always has a warm sausage roll for him behind the bar should he ever want one." Jacob had menace in his eyes.

George knew what Jacob was implying for it had been a long-term rumour in the Purple Giant that Betty and Jerry were something of an item. It was weird for George to think of the two pensioners in that way; mind you, neither of them had seemed to age in all the years he had been coming to the pub. That wasn't to say that they looked young, though, more that they were always old and wrinkled. It wouldn't surprise anyone if the two geriatrics had fallen in love over time, they were essentially part of the furniture of the place; there wasn't a time that George could recall coming in when at least one of them wasn't there. Jerry was always flirting with her over the counter, she had always given him what he loved most – alcohol – and he had always returned the favour with a steady flow of money for, what must have been in George's reckoning, at least a century.

"They were old when our parents used to come in here drinking, how old do you reckon they are now?" asked George, realising that his previous guess of over a hundred couldn't be correct.

"Well, over one hundred, I'd say," Jacob replied as if he had been reading George's mind all along. The duo laughed together as they so often did and talked another half an hour of football, girls and a little more of Betty and Jerry's fabled romance.

Jacob checked his watch before leaping up from the sticky wooden bench they were sitting on. "I need to leave to get ready to meet Annabel for lunch. You sure you don't want to come?" He downed the rest of his pint and George did the same.

"Nah, not today. Money's a little tight. Thanks for the drink."

"We're even," Jacob said as they embraced with a quick brotherly hug and said their farewells.

When George got to the door of his home, he found it was unlocked which meant that his parents were back from the gym.

Immediately after he entered the house and slipped off his shoes (forgetting to undo his laces again), they were on him with questions. The immediate greeting was focused on training and whether their son had played a key role in the game. Then talk turned to why the washing-up had not been done and the conversation was growing heated when George's dad changed the subject with the age-old question, "Who's putting the kettle on?" Once the tea was made, the family retired to the garden to enjoy the sunshine and drink their beverage. After relaxing in the beer garden and now sitting in his own garden, George felt his skin beginning to burn. *Damned ginger gene*, he said to himself. He blamed his dad for his quick-to-burn skin, an obvious target as the curly ginger hair on his father's head was clearly the reason for his own. His dad was taking the necessary precautions, however, and was rubbing sun cream into his skin as soon as he sat down, an action George should really do as often as his dad. His mum, on the other hand, was blessed with sun-kissed olive skin, a colour she had acquired after many overseas business trips in her working life. Unlike her husband she didn't bother with the lotion and George believed this was where he got his laid-back approach in regard to the sunblock.

"Look how long the grass has got," George's dad said to no one in particular.

"You only cut it yesterday, Bryan," pointed out George's mum.

"It needs cutting every day in the midsummer, Belinda," argued Bryan, who quickly got irritated about small details such as the length of the grass.

"Hello neighbour!" exclaimed Dave suddenly.

George looked to his mother and she gave him a telling glance back that said 'Here we go'.

"Grass is getting long," Dave noted to Bryan.

"I know, my garden looks like a jungle," replied Bryan. "You cut yours this morning, I see."

"Needs a mow every day in midsummer," Dave said.

George looked to his mother and she shook her head, anticipating what her son was planning.

"Oh no you don't, you can't leave me with them."

Before his mother had finished protesting, George had gotten up with his cup of tea and made his excuse to leave. She stared after him and, when George was safely back in the house, he turned to look at his poor mother stuck out there with the two of them. She wasn't amused.

While walking towards his bedroom to play some computer games, George's eyes fell onto the unnamed parcel from earlier; his parents had opened the others but left that one, which was strange as they always opened all the mail. The uniqueness of the parcel was predominantly due to the jet-black box with a golden border surrounding the edges. In the centre where the name and address should rightfully be, there was a multicoloured logo. It depicted a green tribal headdress above a purple torso flanked one side by a red sword and the other side by an orange pistol. Upon closer inspection the golden border turned out to be the thread that sewed the parcel together. George raced upstairs to get the tweezers from the bathroom and a pin from his mother's sewing set, then got to work unpicking the thread. Carefully, George unpicked the golden border and when the last of the thread was removed, the lid slid off and a short letter along with three other items fell to the floor, the heaviest of which fell on George's toe. With a squeal of pain he thumped the wall next to him that only served to send a fresh shoot of pain up his left hand. Ignoring the pain and more intrigued than ever, he picked up the objects before the cat tried to eat them. One was a sort of golden medallion or coin engraved with a skull, the second a horseshoe (the culprit for landing on his toe) and the third a pointed blade, presumably from the end of a knife. Perplexed beyond belief, George proceeded to read the letter:

'To Mr George Keen,

You have been contacted by Minotaur and specially selected to take part in a non-governmental expedition. Whilst you are reading, forces you do not yet understand are threatening the very world we live in. Enclosed within you will find three objects, a coin from one of Captain Polyphemus' treasure troves, a horseshoe from one of Johnnie Lang's horses and the tip of one of the warrior queen Kalysta's spears. Bring these items to 54 Langley Road at 10 am on the 26th August if you choose to accept.

P.S. Failure to attend will signify a lack of compliance to co-operate in which a team will be sent to wipe your memory and dispose of any evidence of this letter.

Regards, the Minotaur Human Resources Team'

That's two days' time, he thought to himself, bank holiday Monday. Shaking partly from fear and partly from excitement, George took the letter and the obscure items to his room and hid them in his drawer. Next on the agenda he decided to find his laptop to try and research any sign of who the mysterious organisation could be or who belonged to the names within the letter. Unfortunately, though, when George went to the location he always left the laptop, just next to the sofa downstairs, it was missing. *Great*, he thought. George knew that if it wasn't there then his father must have used it and thus it could be anywhere. There was only one thing for it – to look for it could take forever and yield no result – he would have to go and ask where it was, a task that seemed so simple and easy, however, he knew it wouldn't be. The situation was dire – give up researching the contents of the parcel for the time being or return to the garden and, in doing so, return to the chat with his father, and Dave who, at this point, would doubtlessly be in their element.

Belinda had a smile a mile wide when she saw her son return to the garden; she knew he wouldn't have done so unless he absolutely had to and that made it all the sweeter for her.

George gave his mother a look that said 'Shut up', again using their silent facial expressions to hold a hidden conversation. Watching his father and Dave talk made him realise what real love looked like; even if Jerry was enjoying Betty as much as the drinks she served, it would still be nothing compared to the passion George could see between the two neighbours still talking over the fence. The topic had moved onto football.

"Bryan, Messi's stats speak for themselves, your point is invalid," argued Dave.

"I've told you once and I'll tell you again: Messi has never captained West Ham to a win over Spuds and, for that, Noble will always be the better player." Bryan laughed as he said it.

"The team I support is Spurs, not Spuds, and you're deluded," Dave joked back over the fence. "Next you'll be bringing up the nineteen sixty-six World Cup again," he finished.

George couldn't help but chuckle out loud which got his father's attention. "Tell him, son, Messi or Noble?"

"Noble. Without a doubt. We *did* win that World Cup, Dave." George loved joining in with the banter as much as he pretended he didn't with his mother. "Where's the laptop, Dad?"

"That's my boy." Bryan loved how much he could wind up his neighbour. "I left it by my bed, mate."

George was about to leave when Dave shouted after him, "Take some wipes with you, lad, God knows what he was doing with it in his bed." All the men laughed and Belinda tutted loudly before telling Dave off for his crudeness. George left the garden for the second time and returned upstairs to search his parents' bedroom. It didn't take long to find the laptop when he knew where to look, and it was still open on the page his father had been looking at. George guessed that he must have been up all night looking at holidays on the Internet because the charge on the device was low and several holiday booking sites were open in different tabs. Once he found the cable to charge the laptop and plugged it all in, he was ready to start his research. George began by typing into the search bar 'Minotaur'. After what seemed like an eternity the result was a confusing one; there was no mention of an organisation by that name, only a catalogue of information on ancient Greeks and a ferocious-looking beast. Thinking this was strange, he typed each of the three names featured on the letter into the search bar; however, every investigation came up with the same disappointing conclusion. No one had ever existed that fit their description, with the exception of Johnny Lang, a cattle driver attributed to discovering 'Lost Horse Mine'. Something told him that this wasn't the man referenced in the letter. At a loss of what to do next, George phoned Jacob and arranged to meet at the local coffee shop the next day. The call was short and sweet because Jacob was with Annabel at the time; they had always been friends, but Jacob had recently been trying to up the ante with the girl. The rest of the day faded away as the sun set and George settled down with his parents to watch the latest box set on the TV. He found the fantasy worlds experienced through media far more interesting than the one he lived on and often opted to indulge and explore them rather than go out and experience his own.

CHAPTER 2

The next day George woke up in his own time and got ready to go and meet Jacob in town for coffee. He wore the same clothes in which he went to football training the day before, with the exception of fresh pants and socks. George told his parents he was heading out and Bryan made the usual joke about moths escaping George's wallet when he packed his bag. The day was once again a scorcher and this time George remembered to lotion up before facing the powerful rays. He donned his sunglasses, untied his laces on his shoes so he could fit them on his feet after just slipping them off the day before, and then retied them once they were comfortable. His bag over one shoulder, George set off into the world to begin his walk to the coffee shop. The walk took him past the same workers that had heckled him the day before, so he decided to get his own back and mocked them for having to work across the bank holiday weekend.

"Shame you guys have to work on a day like this, isn't it?" George sniggered. "A bank holiday at that." Once George felt the workers were suitably riled up, he left them arguing amongst themselves about whose fault it was they were behind schedule and having to work on a national holiday. The walk to town also led George through the woodland he crossed with Jacob the day before, the shade in amongst the trees was a welcome relief from the hot sun, however, after a while he found himself wishing for the sun's warmth on his face again. Emerging from the woodland, he was hit with a blast of warmth and blinding light. Within minutes he felt his skin starting to burn despite applying the lotion. This is where George's path diverted from the one he took the day before to the Purple Giant; instead of going across the farmer's field he made a sharp right and followed a dusty trail into the town. Halfway down he had to stand on the grass verge to let a large cattle float pass on its way to the farm. As it passed George felt a gust of wind that cooled him slightly before he was quickly back in the sun's warm embrace again. The lorry was the only traffic he encountered on that road and before long he came upon a busier road that led to the heart of town. George was about to begin the final descent to the shops when a horn made him jump. A convertible BMW swerved to a halt next to him and Jacob's beaming smile invited him into the passenger seat.

"What're you walking for?" asked Jacob who was looking the epitome of cool in his reflective shades, gold necklace and designer watch.

"It's a nice day," began George, "there's no point polluting the planet when you can walk on a day like this."

Jacob guffawed, "You sound like Annabel, 'Ooo, you should drive electric. Ooo, it's not as bad for the planet'. Besides, there's no point driving in the heap of metal *you* do, I suppose, but when you have a stallion like this, any time is suitable for a ride."

Once George was seated and had his seatbelt on, Jacob wasted no time in accelerating off like a Formula One driver. He pulled out in front of an unsuspecting Ford Focus but accelerated so fast that it didn't cause an accident. The speed limit was thirty on the road but that didn't stop Jacob from going sixty. When they got into the town centre a matter of minutes later, he slowed right up and cranked the music up louder: 'I'm in love with the shape of you' the radio blared. Jacob made sure he honked his horn every time he drove past a female that tickled his fancy, which was all too often for George's liking. Despite it going against all that George thought was chivalrous, the girls seemed to like it and often waved to Jacob as he passed. They reached the car park and Jacob ensured he had two spaces free either side of his car so his 'baby' would be safe from scratches. When the car was turned off the radio was killed as the power left the vehicle; the newsman was cut off midway through explaining a landslide that had shaken Nepal. The walk to the coffee shop took less than a minute but in that time they managed to pass two charity shops and three other coffee shops. The town was full of people as it was a bank holiday weekend so, despite the stiff competition, all the shops were busy and, unsurprisingly, there was a large queue at the one they had chosen to visit. There was a table of screaming kids on the left as they entered and, after a quick glance around, it was evident that the only free table was right next to them.

George wanted to buy the coffees as Jacob bought the beers the day before, however, Jacob reminded his friend that he only did that as recompense for the part he played in getting George punished years ago. He told George to go and sit down and let him get these as well. George gave in after Jacob refused to let up and took a seat next to the unruly kids. He quickly glanced across to see what the parents were doing but it was just a mother who had her head in her phone oblivious to the chaos around her. George was on the verge of saying something when a little old lady seated on the table the other side beat him to it.

"Stop that!" she yelled. "In my day you'd have been smacked for behaviour like that."

The kids immediately sat down and were quiet.

That's all it takes, thought George. If only the mother was as capable as that old lady. It didn't take long before the kids became restless again and the racket built up to its previous level. The old lady moaned at the mother and got up and left – the mother either didn't hear her or was too disrespectful to answer, the latter George assumed. Jacob arrived with the coffees just as George was engrossed in watching the youngest child's battle to free a bogey from his nose.

"He's been digging for gold for a whole minute now," observed George. "Give him a couple more seconds and he'll get a slot on the Discovery channel."

Jacob chuckled and handed his friend his drink. Very soon they began to discuss yesterday's football match, most notably George's last-ditch attempt tackle which Jacob didn't seem to agree was as fair as George stated. Then the discussion moved on to Jacob's progress in asking out his lifelong crush, Annabel. It quickly became apparent it was a sore point though, concluding rapidly that, unsurprisingly, Jacob had bottled it again and Annabel was still blissfully unaware of his affections. George was desperate to tell Jacob all about the parcel he had received but was afraid that he would get in trouble for telling anyone and so he chose to leave the matter out of the conversation altogether. The decision was a difficult one but the walk into town had given him time to clear his head and get some fresh air. With the time and space he had, George concluded that he couldn't trust Jacob to not post the secret meeting location on social media. The chat died down for several minutes as George began thinking about what the next day had in store for him. Breaking from his thoughts he realised Jacob was just as quiet. *Something isn't right,* he supposed, *it's been a full five minutes and Jacob hasn't even attempted a bad joke.*

"Everything alright, mate? You don't seem yourself," inquired George.

Jacob snapped out of the trance he seemed to have fallen into and replied, "Err… Yeah, fine, mate. I was just thinking, that's all."

"About Annabel?" George fired back in a joking fashion.

Jacob gave his mate's arm a hefty thump that would undoubtedly leave a bruise in the morning. "No, something else," he murmured as he seemed to fall back into deep thought again.

George took that as a sign to not probe any further and the table returned to silence once again. Accepting that Jacob wasn't really in a talkative mood, George returned his gaze to the kids on the table next door. The boy had stopped picking his nose which he assumed meant he had found the inheritance he was looking for. Having said that, it was now the boy's sister who appeared to be joining the gold rush in the chair next to him. George looked down at his coffee and suddenly didn't feel as thirsty as before.

"Do you think we're alone in this world?" Jacob posed the question out of the blue.

"Mate, I'm telling you, just ask her out and she'll say 'Yes'. You aren't destined to be alone." From Jacob's facial expression, George realised that he completely misjudged the direction of the question.

"Christ's sake, George!" Jacob lashed out, "I'm not talking about Annabel. Stop bringing her into it. I mean, do you think there're forces out there we don't understand? Something more than just us?"

George was completely caught off-guard, he wasn't used to Jacob caring about another human let alone potential alien life. "Well, not really," he began, then something about the way Jacob posed the question troubled him. *Forces we don't understand*, George realised. He looked Jacob in the eyes. After a lifetime of friendship Jacob was like a brother and he could tell when he was hiding something. *Surely not, could he?* George thought about what he said next very carefully. "What've you been reading?"

"I don't read. You know that. I'm not like you with your head in a different fantasy novel each week."

George nodded in agreement. "Yeah, so why the sudden open view of 'forces we don't understand'?" He made the question a mockery.

"Just trying to make conversation, aren't I? Anything to stop you talking about me and Annabel all the time," Jacob said defensively.

George was just formulating a response when Jacob broke in again, angrier still.

"You make everything a joke. Sometimes when I want to have a serious conversation you can't have that with me." Jacob then scraped his chair out from the table and left without another word.

George didn't read into it too much; his best mate was prone to these fits of anger and was always fine again when they next spoke. Instead of chasing after his friend, George just sat their mulling over the last few minutes: *'Forces we don't understand'; why would he use that wording?* Then he was brought back to reality by a family asking if they could have his table.

"Yeah, 'course." He picked up the empty cups and placed them back on the counter, thanking the staff on his way out. George then ventured deeper into town in search of a present for his father's birthday at the start of the next month. Remembering birthdays was normally a tough ask for him but it was never a problem when it came to his father's as it was 3rd September, the day Britain declared war on Germany – a date no history buff would soon forget. His love for history came from his father who had brought him up watching war films and going on trips to museums. His favourite being a trip to Normandy to see the war graves from the D-Day beach landings. It was a very humbling experience for them both, white crosses as far as the eye could see marking the heroes who gave their lives to free Europe from tyranny. George turned the corner and came into view of the store he was looking for, an enormous bookstore with a large statue outside epitomising an open book. The book monolith was a favourite spot for family pictures and the beautiful day had encouraged more people to queue for a snap than George had ever seen before. Walking past the attraction he entered the building and was immediately hit with a cold wave of air conditioning that sent a tingle down his spine. George removed his shades and inhaled the sweet scent of paper. The smell of the books was intoxicating. He breathed in the adventure between the pages and his hairs stood on end as he sensed the general buzz around the departments while people looked to lose themselves in a way only a good book could allow. How he wished to experience an adventure like one of the heroes in his novels, the thrill and danger of the exploration as well as the bonds of friendship made along the way. Anything to break him out of the monotonous cycle of his nine to five. Shaking his head to clear away his daydream of heroism and grandeur, he remembered why he was there and ambled over to the cookery section to browse the potential presents. His father was always asking for new cookbooks recently due to the new vegan diet he was trying. At present, all Bryan had been eating was salads and he was desperately looking for new recipes to vary his meals. The cookery section was full of inviting books with all sorts of different meals that could be cooked on a vegan diet. After picking up and scanning through several books, George eventually settled on a book named 'How's That For a Plate of Grass?' written by a vegan comedian documenting their favourite meals and instructions on how to make them. The cashier was unsurprised by his choice and remarked that he was the fourth person to purchase that particular book this day alone. George placed the present in his bag, receiving joy from the fact he avoided paying five pence for a plastic bag. Exiting the shop felt like stepping off the plane in a foreign country, a dry heat blasted his face in stark contrast to the fresh air conditioned building he was leaving. The queue for a picture at the book statue had not dwindled a bit and, if anything, may have swelled a little more. As George was passing, he overheard an argument between two fathers who both believed their wives and children were next for a picture with the iconic landmark. It was not a difficult objective spending the remainder of the day milling around town looking in his favourite outlets and fantasising about being able to purchase everything he wanted. Before long the day was drawing to a close, the temperature had dropped and George began his walk back home.

Goosebumps had formed on George's arms by the time he reached his front door. Despite living in England all his life he still didn't anticipate the thunderstorm that had ripped across the sky on his journey, marking the end of the beautiful day. It was common knowledge that the weather turned on a dime in the UK, but without carrying around a suitcase twenty-four seven, there was no way to have all the necessary clothes to deal with the weather extremes experienced in a single day. The last fifteen minutes of his walk home George was plodding along in just a t-shirt in the pouring rain.

Belinda was ready with a towel as soon as George got through the door and immediately wrapped her son in a warm embrace to get the chill from his bones and dry him off. She ordered him to go and shower to warm up again but gave a very strict time limit of ten minutes as dinner was almost ready. After showering and feeling the heat return to his body, George changed into his dressing gown and slipped into his comfiest pyjama bottoms. Running down the stairs and into the kitchen he found a freshly cooked stir fry waiting for him. The rice noodles were his favourite part, so Bryan ensured George had more than anyone else. Where the parents lacked in noodles they made up for with extra vegetables: red, green and yellow peppers, chestnut mushrooms, beanshoots, edamame beans, cabbage, carrots and red onions. There were even little vegan chicken pieces in the dish, they tasted exactly like the real thing but were slightly softer. The aroma of the plate was mouth-watering, the different vegetables each adding their own sweet scent to the mix. The first taste was overwhelming, an explosion of flavour; the vegetables gave a crunch and the sweet chilli sauce gave the food an extra kick that left a lasting aftertaste. As always, the family finished far too quickly; indigestion set in almost immediately around the table. Belinda hiccupped and moaned of belly-ache.

Later, the three of them began watching their evening TV programmes together. That night was Belinda's favourite, a show about hospitals. On that particular episode, a lumberjack had had an accident with his chainsaw; the viewer could see the danger coming a mile off but that didn't stop the supposedly experienced worker from forgetting basic safety measures and, as a result, losing his arm. He would have bled out on the scene of the accident, but the ambulance crew saved his life by applying a tourniquet to stop the blood flow. It always made Bryan laugh that his wife enjoyed the show so much because she had a deathly phobia of needles and, naturally, being a hospital show, there were frequent injections on the screen. After the lumberjack had been transported to the hospital, he received the standard morphine shots at which point Belinda almost fainted, and George and his father laughed. When the programme finished, they retired to their respective rooms for bed with images of blood and hacked off limbs still in their heads. Nevertheless, it wasn't the gory show that kept George awake that night, more so the conversation he had had with Jacob earlier in the day and a thousand different scenarios of what he was going to get himself into when he turned up at 54 Langley Road the following morning.

CHAPTER 3

Sanctum
Moanatenger
Captain Quint's Ship

Clunk...clunk...clunk... the wooden leg of Captain Quint always warned of his approach as it thudded on the deck of his ship. The oak limb was as much part of him now as his left arm, and it had been since he had it fitted a year after his duel with the Kraken. The weight being pushed down on the fake appendage still made his stump ache under the pressure, but he kept his pain hidden behind his stern wrinkled face. His beady brown eyes gave no indication of the struggle he dealt with and the grimace on his face was ever present as if to be painted on. Quint was tasked with escorting a merchant shipment of snails from Barren Valley coast to Chungwantanya. The odd cargo was used by the tribes of Chungwantanya to create a purple colour for their textiles and accessories. It was a shipment that had very little importance in reality, but to Quint it was a voyage of great significance. The successful transport of the commodity from one coast to the other across the treacherous waters of Moanatenger would, in his eyes, be a huge victory for a united Sanctum. The evil rule of Dark Snake was enforced from the tip of Liberterra in the north all the way down to the dark godforsaken mountains of Dreadnoque in the south. The land between was a constant war zone, forces of good fighting for a lasting peace and those loyal to the Dark Snake's twisted rule, focused on subjugating the populations of Sanctum to then launch a crusade against Earth.

The echoing sound of Quint's leg came to a stop as the captain reached the edge of his vessel and gazed across at the merchant ship he was guarding. The captain of the cargo ship nodded in acknowledgement and waved a thanks to his guardian. Quint had never failed to successfully achieve his goal whatever it may be once he was on the open sea. He had a one hundred percent success rate in safely escorting his consignment across the waters, even if it had cost him his leg in the past. His ship was named *Relentless* after his own dogged attitude and unyielding concentration on his task. It was a fairly large ship with fifteen cannons and a crew of one hundred and twenty good men he had chosen himself, many of which he had bled alongside in the past. The water was calm which should have been a good thing, but the still conditions were troubling Quint. He was unnerved by the eerie silence; it was as if the very water was holding its breath. The tranquil conditions were also an issue as the lack of substantial wind meant very slow progress. *Relentless* had the oars to power it on through times like this but the cargo ship was not as well suited, relying mainly on the elusive wind. Captain Quint turned away from the merchant vessel and looked at his own crew on board his ship. They were tired after a long journey for they had been sailing a considerable time and it was taking its toll. The usual songs were not being sung and the liquor was at a dangerous low. They had been untroubled on the voyage which was an all-round good thing with the waters always being patrolled by immoral captains eager to prove themselves to their demonic master. However, the easy trip meant that the crew were growing restless and looking for less conventional ways to entertain themselves. The last couple of days had seen a vast increase in sword fights breaking out over trivial things such as the number of birds that had flown by or even who ate the last peanut. The strict rules for conflict on the ship laid down by Quint stated that the winner of these disputes was whoever drew first blood which limited the wounds and drew a line. Nevertheless, that morning two of the crew members were unwise enough to forget the guidelines for conflict and continued the fight after first blood was drawn. After being cut, the loser retaliated with a strong overhead swing of his sword towards his quarry. Fortunately, his opponent saw it coming and was able to raise his own weapon to parry the blow. The fight then continued until the original loser was standing over his opponent watching him bleed from a fatal neck wound. He barely had time to celebrate his victory before the roar of excitement from the spectators died down to be replaced with a harrowing *clunk... clunk... clunk.*

The victor of the duel was given no time to plead his case before Quint had drawn his flintlock pistol and blown a hole in the troublemaker's head. The lifeless corpse fell over the edge of the ship and splashed into the water.

"Clean that up!" Quint ordered one of the onlookers.

The sailor didn't need asking twice and swiftly left to collect a mop and bucket to remove the dead man's brains and skull fragments from the deck. Two other sailors grabbed the man that died of the neck wound and threw him overboard to feed the fish.

"Anyone else forgotten the rules?" the captain threatened the ship with his firearm. "Good! As you were," he laughed at his own power as he limped away.

Quint spat on the deck remembering the farce from earlier in the day. He was about to return to his quarters when there was a shout from the crow's nest. "SHIP!" the lookout yelled down. As quick as a flash the entire crew were massing on the side of the ship where the sentry was pointing. Approaching on the horizon was a ship similar in size to Quint's but with fewer cannons and greater crew capacity. The black mast depicted a troubling image of a yellow head impaled with a red dagger through its cheeks. The man on the mast looked to be screaming in pain, a warning for those the ship was approaching. "*Torment*," gasped one of Quint's crew.

Glob Karver was the name being spread round the ship in gulps and whispers.

"TO STATIONS!" the captain bellowed. The merchant vessel was not in a safe place, it was between the two ships readying for battle. *Torment* was getting closer by the second but Quint's organised and disciplined *Relentless* was in position almost instantaneously. Within a very short space of time the captain had managed to get his crew to place their ship between the approaching evil and the cargo transport. Quint smiled to himself, happy that he had his mission protected. The crew knew exactly what to do and were already in the process of performing their captain's orders before they had even left his mouth. *Relentless* was side on with the approaching *Torment* and began their cannon fire. The sound of battle broke the previously silent landscape, shattering the peace like glass. On the one hand, the first few cannon balls fell short of their target and sent up plumes of water as they crashed into the sea. On the other hand, *Torment* was not returning fire, but instead continuing straight on towards its prey. A cannon ball hit home and made a hole in the front of the enemy ship, but the vessel kept coming. Then on the bow of the ship appeared a small stocky bald man with a large sword in his hand, almost the size of his own body in length. The hairless man was laughing into the face of the incoming cannon fire and begging them for more. Suddenly, *Torment* reached Quint's ship with a bang, knocking the disabled captain off his feet, unable to stay balanced with his wooden leg. Looking up, Quint saw the bald man leap from the top of his ship onto *Relentless*. There was a moment of silence as the murderous captain looked at Quint's crew, wordlessly begging them to make the first move.

Quint could not stay on the deck and struggled back to his feet. "What're you waiting for? Kill him!" he ordered.

The stocky man smiled, revealing a disgusting arrangement of teeth. "Your death is Glob Karver." Then the sun was blotted out by the mass of bodies swinging from *Torment* to *Relentless* to back up their captain. A brawl to the death broke out. For every enemy sailor Quint's crew killed another one seemed to be just boarding. Screams of agony were heard all around the ship, hacked off limbs were littering the deck and the smell of battle was ripe. Destruction made the vessel its home. Quint slew an enemy and tried to see how the fight was panning out. He couldn't tell who was winning with the quick glance he made before another sword thrust his way. He was limited in movement by his wooden leg but made up for it with high quality swordsmanship. Quint parried the incoming weapon and plunged his own sword deep into the insides of his aggressor. He watched as the life drained from his enemy's eyes and then pulled his sword from their belly revealing a blade running red with death.

"We're fightin' 'em back," came an encouraging update from one section of the ship.

"Moanatenger's a free realm," came another hopeful voice.

Quint let out a roar and powered on through the enemy ranks, his sword arm having a mind of its own; it was moving faster than the captain ever thought possible. His right arm was waving around behind him to counterbalance his forward attacks. He pulled his weapon from another stomach and looked for his next victim when a huge sword swung down in front of his vision. There was promptly an immense pain and a hot sensation spread up Quint's left side. He heard his sword drop to the floor along with his left arm. He became dizzy and stumbled backwards away from his limb laying on the deck as spurts of blood erupted from the amputated stump.

"Protect da captain!" came an order from one of the crew.

"Don't let Karver escape!" demanded another.

The stocky man was laughing as he killed those trying to stop his exit. "Retreat!" Glob called to his sailors.

Quint collapsed to the deck once more and his vision became blurry. He pulled a sailor close to his mouth so he could hear him through his weakened state. "The cargo ship?" he muttered.

"It's safe, Cap'n. It's gunna be OK."

Then Quint blacked out as his life drained from his left shoulder, the grimace painted on his face was slightly upturned, however, his one hundred percent ferrying success rate was intact.

CHAPTER 4

Earth
England
East Anglia

Waking up the next day, George was thinking about the location he had to go to later. He knew where Langley Road was but had never been down there, it was just renowned for being full of decrepit old buildings and peculiar shops. It was fortunate the meeting fell on the bank holiday Monday or George would have been unable to attend due to work commitments. Although entirely unsure what the letter could mean, the prospect of setting out on his own adventure made sleep extremely hard to come by. Still in a daze from his insomnia, he opened his wardrobe to choose a t-shirt for the day; after one glimpse outside it was already decided to be a shorts-and-t-shirt-day despite not testing the air temperature yet. As he pushed the different options along on their hangers, he got whiff of a tangy and stale smell. Upon further inspection the toxins were discovered to be coming from under his armpits. The night had been hot and sticky which furthered his inability to sleep but also meant that, despite showering only just before going to bed, he would in fact need to do so again before changing. Pushed on by the foul aroma emanating from his body, George quickened the pace of his search and settled on a t-shirt that depicted an iguana with shades on with the writing 'Bad as iguana be' written above it. The top was another keepsake from his trip to Mexico and, as such, was one of his favourites. The choice of bottoms was far more limited, and it took no time at all for him to snatch up his khaki shorts and head to the bathroom to wash. The toothpaste was the first real obstacle of the day to overcome, it was at that stage where most of the tube had already been squeezed out and it hadn't been done by squeezing from the bottom as his mother always advised, but instead by pushing around the top.

George knew that he was as guilty for that as his father was and now regretted his earlier time-saving scheme. Pressing from bottom to top and repeating a trio of times he finally managed to secrete enough to clean his teeth. The shower took what felt like an eternity to warm up and even when it had there was still a cold drip every five seconds that escaped and fell on George's back, sending a shock down his spine.

Feeling thoroughly refreshed even if somewhat abused by the shower's cruel game with the cold drip, George dried off and got dressed. In his rush down the stairs, he almost ended up cartwheeling to the bottom when he saw too late the cat napping on the middle step. With a swift evasive manoeuvre, he just about landed on the next step down preventing the need for acrobatics at the early hour of the morning.

"That was quite an entrance," chuckled Belinda as she watched her son avoid the cat whilst drinking her mint tea on the sofa. The herbal brew had a lovely smell but somewhat overpowering for the senses so early in the day.

"Want some tomatoes on toast?" called Bryan from the kitchen.

George had expected the question and had his answer on the tongue ready. "No thank you, gonna grab something on my way to town." The morning had flown by and George rapidly found himself needing to set off on his way to avoid being late. The heat was sweltering outside, as he expected it would be, and the burden was worsened by the backpack full of the items given to him in the parcel. In addition, he packed a notepad and a pen in case he found the need to take notes. On the way, George attempted to ring Jacob to inform him that he was busy for the day and thus would be unable to meet up, however, there was no answer on either time he tried his phone. *Must still be cross with me from yesterday,* George decided. The farmer was busy in her field that morning, she was driving her large green tractor around with ease. It never ceased to amaze George how efficiently she could get the ungainly vehicle to turn in tight circles and stay balanced on risky-looking bits of terrain. The farmer noticed George watching her, switched off the engine before bellowing over to him, "No day off for me! Us farmers only get the one time off, I'm afraid."

George was about to inquire as to when that one time off was when she thundered the answer, “That’d be when we’re dead!” then with a psychotic laugh she turned the key and the tractor rumbled back into life to return to work.

“Strange breed of human,” George mumbled under his breath as he continued into town.

When the first line of coffee and charity shops came into view there was a river of sweat running down George’s back between his heavy bag and his skin. He swung the bag off his back to give himself some respite, allowing cool air to blow against the wet patch left on the rear side of his t-shirt. It took a second for George to find his wallet in the bag, but just as he was cursing his clumsiness believing he forgot his money, he found it and felt his stomach growl. A light pain had begun to grow in the base of his belly, the walk only serving to further fuel his hunger after missing breakfast. George stopped to get himself a quick bite to eat from a sandwich delicatessen. Whilst lining up and choosing which sandwich he would be getting today – the sweet chilli chicken, as always – he couldn’t help but notice the cloud of flies floating around and wondered how contaminated his lunch was going to be. George reached the front of the queue and the deli worker was in the process of asking George “What would you like to–” when a large zap startled the worker. The sudden noise was a mystery to the employee, however, George had the rather unfortunate knowledge that the small electrical strike was in fact one of the flies getting vaporized in a fly trap. Worse still, the tray that was supposed to catch the burnt remains was hanging off the bottom rendering it completely useless. Because of these circumstances, George remained hungry for a short while longer, choosing not to get a sandwich as the memory of the cremated fly floating towards the deli counter replayed over and over in his mind. Extremely hungry and no longer bothered what he ate so long as he ate very soon, George decided to grab a steak bake from the bakery across the road. Unsurprisingly, the bakery was packed full of customers and the queue backed out the door; nonetheless the wait went quickly due to the sheer volume of staff brought in for the bank holiday business. The absence of steak bakes for sale highlighted appropriately how the day was panning out so far. A further compromise meant George left with a cheese and onion pasty instead. Greedy in his hunger, George ripped into the pasty with his teeth to try to refuel his body. The lava that leaked out onto his tongue did nothing to improve his mood, only serving to ruin the rest of the meal due to the blistered flap of skin at the roof of his mouth, sending shoots of pain through his face with each subsequent bite.

Following an extremely unsuccessful breakfast, *Perhaps I should have had it at home after all?* he mused to himself, George discovered he had reached Langley Road. Whilst walking down the street and counting down the building numbers, George found his pace increasing faster as he neared the next stage of this weird turn his life had taken: 120, 118… his walk turned more into a march... 98, 92... then a light jog overcame him, 88… 74… eventually George entered a full sprint to reach his destination... *62 and what? No. There must be some mistake.* After checking and double-checking the number on the street said 54 as did the letter, George felt an abrupt drop in his excitement in realising that the whole thing was likely a cruel joke. These new emotions were in direct response to the fact that number 54 Langley Road was, in fact, an old antiques museum that looked almost empty. It contained a sole flickering lamp that was set on the counter, combating encroaching darkness from the rest of the building. Above the entrance was an old, tattered sign that said Roy's Antiquities Store – Moat Ruin. George's immediate thought was, *Who would call their store Moat Ruin?* After getting over the fact the name sounded like a depressing heavy metal band, George decided that he had not walked all the way here for nothing.

His ginger hair was the second brightest thing in the gloomy outlet, so in order to see his surroundings better, George switched on his phone's the torch. When the door opened there was the light *ting-ting* of a bell to signify that a member of the public had entered the premises. Nobody responded to the sound and George began to feel that the building was perhaps empty. He could hear himself breathing amongst the quiet, and the smell of the place was none too pleasant – of damp and rotting. The store was full of all sorts of weird and wonderful items. On George's left was a collection of miniature heads, they all had black hair the length of their faces. Interested in what these were, George read the text displayed under one such oddity:

> *'Displayed above is a collection of shrunken heads. These are real heads that have been shrunken down and kept as trophies after victories in battle. The custom was found to have existed in South America years ago in some tribes. The Pintaki still follow the tradition today; this was a death threat from the tribal leader to myself. I now have it on display here at RAS.'*

Slightly creeped out, but more intrigued than ever, George continued towards the counter, stopping frequently to look at objects and read their captions by torchlight. As he rotated his phone in his hand, different sections of the shop came into view as they were bathed in sudden light. Most notably amongst the objects he stopped to study was a leg. It had been preserved in some kind of jelly. After nearing the limb, it became apparent the foul smell of the building originated from the jelly-like substance the leg was suspended in. George held his nose and began to read:

> *'The leg of a legendary pirate, torn off during his desperate struggle with the great Kraken of Moanatenger. The limb was thought lost until I found it washed up. The captain to whom it belonged remains unaware it is now on display here at RAS.'*

George wasn't convinced it was a real leg and was even less persuaded by the story of it how it got there. Before venturing further into the spooky store, George decided it wasn't a real antiques museum and instead was full of objects and stories of make believe; *Surely they couldn't be real heads and a real leg.* The next two displays he gazed at solidified that belief; the first being a grey tankard with a bullet wedged in the bottom of it. The caption for that particular object was:

> *'The Lucky pint. This cowboy's drinking saved his life. One of my favourites in my collection, this tankard caught a bullet destined for the man drinking from it. Instead of landing in his skull, the bullet got wedged in the tankard. I won it off the tavern owner in a game of five finger fillet.'*

The final exhibit George took time to look at was, at least, from a story he *had* heard of this time. There was a very old looking body armour hung on a manikin. There were several indents and scratches on the artefact which could only be expected, both from old age and previous use. The writing beneath claimed it belonged to St George, the patron saint of England:

> *'One of my less interesting exhibits, originating on Earth, is the armour of St George. This was the very armour worn by the knight when he slew the dragon. Gifted by a friend from another museum to kickstart my exhibition.'*

'Originating on Earth' George read again. *This guy must have lost his marbles.* Turning to leave and now beyond certain that the whole thing was a practical joke, George was faced with a tall, jagged slab of black rock. Unsure how he had missed it to begin with, George moved closer to further inspect the out of place stone. The monument looked hundreds of years old, showing several signs of wear and history. George ran his fingers along the outcrop, feeling in the cracks and crevices; some felt natural but others felt more like chippings as if someone had used a chisel on it. Further signs of tampering appeared when he noticed that all along its edges were black smears from charring, as if an attempt to burn it. Something about the rock was captivating George and he couldn't seem to bring himself away. Round the back of the monument George discovered four moulds; one shaped like a sword; another, a gun; the third, a torso and the last, a headdress. These shapes seemed familiar somehow; *where have I seen them before?* Suddenly it came to him. George fumbled in his backpack for the letter from Minotaur; *yes, there it is,* on the envelope was the multicoloured logo, a green tribal headdress above a purple torso flanked by a red sword and an orange pistol. *Interesting.* George reached out to touch the stone once more, still finding himself being drawn to it by some unknown emotion. He was a fingertip away when there came a tremendous roar.

"Get away from that this instant, young man!" The booming voice had come from the direction of the counter and, to George's surprise, the voice did not match the appearance of the source. A small man pushing five foot four with short, spiky green hair was approaching George and scowling. "What're you doing here? We're closed today," enquired the supposed owner.

George, still shocked by the sudden and aggressive arrival of the man, stammered his reply, "I... I received a… a letter."

"I haven't sent out any letters. Now, unless you're here to buy or sell antiques, I suggest you leave."

Puzzled by what on earth was happening, George began for the exit.

"He's with me, Roy." Another man had appeared by the counter.

George rubbed his eyes, adamant he was drunk at the Purple Giant or dreaming because the weird just got weirder. Roy's supposed acquaintance was none other than Presley, his football coach. Moreover, instead of his usual gym attire, the mountain of a man was wearing a red suit with a green bull logo on his left side.

Roy immediately changed his tone. "Apologies, young man, you can't be too careful these days, Tombstone are growing in power and have made three attempts on stealing the monument in as many months."

George, awestruck, just looked between the two men, wondering who was going to speak gibberish next when Presley piped up again, "Come this way, Mr Keen, you have a lot to learn and see."

George obeyed and followed further into the building whilst Roy retreated to his hiding place in a dark corner of the room waiting for further intruders. Reaching a large painting of a minotaur, Presley reached out and pulled on the ring in its nose and twisted it clockwise. The painting opened up, revealing an elevator. George stepped in and Presley pushed the button which began their descent.

"What's with the suit?" George inquired, too confused to ask any of the more pressing questions on his mind.

"All will be revealed soon. Just follow me," Presley replied.

The elevator doors opened to a small hallway; the walls were entirely white as was the ceiling. George squinted as his eyes adjusted from the dark room they had just left to the dazzling brightness of the hallway they had just entered, which was lit with invasive lights. There were no doors in any walls. After a matter of metres, they came upon a guard dressed in the same red suit as Presley with the green bull on the breast. The guard, armed with a pistol and a Taser, didn't make much of an effort to stop the two of them as they walked his way. Presley ushered George past the guard, missing a step only briefly, to show the guard some identification which the sentry didn't even feint to look at. The further they walked the more apparent it became that they were in some underground complex under the local shopping area. The walls and ceiling were still white but now the borders of the hallway were dotted with doors. George attempted to read the signs of each as he went past but struggled to catch them all. Amongst the ones he was able to decipher were 'Armoury', 'Meeting Room A' and, most surprisingly of all, one that read 'Presley Jones – Head of Operations'. The hallway stretched on for a little while longer after the point where Presley took George through a door marked 'Meeting Room B'. The door led into a large room filled with chairs all facing towards a projection screen with the words 'Minotaur initiation presentation'. The walls were not white in this room but instead were painted with the opposite end of the spectrum – all black. The choice of colour was most likely to emphasise the projection and make it clear to those who would be seated at the rear of the room. Presley flicked a wall switch and the room filled with light as it was illuminated from the ceiling bulbs. George could now see that all the chairs were arranged in a sequence of colours: red, green, yellow, blue, and orange, and this pattern repeated throughout the room. The area stretched back much further than he originally thought, with an open space at the back of the room that was originally shrouded in darkness. Presley beckoned George to a seat when he sat down and waited for further arrivals. When the boy opened his mouth to demand to be informed what was going on and for Presley to explain himself, the only response George got was that all his questions would be answered shortly.

After what seemed like hours but was in fact only a matter of minutes, other candidates turned up. George was relieved to see that they all looked as lost as he was and that none of them had any idea what they were in for. Interestingly, they all appeared to be of the same age as himself. Some were shown in by Presley, some by the strange man with the green hair and the rest by the other people in the red suits. Everyone was told to sit down and wait, the same as

George had been. After what must have passed as ten minutes, the candidates began to move from their seats and mingle at the back of the room in the spacious area.

As the room started to fill a large congregation began to form towards the right-hand corner at the rear of the room. When George went over to see what the fuss was about, he found one of the candidates was in the centre preaching to the others. The speaker was short and fat as well as challenged in the follicle department; nonetheless, that didn't tame his enjoyment of being in the spotlight.

"That's what I found out when I researched this place, anyway."

There were groans of disagreement and some looks of uncertainty as to whether this guy was full of nonsense, but others seemed to believe him.

"What's he telling them?" asked George.

An average height dark-skinned man with a large Afro supplied George with his answer. "Apparently, we've been selected to receive special training to take down hostile foreign governments from the inside… Or was it that we're being sent to win the hearts and minds of Middle Eastern locals to turn the tide of terrorism? Oh no, that was it, we're being lowered to the depths of the ocean yet unexplored."

George chuckled, understanding where this was going. "One of those, is he?"

"Now what gave you that impression?" the young man winked. "Name is Cheikhou, but my friends call me Cheik. Pleased to meet you." Cheikhou smiled and outstretched his hand to shake.

George accepted the offer of friendship and was not surprised at the firm grip of the handshake considering the sizeable bulge of Cheikhou's biceps under his skin-tight grey top.

The door swung open, Presley entered and was trailed by the final two candidates. George didn't believe that the day could get any more surreal but that didn't stop the last two candidates being Jacob and Annabel. Jacob was wearing his black shorts and a floral shirt over a plain white t-shirt. Annabel in her yellow sundress was an unsurprising love interest for Jacob. She was tall and had long, flowing blonde hair as well as bright blue eyes. Unfortunately, her natural beauty was often masked by layers of unnecessary make-up that the poisonous media made young girls believe they needed to reach 'true beauty'. Even girls as intelligent as Annabel could be brainwashed by the need for validation on social media, a toxic trait of the current society.

George ran over to them with Cheikhou close behind. "I can't believe it!"

In disbelief himself, Jacob still managed to call upon his wit. "Come on, Annabel, I told you this secret facility was fully booked; let's go to the one further downtown." Jacob bumped fists with George and was introduced to Cheikhou.

George pointed to his friends and told Cheikhou, "That's Jacob's bird, Annabel," which immediately sent red flushes into the faces of the accused.

"Twenty years of friendship and that's the introduction I get? You're lucky I'm *not* a bird, I'd peck your eyes out," Annabel warned with a wry smile.

Introductions over, they sat in a row awaiting the start of the presentation.

Presley flicked the switch to turn off the lights bringing the projection into full focus. The talk died down and the presentation began.

"Welcome to Roy's Antiquities Store, or RAS, the local base of operation for Minotaur, the only other being in Arizona," began Presley. The first image on the slide show behind him displayed a world map with two red dots showing the base locations: one in their current position, the other across the ocean. "You've all been summoned here today to see if you have what it takes to join an operation of global significance."

"Yes, told you – I knew it!" a voice boasted at the front with triumph.

Presley ignored the distraction and continued. "I have forty of you sitting in front of me today, by the end of the process I'll have five. You're going to undertake three tasks today. After each task half of you will be leaving us."

A murmuration filled the room.

"For this reason you'll be finding out no more about the mission or who we are here at Minotaur unless you're wise enough, fit enough and physically, as well as mentally strong enough to be in the final five."

At that, the murmuration grew to a subdued chatting sound.

"The tasks will be performed in virtual reality suits that'll fully immerse you in your surroundings. Everything will feel, sound and look as if you are just in your everyday bodies; however, due to the risks the tasks pose, you'll in fact just be holographic forms of yourselves, therefore, if you 'die' during one of the tasks you'll be able to simply respawn and try again."

The previous subdued chatting sound erupted into a full medley of shouts and deep conversation.

"SILENCE!" Presley used his booming voice to hush the room instantly. "You're here to prove you have what it takes to save this world from its impending demise, not to act like a group of school kids. If you don't think you have what it takes, then leave now."

Nobody rose; instead, everyone sunk further into their seats attempting to hide from Presley's voice.

"The first task will begin immediately. You'll be in groups of four. The five fastest will progress to the next round. Now, please follow my colleague through the door behind me to collect your virtual reality suits."

One of the men dressed in the red suit with the green minotaur logo showed the candidates where to go. He took the men in one room and sent the girls off with a short rotund lady to another room. Before handing out the others', the employee showed the candidates how to correctly wear the suit by applying one himself. The jet-black spandex clothing was tight, making them difficult to squeeze into for a variety of reasons; Cheikhou struggled the most as he was muscular for his height and age.

When they emerged, all clad in their new attire to reunite with the women, George nudged Jacob who was looking over at Annabel in her suit and said, "Not straying from the mission, are we Jacob?"

"I'm not lowering myself to *your* level!" he fired back.

As quick as a flash, Cheikhou leapt at the opportunity, "No, but it appears you may be rising to it," and with a nod at Jacob's groin, he set all within earshot to hysterical laughing.

Annabel heard the laughter and came over to see what all the fuss was about. She giggled nervously when she discovered what had arisen. The groups for the task were decided by the chair colour the candidates were sitting on. Miraculously it worked out, so George, Cheikhou, Jacob and Annabel walked into the test room together. Unaware of what they were about to face, they were equipped only with the items from the parcel they had brought with them.

The test room was not what any of them were expecting. The four walls were white and in the centre stood four bright purple armchairs with helmets placed on the seats, each with a member of the Minotaur team standing behind them. Other than that, the room was empty. George and his friends were ushered into an armchair each and placed the headsets on.

"Nothing's happening," moaned Cheikhou.

All of a sudden something gripped George's hands and feet and held them tightly against the armchair.

"Your hands and feet are being restrained for your own protection so that you don't lash out and hurt yourselves or a member of staff during the trial," stated one of the uniformed men. "Your virtual self will not be affected by these restraints; once in the simulation you'll be free to move again. Your task is to reach the door and go through it together. Once you've all done this you'll be taken out of the simulation."

Annabel was growing restless. "Just start it already."

As she finished her short outburst, George felt himself becoming very dizzy and passed out. When he awoke, he found himself surrounded by the others who were checking everyone was OK and getting their bearings. They were in a large outdoor grassy area with no prominent features other than the odd tree or boulder – otherwise just flat grass.

Jacob let out a large laugh and pointed at the source of his amusement. "Thought this was supposed to be hard!" he bellowed as he directed everyone's gaze to what was quite clearly a door just a few hundred metres away.

"It can't be that easy, Jacob. They wouldn't just put the door so close. Something isn't right," reasoned Annabel.

Nonetheless, never one to worry about consequences, Jacob ran towards the door, too eager to show the others he was right. Remarkably, Jacob reached the door and opened it revealing a shimmering exit. He put his hand out to feel the strange haze and found it was like touching glass; there was some sort of forcefield preventing him from entering. Jacob then remembered that they must enter together and turned around to return to his team who were still stationary, watching him.

George took a step forward to meet Jacob who was already halfway back when there was a tremendous explosion. The spot that Jacob was just standing in was covered in smoke and when it cleared, he was nowhere to be seen.

"Oh, hell, no!" shouted Cheikhou.

"I'm sure he's fine, Cheik," said George, trying to calm down the others who were quite rightly perturbed by what they had just witnessed.

"Try telling that to *him*," answered Cheikhou whose trembling finger was pointing about two metres to the left of the explosion.

Annabel let out an almighty scream as she processed the small shape on the floor where Cheikhou was pointing. One of Jacob's legs was lying on the ground with small spurts of blood still pumping out the end. Annabel began crying and Cheikhou tried his best to console her, however, he himself was feeling quite sick and scared as well.

"Well, that was a blast alright, but don't ask me to do it again."

George turned around to see the source of the voice and saw Jacob standing with a grin on his face.

Annabel ran up to Jacob and slapped him across the cheek. "Never do that again!" she warned.

"Does someone want to tell me what the hell is going on, please?" inquired Cheikhou.

No one seemed to know what had happened, not even Jacob. Then George reminded them what Presley had said about dying in the simulation. The leg that was on the floor spraying blood had vanished and George explained how he thought Jacob must have stood on a landmine and had now respawned.

"Did it hurt?" asked George.

"Well, it kind of all happened so fast," replied Jacob, "but yeah, just before I reappeared behind you lot grieving the loss of the most important member of the team, I felt a searing pain. It's gone now, though."

Glazing over the fact that Jacob thought he was the most

important member of the team, despite just getting himself blown up within the opening minutes of the first task, the group analysed what they had learnt so far. The door was protected by a minefield and therefore would not be as easy to reach as they had hoped. All of them must enter the door at the same time and dying was not fatal but, in Jacob's words, "Hurt like a lorry to the nutsack," and therefore should be avoided if possible. The avoiding-dying bit was easier said than done as the group each took turns trying to safely navigate to the door. Nevertheless, never could they replicate Jacob's lucky initial sprint which seemed like hours ago now.

Annabel, growing restless after being blown up herself at least half a dozen times, decided a new approach was required. "We were given these items in our letters and we haven't tried to use them yet," she huffed.

This made George think; he had watched loads of war documentaries with his father before and he was sure that he could recall some information to help him cross a minefield. Then it came to him. They used to slowly sweep the ground, prodding it with blades; if they felt a mine then they would mark the position and carefully reroute. George told the group to each retrieve their blades from Kalysta's spear. Confident of his new tactic he then set out testing the treacherous path. In the blade went, making the earth *squelch* when it exited; this continued: in... *squelch*... in... *squelch*... in... *tang!* George had touched the edge of the landmine with his blade and then called to the others for something to mark the spot with.

Annabel ran over to a tree in the opposite direction of the door and tried to break off a branch. Try as she might though, she couldn't remove it from the tree. "A little help, boys?" she puffed questioningly.

"Move over, baby. It's time for the gun show." Cheikhou strolled forwards and rolled up his sleeves revealing his chiselled arms. He got a good grip and pulled downwards quickly. The branch broke off with ease. With a wink, he snapped off some twigs and gave them to Annabel. She handed them out to the group.

"I could have done that," Jacob assured her, disliking the way she was admiring Cheikhou's strength.

George marked the explosive with one of his twigs to show the others its position. The rest joined in and, slowly but surely, began to make progress across the minefield. It all looked to be going very well when, suddenly, Cheikhou cursed loudly and disappeared in a huge *bang!* The chain reaction took each of them out one by one leaving George until last. *Here we go again*, he thought to himself as he embraced his latest death. Once they had all respawned, the markers for each of the located mines had been blown up and the simulation was reset.

This was too much for Jacob. "We tried, George; I think we should give up."

"No," protested Annabel. "Everyone lay out your items that were sent to you in the mail."

Once all the items were on display it became apparent that they had all been sent identical objects, however, the coins seemed to differ slightly. They each had the engraved skull on one side but on the other were differing lines and markings. Annabel noticed two fit together like a puzzle if they overlapped. Then the third fit into place.

"Where's the fourth one?" Annabel asked. She glanced up and saw Cheikhou cowering away. "Where's your coin, Cheik?"

Getting redder by the minute, Cheikhou murmured his reply, "I... hungry... no money... vending machine."

"What?" Annabel was pressing more intently now.

Cheikhou gave up hiding and just came out with what he had to say. "I was hungry on my way here and stopped off at a corner shop, but I had no money on me. Luckily, my favourite chocolate was in the vending machine and so I used the coin from the letter, although I suppose that isn't so lucky now."

Annabel was furious. "You could have cost us the task now; this was beginning to form a map to show the safe route through the minefield."

"That worked?" Jacob asked Cheikhou.

Cheikhou nodded, still trying to avoid Annabel's wrath.

"Sweet," laughed Jacob before being shut down by a glare from Annabel.

"We'll just have to use the map as it is," George said, trying to settle Annabel down.

After another five minutes of Annabel shouting and Jacob

questioning Cheikhou how he used old pirate money to buy chocolate, the group set off following the safe route shown by the combined coins. When they reached the end of the map that they had available to them due to the lack of Cheikhou's coin, they just guessed the rest of the way which was only a short distance. For once, luck was on their side and they reached the door together in one piece. They travelled through the shimmering exit.

The group woke up back in their armchairs with a guard behind each of them removing their restraints. Jacob leapt out of his chair and marched over to Annabel where he grabbed her by her soft blonde hair and kissed her full on the mouth. When he pulled away, he was relieved to see her smiling and she returned the kiss. Jacob turned to George who was watching, gobsmacked by the sudden act of bravery. Then Jacob announced, "Well, if dying has taught me anything it's that love is certainly not something to be afraid of."

They were ushered back into the large meeting room they were in earlier and found they were surprisingly one of the first back. When all the other groups returned as well, Presley appeared and spoke to them again. First, he dismissed the five slowest groups, immediately halving their combined number to twenty people. George watched as Minotaur employees took the eliminated people from the room back into the white hallway with the elevator. Taking note of the dejected looks on the failed contestants' faces, he decided he was determined to be in the final five.

"After that test, you'll all have found that you work best as a team and need each other to overcome tough obstacles," Presley announced.

Annabel glared over at Cheikhou who was purposely avoiding her gaze.

"Next, you'll be doing your duo tests. Please, once again, follow my colleagues to your respective test rooms."

This time they were separated; Jacob was with Annabel, George got put with a British-Chinese girl called Rosie, and Cheikhou had the pleasure of being put with the know-it-all from earlier who turned out to be called Alex. George set off with Rosie towards the test room, but before they got there he asked if he could go to the toilet. The Minotaur worker gave him directions back into the white hallway and to take the third door on the left. George walked straight there following the route perfectly to relieve his bladder; nevertheless, he took a slight diversion on the return trip to try to peer through the window of the room that he noticed the tail end of the eliminated candidates enter. He successfully glimpsed the procedure and found that, to wipe the memory of the candidates' minds, they merely waved what appeared to George to be a sort of metal detector over the face of each person who then asked where they were and what was happening. Once wiped, they were given a story of how they fell and were nursed back to health before being taken to the exit and sent out onto the street. *Brutal*, thought George before remembering Rosie waiting for him in the test room.

Again, the decoration of the task area was the same, as was the mission, however, this time there were two armchairs. They strapped in and embraced the simulation.

When George awoke it was immediately evident that they were in a very different setting to last time. He was in a sort of wide corridor which was dark and damp. The slimy, jagged rock walls were illuminated by a series of torches hung along either side of the tunnel. There was silence apart from the occasional drip of water from the ceiling. Rosie was to George's left and was just coming to terms with her surroundings too, when there was a mighty roar. George turned to see a great hunched humanoid figure with grey skin and massive black eyes chained to one end of the corridor. George got as close as he dared and saw the callous grey hide of the being – which he concluded must be a troll – was cut around the neck where he was being restrained with a large metal collar tied to the wall by a thin rope.

Deciding that the other way was most likely their safest bet, George and Rosie began to walk to the other end of the dim corridor only to halt almost immediately – the torches caused great shadows to dance around the floor in front of them. A couple more steps threw the shadowcaster into vision. What met their eyes was the ugliest, most terrifying monster either of them had ever seen. A very large being with a dozen tentacles sprouting from its yellow pus-filled skin was blocking their way. Just in front of the door at the end of the corridor stood this beast with a twisted and deranged look on its face which seemed to melt into the rest of the saggy, weeping skin.

"You have to be kidding me," breathed George as he looked across to Rosie who seemed just as impressed as he was. Whether it was the fact that the only other occupants of the corridor were so hideous or whether it was general attraction, George couldn't help but realise then how soft Rosie's black hair looked and how her features gave her a tough but pretty visage. The way she carried herself made her seem taller; displaying one's stature is measured in more than just height. From their small discussion on the way to the test room (before he visited the toilet), George discovered she was a gymnast, which explained her lean body. Rosie leapt into action which jolted George back from his daydream. She seemed to be charging the yellow beast with her spearhead out, thus George felt he should do the same. This plan did not reap rewards, however; Rosie was thrown to the side by one of the tentacles and, despite George managing to stab the offending limb, he himself was crushed by a second tentacle. George felt his eyes close as he listened to each of his bones break. He lost feeling in his legs and then his arms before all went black.

"OK, don't take on the giant death machine in open combat," George told Rosie as they each spawned again in the centre of the corridor.

"Agreed," replied Rosie in an apologetic tone. "How about one of us tries to distract it whilst the other opens it up from behind?"

"Worth a try," huffed George. The two of them set off again towards the great lumbering monster and George tried to provide a distraction. He waved his arms and began throwing small stones he found on the floor that must have fallen from the walls or ceiling over time. The monster turned to face George and let out an almighty howl.

"Oh no," whimpered George. "Rosie... Rosie… ROSIE!"

As quick as a flash, Rosie sprinted past him and vaulted a tentacle, another came crashing down towards her, but she cartwheeled out of range. A large leap allowed her to evade another flailing tentacle and now she was behind the beast. Nonetheless, this proved to be less helpful than originally thought as Rosie noticed thick scale-like armour protecting its back. She lunged at it with her blade, but the point just deflected off the armour. The monster ran forwards towards George, and Rosie could see through the behemoth's legs that George had begun a sprint towards the other end of the corridor, yelling for Rosie to help. The great strides of the monster enabled it to catch up with George relatively quickly and it reached out and grabbed its prey, forcing George quickly into its mouth. He was gone. Then something strange happened. The yellow beast spotted the troll chained at the end of the corridor and yelped, retreating back to its own end of the passageway. Rosie had just enough time to clock this before being stampeded by the advancing monster.

"Where were you?" yelled George, positively outraged by the fact that, in his opinion, Rosie just let him become monster fast food.

"I tried but the hide was too thick," said Rosie defensively.

"Well, we're stuffed then," groaned George, "because I sure as hell am not doing that again."

"Not necessarily," Rosie said, scratching her arm as she spoke. "It's just… I don't know if I'm right."

George was slightly apprehensive as last time he trusted her he was chewed six times then swallowed; nevertheless, he had no better idea. After Rosie explained her findings, it was George that had to convince Rosie to follow her own plan after she doubted herself. Reluctantly, Rosie accepted she may be right and led them toward the troll. *She's a lunatic,* thought George as he watched Rosie walk right up to the chained troll. To his amazement, she did not get eaten or harmed in any way. Rosie then proceeded to use her spearhead to cut the rope that was holding the troll back. Once released, she watched as the troll got to its feet and towered above each of them. Convinced that he was about to be killed for the third time in a short period, George backed against the wall. To his surprise, however, the troll simply growled in what could only be described as a thankful tone and set off towards the other end of the corridor.

When Rosie sidled up next to George again, she gulped, "Part one complete. Let's not get our hopes up."

George decided to pat her on the back. "Nonsense, I believe in you." Excited to see the results of her genius, George followed the troll up the corridor. The pus-filled yellow monster saw its foe coming and charged the troll, knocking it off its feet. The collision of the two colossal beings caused the whole corridor to shake and a few loose stones rained to the floor. The troll immediately recovered and pulled one of the tentacles clean off; the open wound sprayed pus over the troll's face, but a great leathery tongue licked the yellow substance straight off. As if spurred on by the taste of the liquid, the troll bit down hard on another tentacle and ripped off some of the flesh, chewing it and swallowing once again. The yellow beast roared in pain as the troll continued its onslaught. After only a few minutes the yelping died down and the troll was left standing, indulging in its meal. A great gash had been opened across the troll's fat belly as the yellow monster had caught it with its razor-sharp scales during the fight.

George and Rosie, who were filled with excitement as well as fear, edged past the troll and exited the door whilst George continually repeated to Rosie how brilliant she was. Unhappy with her reluctance to take the credit and admit her good work, George's admiration for Rosie continued all the way into the meeting hall and the whole time they were waiting for the others to finish as they were the first to do so. They were first by some way as the next pair didn't arrive for another ten minutes; it was Annabel and Jacob. Again, it was the boy congratulating the girl on her wit and dexterity to see them through the trial. The third duo through were girls and the fourth, another mixed pair. George grew nervous for his newfound friend, Cheikhou, who was still not back.

"Who's he with?" Rosie asked.

"Some kid called Alex," George answered. "A know-it-all."

"A dick," one of the waiting boys added.

"Oh no. He was in my first group for the minefield challenge," Rosie told them. "He said he knew how to dismantle them from being in the army cadets. He blew up six times before I made him stop."

There was muffled shouting coming from one of the test rooms.

"What if Alex ruins it for him?" asked George.

"From what I've seen of Cheik so far, he will kill the–" but Jacob's reply was cut short by the return of the man in question. Cheikhou had a big smile on his face. He was being followed by Alex who didn't seem so happy despite claiming the last position in the final trial. Alex was unusually quiet and sported a big black eye which screamed foul play had occurred.

Cheikhou returned to his friends, laughing, "Had to knock him out. He kept screaming and alerting the great ugly dude at the end of our whereabouts. Then he kept killing the chained-up grey guy, thinking he was being a hero. After the third time he got me killed I spawned and knocked his lights out. Then I did it myself and carried him through the door on me shoulders."

Everyone was laughing apart from Alex who was being comforted by the first aid team.

"But you can't get hurt in the simulation," pointed out Annabel.

"Very true, but he came up to me shouting after the task, despite me literally carrying him through the trial, so I had to hit him again." Cheikhou ignored the disgusted looks on the girls' faces and instead ran with the reactions of George and Jacob who had fallen off their chairs laughing. The wait for the last pairs who were going to be eliminated was tedious but went by in the end. The time was passed by discussing what the horseshoe could be used for in the final round after both the coin and the blade were used in previous trials. Annabel was explaining her theory when Presley entered the room and again began by dismissing the failed contestants.

"Congratulations to those of you who have reached the final task. Well done for realising the moral of the last task which was that, even when armed with a weapon there can be other ways out of conflict. You also determined who your enemies were and showed bravery and instinct to release the troll."

"It's easy when you know how," piped up Alex with his chest puffed out.

Presley continued, "I especially applaud Cheikhou who had the initiative to first sense weakness in his partner and then show them where they could be of best use, which, as Cheikhou discovered for Alex, was laid out on the floor out of the way."

The room once more burst into applause and merriment at Alex's expense as he reddened and sank down into his seat.

"The final task will be performed individually and afterwards, therefore, we'll have our five final candidates that will be trained and deployed in the field. Nonetheless, before we proceed to the last mission, you must be hungry, so follow me to the canteen," Presley said, concluding his speech and leading the way to the refreshments.

It was apparent upon entering the door labelled 'Meeting Room A' that the building did not in fact have a canteen. The table normally used for meetings and discussions had been transformed into a buffet. There were platters of sandwiches, their contents ranging from salmon, to egg, to cheese, to beef and to watercress. Little bowls of different flavoured crisps were dotted around the table as well, some spicy and some salted. There was fruit in abundance; bananas, apples, melons, grapes, exotic options like papaya and star -fruit, as well as many more. The drinks were entirely non-alcoholic, much to George and Jacob's displeasure, but were still varied enough to cater for the remaining candidates; fizzy soda, water, squash, fruit juice and even tea and coffee. Alex led the charge to the food and soon filled his plate up with all sorts of crisps and sandwiches. Giving the fruit a wide berth, he reached for the fizzy drink and cursed as it flowed like a volcano from the top upon being opened. Alex's misfortune was met with a huge cheer from the other candidates who followed to get themselves food and drink. When George and his friends each collected the refreshments they wanted, they sat on the black swivel business chairs used for the dinner party and pulled them up to another of the meeting tables.

"That's a lot of fruit, Rosie," noted George who had invited her into the little clan they were forming.

"Fruit's healthy for you," she said, stating the obvious, "it helps strengthen the body and–"

"The only things I want strengthening are these guns," interrupted Cheikhou, who was showing off his already muscular arms whilst eating his protein-packed beef sandwich. Jacob nudged Annabel's arm to stop her admiring Cheikhou's physique. She snapped out of her gaze and whispered a small apology at her new partner.

"Can't blame 'em for looking," howled Cheikhou.

The laughter died down as Alex approached their table. "Please can I sit with you?" he asked.

"No," replied Jacob, George and Cheikhou in unison.

"Please, they won't let me sit with them," he begged, pointing at the other table that had formed.

Annabel told the boys off for being so cruel and looked at Alex, "Of course you can si–" but before she had finished, Alex had sat his fat cheeks next to her and began eating.

"Fwrankshh," Alex said through a mouthful of salmon sandwich. The mistake of allowing him to sit there soon became apparent when he did not stop speaking through mouthfuls of food and refused to accept that he needed Cheikhou's help in the previous task.

After having enough food sprayed over him from Alex's overlarge mouth, Cheikhou stood up and threatened to punch Alex again if he did not move.

Rosie was trying to settle Cheikhou down whilst Jacob was egging him on when Presley returned and told them it was time to be taken to perform their individual tasks.

Alex leapt up and almost bowled Cheikhou over with his weight when he waddled past him to be the first to enter the simulation.

On the other hand, before Rosie was happy to start the third simulation, she posed Presley a question: "Are these items you have given us genuine?" She explained her doubt. "Because if so, then why do the coins of an ancient pirate have the answer to a test we have done today on them? Also, how many spears does this – Kalysta, is it – have?"

Presley chuckled at the young lady's quick observation. "We can't pull the wool over *your* eyes, can we? You're right, Rosie, we made the items and sent them out for the purpose of the test. For example, the coins were altered by the simulation to show the path no matter what groups you were put in. Nevertheless, the real items *did* exist and so did their owners. Unfortunately, we don't have the real items in our possession."

The group took a while to accept the truth of the situation and realise that it was foolish for them to have ever thought they each had the same original items from the supposed legends. George set off to find his simulation room, confident from previous successes and eager to find out what his solo task had in store for him. The walk to the test rooms had, on previous trips, been with friends and, without them, George found his palms sweating about what awaited him. On the positive side, George found that walking alone and without distractions he was able to take in much more of the secret facility.

Peering through doors to uncover their secrets, he saw sleeping quarters for the workers that might have missed the last train or bus home after a long day of whatever they did here. A particularly large room contained computers that seemed to be monitoring activity around the world, as if they were looking out for a sign of life from a distant foe. Most interestingly to George, he spotted a large red door at the end of the hallway they had not yet reached with the words: 'DO NOT ENTER UNLESS AUTHORISED' written in large black letters across the front.

"What's behind there?" inquired George to Presley who was a little way ahead of him.

"Huh? Oh that," he began, seeing what George was pointing at having evidently been woken from a daydream, "it's beyond top secret and I couldn't tell you even if I wanted to, I'm afraid."

"Oh, OK," sighed George, a little dejected but still longing to know more about the place.

Presley suddenly let out an almighty laugh which, from someone of his stature and appearance, was almost as scary as if he had just roared with rage. "It's the janitor's cupboard, boy. He wrote that on the door for a joke."

As he finished his explanation the door opened and an old man with shaggy grey hair wearing a worn hat stumbled out. He was holding a broom and pink feather duster, muttering to himself about youths making the place dirty and not wiping their feet.

George chuckled his way to the test room and sat in the chair provided, placing the headset on. He didn't even jump when the restraints swiftly held him to his chair. *I can handle whatever they throw at me*, and with that thought George surrendered to the simulation.

When he came around, George found himself in a room very similar to the one he had just left apart from there being no chair in the centre. The room was completely empty and there were two doors at the far end; one was closed whilst the other was wide open with bright rays of sunshine coming through. George approached the closed door first and began to feel cold. As he got nearer to the door, he noticed there was no handle and it was decorated with a large painting of a minotaur holding a ball of light, the words

Semita salvatoris were written below. Curiosity took over as George reached out to touch the painting and feel for a way to open the door; however, as soon as he made contact with the barrier, a chill shot through his spine and a tear trickled down his face. George quickly retreated but found that he could not remove his eyes from the passageway whilst thinking, *What caused such a powerful reaction?* A bitter taste of salt woke him from his daydream as the tear rolled down onto his lips. Unable to quite bring himself to face the closed door yet again, George proceeded through the already open passage. Immediately, the differences to the previous door were apparent; there was a warmth from this entrance and the sudden heat seemed to ball in George's stomach as if he had just eaten a warming meal on a cold winter's day. The sun was shining strongly amongst the clear blue sky and George had to protect his eyes from the brightness in order to take in the rest of his surroundings. All of a sudden he realised where he was: the woodland near the farmer's field – one of his favourite places growing up. He had many happy memories here, one being his twelfth birthday party; it was hot that day, too, if he remembered correctly. Then someone ran 'through' him as if he were a ghost. Judging by that, he would be unable to interact with anyone here. George peered at who had just passed through him and his stomach lurched. Sure, he had just seen the impossible. George followed a young girl carrying a Frisbee back to her friends. George's heart leapt but his brain ached at the exact same time. The young girl holding the Frisbee was a younger Annabel and the friends she returned to were him and Jacob. Frantically scanning the scene, George spotted his family and friends holding presents.

His father, a packhorse for the day, was carrying all the bags and new toys whilst his mother was holding a balloon with 'Twelve today' printed on it. George witnessed his younger self enjoying a packet of crisps under a large tree. *Jacob used to climb that tree three times a day*, George chuckled to himself, *his earliest attempts of showing off to Annabel.*

Further analysis of the scene revealed nothing that would constitute a challenge like the previous tasks that day. *It doesn't make sense, why would the door bring me here – to my happiest memory?*

George sat and watched for a while as Lincoln turned up and

started a game of football. Even then he was showing vast amounts of talent for the sport. As soon as they grew tired of football, the four of them played a game of tag which took them all around the field, weaving between the trees. Unable to run any more, they sat down dripping with sweat, a brief pause to refresh themselves for the next activity. Annabel was presently studying to become an environmental scientist, however, even back then she showed her care for the environment around her as she broke from the group to pour some water onto some particularly dehydrated plants. "For the bees," she'd told them. "Without the plants they'll die and without the bees *we'll* die."

Before long, the afternoon had become evening and the sun was a gentle glow on the horizon. George watched as his younger self argued with his mother to stay a bit longer before the debate was abruptly ended by a large kiss on the head from his father.

Bryan then hoisted his son over his shoulders and carried him off into the sunset like the end of any good cowboy film.

Back to the present, George stood and shook out his legs, trying to reignite the blood flow that seemed to have slowed judging by the piercing pins and needles his lower body was experiencing. George turned to exit through the door which he entered earlier, however, the simulation began to whir around him and then reformed into a new scene. He was no longer outside but in an unfamiliar house; there was a purple fluffy rug on the floor and a flat-screen TV on the wall. The wallpaper was floral and the light filling the room came from a dusty old lampshade swinging to and fro in the slight breeze from the open window. The black sofa and armchair were empty but two large depressions in the seats showed that two people had been sitting there recently.

A young woman walked into the lounge looking dishevelled and hot from working away in the kitchen. "Dinner is ready, darling. Sky, come and eat with your father and I."

Quick footsteps echoed through the house as a child ran out of their room and down the stairs to obey their mother and take a seat at the table. The mother and daughter looked alike in all but the hair; the mother had chestnut brown curls whereas the daughter had shoulder-length, fiery ginger hair. *I sure hope I don't pass my hair on to my daughter,* George thought to himself as he looked in the mirror hanging just behind him. Wondering why he was here, George made for the front door next to the staircase but, as he reached the door, the father of the girl rushed downstairs running straight through where George was standing. *Yep, that's me*, George admitted to himself as he followed his older self to the kitchen and, by the looks of it, to his family. George was dumbfounded again as he had been whilst observing his twelfth birthday party. *They're so happy, is this my future? If it is, I don't want anything to change*. When the meal was finished, George watched the family retire to the lounge to partake in some evening TV, still laughing and smiling as they went. Excited about his future with a beautiful wife and an adorable kid, he decided to take his leave. This time when George made to return to the room that he'd begun the task in, he succeeded. Surrounded by the white walls of RAS again, he turned to look at the duo of doors once more. The pathway he had just been through closed for the first time. On the door which obstructed it was a painting of a skull with the words 'A joyful death' written underneath. Stumped by the picture and accompanying words, George pondered its meaning; he had just been through that door and there *was* no death, only his birthday party and a future happy family.

"Confused?" boomed a familiar voice behind him.

George was startled by the sudden intrusion on his thoughts but quickly regathered his composure in time to ask Presley what the doors meant and how he was to proceed.

"The door on the right shows your happiest memory and the future you may have if you choose *not* to join Minotaur. It therefore also serves as a reminder to all what you may sacrifice if you choose to join Minotaur – that life and all associated with it may be lost. Nevertheless, to go back to your family and live happily – thus not join Minotaur – would be sentencing mankind to death, hence 'A joyful death'. If you choose to join Minotaur and help save the world then choose the left door and the *Semita salvatoris* or 'The path of the saviour' will be made."

The strong emotions felt when George originally touched the left door made sense now; *however did my body know to react with such pain and anguish before I even knew where it led?*

When George turned to voice his thoughts to Presley, he was gone and the door was just closing behind him, leaving George in silence to ponder what he hoped would be the biggest decision he would ever have to make. The urge to merely choose the door on the right promising happiness was very strong; nevertheless, after what seemed like hours of procrastinating – but was, in reality, only a matter of minutes – George came to the gruesome conclusion that he would have to give up his friends and family in order to choose the door on the left and try to save mankind from its fate. *You always wanted adventure, George, a chance to be a hero, well now I guess I've got to go through with it... Now, just to figure out how to actually open the door*, George wondered to himself. He first began by ramming it with his shoulder a couple of times but soon grew tired of that method when the door wasn't even shaking, and his arm became very sore very fast. Kicking and punching yielded the same disappointing results. *What would Annabel and Rosie do? They would have been through here ages ago.* Frustration building after each attempt to open the door showed the same failed result time and time again. George just slumped to the floor and thought back on the day's activities, trying to find some clue as to how to open the door. George knew that each item they received in their letters had proved the way to solve the task before, yet he had gotten the horseshoe out a quarter of an hour previously and all attempts made with the item had failed. He had tried knocking the door with the horseshoe, waving it across the seal of the door and he had even attempted to place it on his own foot but discovered quickly that a human's foot is very different to a horse's hoof. He became dejected and furious that the best and easiest option, the right door, was easy to choose whereas the option only a fool would take was so hard to unlock. Taking a deep breath, George racked his mind one final time to find a way to open the door. George stared at the minotaur painting; it had the big shaggy coat of fur, large green eyes and two enormous arms holding an equally gargantuan axe, yet somehow, some way, something was missing. *That's it. Got it!*

George shot to his feet and found the horseshoe he had thrown at the opposite wall just seconds ago in anger at the situation. He picked it up and carried it over to the paining.

George prayed and shoved the horseshoe into the minotaur's nose. *BINGO!* The horseshoe clicked into place and George twisted the makeshift nose ring ninety degrees, just as Presley had done earlier in the day to access the secret elevator. The door swung open and George spotted something fly towards him. There was a flash of pain and then everything went black for a millisecond. When his vision returned after the brief assault, he noticed Presley on the opposite side of the door. He pulled George through and embraced him like a long-lost friend.

"Sorry," he whispered into George's ear. "Sorry it had to be him, lad."

George pulled away and looked up into his old football coach's face, a man he had always despised for being harsh on him at practise and during games, yet now he was the leader of some secret task force to the save the world. Stranger still, as Presley released him and sent him to the meeting room to await the others, George was sure he saw a sparkle in Presley's eyes, a shadow of a tear that a man of his size and stature would never be expected to shed.

As expected, Annabel and Rosie were already there when George reached the meeting room.

"So, you've chosen *'The path of the saviour'* as well, have you then?" George asked them upon entering the room, making sure to used exaggerated inverted commas near his head as he said the 'path of the saviour' part.

"Yes, and don't mock, it's serious!" Annabel shot back. "Roy held my hand as I made my choice and walked through the door with me."

George was trying to remember who Roy was; he had met so many new faces that day.

"The one with the green spiky hair," Annabel barked with unnecessary force, seeing that George was struggling to remember. Annabel continued, "I have known him for as long as I can remember. I always used to come into his shop to see what weird and wonderful artefacts he had acquired in the week. There was this one time that..." but she tailed off on noticing that the others were not the slightest bit interested.

"Hang on a minute," started Rosie, "so George knows Presley, and Annabel, you say you know this strange Roy gentleman." Ignoring the glare she received from Annabel for calling Roy strange, Rosie carried on. "Well, a familiar face came into my room to help me make my choice also, Yuanli my gymnastics teacher."

"Did you both feel pain as you opened the door?" asked George, concerned that he would be the only one.

"Yeah," the girls replied in unison.

"It lunged as quick as a snake," added Annabel.

"Yeah, and made a cracking sound as it snapped though the air," Rosie remembered.

"Whatever it was, it hurt for such a small amount of time and none of us have any marks of harm," George finished.

Before this information had time to sink in, Cheikhou swaggered into the room laughing and shouted behind him, "Yeah, see you later, Carlton!"

George barely had time to open his mouth to ask the question as Cheikhou answered it immediately in an excitable voice.

"You won't believe who I just saw."

George resisted the urge to sarcastically reply 'Carlton'.

"Carlton. He used to be a safari ranger on the reserve near me before I moved to England. He let me ride shotgun with him on trips to tend to the animals and intercept poachers."

Rosie couldn't help herself and asked the question that had been brewing in her mind since Cheikhou mentioned Carlton. "What's he doing here, then?"

Cheikhou smiled his signature big smile and replied, "I'm getting to that, honey; give a brother a chance to finish his sentence, will you?"

Rosie flushed pink and reprimanded herself for not giving him time to finish.

Cheikhou ploughed on with his story. "So, yeah, Carlton comes in the room when I was choosing my door and, obviously, I was shocked to see him so I asked why he was here. He said that he's my guardian and that each of the five people that will join Minotaur have had guardians looking out for them since we were much smaller versions of ourselves." Cheikhou judged by the looks on his audience's faces that they, too, had each received a visit from their guardians in the room with the doors.

"Suppose we're just waiting on Jacob now then," sighed Annabel, who looked slightly more worried than the rest about her new-found boyfriend's fate.

"He'll be along shortly!" boomed Cheikhou. "Tell me about your guardians, then."

Before anyone had time to fill Cheikhou in, the door to the meeting room swung open and Alex was pulled in by a plump fat woman with tight blonde curls that was moving surprisingly fast for her stature. Alex had tears streaking down his face and the rotund lady did not seem impressed.

"Alex, you great baby, you made the right choice. They wouldn't be able to do it without you."

The group cast disapproving looks at the statement to each other.

"I'll deliver an extra pot of ice-cream to your house this week so you can hide under the covers while moaning and comfort eating," and with that she gave Alex one final clip on the ear and stormed out of the room, muttering something along the lines of 'embarrassing' and 'disappointing'.

Rosie, Cheikhou and George were chuckling at Alex's expense but Annabel suddenly shrieked at them, "Don't you see? He's the fifth member of our team. Jacob hasn't made it."

Rosie confirmed Annabel's suspicions. "She said she would deliver ice-cream to his house, she must be Alex's guardian, his local delivery driver."

"Yeah, she said something about always looking out for me; I did wonder why she was always the driver who delivered our weekly shopping. I am even made to call her Auntie Barbs," moaned Alex, apparently unaware at how much the rest of them wished he wasn't there and that it was Jacob instead.

The door to the meeting room opened again and all the failed contenders who didn't make the final five were ushered into the room.

Jacob dragged his feet to his friends with his head hung low. He immediately went to Annabel, "I entered the door on the right and saw the moment we kissed after the first task, and then the simulation changed and you and I were getting married; George was best man. It was perfect." Yet the happy story was being told with a sullen voice. A telling voice, one which all but confirmed he picked the door on the right.

Annabel kissed Jacob and explained how they all had guardians. When she got to George's guardian, Presley, she paused and glowered at George, "How come Presley had to be your guardian? He has known Jacob just as long and Jacob was always braver and stronger." Annabel was choking on her words now as she forced back the tears.

Jacob then rounded on George as well, "I thought we were best mates? You couldn't have told me about all of this!"

George tried to explain he didn't know about any of it, but Jacob continued, "I always told you that you were Presley's favourite. You're a fool if you think any of this is real; don't worry, I know you'll come crawling back to me."

Cheikhou took George by the arm and pulled him aside, "They don't mean it, man, she's just sad for Jacob and he's bitter that Presley chose you instead of him. Just leave them to it."

The guardians entered the room to congratulate the respective youths they had shadowed the last couple of decades and, at the same time, the workers tasked with wiping the memories of the failures entered also.

George followed Cheikhou, Alex and Rosie over to speak to their guardians and be introduced to each other. As the group was walking away, they could hear Jacob saying something about revenge and Annabel seemed to have lost control of the situation, too. She was trying to calm him but finally he pushed her away and stormed from the room.

Presley barked orders to stop him, reminding the other workers of the dangers of leaving the base without having their memories wiped. A set of men and women dressed in the signature red suits went sprinting after him. Jacob swivelled round, laid out the leading chaser with a strong right hand and crashed through the door to try to escape.

George could only guess that Jacob asked Annabel to come with him but, displaying the exact same strength of will that had been tested minutes earlier, she refused to leave her newly formed Minotaur team, despite how sad she was.

Annabel stomped back over to where George and the others were standing and just slumped down in a chair near them, crying into her arms.

Rosie broke from the group and went to comfort her.

Alex tried to chip in but only made matters worse with his suggestion to share the ice-cream Barbara was bringing him with her.

Roy was most successful cheering her up when he gave her a ring set with a beautiful stone, "Now you know I'm your guardian, here's a little present I've been saving for years."

Annabel managed a weak smile and whispered her thanks as she slipped the ring on, however, the smile never reached her eyes which were still full of tears.

For the final time that day, Presley announced himself to the room, demanding complete silence. "Congratulations and, most importantly, thank you to all of you who have shown the bravery, commitment and strength to join our cause. I'm aware that, at the moment, this will all seem very alien to you, perhaps even a little silly. I can guarantee you that nothing about this organisation is to be taken lightly, you are now members of Minotaur and, as such, have given up your lives to the protection of this planet. We'll meet again next week. I will give you a full debrief then in which you will be informed on what we do here and why. The week leading up to that meeting you should fill with joy and happiness. Give up your jobs and live it as if it is your last week on this earth, because in the reality you know of now, it will be." He was halfway through proclaiming his congratulations to the final five and wishing them all the best of luck in their new duty when a worker in a red suit ran into the room and whispered something inaudible into his ear. Presley's eyes shot open and he dismissed the worker with the wave of an arm. His mind clearly on what he had just been informed, he quickly rounded off his speech by setting the next meeting day which was the coming Sunday in the same location. He also referred the group to a lady at the back of the room who would take their sizes in order for suits to be made in their shape. Then, when the instructions were given out, he marched from the room in pursuit of the man who had just spoken to him.

Whilst George was waiting for his turn to be measured, he was left to wonder where Presley had just had to rush off to in such a hurry. He hadn't come up with an answer, and just prayed it had nothing to do with Jacob, when his turn to be measured came. The lady that measured him was the woman called Yuanli, Rosie's guardian. The lady was British-Chinese and had long black hair that reached halfway down her back. Her face looked younger than her years and George was immensely surprised when she said she was fifty years old; he wouldn't have placed her a day past thirty. Her slim body and lack of wrinkles hid her age remarkably. She was a very nice lady, complimenting George on his hair, something very few people did, and measuring the awkward areas around the groin as fast as she could, making light of the action when she did.

When all sizes had been taken, Annabel was the first to notice the time and when she exclaimed it to the room, they all decided it was best to head home for bed. The five new members of Minotaur said their goodbyes, littered with yawns and the occasional sob from Annabel.

George exited Roy's Antiquities Store that night with a great smile on his face; he was meeting Cheikhou in the week so they could get to know each other a bit better in less extreme circumstances. Additionally, he was immensely proud of himself for enduring and thriving in the day's activities. He started up the street towards the woodland near his house, humming under his breath and buzzing for what adventures awaited in the future. George was completely unaware of the watching eyes from the bush across the road.

A gruff voice barked, "Is that him?"

The shaky voice of Jacob replied, "Yes, that's him," in a tone that implied the voice was not shaking through fear but rage.

George hated walking in the dark and liked it even less when he had to go through the forest. He always felt like there was someone watching his every move, waiting to pounce on him from one of the trees or behind one of the big bushes along the woodland floor.

There was no light in the forest, so he had to get out his phone to use as a torch. It was the same idea he deployed in the antiques shop earlier in the day, a moment which felt like a lifetime ago to George after such a busy day. The light illuminated the forest for a few seconds before the phone died with a merry tune to signal the end of the battery life. He was once again plunged into darkness. It took a few seconds before his eyes adjusted enough to see the path by the faint moonlight that was infiltrating the trees. Nothing could be done about the black shroud of night and this was the only way home, so he ploughed on regardless. It was a path he had travelled many times in the dark but normally he had the added bonus of being drunk, coming home from the Purple Giant, so his fears were nulled. A rustle of leaves in a tree to his left made him look up in alarm but there was nothing there, *just the wind* he told himself. After a couple of minutes of walking there was a scream to his right, hidden behind a row of oaks. His walking pace became brisker and another minute of travelling was followed by a howl a little further forward. George quickened his stride once again and found himself almost jogging. He could see the faint glow of a street light in the distance, a safe haven marking the end of the vegetation, promising to banish the demons away.

He was getting close to salvation when, suddenly, his path was blocked. George fell to the ground in shock as a gaunt figure dropped from an overhanging branch onto the path. The creature stepped into a slither of moonlight which revealed it was naked save for a scrap of cloth covering its genital area. It had thin wisps of brown hair sprouting from an otherwise bald head. The creature was so emaciated that it looked like a rib cage wrapped in pale mottled skin. The beast's hands were tipped with long razor-looking claws that could easily rip through tissue and tear away flesh. It fixed its stare on George with big black eyes, no white to be seen. As it took a step towards its helpless prey, another figure came charging from the surrounding foliage and tackled the monster to the ground. A quick scramble ensued where the skinny monster attempted to escape its aggressor, but it was no match for the larger figure who smashed its skull into the forest floor until the contents of its brain were feeding the soil. Wailing a final time in a blood-curdling screech, the creature died. The mountain rose and stumbled into the same slither of moonlight the creature had just evicted. Presley came into focus covered in blood, none of it his own. He looked George in the eye and said a single command, "Run."

George stood motionless as Presley bowled him out of the way to deal with another of the creatures that was creeping up behind the unsuspecting redhead. Once he recovered from the initial shock, George didn't need asking twice. He sprinted for the safety of the street light and bathed in its bright embrace when he stumbled into the open. He didn't look back, instead opting to continue running to his home.

He crashed through the front door and locked it behind him, then he checked all the other doors were locked in the house as well as the windows. The next logical step for George after a major event in his life was always to ring Jacob. Knowing his phone was dead, he used the landline, however, when he rang, the phone went straight to voicemail. George was still shaking when he got into bed and wondered to himself, *what have I signed up for?*

CHAPTER 5

When George awoke the next day, he was hoping that the previous day had just been a bad dream. The first action he performed was removing his mobile from charge to check his contacts. Cheikhou was in there that meant that the day had definitely happened; nevertheless, he decided that surely the creature of the evening was just a nightmare. The second action of the day was to phone into work and resign on the spot, nothing had ever felt so sweet. Hearing his manager on the other end of the phone shouting and complaining that he couldn't do that took a place in George's top moments of his life so far. Not wanting to waste the opportunity, he milked the phone call to its maximum, telling his manager exactly what he thought of them and pointing out all the discrepancies in the workplace. When the call ended, George's eyes were watering with laughter and his manager's were watering with rage. There was only the briefest moment that George second-guessed himself, wondering if he had imagined the part of the previous day when he was told he could give up his job, the same as he had convinced himself he imagined the creature from the night before. A weight off his shoulders, George wondered how to begin his last week of freedom before embarking on the journey with Minotaur.

The weather was once again as nice as the other holiday destinations around the continent so, to make the most of it, George decided he would go to the beach and open up the beach hut. He tried Jacob's phone again but still got no answer. He then tried Annabel and a few other friends. After several phone calls it turned out that only Annabel was free after making the difficult decision to suspend her studies which were the building blocks for her aspiration to become an environmental scientist. To start with she was unwilling to come, opting instead to see if Jacob would meet her. Nevertheless, after she failed to get hold of Jacob as well, she messaged George and asked if she could still come. After packing lunch, sun cream, towel, hat and sunglasses, he left the front door and walked to his car.

When George first entered his car, it felt like climbing into an oven. The all-black metallic shell absorbed the morning heat and made the air stuffy and difficult to breathe. As soon as the engine was turned on George opened both windows to let some air into the car. This made little impact nonetheless as, until the vehicle got moving, the only air that surrounded the vehicle was the same hot, dry air that currently occupied the interior. The radio blared into life still playing the CD from George's previous journey, *'It's my life... It's now or never'* sang the singer through the speakers. George felt a shiver run down his spine as the false memory of the night before replayed in his mind. Shaking his head, he locked the doors to the car and set off to pick Annabel up just around the corner.

The drive to her house took less than five minutes and George pulled over and beeped his horn to alert her of his arrival. She leant out of the window with a towel wrapped around her and shouted down that she would be ten minutes. George grumbled to himself, but the time soon flew by whilst he rocked out to the tunes in his car. He heard a door slam shut and looked up to see her emerging from the house, taking pictures on her phone and uploading them to the internet. Her blonde hair was flowing freely all down her back, she wore a crop top which exposed her toned abdominal muscles and her long legs were almost entirely on show in a short denim miniskirt. Amongst the jewellery on her hand, she was wearing the ring that Roy had given her the previous day. George had always felt an attraction to Annabel, much like his best friend; conflict was avoided, though, as they made a deal many years ago that Jacob could attempt to win her affections in lieu of himself.

She reached the car and tried to open the door, but it was still locked where George had panicked earlier. She tapped on the window and shrugged her arms.

Apologising, George unlocked the vehicle.

Annabel opened the car door and sat down in the passenger seat. "Sorry about the wait," she said.

"No worries, as long as you have the approval you need from the hoards on social media." That just earned him a slap on the arm.

Annabel was not as into rock music as George, so she changed the CD to Robbie Williams which suited them both.

They hit little traffic on the way to the beach, although George still begrudged the small amount they *did* encounter, blaming the wait for Annabel.

"Really need to fix the air conditioning in there," George admitted whilst locking the car.

"Yeah, travelling in a furnace isn't ideal," Annabel huffed as she removed a sticky strand of hair from her forehead.

Improving their mood, they noticed the coast was quiet the day after the bank holiday weekend due to everyone returning to their work or education. An immediate advantage presented itself when George managed to park close to the beach hut, meaning the walk wouldn't be too far.

A seagull sang overhead whilst George struggled with the stiff doors to the coastal abode. When he finally forced them open with a grunt, he made a note that he would have to oil up the hinges next time he came, the same memo he left every visit. The hut was located near a water pump, so George took no time to go and fill the kettle ready to make a cup of tea. Hobbling back with the kettle, trying not to spill its contents, George almost tripped when he saw Annabel had stripped down to her bikini and begun to sunbathe. *God, Jacob, where are you?* he wondered to himself, trying to avert his eyes from her figure. They both wanted a cup of tea and George began cooking the bacon that Annabel had brought for their breakfast. When he was happy that the meat was cooked, he buttered up some baps, put the meat between the bread and smothered them both in tomato sauce. Annabel accepted hers graciously and they sat together just people-watching in the blistering heat whilst they ate their food. It was only a matter of time before Annabel broached the question of where George thought Jacob could be. "Why would he miss this?"

"He's most likely at work, he doesn't have a free pass to give it up like us, remember?" George knew his best mate didn't work Tuesdays but, ignoring Annabel a day after finally admitting his love for her was not a smooth move in his eyes so he covered the best he could.

"But why isn't he answering his phone?" she shot back.

"Maybe it's dead. Maybe he's still sulking. Give him a few days.

You know how he gets."

"I suppose," she allowed. "I'm busy tomorrow but Thursday I'll go to his house if he still hasn't answered his phone by then."

"Yeah, OK. That's the day Cheikhou and I are going paintballing so you will miss that, though."

On the one hand, Annabel didn't seem too worried about missing that particular activity, but on the other hand, the small talk about Jacob seemed to put her mind at rest. Now she had a plan there would be no need for her to worry for a couple of days. They spent most of the day simply sunbathing and people-watching.

One particular group of yobs offended Annabel the most, "Uncultured swines," Annabel groaned.

George had also witnessed the group take turns launching their rubbish into the sea, adding to what was increasingly being known as the world's largest waste dump.

Although he didn't agree with the act, he still grumbled to himself when Annabel insisted on retrieving the refuse. Further people-watching was broken up only by the odd dip in the sea and the even odder appearance of 'Sharky', a local nutcase who spent every day scanning the coast for fossils and talking to unsuspecting beachgoers about whatever was troubling him that particular day. He got the name 'Sharky' from the back of the football top he wore at all times; no one knew his actual name. Unfortunately for Annabel and George, the shells were troubling Sharky that Tuesday.

"Hey guys, have you seen all the shells today?" he started.

George made the mistake of looking up first. "Oh, hi. Yeah, there's a lot, isn't there."

"Enough to make a fort, I'd say!" Sharky shouted back, scanning the beach.

"Maybe," replied George.

"I reckon the crabs are planning an all-out assault. The shells are their scouts," whispered the madman. Annabel let out a small giggle and Sharky shot her a crazed look. "What do you know of the attack?" he barked.

Annabel cursed the ease at which she laughed, this time resulting in her being dragged into the conversation. She was far too clever to be stuck for long, however, as she leaned in and ushered Sharky closer, saying, "The attack's happening at the pier in a half-hour." To add extra effect, she jumped to her feet and pointed in the direction of the phantom danger, "Go, stop the assault, save us all!"

Sharky ran away with his new orders whilst George thanked Annabel for her good acting. Scared that he would return, they decided it was likely time to leave. As quick as they could they collected their belongings and retreated to the car before Sharky called for reinforcements.

The CD finished halfway back to Annabel's house and so they listened to the first few songs again.

"Thanks for coming!" George shouted from the car when Annabel got out to leave.

She didn't respond as she analysed the many notifications coming through on her phone now the signal had returned. "He hasn't 'liked' any of the pictures I put up this morning!" Annabel called back.

"What about the other three hundred people? Surely, they mean something?" George tried to console her.

"It's six hundred now but none are him. I don't know why I do this to myself; I don't feel any better for the validation, not when the one person I care about ignores me," Annabel said, her shoulders sunk.

"Don't keep doing it then," George muttered to himself.

"What?" Annabel cupped her ear.

"Thursday. Give him 'til then, he's crazy for you!" George shouted back.

Annabel nodded and gave her thanks before disappearing into her house.

Alone once more, George locked the car from the inside before driving home. Whilst passing the forest his hands tightened on the steering wheel and his foot grew heavy on the accelerator, he wasn't going to chance another meeting with the monsters that attacked him, imagined or not. Once home, the rest of the night flew by as the day had, and George found himself surrendering to the sea air in his lungs pulling him into a deep sleep.

George woke on the day of meeting Cheikhou, relishing his morning stretch. He felt good which he savoured before the inevitable aches and bruises the paintballing would reward him. The day started similarly to every other one for George – the overwhelming stench of the fresh incense stick lit by his mother and the inadequacies of his curtains, again being the main reasons for his early rise. Nonetheless, the constant thoughts and feeling of excitement running through his mind were also no aids in trying to get lots of sleep. George threw on some old and tatty clothes: stained tracksuit bottoms covered in paint from years past and a jumper full of holes, some from constant use when the jumper was in fashion, the rest no doubt caused by moths in the cupboard.

"Alright One-eye Pete, round for breakfast?" joked George's father, taking the mickey out of his worn attire.

George turned to see his father was already at the breakfast table with half a bowl of porridge, a quarter already eaten, the rest dribbling down his chin.

"I'm dressed like this because I'm going paintballing with a mate today. Saving that for Ron?" replied George to his father's sarcastic comment.

George's father immediately wiped his chin knowing full well that they knew no one called Ron and that George must be referring to the porridge dripping down his chin, 'saving for later Ron'. The father and son banter finished as abruptly as it started when George's mother entered the room fully dressed and began berating her husband about needing to leave for town in the next five minutes to meet her mother.

George continued assembling his breakfast which, for this morning, was a poached egg and some baked beans. Whilst the beans were cooking George tried ringing Jacob again. The monotonous voice of the answerphone came through the speaker as it had every time since he stormed out of RAS on the Monday. George thought his mate would have realised he was silly to have reacted the way he did, but obviously he was wrong. Nevertheless, Jacob always came back to him after a fallout, the only worry was that it was never after this long. He gave a silent prayer, *please let him be OK.* "Good luck, Annabel," he muttered when he remembered she was actively searching for Jacob that day.

Having never been paintballing before, George was a little

apprehensive whilst he left the house and walked to where he agreed to meet Cheikhou, but when he saw his mate's big grin he was immediately eased of his worries and came to the conclusion that Cheikhou would not let him get hurt. Standing next to Cheikhou was Rosie, who had obviously decided she quite fancied joining in the day's activity as well. George didn't know how he felt about this as he didn't want to make a fool of himself in front of her.

Rosie spoke first, "Annabel isn't coming, she's walked to Jacob's to see him and talk over what happened Monday."

George nodded, despite already knowing.

"Alex isn't coming then?" inquired George.

Cheikhou's overexaggerated laugh, even by his standards, gave George his answer.

"No, Cheik decided not to invite him, which I think's cruel as he's a part of the team, like it or not." Rosie glared at Cheikhou but the look only propelled him into further laughter.

The three of them jumped into Cheikhou's car and set off for their destination. During the journey George discovered that his new-found friends were both avid paintballers and went at least three times a year. He also learnt that the bruises don't stay long but the little pellets hurt like hell when they hit you. The time in the car did nothing to settle George's nerves and the prospect of embarrassing himself seemed to grow more likely by the second. George watched his legs bounce until he felt the car come to a stop. He looked up to see if they were at their destination, but they were just waiting at some traffic lights.

"Not long now!" Cheikhou shouted into the back as they set off again at the green light, "Just a little furth – WHAT'RE YOU DOING, YOU TWAT?"

A large Land Rover had jumped the lights to the right of them and almost crashed straight into the side of their car, but Cheikhou managed to manoeuvre them out of danger with some evasive driving. When they turned to confront the reckless driver, the vehicle had accelerated away.

George shook his head and patted Cheikhou on the shoulder, congratulating him on his dexterity behind the wheel.

"Good job I wasn't driving," Rosie panted, "I couldn't have done that."

After setting back off it wasn't long before they reached their location. Cheikhou was still fuming when he exited the car and Rosie was the victim of his anger on the one hand, after she pointed out that his unsavoury language moments ago was unnecessary. Cheikhou, on the other hand, insisted quite the opposite and said that it could have been much worse.

The fire in his belly was reignited with gasoline minutes later as they entered the compound and Alex was standing there with what must have been his father, a little shorter, equally round but down to just a few wisps of hair on his liver-spotted head.

"Hey guys!" Alex shouted across, waving his arms.

"Hey Alex!" George took on the burden of going to talk to him.

Alex was his usual self for the following ten minutes telling George about all the times he has been paintballing before and that him and his father come weekly and take part in tournaments. Apparently, Alex set a new record for eliminations in the last one when he single-handedly took the enemy flags one by one during a competitive game of Capture the Flag, a game which Alex told George he would find out more about later. George was finally relieved of his duties when Rosie called him over to collect the camouflage suit he would be wearing for the day as well as his gun and ammunition. George looked around and saw around twenty further people who would be partaking in the fun, a mix of younger kids and older people; he was certain that one guy with a scar down his cheek must be ex-military and that led George to wonder how he stood any chance against these guys. They were then ushered into seats to watch a training video telling them how to load the gun and instructing them on safety during the day. The video ended with a final warning not to shoot when the helmets were removed, with a clip of an egg being hit by a paintball throwing yolk and egg white everywhere, the words 'That could be your eye' flashing up to finish off. George was shaking slightly by the end of the video and Alex was not helping with his constant stories of the times that he had been shot in the ear and went deaf for a month and when he was winded and couldn't breathe for a few minutes. The horror only grew when the group of them arrived at a desk which was offering to sell pyrotechnic grenades and large paintball miniguns.

Alex filled up with grenades and George watched as the largest man in the group thumped up to the counter and asked to purchase the minigun. It looked small in his bearlike arms but when he came thumping back past where George stood, he saw that the gun was almost as big as he was. The only man that bought more items than Alex was the guy with the scar on his face, who was the last to leave the counter. He purchased the rest of the pyrotechnic grenades as well as a few small contraptions that, on closer inspection of the label, George discovered were paintball landmines. The teams were then separated into blue and red.

Cheikhou, Rosie, George and 'Scarface' were part of team blue, whereas Alex, his father and the bearlike man joined the others on team red.

Rosie warned Cheikhou not to just go after Alex, but he dismissed her with his characteristic laugh. George was just pleased that he had Scarface on his team. Deciding that he was his best avenue of a safe and successful day of paintballing, George struck up conversation with the gent. "Hi, my name's George," he greeted, sticking out his hand.

The mysterious man shook it and replied, "I'm Greg, but call me Razor; that's what the guys back at base call me."

Excitement was building in George. "OK then, Razor, I'm going to stick with you. Just tell me what you need me to do."

"What I need you to do? I don't know, I've never been here before either." Razor seemed taken aback by George's faith in him.

"Oh well, yeah, but you can call upon your skills from work, can't you?" winked George with a tone of anticipation.

"Well, yes, but I don't think that my vet skills will serve me now," replied Razor.

"OK, you might be a bit past it, but I have heard that the vets are even tougher than the current soldiers." George was growing restless of Razor playing dumb, he was going to need his help.

"Current soldiers? Oh no, not an army vet, son, I'm an animal vet. What made you think I served in the army?" Then he realised, "It's the scar, isn't it? Well, sorry to let you down but that was a particularly nasty tabby cat I met a few years ago; the guys at work have been calling me Razor ever since," he laughed but George did not.

"Well then, Greg," George was not prepared to call him Razor now that the reason behind the nickname was revealed, "why did you buy all them weapons, then?" George asked with a final plea that perhaps Greg from the vet's might have a hidden talent as a bomber.

"I've no idea. Just wanted to see what they did; should be intriguing, shouldn't it?"

With that, George walked back towards Cheikhou and Rosie, ready to start the day's proceedings. The talk with Greg had taken place during the walk from the base camp into the woods where the games would be played. Each team had a leader who explained that the first game was just a Team Deathmatch. Both teams play until one entire team has been eliminated. If you were hit you were eliminated, simple as that. The whistle blew and the game began.

George sprinted for the nearest tree and threw himself behind it with such force that he was sure that he heard it creak with the impact. Cheikhou and Rosie advanced towards the enemy, weaving between trees for cover, and Greg had run wildly towards the enemy lines shouting at the top of his voice. The combination of the tatty clothes and the camouflage suit, as well as the protective mask, was quite claustrophobic, and George struggled to breathe in his hot, sweaty prison. After Cheikhou and Rosie had advanced out of view, George decided it was safe to follow in the direction they went. The first game was played at quite a small location and therefore it was not long until George once again found his team. The first member of his team he spotted again was Greg, covered in paint and trudging back towards the safe zone where you were to go if eliminated. Despite the hammering he seemed to have received, George saw the hint of a smile through all the paint covering Greg's mask. "Get in there, the guys need you!" shouted Greg as he passed.

George scanned the woods for his friends and saw Cheikhou about to be shot by an enemy. However, at the moment Cheikhou would have been eliminated, a paint pellet hit the attacker and Rosie rushed in and shouted to Cheikhou something sounding like, "Saved your life!" through the clamour of the battle. George rendezvoused with them behind the wooden fence that had been erected for synthetic cover. He didn't need Cheikhou to explain that they were losing the fight. He had seen many more of team blue than team red walking to the safety zone with their guns held above their heads to show they were eliminated. Cheikhou explained that Greg had run into the middle of the open space in front of them and was just yelling, firing this way and that, trying to eliminate as many as possible. He also said that he was almost hit by one of Greg's bullets himself but dived out of the way just in time. The blue team leader saw them huddled together and shouted over to them to split up and try to take some of the enemy down. Taking his advice, they all split from the spot instantaneously. A member of red team had been encroaching on their position from the direction George ran in and, when he came face to face with his foe, he froze and the enemy team member didn't. The shot hit George straight in his chest and the impact felt as if he was stung. The red team member sent a hasty apology in George's direction which he thought a bit odd, and then he ran on and rolled under the pellets being fired at him by Cheikhou. Out of the roll he raised his gun in one swift motion and shot Cheikhou, too. George had not stood yet to go to the safe zone as he was in awe at the skill and ability of the opposing player.

Rosie turned when she heard Cheikhou swear after being eliminated to see what was wrong. The millisecond pause allowed the red team member to place a pellet just above the ankle onto the lower leg. Rosie turned out to be the last of team blue and so the reds won. The three of them joined up and looked across to the red team member who eliminated them all, wondering who it had been. When he finally took the mask off during the refreshments before the next game, he was revealed to be Alex, much to Cheikhou's annoyance.

He came over to them with a smile that said 'Sorry' but with a 'Told you I was good' tinge to it. Cheikhou, surprising no one, was the first to open his mouth. "Yeah, yeah, very impressive how you can move so elegantly despite all those extra pounds you carry compared to the rest of us. I bet you have the whole *A-Z Encyclopaedia on Paintball* shoved down there," he pointed towards Alex's rotund belly.

George laughed but Alex brushed it off. "It helps to have extra padding when you get hit, not that I know how that feels, hey guys?" He tried a wink at Rosie but his fat cheeks made the wink look more like a wince.

"I can show you, if you want?" Cheikhou lurched forwards but was stopped by several factors; one, Rosie was holding him back; two, Alex's father was approaching, and three, the last chance for a toilet break had been called by one of the marshals before they went out to play the second game.

George and Alex went off to the toilet and left the others to meet Alex's father who was not like his son in personality. The last George heard previously, out of earshot, was Alex's father saying, "It's so nice to meet some of his friends, Alex told me a lot about you two after you met Monday; he seems particularly fond of you." George didn't need to look back to know he was talking to Rosie.

On the walk back from the toilet George turned to Alex and stated how impressed he was with his performance in the first round and apologised for Cheikhou who had seemed to have taken a particular dislike to Alex.

Alex's reply far from helped his case: "Thanks, Georgie man, but I know that the best can become targets of the less talented, sometimes. One day you both might be on my level."

The second game was Capture the Flag, the stipulation Alex allegedly set a record for eliminations in during his most recently played tournament. The object of which was to collect all four of the opposing team's flags and protect all your own at the same time. The teams were separated again, and this time George promised the others he would go with them straight away; Rosie kept pointing out that they were outnumbered in the first round after his late arrival and Greg's antics. Before the round began, they were allowed to choose their starting positions. Again, the game was in the woods but there were more man-made additions this time. A blown-up car was in the centre and next to that was a building like an old pillbox, the marshals had said that taking and holding this position was key to winning as it covered all the flags for both teams. There was a flag for each team in the pillbox and the rest of the flags were on synthetic walls in each corresponding team's base. Rosie and Cheikhou were guarding one flag, and George had somehow been roped into guarding a second flag with Greg. The other flag was guarded by four team members as it was nearest the enemy side, the rest of the team were to try and take the pillbox as well as the enemy flags. Greg laid his paint mines round the defending sectors to add some extra support, though whilst he laid one down it exploded in his face. After cleaning his mask and checking if he was OK, the blue team leader sent him back to George. The whistle blew and George had to tug Greg back to the floor after he went to sprint into the action again. The battle for the pillbox was won by the red team after a charge led by Alex and his father crushed the blue attempt to take the strategic location. George saw that this enraged Cheikhou who was being calmed by Rosie. Whatever she was saying was not working because Cheikhou jumped up and ran at the pillbox, firing through the slits in its walls, trying to take back the position. Pellets rained down on Cheikhou but he kept advancing, somehow avoiding getting hit. To George's surprise, there were actually red team members leaving the pillbox with their guns above their heads where Cheikhou was eliminating them. The heroics of their team-mate gave the blue team another spurt of bloodlust, so they joined Cheikhou in his advance and eventually reached the perimeter of the bunker. George saw Alex climb through a hatch on the top and eliminate two of the blue team before quickly sliding down the other side to avoid the retaliation of the other blue team members. George's squad took the bunker as Alex retreated to his team, but their charge had cost them two flags; the furthest one forward was captured during the initial battle for the pillbox and when Cheikhou left Rosie, she was eliminated by a group led by Alex's father. When Cheikhou found out Alex had got one over on him again, the win at the pillbox seemed pointless. Nonetheless, the blue team managed what the red team couldn't and kept hold of the pillbox, and the marshals were correct to say it would prove vital. Any approach on the flag that George and Greg were protecting was instantly stopped by the rain of pellets from the central position. Realising this, George and Greg left their flag to be protected by the pillbox and began a flanking manoeuvre on the red team. George led Greg through a trench that encircled the battlefield. Halfway round they met resistance, but George picked up his first two eliminations and Greg his fourth. His mad charge during the first game had merited results eliminating three, foolish as it had been. When they reached their destination, they were hiding behind a wall and they could see the remnants of the red team huddled, trying to figure out how they were going to turn this around.

Greg whispered, "I've got this," to his left, despite George being on his right. He then proceeded to take out one of the paint grenades he had purchased earlier, trying to remember the instructions he was given. Greg turned the end once and counted to five, ready to throw the paint bomb, *one... two... three... fo–* but the bomb went off prematurely and covered Greg in paint. The red team realised they were there and hit Greg with a few more paintballs for his idiocy.

George saw Alex take one of his team to come and finish him off, he turned to run but slipped in the mud and, before he could rise again, Alex was standing over him with his team-mate. George went to admit defeat but, as he opened his mouth, two paintballs hit Alex in the chest and the other guy was hit by two more.

"Get up, buddy," Cheikhou instructed, rushing past and lifting George to his feet. "We saw you and Greg and thought it was a great idea; we have left two in the pillbox so they think we're still there."

As Cheikhou got to Alex he stopped and looked at him, about to make a remark, but Alex spoke first.

"There was mud on my visor, I thought I'd give you a chance. Obviously, I let you eliminate me as I saw you were getting jealous; didn't want you to stop enjoying yourself just because you aren't the best here." Snorting, Alex got to his feet and went over to the area for eliminated players.

"Was that two or three excuses?" Cheikhou asked George.

Once Alex was gone the blue team easily acquired the remaining flags and claimed a victory.

At the start of the third and final game, Rosie had still not forgiven Cheikhou for ditching her, despite his heroics that came from it. She refused to protect Cheikhou during the next game as he didn't protect her in the last one. Normally this wouldn't be a problem, but this final game was Eliminate the Leader in which each team kept coming back after being shot until their leader was eliminated, and team blue's leader was Cheikhou.

The red team instantly appointed Alex and so the tie-breaking game was to be Team Alex versus Team Cheikhou.

George eventually persuaded Rosie to do her job to protect Cheikhou just so she didn't harm everyone else's chances of winning. The leaders were not given weapons as they were just to be protected, however, in the centre of the game were red and blue guns. If the corresponding leader reached their gun, then they could use it. The whistle blew to start the final game and both teams seemed to have the same idea to try to get their leader to the gun of their colour. The massive bearlike man rushed forward for the red team with his minigun, the blizzard of bullets pinned the blue team down whilst Alex rushed for his gun. No one on George's team could move until the gun slowed and the bullets stopped flowing, then everyone on the blue team shot the large menace at the same time. The behemoth roared in pain as a flurry of bullets hit his midsection; instead of going to the eliminated area to come back on he was instead taken to the medical tent due to the sheer number of pellets he took. The fight that broke out afterwards lasted around fifteen minutes with both leaders not risking exposing themselves to get to their gun. Alex had failed in his initial charge, his large frame making him too slow to make the most of the opportunity. The fact that the game allowed people to keep returning after being shot meant that they reached stalemate; neither team seemed to be making progress.

George had gotten much better and was now up to eight eliminations but that wasn't enough to break the stalemate. The two teams began to tire as the deadlock continued for another five minutes and both teams were ready to accept a draw, apart from the captains who were as eager as ever. The marshals called time and decided that if everyone was OK with the decision, they would now determine the winner by a one-on-one battle between Cheikhou and Alex. It would be a cowboy-style duel and they would both be given a special pistol-shaped paintball gun. They were warned that the pellet in the weapon packed a punch and hurt a lot more than the other pellets but neither of them believed they would be on the receiving end of it, so they agreed to the change in ammunition. The red team lined up horizontally behind Cheikhou and the blue mirrored them behind Alex. Rain started drizzling from the sky but soon became a downpour.

There was silence as the two champions faced each other and stared one another down.

Cheikhou broke first and reverted his gaze over Alex's shoulder, looking slightly worried for the first time today.

Alex noticed the loss of eye contact and gibed his opponent, "You know you can't take me. I can beat you with a blindfold and my hands tied behind my back."

Cheikhou didn't react, instead continuing to gaze over Alex's shoulder. They turned back to back and began walking in opposite directions towards the opposing team. When the marshal shouted 'NOW!' they would turn and try to eliminate the other person. Their guns were held in holsters by their side so their drawing speed would be important as well as their accuracy on the turn. The holsters burnt into the sides of the champions like hot coals in their pockets. The ground had turned to mud from the rain and squelched under their shoes, and Alex's heavy breathing was the loudest sound other than that. The marshal shouted and the opponents turned to face each other. Cheikhou was much quicker in drawing his weapon and fired off a round almost as soon as he had turned. Alex was slower but still fired in response. Silence fell again but was broken very fast when Alex began to gloat, singing, *"Simply the best, better than all the rest."*

Screaming erupted when Alex won. He ran over to rub the win in Cheikhou's face but when he reached his opponent he was thrown out of the way.

Cheikhou moved Alex aside with ease so he could look past his heavy frame and sighed in relief, "My shot found its mark, thank goodness."

Alex turned to see what Cheikhou was on about and saw George standing over a hooded man holding a knife.

Cheikhou shouted across, "I saw him sneak in behind you during the face off with Alex, that's why I broke my stare! I didn't recognise him from today and then saw the knife by his side. I didn't want to spook him into something rash so didn't shout out but waited for my time. As soon as the marshal shouted 'NOW!' I unhooked my gun and fired my pellet at his head, aiming to knock him out!"

His shot had been spot-on and hit the assassin straight between the eyes. Upon closer inspection the man was not recognisable to anyone and his motives for trying to attack George were not yet known. They tied him to a tree and waited for him to wake so they could question him.

Ideally, they wanted to interrogate him before the police did whom Greg had already phoned. In the meantime, everyone congratulated Cheikhou on throwing the game to try to save his friend's life. Alex didn't accept he had thrown the game, though, saying, "He would have lost either way." He tried to tell anyone that would listen.

Cheikhou was awarded with the winner's medal for the 'Player of the Day' due to his quick thinking, despite not actually winning the face-off.

Alex kicked up such a fuss that he'd won that Cheikhou threw the medal at him.

Alex snatched it up, saying, "At least you know who the real MVP was."

The mystery man had not awoken for a strangely long time, so Rosie went over to check on his condition. A scream informed the others that something wasn't right.

George, Alex and Cheikhou arrived at the scene perplexed by the cause of the commotion as Rosie was fine and the man was still tied to the tree.

George walked closer and saw the reason for Rosie's horror. The man was dead, lying with dried spit around his mouth and some white foam on his dark-coloured lip. Looking closer at the white frothy spittle, George suggested it looked like a severe reaction to something.

"Looks like cyanide," piped up Alex from the back. "Whoever this guy was, he didn't want us to know".

The four of them looked at each other and came to the same conclusion that whatever he was there for it must have been related to Minotaur. Lying next to the corpse was a small purple flower, half of the petals removed. Upon closer inspection of the man, they saw that he had a purple stain on his hands, likely from the same flower.

Rosie then noticed there was something in the man's mouth. Lowering herself to his level, she carefully leaned forward and reported that it was some chewed petals. "That explains why–"

"I reckon that's why his lips are so purple," Alex butted in.

"–his lips are so dark," Rosie finished.

"The flower must be–" started Cheikhou.

"I reckon the flower's poisonous; I know all about dangerous plants," interrupted Alex once again. Cheikhou didn't finish his sentence like Rosie had, instead fixing Alex with a warning look.

A vibration came from the man's jumper pocket that killed the conversation dead.

They all stared for a moment, unwilling to approach the corpse. Eventually, George rummaged around and found a phone and a scrap of paper. There was no caller ID. George answered but remained silent in order to hear who was on the other end.

"Is it done?" a thick, southern American voice asked.

"Hello, who's this?" George asked.

The connection died with a buzzing sound and the phone became hot. George dropped it before it exploded on the floor beneath them.

"What's the paper say?" Rosie asked.

George unfurled it and discovered it was a return plane ticket to the state of Georgia. "Day trip."

A siren cut through their confusion and the group turned in unison to watch a duo of cops walk towards them.

"No word about Minotaur," whispered George as he tucked the ticket back in the man's coat.

"Agreed," the others said together.

As the police approached with a cocky swagger, their features came into vision revealing a man and a woman. The man was much older than the woman, he had a bushy moustache which boasted more hair than the rest of his head and he made up for what he lacked in height around the waist. The woman looked to be quite new on the job and stayed one pace behind her partner at all times in order to follow what he did in an apprentice fashion. She had a prominent nose and a snort to go with it as she laughed at something the older man said. Her eyes were small and beady, which were swallowed by her chubby cheeks; her only redeeming feature was long, velvety chestnut hair.

When the cops reached the group the man spoke first, reaffirming he was the leader. "What happened here then, guys?" he began whilst giving Cheikhou a look-over.

Alex stepped forward to lead the conversation, pushing George out of the way. "Hello officer, I'm Alex. I have a lot of respect for the work you do and thank you for your service." He reached out a hand for the policeman to shake.

The moustached man laughed and, when he did, the female officer followed, her cheeks wobbling with joy. "Thank you, young man."

The female spoke for the first time, "We're going to question each of you one at a time; we would be happy to start with you."

George watched Alex walk off and waited with the others, observing the questioning from afar.

"It's like the three little piggies," Cheikhou joked.

This time even Rosie allowed herself a little giggle.

When Alex returned, he refused to give up any information to help prepare them for what to say in order to align their alibis to avoid mentioning Minotaur.

Rosie went next and was finished in half the time it took Alex, most likely because she wasn't trying to tell them how to proceed with the investigation.

George followed after; when he reached the police car where the questioning was taking place, he saw they were both leaning on the bonnet enjoying a box of cream cakes. "Rokay, letch get goin'," the man spat through a mouthful of éclair. "Do you know the deceased man?" was the first question.

"No, I've never seen him before in my life," answered George.

"Am I correct in thinking that you were the target for this man before he was shot?"

"Yes, I didn't see him coming but my friend, Cheik, shot him when he saw he was holding a knife."

"I see," said the male officer. "Is that Cheik over there? The coloured chap."

George nodded but didn't fail to notice that Rosie and Alex weren't with him, he was standing alone and so the addition of 'coloured chap' was unnecessary.

"I should like to talk to him very much," he said in a suspecting voice. "Call him over for me, will you?" The moustached man glanced at his colleague, giving each other a look.

George left and came back with Cheikhou by his side. The older man stepped back and let his colleague question the final person.

"Hello Cheek, I'm Officer Porco. Do you mind telling me what you're doing here today?"

"It's Cheik, like the bank payment. I just came for some paintballing," he replied, calmly forgiving the mispronunciation of his name.

"Are you aware that a paintball gun is considered a weapon and it is illegal to fire it at someone who is not actively in the game with the correct protection?" she probed.

"What do you mean?" Cheikhou shouted, "He was going to stab my friend!"

The young officer reached for her Taser. "Don't get aggressive with me, you won't find me such an easy target."

Behind her the older man put his hand on his truncheon.

"I can't believe this. I was saving my friend; you know I just knocked him out, don't you? He committed suicide with a poisonous flower," Cheikhou protested.

"Is that a threat?" Officer Porco screeched.

Cheikhou didn't know what he had said or what to do next so he just threw his hands in the air and said, "Look for yourself." He led the way over to the body with Officer Porco following, her hand resting on her Taser holster.

The moustached man came, too, as backup for his colleague George suspected, more than to try and confirm the suicide.

A few minutes analysing the corpse meant that the police finally stopped suspecting Cheikhou of murder; however, they never apologised for the unnecessary aggression. During the analysis another team turned up to remove the body and take it away for a post-mortem.

The group dismissed, Alex went home with his father.

Before starting for home, George tried to ring Jacob and Annabel to check they were OK but neither were picking up their phones. Whilst George was failing to contact his friends, Cheikhou and Rosie used their mobiles to report what had happened to Carlton and Yuanli, their guardians. When they got off the phone, they both corroborated that their fellow guardians told them to head for home and await further instructions. They hurried into Cheikhou's car and began the route home.

During the journey another long conversation began when Rosie breached the idea that the car that jumped the lights on their way to paintballing was not an accident but was, in fact, most likely another murder attempt. George refused to believe this and was still hoping that the man at paintballing was just a random psycho and had nothing to do with Minotaur. Nevertheless, he wasn't convincing himself let alone the others.

For the second time that day talk was halted by the sound of sirens. They were distant to begin with but within seconds were directly in Cheikhou's rear-view mirror. He pulled over to the left to let them pass and a police car shot past at dangerous speed. "I've had enough of police for today," moaned Cheikhou as he pulled out to continue the drive.

The afternoon had become evening by the time Cheikhou had driven back to each of their houses and dropped them off individually. This process took a while as they wanted to make sure Rosie was safe back in her home before going to deliver George.

When Cheikhou pulled up outside the Keen residence, he gave George a fist bump and said "Take care, brother. I won't be there tonight to help if anything goes wrong." He meant it as a joke but the look in his eyes showed genuine fear for his friend.

"Thanks, Cheik. You saved me today. I can't stop thinking about it. What if you hadn't seen?"

"I did see and that's all that matters. Go rest. Carlton said not to delay, and I have a long drive of my own still to come. I won't have you repaying me by making me food for the bogeyman," Cheikhou said, managing a laugh this time.

George left the car and entered his house, reassured by the echo of Cheikhou's laughter ringing through his head.

CHAPTER 6

Earth
Mexico
Mexico City

The wind was howling and most of the shops were closed due to severe weather. The metal shutters in the out-of-use doorways were clamouring, a constant drumbeat as the fast air rattled the material. The rain was hammering down and the street had become a newly formed river. The litter of the city was travelling down the road, swept up by the constant water. Crisp packets, bottles, carrier bags and even a small bin were racing down the road, performing their very own entertainment for those watching on. The dark sky showed no sign of the weather relenting; if anything, the rain was beginning to fall faster and heavier.

"Why did we have to come in hurricane season?" grumbled Lee to his friends whilst grimacing up at the grey carpet of unforgiving clouds.

"We didn't know there was going to be one today, did we?" Harry snapped back. "Besides, the season stretches on until November. We can't wait that long. If we're going to prove our loyalty we need to show we can get a job done."

"Just relax," pleaded Scott who was watching the small bin dodge and weave round other floating debris in the makeshift river. "The messengers said that the first stage of their leader's plan was to increase natural disasters on Earth. Only then will the planet be weak enough to assault."

The trio were sitting in a bar along what was, up until recently, a busy shopping street. The sheer excess of water had put an end to any browsing however, and people were currently taking cover in whatever opening they could. Those that were unfortunate enough to have been unable to reach a safe haven were using the tops of cars, bus stops and even street lights as pontoons to keep them out of the flood.

"We aren't going anywhere any time soon," pointed out Scott whilst taking a sip of his Corona. "So how about we make this interesting?" He signalled for the waitress to come over and ordered a tray of tequila shots. The waitress was very snappy in her task; it didn't take her long as the bar was almost empty.

"You Americans are stupid," she tutted when she lowered the drinks to the table. Most of the locals had left the bar when the rain started but the three American men stayed and were now trapped in the outlet.

"You love us really, honey," smirked Scott as he paid for the drinks. He winked at her to thank her for her service as he slid his card back into his wallet.

"OK, what's your idea then?" asked Lee who was already sceptical, faced with the liquor on the table.

"We each bet on a floating piece of trash as it passes that car," Scott declared, pointed over to a small green vehicle that was doing well to withstand the water. "Whoever's trash passes that taxi last has to do a shot," he added, finishing by pointing at a deserted vehicle further up the road.

The other two nodded in agreement; they had to do something to pass the time as they couldn't leave in the current conditions.

"*Idiotas!*" they heard the waitress exclaim in her native tongue over at the bar.

All three chose their first bit of rubbish and began the first race. It was fitting that Scott lost the first round as it was his game; the loss came when he chose a bottle that sunk mid-contest. The second and third competitions ended with Harry having to drink. After the two shots the man began to loosen up after his earlier outburst at Lee. The fourth and fifth races left Scott drinking again which meant Lee remained unbeaten. Now there was only one shot left of the original six and both Scott and Harry were determined for Lee to lose. The three tequilas in quick succession were beginning to get to Scott and he was struggling to focus on the debris to choose a suitable champion. After several false starts when he chose an object that wasn't visible or tried to cheat by choosing an item already ahead, the final competition began. This time Scott had chosen a sombrero that must have washed away from a clothing store further up the street. The hat was easily in the lead with both Lee and Harry's objects lagging behind. Scott turned to his friends to make a cocky remark when his traditional Mexican headgear collided with a lamp post and flipped over. The upside-down sombrero started to fill with water until it sunk below the surface, allowing his friends' chosen objects to float past with ease. In disbelief, Scott swore at his laughing mates and swigged the final shot. Moments later his head hit the table and he was snoring loudly in defeat.

A cold glass of water brought Scott round and, instead of being faced with torrential rain, he was eye to eye with a very angry-looking Mexican lady. "Moron. Idiot American!" she yelled as she threw another cold glass of water over his face, provoking another fit of laughter from his friends.

"*Lo siento señorita*," Harry apologised to the angered waitress in her local tongue to show he meant it. He then thanked the bar staff for enduring the trouble they had caused and dragged his hungover friend out of the establishment.

The weather was the polar opposite to when Scott had collapsed: the storm had passed and the sun was beating down in all its glory. The heat was now unrelenting, mixed with the smell of sewage that had overflowed in the temporary river – it was enough to make Scott gag. Unfortunately, gagging wasn't enough, though, and he proceeded to spew up on the pavement, receiving disapproving looks from passers-by as he did so.

Harry marched off into the distance.

"Let's get you outta here," groaned Lee whilst pulling his drunken friend along forcefully. "Get these down you," he ordered, passing Scott a bottle of water and a chocolate bar.

He rammed the chocolate down his throat and chugged down the water, spilling some on his navy blue shirt in the process.

Harry returned with a new shirt, a pink one adorned with orcas. He helped his friend change out of his soiled clothes and threw them in the nearest bin.

"Better?" asked Lee, hoping for a miracle recovery.

"Yeah, loads," Scott replied. He always had been a heavy

drinker and had the most amazing recovery technique that his friends soon learnt to help him with: a glass of water and some chocolate and he was pretty much cured, save for a thumping headache.

"Good, because we want to hit the museum now and we need you ready. The local police are busy clearing up the damage from the storm; it could work in our favour after all." Lee led the way to their parked vehicle and gave a silent prayer that it had survived the flood. Luckily, the small maintenance van had held firm and was exactly where they had left it. Lee drove seeing as he was the only one that hadn't been doing tequila shots due to his exceptional choice of Olympic-grade debris. He fumbled with the keys and rammed them into the ignition. When he turned them, however, the engine failed to start.

"Maybe it's flooded," Scott remarked with a smirk on his face.

Lee ignored him and tried again; this time the machine burst into life and the last leg of their journey could begin.

In the back, Harry was changing into a work uniform: a dark blue boiler suit with a hundred-and-one pockets for a variety of tools and gear.

Scott sat in silence trying to sober himself up ready for the main event; he couldn't let them down now, not with the stakes as high as they were.

The drive was a short one and within minutes they pulled up outside their destination. The museum had remained open during the storm and, as a result, was still very busy when the trio arrived. It was full of people that thought they would have a look around to avoid the weather.

Opening the door to disembark outside the historic building, Harry stopped momentarily in order to take in the architecture. White marble pillars were erected outside the entrance holding up an ornate golden dome engraved with the date of construction and the names of the founders of the original displays. The museum towered above the buildings to its left and right, highlighting its superiority in importance and design.

Scott gave Harry a small push to clear the door and speed along proceedings. When they were both out of the van and the door was closed, Lee proceeded to his next location leaving his friends to begin.

Harry took the lead and walked confidently through the entrance heading straight for the reception desk. "*Un momento por favor. Un problema*," he puffed whilst laying his large bag of tools on the desk in front of the unsuspecting female receptionist.

Scott nodded at his friend to acknowledge the plan had begun and headed deeper into the museum. His head was still banging from the alcohol earlier but the adrenaline was powering him on. He walked with purpose towards the section of the museum with the exhibit he was after; however, the looks he received from people he passed gave him an inkling he may have been drunkenly stumbling rather than walking. He was apologising profusely every time he accidentally collided with someone he saw double of.

Security guards were beginning to watch his movements; his drunken antics were drawing attention. *Pull yourself together!* he scolded himself.

One of the guards was beginning to close in on him to confront him when the lights in the building extinguished.

A smile played across Scott's face as he thanked Harry for completing his part of the plan. In darkness, Scott was able to bypass the security guard and, moments later, an announcement rang through the museum for everyone to be evacuated due to a problem caused by the storm. Everyone was streaming in the opposite direction to Scott as they were rushing to the exit in slight panic. He battled through the human current eager to reach his target. Once clear of the mass of human bodies, Scott was able to get his bearings and realised he was exactly where he needed to be – ahead of him was a huge sign welcoming him to the ***Aztec History*** section. Navigating his way around without other tourists was much easier and it took no time at all to reach the artefact he was sent to acquire. Placed atop a waxwork figure of the famous Aztec leader, Moctezuma II, was an elaborate feathered crown made up of quetzal and other brightly coloured feathers. The bright blue and green plumes emerged from a golden helmet, an accessory worthy of the emperor it belonged to. Scott reached out to take it but quickly pulled his hand back realising there was likely to be an alarm on the exhibit.

"Oye tú, deberías haber dejado el museo! ¿Qué estás haciendo?" a guard shouted.

Scott was unsure of what he said but the tone of voice implied he had seen what Scott just attempted. The guard was reaching for his communication device to warn of an intruder when he was attacked from behind.

Scott saw a leather arm wrap around the officer's neck like a boa, constricting his airways and pulsating with each exhalation to tighten its grip. With an audible thud, the man fell to the ground revealing a terrorising figure behind.

The aggressor was wearing a wolf mask with blood-red eyes and sharp teeth. Red wiry hair was hanging down around its head and it wore a black leather trench coat. The horror stomped towards Scott who was paralysed with fear. The alcohol wasn't helping the appearance of the aggressor as his drunken vision twisted and blurred the villain's features. The wolf grabbed the headdress which set off an alarm. "Extraction?" the figure snarled.

Scott remained fixed to the spot until the wolf grabbed him by the arm. With a start he snapped out of his trance and led the wolf to the back exit. The alarms were blaring out and police sirens could be heard when they reached the locked back door. Scott tried to open it in his weakened state but couldn't. "We're doomed," he wailed, giving up hope.

The man in the wolf mask grunted and shoved Scott aside. With a growl and a kick, he forced the door open and saw a man waiting in a maintenance van.

"Who're you?" Lee was startled at the man's harrowing appearance.

The demon in the leather trench coat threw the headdress through the open window and ordered, "Keep it safe! We'll come for it!" Then he disappeared into an alleyway opposite to flee the approaching law enforcement.

Harry opened the back of the van and pulled Scott in.

Lee accelerated and drifted round the corner, narrowly avoiding the police arriving at the back door.

CHAPTER 7

Earth
England
East Anglia

Presley was just finishing the late afternoon football training with the under-sixteens, a miserable afternoon with both goings-on and weather. The grass was sodden after torrential rain and the under-sixteens had been messing around for most of the session again. The match to finish the lesson was nothing to write home about; there were no bright talents in the young group that replicated the kind of ability and potential shown by Lincoln in George and Jacob's group. More time was spent extracting footballs from the surrounding bushes than actually playing on the pitch; for this reason, Presley was actually happy to be leaving to check in on his Minotaur team this evening. Keeping tabs on a resurgence of an evil organisation hell-bent on humanity's destruction had to be easier than the time he spent with the adolescent morons that occupied his afternoon. Presley knew Tombstone were planning something; he had never seen screamers on Earth until the night he saved George in the forest. Somehow, Butcher and Amazon had made it to Earth and now screamers were with them, too; the fact that Tombstone had crossed the veil between worlds meant time was running out. Fortunately, he made easy work of George's assailants, and the attack came at night, that way no one saw any of the strange creatures before a team came out to collect the bodies to burn them back at RAS. He had enough to worry about without having to deal with the fallout the discovery of such monsters would cause.

Following his class' dismissal, Presley began his walk to his car and halfway there his phone began to buzz. It took a second to wiggle his mobile out of his pocket but when he did the screen displayed the flashing name 'Yuanli'. His colleague told him how Rosie and her friends had been attacked but fortunately thwarted their aggressor. Nevertheless, when he heard Annabel was unaccounted for he ran the remaining distance to his car and hurried the engine into ignition. Presley was in such a rush that he pulled out without checking his mirror and was met with the loud honk of an aggravated driver. Presley hung out of his window to make his apologies but was unable to stop the relentless crude hand gestures and foul language being thrown his way. Giving up trying to appease the now red-faced and gasping man in the car behind, he accelerated hard and made his way out of town. Again, not concentrating, Presley ran a red light whilst trying to phone Roy. As Roy picked up, his 'hello' was drowned out by the shriek of a siren to Presley's left. Presley suspected Annabel to be in danger and thus was not willing to stop for the pursuing law enforcement officer.

"Roy. It's Presley. Do you know where Annabel is?" he panted through his building adrenaline.

Roy didn't grasp the gravity of the situation and his answer was not as snappy and relevant as Presley required. "Er... I believe she went for a date with Jacob. You know, I don't know what she sees in him, I think he has a monobrow forming, not to mention his–"

Presley cut him off sensing Roy's lack of understanding of the magnitude of the issue. "George and the others have been attacked. Annabel isn't accounted for. I need to find her!" shouted Presley, struggling to make himself heard over the siren encroaching on his car.

"Is that a police car I can hear?" inquired Roy.

"Yes. Find Annabel and send me her location when you do." Presley cut the call and focused on losing the pursuing police car. He took a sharp left and then a sharp right, but the policeman replicated his every move and was not losing any ground on his prey. Just when Presley thought it couldn't get any worse, a second police car joined the fray from his right forcing Presley to make an unwanted left turn heading away from Annabel's likely location, which he supposed might be near Jacob's house.

The chase continued out of town and into the countryside. The twisty and winding country roads meant that it was hard to maintain a fast speed and Presley was going to be caught any second if he didn't take drastic action. "OK. Let's play!" he shouted to his empty car. He turned right into a quarry and began weaving between the piles of rocks, taking the police deeper into the maze of materials. Rock dust was spraying all around the car which made visibility almost impossible when combined with the evening light. Presley doughnutted on the spot to build up a dust storm and create a makeshift smokescreen from the pursuing law enforcers. He could hear the sirens right next to him but the drivers were unwilling to enter the dust storm in case of collision. Presley drove in the opposite direction to the sirens and came out between two large mounds of built up rock either side. He continued between the synthetic valley until he spotted a furrow in one of the mounds. He quickly turned into it and killed the engine and lights. Moments later two police cars zoomed past, unable to spot their prey hidden in the dark shadow of the mound, protected by the cloak of night. Presley gently reignited his engine and reversed out.

Unbelievably, the police had turned around and were facing him once again. He was a deer in headlights, almost literally. Putting his foot through the accelerator, he shot off in the direction that he had just come from. Unsure of where to go next, he turned a corner and was met with the sight of an oncoming large truck filled with loose chippings in the rear. He managed to swerve out of the way but the truck, in its efforts to avoid collision, tipped over onto its side and slid horizontally. The first law car to come round the corner crashed straight into the back of the upturned truck and became buried under a pile of rock. The second car screeched to a halt as it drifted round the bend. The driver leapt out to help their colleague out of the wreckage.

Presley took the opportunity to spin round and build up speed towards a ramp heading in the direction he hoped was the exit. Presley nailed the trick and, as he shot through the air, he felt he was travelling in slow motion as he took in the scene below him. The policeman that crashed into the truck had blood trickling from his head but seemed to be OK, talking to his colleagues who were checking him over.

Presley's main worry was that he was unable to identify the condition of the quarry worker from the truck. That was until he heard a sudden yell.

"Hell, yes. Take that!" The quarry worker was tall, covered in tattoos and had a long, brown beard. Aside from miraculously being unharmed he was also chuckling away at the sight of the disgruntled policemen. He gave his hero a quick thumbs-up and rushed to open the gate for Presley to speed off in search of Annabel.

Police now well and truly lost, Presley had time to drive to RAS and speak with Roy face to face to see if he had made any progress in locating Annabel.

Upon arrival, Roy was still none the wiser, however, after around five minutes his phone rang and it was Annabel. Roy almost dropped the phone in his haste to answer. "Annabel, it's me; are you OK?" Roy could hear a soft rumbling in the background, like a car engine.

Annabel's voice crackled through the phone. "Roy, oh thank God!" she panted.

"Where are you? Are you OK?" Roy could tell from the sound of Annabel's voice that the answers would not be good.

"I don… I'm scared… they've taken me," Annabel wept sporadically.

"It's OK, try to stay calm. Who has you? Where're you?" Roy repeatedly asked whilst trying to keep the fear from his own voice.

"Jacob wasn't... I was walking home and… and…" Annabel couldn't think, her usual brilliant brain was scrambled.

"Listen to me, list... Annabel, I'm here... you just have... Annabel, please... Answer my questions." Roy felt helpless from his side of the phone whilst the girl he was tasked with protecting was panic-stricken and in harm's way in a place he didn't know, taken by a thief he couldn't identify.

"Car… boot... he was so strong... filthy... massive. I couldn't stop him, he just took me," Annabel stuttered whilst she relived the kidnapping. "Roy, they said–" Annabel's disjointed report suddenly cut off as the sound of rumbling stopped in the background. "… They're coming... please... HELP!" Her feeble whispers were replaced by the desperate screech of her final word.

Roy shouted instructions down the phone. "Stay calm, Annabel! I'm coming. Listen, you need to take the stone out of the ring I gave you and press the button underneath. It'll activate a tracker. Annabel, do you hear me?"

There was no reply, but Roy heard voices through the phone that weren't Annabel's. Then there was a crack and a buzzing sound which replaced the strangers' voices. Roy glanced down at his phone and felt the hot sting of a tear escape his eye.

"That voice…" Roy stated to Presley, "…the description."

"No wonder they didn't bind or search her. If he took her then fear would paralyse her enough," Presley grimaced.

"They underestimated their target, though. My Annabel's too smart to be left untied." Roy said the words but struggled to even convince himself to have false hope. Turning to his computer and activating the tracking system, Roy crossed his fingers so tight that his knuckles turned white. Every second that Roy stared at the monitor and Annabel's name had not appeared was another punch to his gut.

Presley embraced Roy and tried to console him; it would be impossible to find Annabel now.

Despite the awful situation Presley knew they had little time to grieve. "Roy, the others still need to be warned and gathered up to prevent any more kidnappings, it is obviously Tombstone's work."

"There was another attempt on George's life today, as well. I thought that the other night would be a one-off attack, but they are growing bolder and more aggressive."

Roy was wailing and spurting out reasons why he was an awful guardian and that he should have taken more care.

There was no time for weakness and, as a result, Presley slapped his friend round the face; a punch from his large hands, however, would have done more damage than good.

The slap brought Roy back and he composed himself to listen to his superior.

All of a sudden there was a loud beep, followed by another one and then a continuous beep.

Presley and Roy turned to see a red dot appearing on the tracking system with the name 'Annabel' underneath it.

"That's my girl!" shrieked Roy, trying to stop his tears which had begun again.

All in one swift movement, Presley turned around and threw on his coat. "I'll go after Annabel. You go and get George. Send the other guardians to get their charges and bring them back here for immediate debrief. We can't wait any longer, we must take them to start their training."

Roy nodded his understanding and Presley left to track down Annabel using the same tech Roy had on his computer but adapted for phone use. The only diversion Presley made before rushing straight to his vehicle was to visit the armoury. Opening the door, he was met with a great array of guns, some large for full-scale firefights and some smaller for more covert operations. Nevertheless, Presley ignored them all and gazed with a smile on his face at the middle of the wall where two worn and well used gold engraved black pistols were hung. Both had the green Minotaur symbol on them and each bore the name of a Greek god; the left one had 'Thanatos' scribed on it, the Greek god of death, and the right-hand weapon was engraved with the name 'Hades', the god of the underworld. Presley took the akimbo pistols, gathered some ammo, helped himself to two grenades before closing the door behind him and set off to the garage that was home to the collection of vehicles at Minotaur's disposal. After navigating his way through the underground corridors beneath RAS, Presley eventually came to a black door. As he reached for the handle the door swung open and Barbara, Alex's guardian, came tumbling out covered in oil.

"I've just done the pre-mission checks on the truck. I can't believe them poor kids are going to be whipped away from their families at such short notice, they shouldn't have to be the ones to fight Tombstone." She was in a hurry so didn't stop to chat with Presley.

He turned to calm her but she was almost already out the corridor, *Man, she's fast for her size*, Presley thought. "Have faith, Barbs!" he shouted after her.

Her response was a loud grunt and she disappeared round the corner.

Presley put the meeting with Barbara behind him and refocused on the task at hand. He stepped foot inside the garage and saw a selection of black 4x4s lined up in a row. In the centre of the open space was the truck ticking over with a soft rumble where Barbs had left the engine on, presumably ready for a quick exit should the need arise. Presley walked past all the cars and headed straight for a dark corner of the room. In amongst the darkness was a white sheet with a large bump underneath it. Presley grabbed the sheet and ripped it off in one swift movement, throwing it on the floor behind him to reveal an obsidian-coloured Harley-Davidson with a large silver metallic exhaust down its left flank. The front of the bike was dominated by a giant minotaur skull-shaped headlight; there were holsters for his akimbo pistols near his seat. Presley sat on the bike and retrieved the key from his pocket. Upon inserting it into the bike, the engine roared into life drowning out the soft rumble of the truck nearby. By now, the dark corner of the room was fully illuminated by the minotaur headlight and within the newly lit room Presley saw Roy opening the shutter to the outside world. Presley slowly approached the shutter and stopped to speak to Roy one last time.

"You take charge of George and the others, Roy. Just get them to Arizona and start their training. Don't expect an easy ride, though, friend, the assault on George and the kidnapping of Annabel proves that the war in the shadows is over. Tombstone have reached their full strength and are ready to make their move to destroy the free world. We can't let that happen."

Roy took in the instructions and shook his head. "I'm not ready. *They're* not ready, Presley. Tombstone will have their dark demise; we can't stop them, they have–"

Roy was cut off by the sharp sting of a Presley slap to the side of his face. The force of the impact made Roy's eyes water and he looked up with new determination in his face. "I needed that."

Presley put a hand on his friend's shoulder. "Roy, I'll save Annabel, don't threat. Now just make sure her friends get to Arizona safe." Presley put on his helmet which, again, bore the green minotaur symbol on its crown and gave a final nod to his friend. Looking up at the full moon in the sky through the shutter, Presley revved his bike. The thunder that came from the machine made Roy stumble back and Presley accelerated off into the night.

CHAPTER 8

Earth
England
George's house

George closed his front door after returning from paintballing and was overwhelmed with the aroma of dinner, the sweet smell of tomato filled the air along with a vast array of spices and herbs. The source of the smell was a freshly made lasagne cooked with soya mince, the same great taste with the added health benefit of no red meat. The table was set and George's father was just serving up his own portion after he had served his wife her share. They seemed to be listening intently to the radio and didn't notice their son at first.

George tried to decipher what the lady on the radio was saying which engrossed his mother and father.

Bryan took a step back when he finally saw George, alerted by how quietly he had crept up on them. "High-speed police chase going on heading towards the old quarry," he said, confirming what George thought he overheard on the radio. "Help yourself, son," Bryan remembered, pointing to the lasagne on the stove. "How was paintballing?"

"Errr, yeah, it was good, thanks. It doesn't hurt as much as I thought it would." They had agreed to keep the possibility they were being hunted by murderous members of a secret organisation to themselves, trying to save panic by not telling their respective parents.

"Were you good?" inquired George's mother. To Bryan she added, "Oh, I bet he was good, he always does well."

"I was OK, Alex was the best and Cheik was very good, too." George failed to mention he was outperformed by Rosie, childishly assuming it embarrassing to be shown up by a girl in an activity involving guns. He then proceeded to explain how each game unfolded, changing only the one-on-one showdown at the end so it concluded with Alex shooting Cheikhou without the interruption of a deranged killer.

"Remind me why you are not at work this week, then?" requested Bryan and, at the exact same time, Belinda asked a question.

"Who are these Cheik and Alex people? Where were Annabel and Jacob?"

George elected to answer his father first. "A new opportunity has come up, remember? I've left my old workplace before starting at the new place next week." Intercepting the next question before it even left his father's lips, he continued, "And again, I'm sorry but I can't tell you anything about my new line of work, it's top secret." Then George proceeded to answer his mother's question. "Alex and Cheik are going to be working with me at my new job. I went out with them for some team bonding before we begin properly next week." Coming up with an alibi for why his best friend was absent was more difficult, he knew he would have to bend the truth somehow and his mother could always see through his lies. He continued, "Jacob wasn't allowed to come because he isn't part of the workforce." George felt his insides tighten, hoping she would swallow the lie. The good news was that she didn't inquire any more about Jacob, instead she shouted allegations of what her son's secret job could be. "I told you, Bryan, he's been recruited by MI5!"

"More likely he's become a drug dealer," Bryan muttered dryly, displaying the usual confidence in his son.

George ate his dinner as he listened to his parents batting backwards and forwards over the likelihood their son was the local Pablo Escobar. Their argument ended as abruptly as it had started with them allowing their predictions were unlikely to be true, they would just have to wait to find out. The main topic of conversation then moved on to the fact that another museum had been broken into, this time an old tribal headdress had been stolen from the Lost Tribes of the World Exhibition in Mexico. The reason this was brought up was that it was the third in a strange string of museum break-ins that year. The end of the previous week saw a sword stolen from a London museum, and at the start of the year an antique gun was taken from an American West Exhibition in California. George had taken little to no notice of these criminal acts upon first hearing them, but whilst listening in to his parents discussing them, he couldn't help but feel the items stolen seemed familiar somehow. He shovelled down the rest of his dinner and rinsed his plate ready to wash up later. The information on the radio about a flood in Siberia killing numbers of locals disappeared from audible range as George ran up to his room and took out the letter from Minotaur. Twisting it in his fingers, he found the abstract logo on the front of the letter and studied it for a minute. Whilst gazing at the logo, George racked his memory to piece together what was troubling him. The logo showed a sword, a torso, a headdress and a gun. Whilst poring over the document, George also remembered the monument at RAS which had the same shaped moulds. Museum artefacts matching the same descriptions had all recently been stolen, the only exception was the purple torso on the letter, *some sort of armour and most likely the next target*, George presumed. Then it dawned on him, "They're keys! The monument must be some sort of stone safe!" George shouted to his empty room. It seemed to George then, that even with his little knowledge of what was going on, whoever Minotaur was designed to stop, they were failing. All they had was the monument, but the opposition had at least three of the four keys to open it which meant soon they would be coming for… *KNOCK... KNOCK!*

George heard his mother answer the front door, "Hello," but then the situation seemed to turn quickly. "You can't just barge in here... HEY!... Honey, help!"

George's father could be heard arguing, "Get out! Who do you think you–" but before his father could finish, Roy came bursting into George's room.

"Come with me!" Roy was almost as green as his hair and looked extremely distressed. "I'm sorry about this but, given the circumstances, we can't wait to meet later in the week, we need you all at my store now for a debrief."

George wasn't prepared for the sudden invasion of his room. "What're you doing here?"

"I'll explain on the way. Say goodbye to your parents, we haven't got long, and I don't know when you'll be back here again." Roy frantically paced the room and his eyes were red and puffy as if he had been crying.

"OK," is all George managed as he stumbled round his room looking for clothes to take, it sounded like a long trip.

"You have no time for that!" Roy squealed in an exceptionally high pitch. "We'll provide your clothes, just say goodbye, you'll regret it if we run out of time." Then he pushed the young man out of his room.

George stumbled down the stairs, questioning what type of goodbye he needed to say, a casual 'See you later' or a 'Thanks for everything'-style farewell? Just before he reached the room in which his parents were being subdued by large Minotaur workers, Roy touched his shoulder and gave George a look which confirmed the type of goodbye it would have to be.

George tilted his head to the side as he felt all power leave his body. He was a child again, filled with the same dread and fear as when he used to lose his parents in a large supermarket. The lip went first, beginning to quiver, and then the eyes welled up with sharp searing tears, they burned the inside of his skull until he felt the heat of his sorrow tumble down his face. George could taste one of the bitter tears roll over his top lip and enter his mouth as he embraced Roy for an encouraging hug. Annabel's guardian pulled away first and pushed George through the door to his parents for their final goodbye, a moment that no person George's age should have to have with their parents. He entered the room an emotional wreck and the Minotaur workers released his mother and father who immediately ran to him. Straight away George was met with his mother's accusations, "You're a drug dealer, and now this lot have come round to rough us up!" she screeched, both disappointed and scared.

George couldn't help but smile at his mum's certainty, "Look what you've done now, Dad," he said as he shook his head and felt further tears roll down his face.

Bryan was next to speak. "What *is* this, son?" he asked with his hands on his hips and his brow furrowed.

"I have to go away for a while," George replied to them in a croaky voice.

"Your son is part of a team that's going to save the world," Roy said, coming to George's rescue. "His mission is top secret and, as such, can't be discussed. You should be immensely proud of what he has taken on. I regret to say, though, this is his goodbye to you. I'm sorry it had to be your son." Roy rounded up the Minotaur workers and ushered them out so George could be alone with his parents for a while.

"We've always been proud of you," Belinda started.

"Always," Bryan agreed.

"I love you guys so much!" George said, breaking down further and he hugged them together in one big embrace. "Thank you for all that you have taught me, I couldn't wish for better role models and, more importantly, two better friends." They all hugged tightly and told each other how much they meant to each other; there was a lot of crying and even some reminiscent laughs but, before long, Roy was back in the room to take George away from his mother and father for possibly the last time.

Bryan hugged his son tightly and let go, giving George an affirming nod of confidence and hope. "I'll see you soon, lad," he croaked through tears.

Roy had to separate Belinda from her boy, she was reluctant to let him go. In the end she had to be restrained by Bryan whilst she punched his chest and swore as George was dragged by Roy out of the front door.

Just before George was piled into the waiting car, he felt something brush against his ankle. Looking down through watery eyes, he made out the shape of a small fluffy creature. He leant down to give a final stroke to his cat, taking a moment to feel the warmth and comfort the soft black fur gave him. "Goodbye," he whispered to his lifelong pet, his house, but mostly his grieving parents within.

George sat silently brooding in the car trying to recover himself.

Roy took a long moment for George to take it all in and sit alone for most of the car journey before justifying to him what he'd made him do.

"The others are being retrieved by their own guardians. I was sent to you because Presley was required for Annabel – she's been taken."

Finally, George found his voice of sorts, "Wait? What?"

Roy looked grim but was trying to sound positive. "She'll be alright. Presley's going after her. There isn't a task in the world I wouldn't trust that man with completing."

The news was too much for George to take and, with the rest of the day's dramas, he passed out through a combination of fatigue, shock and fear.

George's head was thumping when Roy shook him awake to inform him they were at the store.

Roy helped George out of the car and stabilised him before going ahead to open the door to his antique shop to usher George in. The shop was as dimly lit as last time with the only light being thrown into the room by the solitary lamp on Roy's desk. George was led past the shrunken heads and the large mysterious monument. *What secrets are you hiding?* George wondered to himself whilst passing the rock slab. They continued walking until they reached the minotaur painting at the rear of the shop. All George could concentrate on were his recent deductions about the stone. *I need to tell Roy about the museum break-ins.*

"They have three of the keys to the monument, don't they?" he inquired. "What's in there that's so important, anyway?" he moaned, still groggy from his nap in the car.

Roy turned with a look of surprise painted on his face, "You know about the artefacts to open Jedrok?"

"If that's what the rock is called then, yes, I've recently put two and two together," confirmed George. As he spoke, he noticed Roy look across to the armour he had on display, the one that was allegedly previously worn by St George when he killed the dragon. "That's the last key, isn't it?"

"It fits the mould," agreed Roy. "With both the last artefact and Jedrok here, it means–"

"They're coming," George finished, looking panic-stricken towards Annabel's guardian.

Roy nodded grimly and fumbled with the nose ring in the minotaur painting in trying to open the secret elevator, but the fear in his body was making his hands shake too much.

George grabbed the nose ring firmly and gave it a twist. When the elevator opened they climbed inside to begin their descent to the underground facility.

"Are we safe down here?" George asked, his voice shaking from the thought of an unknown enemy closing in through the cover of night.

Roy didn't reply, he was on the phone to someone else. "Have it ready. We're leaving tonight… NO, TONIGHT! The hour is late, Jedrok has to be moved and their training must begin." With that, Roy hung up the phone to his mystery contact and the elevator door sprang open with a sudden *'ding'* that awoke George from his thoughts.

George squinted as he adjusted to the bright white lights of the hallway.

Rosie was sitting cross-legged on the floor, red in the face, with her black hair sticking to her forehead. She was crying while being consoled by Alex and Cheikhou, the latter of which got to his feet and ran over to George. "Thank God you're alright. Have you heard about Annabel?"

George nodded with a grimace.

Roy broke up the meeting by rushing past them and opening the door to the room where they were briefed for their tasks. "Come on, hurry! You can worry for Annabel when we have more time! I've told George already, Presley's gone after her and he'll not fail to bring her back. Now get in here, we haven't much time!"

George led the procession into the room and took a seat at the front whilst the others followed suit behind. The room was unchanged since he first encountered it days ago, apart from the number of chairs that had been reduced to five for each of the new Minotaur members. Annabel's empty seat felt as if it were emitting cold air, a vacuum that sucked away hope and encouraged despair seeping through the entire room.

Roy closed the door and turned to see four sets of confused and expecting eyes gazing back at him. *Presley should be doing this*, he told himself.

"OK, I'm sorry for the abrupt and panicked start to your time with Minotaur but the current circumstances gave way to desperate measures. Tombstone have succeeded in locating and attaining the penultimate artefact required to open Jedrok."

"That means 'second to last'," Alex blurted out before quickly sinking back into his seat under the glare he received from the other three.

Cheikhou was secretly happy for the definition but would never have let it show.

"That's not the bit that confused me!" George admitted, rubbing his head.

Roy shook his head, thinking, *They're lost; Presley could have explained better*. "Right, Tombstone, Jedrok, you don't know what I'm talking about." Roy flapped his arms and rushed over to press a button in the wall. Doing so lowered a projector from the ceiling with a whirring noise that broke the otherwise silent room. In one swift turn Roy reached into his pocket pulling out a remote and faced the four young adults before him. With a gulp he clicked the remote which both dimmed the lights and projected the beginning of a slide show onto the wall behind him. Hastily, he skipped through the slides dominated by a large word in the middle, 'Gaia', with text and images all around it. "No time," he muttered to himself. Then he flashed past paintings of three abstract individuals, none of whom seemed friendly. "Oh dear, no, not now. That's no good for morale," he tutted. "Ah, here," he breathed finally. "Sorry about that, a lot for you to learn down the road."

The slide Roy paused on contained images of two paintings. The left-hand artwork showed a man with slick, greasy black hair and a hooked nose; he seemed taller than average and was emaciated to the point that his bones could be seen through the skin in his neck and face. The man also had piercing green eyes that George could have sworn were staring straight at him sending a chill down his spine. This was the image Roy chose to speak of first. "The man on the left is Horatio Petrov, or should I say *was*, he's now unfortunately dead. Horatio was the latest and possibly greatest in a long line of Petrovs, leader of Dreadnoque and keeper of Gaia. He made sure that it was always used for its core purpose, to keep Earth and Sanctum stabilised. He performed his duties admirably and without issue, that's until he was betrayed by his own wicked daughter."

"What's this Gaia?" Rosie asked.

Roy stopped to think for a moment and replied, "Everything.".

"And Sanctum?" George asked.

It's too much, Presley, Roy panicked. "I promise I'll explain further when we have more time. For now, all you need to know is it's a world whose fate is linked to your own."

George had managed to remove his gaze from that of Horatio

and look at the picture to the right of the presentation, "Is that his daughter?"

Roy looked over his shoulder to analyse the second painting on the screen and nodded his head. "That's Sonya Petrov or Dark Snake. She's not been called by her proper name since her father's death. She's the founder and barbaric leader of Tombstone."

"Tombstone," Cheikhou repeated, "I'm guessing we aren't on hugging terms with these guys."

"Dark Snake named her group Tombstone to signify the death of mankind and begin her conquest to subjugate Sanctum before moving onto destroying Earth itself," Roy explained.

"Ah, so ass-kicking terms," Cheikhou confirmed.

George studied the picture and found she had the same piercing green eyes full of greed and malice as her father. The black hair was also passed on, but Dark Snake had long hair and it wasn't greasy like her father's. The last standout feature was her teeth that looked unnaturally sharp and pointy.

Roy noticed where George was gazing and explained, "She isn't called Dark Snake for nothing. When she betrayed her father she was labelled for her slimy and malicious deeds. She took the name as a brand and used Gaia to infuse herself with snakelike qualities – them teeth are part of them qualities."

Cheikhou shrieked, "I ain't messing with no giant snake. No, I'm not!"

Rosie reminded him who was at stake. "You will if it helps rescue Annabel, you coward."

"I have a story for you about snakes if you think I'm a coward," Cheikhou said back, trembling in his seat.

"Another time, Cheik," Roy pleaded. "The good news, however, is that Dark Snake didn't anticipate the inhabitants of Sanctum fighting back. Gradually, people rallied to fight against Tombstone's evil rule. They gathered under the name of Minotaur and have been fighting in Sanctum ever since."

"People will always rise up against oppression, it's in our nature to fight back," Cheikhou announced.

"Agreed," Roy said as he pressed his remote, bringing the next slide up to reveal a picture of the monument Roy had stored upstairs.

"I can tell by the murmuring in the room that you recognise the rock in the picture. Jedrok is its name. Like I mentioned earlier, there's more to the monument than appears. It's a stone treasury containing the most powerful weaponized items from Sanctum – the indestructible armour of Henry Salvatore, making the wearer invulnerable save for their head and legs; the whip of Johnnie Lang which gives the ability to bend those who've experienced its sting to the users will, making them slaves to your every command; Kalysta's mask, Ufakazi – it means 'all-seeing' in her native tongue. We know little about this one with Kalysta keeping many of its secrets to herself. From what we understand it gives the wearer the ability to see with the eyes of all those loyal to them, no matter the distance they're apart. Finally, but by no means least, Stormsbane, a sword that's sharper than any other, it cuts through enemies like butter. It's rumoured to be the only weapon that can penetrate the armour of Henry Salvatore, although both items are yet to be pitted against each other."

Roy raised his voice as George and the others began talking amongst themselves trying to see whether to believe his words. "The origin of the weapons is not something we have time for at the moment; you'll learn far more about them at a later date. For now, all you need to know is that Tombstone have three of the four artefacts required to open Jedrok and the last one they need, as well as Jedrok itself, is in this very building. That's why time is of the essence."

"I'll protect Jedrok. I'm the strongest here and have the best chance of success," Alex said rising to his feet.

Rosie sunk deeper into her seat and said, "I don't see how I'm going to be much help."

Roy turned to Alex. "It'll be down to all of us to make sure Jedrok and St George's armour stay safe. We'll take it with us as they're no longer safe here. Tombstone will be throwing everything they have got at obtaining the monument so they can get the weapons inside."

"Taking it with us?" George questioned. "Where exactly are we going?"

Roy sighed in exasperation at the question. "We're taking you to Arizona now to receive your training. Then we'll transport Jedrok and the armour to Magellan Castle in Liberterra where we have the best chance of preventing Tombstone reaching it."

George was about to ask another question when the door swung open and Carlton, Cheikhou's guardian, came wheezing into the room.

"Jedrok and armour are loaded into the truck and we're ready to go," he puffed.

Before anyone could speak Roy had ushered everyone back up the elevator and through the shop, past the gaping hole that used to be filled by the stone slab, and into the street. The truck to which Carlton was referring was parked right outside the building and couldn't look more out of place. It was a large green army truck with rows of seats looking towards each other under a canopy in the back. Between the seats Jedrok was tied down with rope so it wouldn't move during transit.

George climbed into the back and the others followed along with Carlton and Yuanli.

Roy sent Barbara to start the engine and get ready to drive. Before going to take his seat Roy turned to look at the young adults in the back. "Are you ready?" he asked apprehensively.

A harsh cold wind howled through the streets and knocked over a dustbin across the road from the truck.

Rosie pulled her cardigan tighter around her body to fend off the chill.

You wanted adventure. Well, now you've got it, George thought to himself. Then he looked from Cheikhou to Rosie to Alex and supposed they were probably thinking the same. In unison they turned to Roy and nodded their heads.

Roy gave a thumbs-up to Barbara at which point the engine roared into life. Annabel's guardian took his place in the cab and felt a tear trickle down his face as he said goodbye to his Antiquities Store for the final time and watched it fade into the distance.

CHAPTER 9

Earth
England
The countryside

Meat Loaf's *Bat Out of Hell* was playing in Presley's helmet speakers as he roared down the country lanes leading to the red beeping dot of Annabel's tracker. Tombstone had taken Annabel a long way out of town and Presley had been driving for forty-five minutes since he left RAS. The roads were eerily quiet, and Presley had seen no sign of life for the last ten minutes of his journey. He knew that animals have a good sense of danger, and the lack of wildlife gave him an idea he may have been nearing Annabel's location. He slowed down and activated the 'Sneak' mode on his bike. It was credit to how good a mechanic Barbara was that she managed to fit the monster of a machine with a suppressor that made the engine impossible to hear at more than one hundred metres away. Barbara hated every minute of her delivery driver work and lived for her spare time when she could tinker and adapt vehicles back at RAS.

It was only another couple of minutes before Presley arrived within five hundred metres of Annabel's location. He turned off the engine and the growling that filled the night disappeared into an eerie silence. The leaves rustled gently in the breeze. *Lack of life, deathly quiet, legions of Tombstone are definitely near,* thought Presley. He got off the bike and took his akimbo pistols from their holsters. He led his vehicle off the road and hid it behind a nearby tree. Then he crept towards his target hugging tight to the bush bordering the road until he came to a mansion on his right. Crouched down to avoid being detected, he approached the house and shimmied over an outer wall, throwing himself behind the nearest oak to scout the building. The tracker pointed to the fact that Annabel was in that mansion and so Presley had no choice but to find the best way to infiltrate the private property. The entire windows were lit along the front of the building which most likely meant that it was full of people – people that would not want him to retrieve Annabel.

There were three storeys to the building and atop the roof were a series of chimneys, though only the largest on the right wing of the mansion had any smoke appearing from it. Presley thought that the smoke was most likely the source of the pungent stench that shrouded the area; it wasn't the nice homely aroma of a log fire however, it was emitting a nose-shrivelling reek of searing flesh and burnt hair. Presley gagged and covered his face with his arm to try to gain some respite, but the smell penetrated through. Unable to focus on his assault before he rid himself of the odour, he called upon a trick that Yuanli, Rosie's guardian, had taught him. She was an expert at controlling her mind through her mastery of gymnastics and martial arts. He began by reminding himself of why he was there: *I need to find Annabel and save her.* Then he listed his top priorities: *find a suitable entrance and exit, don't get spotted and safely extract Annabel.* Finally, he synchronised his breathing and his body the way Yuanli showed him. The nuisance of the smell was eradicated and he was in the zone, ready to begin the rescue. The night was clear so the light of the full moon illuminated the garden he was standing in. Presley mapped out in his mind a clear route using the trees as cover which would enable him to get within metres of the door to breach the building. He quickly ran behind the first tree and then easily reached the second tree. Next, he ran to the third tree but halfway to his safe haven he heard a shout.

What was that?

When Presley reached the oak he slowly edged round it to get a better look at the entrance to the mansion and spotted a group of three men that he failed to see in his starting position. Judging by the accents they were American. In response to the shout that came from one of them they were beginning to gather their weapons to come over to Presley's position to check out the disturbance.

The shortest of the three spoke. "What did you see, Dom?"

A taller but fatter man replied, "I thought I heard footsteps."

Then the third man entered the conversation. "It was probably just a squirrel."

"A squirrel doesn't make as much noise as that," the man named Dom said who was leading the search and was closest.

"Well, it won't be a racoon or, more importantly, a bear, as they don't get them here."

Presley slowed his breathing to make as little sound as possible and reached into his jacket pulling out a pair of enhanced silencers to place on his guns' barrels. During her time working for Presley, Barbara had channelled her love of engineering vehicles into weaponry, also. Transferring her technology used to mute the Harley-Davidson onto the guns had been easy for her. Slowly and silently, Presley screwed the improved attachments into place on his firearms and waited for the leading man to reach him.

Dom reached the other side of the trunk behind which Presley was hiding, suddenly stopped and turned to his fellow guards saying, "Can't see anything. Must've been a falling branch."

Dom's colleagues turned away to walk back to their post and Presley took the opportunity to pounce from behind the tree and grab Dom. He quickly knocked him out in a choke hold, lowered him to the ground quietly and began his advance on the other two guards. Just as he was nearing the smaller man, the guard turned and said, "I hope one of his monsters hasn't escaped." He finished his sentence and saw Presley standing a few feet away with Dom unconscious behind him. He tried to warn the third guard but, before he opened his mouth, Presley had raised his silenced pistols and shot the remaining two guards through their skulls. A murmur came from behind him, he turned and fired two bullets in quick succession into Dom. *The 'no casualties approach' never works,* Presley thought to himself as he entered the mansion.

There were rooms to Presley's left and right and a large marble staircase with mahogany railings ascending. The staircase also went downward into darkness. Presley decided that any damsel in distress is always stored in the highest room, so he approached the staircase. Before beginning his ascent, though, he heard awful blood-curdling screams erupting from the depths of the mansion. Unable to ignore the horrific sounds coming from the basement he decided to take the stairs down instead. When Presley stepped off the bottom step an automatic light came on, first nearest him and then another two lights came on further away until all the lights were on in what appeared to be a large hall. Taken aback by what he saw, Presley almost fell over the bottom step which was directly behind him. The hall was full of cages with all manner of distorted and tortured human figures. It didn't take Presley long to figure out that these were the monsters the small guard was referring to. Each cage was home to an abomination that was formed by Gaia in the hands of Dark Snake. She had tested her ability to use Gaia's powers across worlds on these poor people and turned them into horrific mangled bodies with animalistic features.

The hall smelt of excrement, fear and death. Some of the occupants of the cages had died and were rotting in their cells whilst the other demonic creatures formed by Dark Snake were salivating while gazing at the decaying corpses. The blood-curdling screams Presley had heard must have been the tortured minds of the trapped beings, struggling through pain and urges to go against all of mankind's boundaries. The cage nearest Presley was home to a woman who had been manipulated and tested on with dire consequences. Her back, which at first appeared to be covered in armour, was in fact where her ribcage had been twisted round to her spine to form a hard surface similar to an armadillo. In addition to her rib cage, she had grown more bones along her back that had ripped through her skin in order to form the hard exoskeleton. The area surrounding each of the exit points where her bones had breached the skin was yellowish and, upon closer inspection, pus-filled and weeping. Presley noticed a label which read 'Success'.

How can that be deemed a success? wondered Presley. His internal monologue was broken as he heard a whimper from his right. Presley spotted a man who was clearly dying, his label read 'Failure'. The experiment had lifted and enlarged the man's nose and formed a kind of horn. The subject's breathing was clearly compromised, and the movement of the nose had left the man unable to close his mouth, which was full of maggots, and he had flies eating his face. They were through the flesh in most places, leaving mostly bone.

With a final gurgle the man died there and then, right in front of Presley.

Unable to move on from the hall, Presley continued to look in the cages. The next one he came across was another woman; at first Presley couldn't tell what was wrong but then she lunged at him and hissed with a forked tongue. She slammed into the bars and fell to the ground, but the brief lunge was enough time for Presley to have seen the irregularly pointed teeth that filled her mouth. The label said 'Success'. Again, the woman hissed and opened her mouth; this time Presley saw the venom glands in her gums and didn't chance getting any nearer. The next cage was silhouetted and Presley couldn't quite see its occupant. He edged nearer until a tail tipped with a venomous stinger pierced through the shadows. Presley fell backwards landing on his rear in the desperate attempt to avoid being hit. As he watched the creature retreat into the shadows, he had conflicted thoughts with regards to gathering as much information on Dark Snake's experiments as he could and going to save Annabel straight away. The intelligence on Tombstone's weapons could be vital in the battles to come. These specimens were proof that Dark Snake was trying to use Gaia to make monsters on Earth. In Sanctum, the success rate of using the item would be one hundred percent but her inexperience at using the powerful artefact meant she was unable to use it successfully across worlds, explaining the failures in the room. These mistakes gave Presley hope that she would be unable to create an effective army without conquering Sanctum first, meaning that the conflict could be stopped before ever reaching Earth. In order to beat Dark Snake, Minotaur would need their full strength. Presley turned around and went back up the stairs to find Annabel, unable to risk the possibility she was being tested on at that very moment.

CHAPTER 10

Sanctum
Chungwantanya
Dreadnoque and Chungwantanya Border

A bead of sweat ran down Oleyake's neck, the humid conditions of the forest were always making the young girl perspire. She was a child in a small Obiri tribe settlement on the edge of Chungwantanya. The hot sticky weather would be enough to make anyone sweat, but Oleyake had been playing catch with one of her friends as well. She wasn't very good so every time the small ball was thrown to her, she had to run after it as it rolled away. She bent down to pick it up for the latest failed catch attempt and felt the toy in her hands. It was made from the skin of their meal the night before. The animal pelt was wrapped round a small stone and tied together with thin vines from a tree. Oleyake could still feel the rough edges of the stone underneath the hide, but it would have to do, there were no smoother rocks around. Her throwing was much better than her catching and so when she released the ball it was easy for her friend to scoop it out of the air and return it. Again, Oleyake failed to catch the projectile but this time she couldn't be bothered to fetch it.

"Let's play something else," she droned as her arms fell loosely at her side.

Her friend agreed to the change of entertainment, and they made their way to the river hand in hand. Their parents warned them not to cross the river as it marked the edge of their settlement. The jungle was no place for a child away from home. Bearing their boundaries in mind they jumped in the river and began to play.

The chilly flowing water immediately cooled their bodies and felt blissful as the sweat washed away. Oleyake splashed her friend and he retaliated with a splash of his own. When the water hit her in the face she turned around and began to cry. Nevertheless, when

Oleyake's friend came to see if she was OK, she stopped her act and turned, throwing herself on top of him, tackling him under the surface. They erupted from the water giggling and pushing each other whilst the contents of the river spilled from their mouths in coughs and spits. Their laughter had only just died down when they heard a splash behind them. They spun round to see the source of the sound and saw a lizard exiting the water and running into the jungle.

"Wow, that was massive!" Oleyake's friend observed. "Let's go and get it."

Shaking her head ferociously, Oleyake panicked. "We can't. It's out of the boundary."

"That could feed us for days," her friend reasoned.

Oleyake knew he was right but was wary of her parents' warning not to leave their settlement edge. Then, without further conversation, her friend leapt out of the river and pursued the lizard.

"No! Come back!" she begged. She could hear him getting further away and knew he had ignored her cry. Afraid but unwilling to let her buddy go alone into the unknown, she left the safety of her settlement for the first time and tried to track her friend down. She used the skills her mother had taught her and looked for broken branches and trampled vegetation. Oleyake's playmate was not being very stealthy according to his tracks – she could easily spot the route he had carved himself through the jungle. Brushing past bushes and ducking under tree limbs, she finally found her friend waiting behind a large brown tree with great big green leaves.

"It's over there," he pointed, unaware of how angry Oleyake was with him. The lizard was big and would serve as a brilliant dinner for their families over the coming days if they could catch it, but it wouldn't be easy. The dark green reptile was chewing on a small plant with a red flower; it seemed completely unaware it was being watched.

Oleyake looked left to tell her friend to turn back but he was gone again. Muttering to herself, she scanned the terrain for any sign of him. She thought she could see him behind a tree a little further up, so she slowly crept towards his supposed location. As she was sneaking through she caught her arm on a thorn and it gave her a nasty scratch. Dark red blood began to seep from the wound and drip onto the forest floor. The fluid was soaked into the ground almost instantaneously, quenching the jungle's thirst for blood. Oleyake cut herself again as she progressed, this time on a sharp stone on the ground. The leaf-littered earth eagerly lapped up the blood from her weeping foot. Already hurt and regretting going against her parents' orders, Oleyake was not happy at all when she reached her friend once more. Her worries were not shared by her adventurous peer, nonetheless, and her pleas fell on death ears. "Mum's right, boys don't listen," she grumbled to herself. Oleyake noticed her friend was about to make his move, in his left hand was a stone that she assumed he'd use to club the animal to death.

"Like a jaguar lying in wait," he uttered as if to psych himself up, then he exploded from the foliage and launched his body towards the lizard. He landed with a thud next to the lizard and smashed the stone down where the reptile's head was, however, the animal was too fast and dodged the blow. Spooked, it accelerated off into the bushes, ensuring it wouldn't be feeding the tribe that night. A deep laughing sound came from the jungle next to him and a start of a scream could be briefly heard before it was cut short. Oleyake had a hand round her mouth which had prematurely halted her shriek. It was the strong hand of a man that was scarred from multiple cuts in the past. The source of the deep and menacing laugh emerged from cover, clapping. The amused man was black as night and had long dreadlocks past his shoulders the same colour as his skin. His clothes were shaggy and torn, the material was not from Chungwantanya. His smile revealed a mouth with very few teeth, but the strangest thing about the man's appearance was the dolls hanging from his rags. The dolls varied in hair colour and clothing as well as other physical differences.

"Nice try," he sarcastically clapped, referring to the attempt to get the lizard.

Oleyake was thrown next to her friend at the feet of the strange man.

"Let me take ya home," he offered softly. "Which way izit?"

Oleyake was relieved that the man was going to help them so she pointed in the direction they came from and led the way back to the settlement.

Her friend protested but he had caused enough trouble already; she wasn't going to listen to him anymore. Crossing the river, they returned to the boundaries of their settlement and emerged into the open flatland where the huts were located.

Oleyake picked up the small ball she had been playing with earlier and felt the rough stone underneath again.

"Thank you," she said to the strange man with dreadlocks, grateful for his escort back home.

"Ya welcome, me child," he replied, revealing his gap-toothed smile again.

Oleyake went to run away but he had her dress firmly in his hands. She was pulled back.

"I am Voodoo," he announced to the camp.

The tribespeople looked at him with fear, noticing him for the first time,

then Oleyake's parents emerged from their home. "NO!" they screamed. "Get away from our daughter!"

"Much obliged," he cackled before pulling out his ceremonial dagger and plunging it through the young girl's heart. He threw her body to the ground and embraced the bellows from her distraught parents.

"Kill dem all!" Voodoo ordered the squad of Chungterror tribesmen he had brought with him.

Eager to impress, they set to work slaughtering the peaceful village.

Voodoo stood laughing, bathing in the hideous squeals of the helpless villagers.

CHAPTER 11

Earth
England
South-east

George awoke and the truck was rumbling along in the countryside somewhere; everyone else was awake and deep in conversation. George hoped he hadn't been the only one to fall asleep on the journey.

Cheikhou noticed George wake up. "Morning sleeping beauty. I thought we'd need Alex to kiss you with his froggy face."

Everyone chuckled apart from Alex who tried to defend himself with a comeback.

"Actually, it was the princess that kissed the frog, so maybe Rosie should kiss *me*." This proved to worsen his current situation as he turned beetroot-red and Cheikhou continued to roar with laughter and make fun of Alex's knowledge of princess fairy tales.

Carlton gave Cheikhou a disapproving look and went to Alex's defence, "Remember you weren't always the cocky man you are today, Cheik! Don't forget the incident with the meerkat…"

This did the trick as Cheikhou abruptly ceased laughing and, for the first time, seemed to become a little embarrassed himself. "I was young and didn't know it was a meerkat."

Carlton laughed as he recalled, "You were sixteen and almost wet yourself."

Rosie was intrigued along with everyone else in the truck. "What happened?"

"Don't you dare!" warned Cheikhou who was beginning to panic, his voice a little high-pitched through concern.

Suddenly, the window between the cab and the trailer where they were sitting opened and Roy put his head through. "You have to tell us now! Come on, Carlton, we all know Cheik needs taking down a few pegs."

Carlton began telling the story, much to his acquaintance's displeasure. "We were on patrol on the nature reserve. I'd taken Cheik with me as I sometimes did and the day had been quiet. We were just coming up to the grazing area for the rhinos' usual spot but something was wrong. The further we entered into the usual rhino territory the stranger it got when we realised they were missing. I told Cheik to get out and check out the area to see if there were any signs where they'd gone. After he'd looked for a while I decided to stop the vehicle and get out to help him spot any trails or disturbances."

Cheikhou tried to pipe up but was hushed by the others waiting for the rest of the story.

Carlton continued. "I walked a bit ahead of where Cheik had already searched and analysed the ground. Sure enough, there was nothing there. Afterwards, whilst pretending to continue searching, I set a trap and planted a pile of lion scat that I collected earlier in the day. Naturally, I required a second pair of eyes to confirm the faeces was indeed from a lion, so I called Cheik over to take a look. He ran over, eager to impress, and studied the area I'd brought his attention to. All the colour drained from his face when he saw the pile and he turned to me, panic-stricken."

Carlton had them smiling already but the merriment quickly followed when he imitated Cheikhou's girly squeal, "'Why are we hanging around? They could be anywhere!'"

Cheikhou was less than impressed by the voice Carlton used to imitate him, but it had the others in fits of laughter.

"Carry on," pleaded George through teary eyes.

Carlton obliged and moved on to the next part of his story, "OK, so on the one hand Cheik was panicking, worried about an imminent lion attack. On the other hand, being the brave ranger I was, I ploughed on into the nearest bush and disappeared from Cheik's sight. I heard him about to follow but I yelled 'Don't move, its over here!', then I let out a fake yelp. The shriek that Cheik then made was as if his balls had been trapped in a blender. It was lucky we were in an open reserve as it would have shattered any glass in the vicinity. The joke was going to be over then, but fate delivered Morris to me at that time, truly making it a moment to never forget." Seeing that, obviously, the guys didn't know who Morris was, Carlton explained. "Morris is the leader of the local meerkat gang. I picked him up and began to make my way back through the bush to Cheik, rustling the leaves as much as I could. His yells got progressively louder and high-pitched the closer we got. Finally, before I exposed myself, I sent Morris out from the vegetation and Cheik screamed one last time. Then I fell out of the bush laughing as Cheik realised he'd been tricked. Strangely, he didn't find it as funny as I did."

The story was a success, the whole truck was shaking with amusement and Cheikhou was quietened in the corner, not used to being the butt of the joke. Nevertheless, once he knew there was no stopping the story, he began to smile and enjoy the memory with the others.

"So, where were the rhinos then?" George asked.

Cheikhou answered in a tone that suggested he had still not quite forgiven his guardian. "Carlton moved them earlier in the day to a new place to avoid poacher movements; it was a set-up from the start." Unable to bear having to be the only one getting the mickey taken out of, Cheikhou recalled the moments immediately after the prank so the others had the full story. "Once I'd finished screaming – I won't deny it, any of you would have done the same – I found the lion shit and launched it at Carlton's head. It was a sweet shot, exploded right on his forehead which, granted, isn't a hard target to hit. Still, I feel I got my revenge watching Carlton pick bits of crap out of his hair for the rest of the day."

Rosie was the last to finish giggling and thanked Carlton and Cheikhou for improving the mood in what was otherwise an undesirable situation.

Roy understood the importance of the morale boost and was eager to keep the mood light and the attention away from Annabel's empty space next to Alex. "Anyone else have a funny story to share?"

Yuanli looked over to Rosie with a nervous glance, and at first Rosie didn't realise. Then she caught Yuanli's eye and came to terms with what was about to happen. "Oh no, come on, you can't tell them that story!"

Yuanli gave an apologetic shrug and smiled. She looked so young after years of martial arts and gymnastics. It gave her a radiance that would be associated with a woman half her age. Yuanli ignored Rosie's plea and embarked on her story regardless.

"So, I was going to meet Rosie at the gym. She wanted to put in some extra one-on-one training to improve on some areas she was struggling with. I arrived a little earlier than agreed and therefore was not surprised to find the gym empty. I changed into my workout gear so I was ready before Rosie arrived."

Carlton sat up at that point and showed great interest in that part of the story. "How about you tell us more about your workout gear, eh?"

Yuanli glared disapprovingly in Carlton's direction, and he sank back down into his chair under her burning gaze.

"Anyway, about fifteen minutes after Rosie was due to arrive, I decided to go and begin working out myself, planning to stop when Rosie finally turned up. As I walked through the apparently deserted gym, I heard a faint whimper coming from the corner. I stopped and put all my attention into listening out for the noise again. I quietened my breathing and ignored the background buzz of the lights. Listening very hard, I heard the struggling noise again; this time it sounded a little familiar. 'Hello!' I shouted to the gym I thought to be empty moments ago. The voice came again, louder this time; 'Help!' the voice squealed, 'Help me!' I approached the source of the SOS call and found, yeah you guessed it, Rosie."

Everyone chuckled in anticipation of the rest of the story and Yuanli relished having the full attention of the truck – Rosie was even laughing despite having her face behind her hands.

"Rosie was lying on the weight bench, unable to get up because she had a barbell with huge weights on it for her size, lying across her chest. She was pinned down and completely unable to move. My immediate thought was that she must have been there at least fifteen minutes. She couldn't have come in after myself, I would've seen her, meaning she was there before I ever arrived. The weight of the barbell was pushing down on her lungs, which is why her voice was whimpering and initially too high-pitched to understand. I ran to her aid and, with an almighty push from Rosie and an equally great effort from myself, we lifted the barbell off and returned it to the rack. Rosie rolled off the bench and got up to thank me, however, her voice sounded as if she had been breathing helium for the past half an hour, so the whole situation ended with an undecipherable thank you speech audible only to dogs. Nevertheless, she then went on to train harder than ever and achieve a grade above anything the gymnastics group has seen before, even managing to outperform athletes twice as experienced as her at competition level." Yuanli smiled and nodded in approval at her student. George couldn't help but admire Yuanli's ability to tell the embarrassing story but end it in a way that would praise Rosie and fill her with confidence however much drained she must have felt from the previous anecdote.

"Still never won a championship though, have I?" Rosie sighed as she picked her nails.

"You surpassed anyone in your age bracket, you only lost to those who'd been doing it all their lives. You even beat some of them, like I said." Yuanli battled to try to get Rosie to see her worth.

"It's never easy seeing others claim glory when you've tried your best," Alex added, attempting to sympathise with Rosie. "I often feel bad when I look down on them from the top of the podium, medal round my neck, crowd chanting my–" Alex was starting to recognise the look Cheikhou got before hitting him, but this time he still stopped a little too late to prevent the gut blow, driving the wind and the rest of his words from his mouth.

"Ignore him," George whispered to Rosie, shaking his head.

"I envy him. I could never be so confident," Rosie chuckled.

CHAPTER 12

Earth
England
Tombstone testing facility

Presley crested the top of the stairs as a pair of guards entered the room further down the corridor to his right. He quickly pivoted and silently ran up the next flight of stairs, sticking with his original plan to check the top floor first. Slightly shaken by what he had just seen in the basement, Presley was not his usual self and, upon reaching the top level, he failed to check the hallway and ran straight out into the open.

A guard saw him and shouted "Intruder!"

Presley regained his composure and, by the time the word was out of the guard's mouth, he was lying on the floor with multiple bullets in his chest. Barbara's improved silencer did a good job of muting the bullets but the sound the guard made when he crashed through a table and knocked a vase to the ground removed the option for further stealth. The damage was done and Presley's presence had been alerted to the other guards. The sentries weren't the only ones who knew of Presley's presence; screams of "Help! Please, someone… help!" could be heard from the room the dead guard had been standing outside. Presley ran to the corpse, scooped a set of keys from his belt and burst through the door he was guarding. The sight that met his eyes was daunting. The floor was covered with prisoners of all ages shackled to the wall with metal chains. They were in varying conditions, some looked to have arrived recently whereas others were malnourished and weak, the chains serving to hold them upright more than hinder their escape.

A shout came from the mass of bodies that broke Presley from his disgust at the scene before him

"Presley. Oh thank God. Help us."

He glanced where the sound had come from and saw Annabel with tears streaming down her face but smiling in the way that only she could, a smile that brought light to a dark place and banished all cold with her wave of warmth and happiness. The blissful reunion was over quickly, however, as the guards could be heard thundering down the corridor. Presley slammed shut the door and set to work unlocking the chains with the key he had swiped. As he freed them, the prisoners rushed to hold the door closed whilst the guards banged and pushed from the other side.

Presley used the respite given to him to talk to Annabel. "Are you OK? Have they hurt you?"

"I'm fine now, but the other prisoners told me that they're testing on us and turning us into monsters. I don't understand; who are these 'people'?" inquired Annabel.

Presley shook his head and replied, "These are the people we at Minotaur have been tasked with stopping and the evil you and your friends have been enrolled to prevent from spreading. I'll tell you more on the journey then give you a full debrief in Arizona."

"Arizona?" exclaimed Annabel. "What do you mean?"

The door creaked while the prisoners were holding it shut – Presley overheard one murmur his lack of optimism in holding it for much longer.

He took Annabel by the shoulders and looked into her crystal blue eyes. "You have to trust me and help me get these people out of here. I promise all will be explained later. Just help me with this now."

Annabel nodded but still looked apprehensive. "What's the plan then?"

As she asked the question a great roar emanated from the other side of the door and the guards stopped pushing. The cease was followed by shrieks mixed with growls and a loud cracking sound. The door was then abruptly ripped from its hinges and the prisoners that were holding it shut were thrown to the floor. A mountain of a man stooped down and entered the room. He was wearing a white turban that was specked with blood as well as a vest stained with both blood and food. Thick, matted black hair covered his exposed arms, neck and the top of his chest. A prisoner ran at him with a shard of the broken door and began to stab wildly, but the brute just parried his attempted advances and caught the prisoner by the throat. With a vice-like grip he lifted his aggressor from the ground and squeezed. There was a snap and the prisoner's head tilted back exposing a white neck bone sticking through the skin. The dead prisoner was then dropped to the floor and the behemoth stepped over his lifeless body.

Presley emerged from the crowd and said, "Of all the ugly shits in this world, Butcher, you must be the ugliest. I think it's the slab of meat you call a face."

The beast looked to see the source of the taunt. "Arghh, Presley. Maybe this day wasn't such a waste after all," growled the large man. He charged but Presley sidestepped the attack and whacked the brute on the head as he passed.

Presley attempted to draw his pistols but was pounced on before he could complete the action. The pistols flew across the room and Butcher threw Presley on the floor. A ground and pound manoeuvre followed as he proceeded to pummel into Presley's face with his paw-like hands. Presley's nose broke and the pain gave him a surge of adrenaline to throw Butcher off him. Both men stood up and regained their fight stance. Presley's eyes were watering from his shattered nose but through the blur he launched a flurry of punches and a powerful spinning kick that caught Butcher off-guard. The foot connected perfectly but the bearlike man just swayed a little and then roared, releasing a foul stench from his mouth. Butcher proceeded to attack again. Presley succeeded in deflecting the first few attacks but then the sheer power of the advance broke through his defences. Butcher was backing Presley up and connecting with his punches now; Presley's face was turning red where cuts and bruises were beginning to replace his usual features. The Minotaur leader's eyes began to close in defeat but then he saw Annabel moving behind his opponent.

She was going for the guns.

Presley dug deep and spat a mouthful of blood and a few teeth at Butcher's face.

The response was just a harsh and spiteful cackle. "Minotaur's greatest weapon, so feeble and broken."

A loud *bang!* echoed round the room.

Butcher staggered back and roared.

Annabel had reached one of the guns and fired it in the direction of Presley's opponent. Her lack of previous experience with firearms meant that the aim was off and her shot hit Butcher in the leg. A second *bang!* and Butcher roared again, this time the shot hit his arm. The gun was out of ammunition and Annabel was unsure how to reload but the two shots had done the trick.

Butcher with his tough bearlike skin and bestial resilience did not fall to the ground but sensed his weakness and limped out of the room as fast as his wounded limbs would carry him.

Annabel rushed over to Presley to aid him, but the Minotaur leader was already on his feet. His leadership qualities demanded he show no pain when others were dependent on him to get them out; he knew instead he must be strong.

"Fanks, Anabwel, ba' I 'ad 'im wight where I 'unted 'im," Presley struggled through his heavily bleeding mouth with less teeth than moments before.

Annabel turned to the prisoners and told them to run and save themselves. Then she put one of Presley's arms round her and walked him out of the room, down the stairs and out of the mansion. Their path was clear, the escaping prisoners had overwhelmed the few remaining guards, leaving them beaten on the floor.

Presley was shaking but managed to point Annabel in the direction of his hidden bike. As they exited the gate to the mansion there was a tremendous explosion, the force of the detonation threw Presley and Annabel off their feet and into the dirt. Brushing themselves off, they turned to survey the damage and saw the foundations of the historic building had been blown up causing the bricks to collapse to the ground in a mound of debris.

"Dey wigged da base ta expode," guessed Presley. "Tombsthone are not yet ready for Earth ta see da monstrosities dey've been workin' on."

Stumbling together the rest of the way to the bike, Presley took his arm from Annabel's shoulders and opened the vehicle's storage that had the appropriate gear for Annabel to ride the bike, too. Annabel walked over to admire the bike and saw Presley getting her clothes out. She reached for an item that she found interesting. "Kinky holidays away or a love for horse racing?" she asked, trying to lighten the mood, but Presley snatched the item from her and shoved it back in the bike with a grunt. Whilst waiting for Annabel to change into the motorbike gear behind a bush, Presley decided to ring Roy to tell him the mission was a success. Unfortunately, when Presley pulled out his phone it was completely smashed in the aftermath of his brawl with Butcher. *Bollocks*, he thought as he launched the broken device into the bush a little further from Annabel's changing area.

When she emerged from the vegetation, Annabel put her other clothes in the place where the protective gear was stored previously and tried to get another look at the weapon or toy Presley had snatched away moments before.

Again, he intercepted her snooping and a brief argument began about Presley's fitness to drive that he won on account of the fact it was unsafe to stay where they were and Annabel could not drive a motorbike. As they set off to meet the others and go to Arizona, Annabel grasped Presley tight and whispered, "Thank you."

Presley groaned and said, "Ahh, noth la wibs."

Annabel giggled and the bike sped off. The sun was rising and the chill of the night seemed to be replaced by light warmth from the morning rays.

CHAPTER 13

Earth
England
South-east

Why hasn't he messaged yet? Something has to be wrong. These thoughts ran through Roy's mind as he bounced up and down in his seat over the bumpy roads Barbara was taking them down.

"Ouch, my head!" shouted Alex as he rubbed his skull for the fifth time in as many minutes. "Slow down a bit!" he pleaded.

Cheikhou was also finding it an uncomfortable ride. Nevertheless, if it was causing Alex discomfort then he was all for it. "Nah, speed up, Barbs!" he bellowed over the loud sounds of the truck impacting the ground. They had been driving all night and were nearing the private airfield where their plane to America was waiting. The hustle and bustle of the night before felt like a lifetime ago. Barbara wasn't driving slowly but the journey seemed to be lasting days. The joy brought by the stories during the night drive had worn off and everyone was either asleep, unable to stay awake after a full night of travelling or sitting in silence, most likely thinking about Presley and Annabel, the same as Roy.

"Shouldn't we have heard from them by now?" Rosie asked her fellow passengers.

Yuanli and Carlton merely answered with their snores and George, Cheikhou and Alex didn't know how to respond.

Roy hated having to be the leader and answer difficult questions but he didn't neglect his role. "I won't lie to you. If we're to build a strong trusting squad, there can be no holding back of information. The lack of contact is worrying me. It isn't like Presley to not check in with his team."

"His phone might be broken or out of charge," suggested George, trying not to let morale drop too far.

"It could be, and hopefully that's all it is," agreed Roy.

"It's a shame I'm not there with him."

Everyone looked in disbelief at Alex, unable to accept that he still had the energy to boast. Alex thought the looks he received were because his friends didn't know what he meant. "I could have fixed it for him," he added, to clear up any confusion.

George shook his head and looked out of the back of the truck. The day was off to a bright start weather-wise, the morning sun already having warmth to it and there wasn't a cloud in the sky. George let the rays bathe his skin and he closed his eyes to focus on the light breeze which freshened his face. He relaxed by listening to the birds singing in the trees lining the dusty country road they were travelling down. As he opened his eyes again, he was blinded by the sun. He squinted and blinked a few times to clear his eyes from the shock, but he was seeing colours flashing in front of them and shapes were shooting across his vision. Then he thought he saw something in one of the trees, or more like some*one*. He quickly rubbed his eyes and looked back at the tree, but the figure was gone. *Wow, that sun is bright this morning*, George decided as he blamed the light for the tricks being played.

"Damn!" Barbara yelled as the truck slammed to a stop.

George's head whipped swiftly forwards and backwards due to the emergency brake. Rubbing his sore neck, he looked around and checked everyone was OK. Fortunately, there were no injuries, however, Carlton and Yuanli were startled and frantically taking in their surroundings after being awoken from their respective slumbers.

"What happened?" inquired Cheikhou.

"Tree in the road," Roy answered.

"I was coming round the corner and there it was," shouted Barbara, who was trying to explain why the stop was so sudden and unexpected. "There hasn't been any wind, I don't see why the tree should be on the ground," she moaned.

"Shouldn't have been going so fast," Alex piped up.

"Oh, do shut up, Alex!" she retorted.

"'Yeah, do shut up!'" Cheikhou laughed as he mimicked Barbara's voice.

His laughter soon died down however when Rosie let out a

blood-curdling scream.

George followed her eye line to see the source of her displeasure and what he saw filled him with dread. Standing outside the back of the truck was a creature very similar to the one that attacked him in the forest before Presley saved him – *but that was a bad dream*, George said to himself. The figure had thin wisps of hair, razor-like claws and a naked body save for a scrap of cloth covering its genitals. It just stood staring with its big black eyes, then the creature howled. Before anyone had time to react to the monster outside the truck, an arrow smashed through the windscreen and just missed Roy's head. The shaft wobbled in the chair Roy had vacated seconds earlier to check on the commotion at the rear.

"Everyone out!" barked Barbara. "Out of the truck now!" Just as Barbara opened her door and stepped outside, an arrow wedged itself in the driving seat.

Yuanli was first out of the vehicle having exploded from her seat and rolled towards the skinny beast. Before the creature had time to attack, Yuanli was back on her feet raining blows down on her victim. The creature didn't stand a chance, Yuanli beat it to the ground whilst it screamed. Then in one swift movement she pulled a knife from her boot and rammed it into her opponent's skull. A final shriek and the creature died. Sensing she wasn't safe yet, however, Yunali cartwheeled to her right just in time to avoid an arrow which was destined for her ribs. In the time it took for Yuanli to get rid of the terror, the rest of the group had left the truck and were taking cover on the opposite side to the archer.

"We need to stop them arrows!" commanded Roy.

"I'm on it," growled Carlton before sprinting into the trees at the roadside.

"He's gone the wrong way," whispered Alex to George.

George didn't answer, not presuming to know Carlton's attack tactics.

Yuanli was rolling backwards and forwards, evading arrows raining down around her. "Why doesn't she take cover?" George asked.

"She's distracting the archer," Barbara told him.

George was in awe of the bravery and agility of Yuanli;

everything about her was simply amazing as far as he was concerned. Nevertheless, whilst admiring her, he witnessed something that worried him. "There's more," he groaned.

Rosie spotted the three creatures approaching her guardian and didn't think before sprinting to her role model's aid.

Roy swore at her naïvety. "Come on, Cheik," he said as he pulled him along while he went to help Rosie.

George was left with Alex and Barbara in cover and was in no rush to join the fray. He observed as Cheikhou ripped a creature from Rosie and smashed its skull into the floor the same as Presley had done in the forest. The creature cried out in terror but no help came from the other monsters who were attacking Roy. Just as Roy was beginning to become overwhelmed help from Cheikhou and Rosie relieved him. George was so engrossed in the combat with the monsters that he failed at first to realise the arrows had stopped falling.

Then Alex tapped him on the shoulder and said, "Come on, the archer isn't attacking anymore."

Once George arrived with Alex to help Roy, the combined assault was too much for the creatures who were subdued and killed in a fit of screams.

"Woooo, what the hell were they?" boomed Cheikhou who seemed more excited than shaken by the conflict.

"Screamers," replied Roy. "Minions of Dark Snake."

"You're bleeding," Yuanli said as she worried over Rosie, half-thanking her and half-telling her to be more careful next time. In truth, the cut was very shallow and Rosie was lucky it was only her arm, the weaponized claws on the screamers could easily puncture a vital organ or major artery. "Where's Carlton?" Yuanli questioned after dealing with Rosie.

"He went to stop the archer," Cheikhou told her.

"Well, he obviously succeeded but why isn't he back?" Alex wondered. As soon as he asked the question, they heard a yell from the direction in which the arrows were coming from moments before. The voice was not high-pitched and spine-chilling like the creatures they had just dealt with, the call for help came from the distinguishable African accent of Carlton. The group ran together to where the voice was emanating from. Barbara was first through the vegetation to discover the source of the call.

When George emerged through the brush, he saw Carlton laying in a pool of blood.

"Get them out of here!" Yuanli shouted to Roy.

Cheikhou deflected Roy's incoming arm and completely overpowered his attempt to remove him from the scene. "What happened?" he demanded to know.

Carlton was in a bad way but was still able to tell them how he got in the state he was in. "I hid myself in the cover of trees. I used the vegetation to get within striking distance of the archer and as I got closer I saw the bald head. The accuracy of the arrows that were falling and the characteristics of the attacker – I knew it could only be one person."

"Amazon," Roy said, breathing in despair. He looked around frantically and pushed the others away. "Get back to the truck."

"Who done this?" Cheikhou demanded to know. "Who is this Amazon?"

Yuanli and Barbara helped Carlton to his feet and began applying first aid whilst he told them what happened next.

"I knew I'd be no match for her but needed to stop her shooting you down, so I jumped on her from behind. I knocked the bow from her hand and knew you'd be safe. It didn't take her long to throw me off and pull out two small knives, though. I tried to parry her advances but she was too fast. Every attack I dodged another two found their mark. She was about to finish me when she heard you guys coming and ran."

"I'll make her pay," Cheikhou said as he screwed up his face and looked in the direction she ran.

Roy seemed to grow in presence and power as he pushed Cheikhou away and commanded the group once more, "I said, get back to the truck now!"

Yuanli and Barbara convinced Cheikhou that he needed to listen if he wanted Carlton to receive proper medical care.

Carlton had multiple cuts which was the reason for the pool of blood, but he had somehow done well enough in his defence to prevent any stab wounds meaning no major parts were damaged.

"I'll be fine," Carlton said, wincing as he began walking back to the truck. "Cheik, please, for me – don't follow her, you don't understand who you're dealing with."

"Now I see where you get your strength from," George said as he nudged Cheikhou's arm as they returned to the vehicle.

Yuanli loaded Carlton back into the truck and ensured he was comfy in his seat, then she went to help the others remove the tree from the road. Together, but mostly thanks to Alex and Cheikhou, they managed to roll the tree out of the way and clear the route for the last leg of the journey to the airstrip.

"What're we going to do with those?" inquired Rosie, pointing at the dead corpses of the creatures.

"We'll have to burn them," suggested Roy, who had already begun piling the screamers onto one large bonfire.

Barbara pre-empted the need to remove the bodies and had already gone to fetch some spare fuel for the fire. The sweet tangy smell of the fuel filled the air as she drenched the monsters in the liquid. Unfortunately, the aroma was instantaneously replaced by the most sickening odour of burning flesh when she flicked a match onto the bonfire of corpses.

George could feel the stench clinging to the inside of his throat and burning his nostrils but for some reason the fire had him entranced as he began thinking of the journey he had got himself into. Each leap of flames dragged him further into his thoughts as he remembered his parents crying as he was leaving, the near-death experience at paintballing but, most of all, whether he would ever see his best friend, Jacob, again. The hypnosis ended when George noticed one of the screamer's eyeballs explode under the heat; not only did it serve to bring him out of his daze but he also proceeded to throw up on the spot.

Yuanli gave him a rag to clean himself up and helped him back to the truck in the same caring manner she had done for Carlton moments earlier.

Happy with their work, the group returned to the vehicle ready to depart.

"She was after Jedrok," Roy told the others as he patted the rock. "They aren't getting it that easy." Suddenly, though, he went white.

"NO!" was all that was required to inform the others something was awry. "They have St George's armour," he whispered in defeat. "Amazon must have grabbed it when we were tending to Carlton."

"Whilst we have Jedrok they can have all the artefacts needed to open it," said George in a hopeful way.

"Let's get it to a more secure location then," Barbara instructed as she put her foot on the accelerator and began the last part of the drive. The vehicle lurched into motion and almost immediately jumped and shook as a pothole marked another poor part of road.

Carlton groaned and pleaded, "Take it a bit slower, Barbs, you're going to finish me off!"

They all laughed.

CHAPTER 14

Earth
USA
Wyoming

'Good morning my fellow patriots and welcome to another beautiful day here in the U S of A.'

The morning wake-up call from the radio brought Deacon out of his slumber, the same as it did every morning. Deacon was not one to stay in bed wrapped up in covers, when the alarm went off it was time for action. Deacon decided from a young age that a get-up-and-go attitude would get him wherever he wanted in life, and so far it had. As he pulled on his running gear and checked he looked presentable in front of his smudgy body length mirror, he knew that the reflection gazing back at him was the same person who finished top of his class at school and, as such, managed to become the youngest fireman in Wyoming history. He had received multiple awards across his illustrious career so far, all for amazing feats of bravery and skill in the field. Breakfast was the same as every other day, a bowlful of oatmeal which warmed his insides and fuelled him for the busy day ahead. The man on the radio wasn't lying about the weather; as soon as Deacon left the safety of his house he was met with a wave of heat that dried his eyes and made him cough. That wasn't going to be enough to stop Deacon, though, he needed to be at work in fifteen minutes and to get there on time he had to run. Physical activity wasn't a chore for Deacon; in his spare time he often attended the gym to improve his physique. At six foot two inches he was a tall man with a full head of soft blonde hair. The constant workouts and nature of his job meant that he was in excellent condition. He began running along the pavement, sprinting from shade to shade under the trees bordering the road like sentinels at a palace. He reached the end of the road and spotted an elderly lady neighbour on her doorstep.

"Morning, Pat!" he shouted to her in passing.

"Morning Deacon!" she replied through a mouth without teeth, giving him a gummy smile and watching him until he was out of sight. He was used to seeing her on the journey to work each morning; she always set her alarm to watch the toned figure of a young fireman run past. One particular day he was sure he heard her murmuring something about being sixty years younger. Pat wasn't the only regular spectator in the morning, however. Bennie, a golden retriever, was also in his usual spot. Unlike when he jogged past Pat when he normally sped up, when he reached Bennie he would always slow right down and pat the dog on its head. Deacon reached into his shorts pocket and pulled out a handful of treats.

"There you go, boy," he whispered as he handed them over to the retriever excitedly wagging its tail. That particular morning he spent a little too long with Bennie and ended up having to double his efforts to reach his workplace on time. When he crashed through the fire department doors he was dripping with sweat and was met face to face with Hanza, the receptionist.

Hanza looked up and shook his head. "Why do you always get here an hour early?" he asked in disbelief.

"Get everywhere an hour early and you'll always be a step ahead of the game," he told Hanza in the same way he did every day. He patted the desk, winked at his colleague and made his way to the showers. When he had washed and freshened himself up he changed into his fireman uniform and sat listening to the radio, awaiting both a call for help and his colleagues to turn up. The rest of his squad arrived on the exact minute they were supposed to begin work; they didn't share the same attitude as Deacon. His team were only just ready for deployment when the first call for aid came.

Hanza finished on the phone and shouted, "Wildfire! I'll send the co-ordinates en route."

Deacon led the charge to the emergency vehicle and had the engine started by the time the others had reached their seats. He put the sirens on and waited for the shutter to open to the outside world. As soon as he was confident he could fit the large fire truck through the gap, he accelerated off to the scene of the disaster. The respect for the emergency services in the USA was evident by how fast other vehicles cleared the road to make room for the firemen to pass. The coordinates had come through from Hanza and, with lack of obstruction in their path, they reached the fire in no time. Arriving at the site they discovered there was already another team there tackling the blaze. They had contained it to a relatively small area by quickly removing the vegetation from around the edge of the fire, thus removing the fuel for it to spread easily. Now it was down to Deacon and his team to kill the blaze entirely. They removed the hose from their fire engine and began pumping water towards the back end of the fire. One of the first rules they were taught in tackling wildfires was to aim for the small outer rim of the fire first and ignore the main middle blaze for the time being. The idea was to gradually force it into the middle, not allowing it to spread any further. Recruits were always given horror stories of wildfires, their ability to spread very quickly and become out of control, that way they never underestimated their opponent when they reached a burning forest. The smell of the fiery wood was intoxicating, it filled Deacon's nose and gave him a tingle down his back. *This is what I was born to do*, he thought to himself. The sound of crackling wood and the rush of water from the hoses was overpowering but Deacon was convinced he could hear something else, a faint growling and roaring. All of a sudden he spotted the source of the noise and then, quick as a flash, it was gone again, hidden behind the leaping flames.

"There's a bear cub in there!" he shouted to his colleagues.

At first they didn't hear him, but after repeating himself, they got the message, nevertheless, instead of directing their efforts towards saving the 'bear' they continued to attack the area they were working on.

"We need to get it out!" he screamed to his squad.

"No, we need to kill the fire and the best way to do that is to focus our efforts on this spot here!" Mark barked back.

Deacon made a split-second decision and convinced himself that lives that were in danger in the present outweighed those that could be in danger in the future. There was no way that he would be able to clear a path to the cub on his own with the volume of water coming from his hose, so he had no option but to enter the fire himself.

Mark saw Deacon turn off his hose and swore at him, yelling

repeatedly, “What’re you doing?”

Deacon turned to his team member, looked him dead in the eyes and replied, “My job.” Instantly after he threw himself into the heart of the fire. He disappeared from Mark’s view as he was swallowed by a large orange mouth.

CHAPTER 15

Earth
England
South-east

Cheikhou cracked his knuckles and narrowed his eyes as he watched Carlton shift uncomfortably in the seat opposite him. “You should have let me hunt her down,” he said, angry at his own failure to get revenge for Carlton’s injuries.

“You aren’t ready,” Yuanli reasoned. “Amazon’s skill as a warrior far outweighs your own.”

Cheikhou punched the empty seat beside him. “You underestimate what my anger can achieve.”

The truck stopped abruptly, Roy jumped out and climbed into the back placing himself in the empty seat beside Cheikhou. In his hands were three laminated pieces of paper. As he looked down at the first picture on the top sheet the truck rumbled back into motion. “When Minotaur formed it was the people of Sanctum saying ‘no’ to Dark Snake’s attempt at bringing us all under her evil regime. Unfortunately, the resistance gave birth to some of the most vile and dangerous villains either of our worlds have ever seen. Dark Snake began to recruit warlords to lead her assault on mankind and dispense of the trouble she received in Sanctum. She collected them during the war, choosing the most vicious, brutal and cruel people who proved themselves with their devotion and willingness to enforce her will upon others.”

Roy placed the top laminated page on Jedrok in view of everyone, revealing a picture of a hunched over, dark-skinned man with few teeth, shaggy clothes and long black dreadlocks. Amongst his saggy face were two mean bloodshot eyes hinting at a past full of torment and hurt.

“What’s that on his clothes?” asked Rosie who initially thought she knew the answer to the question but was lost as to the reason for their presence.

Roy traced the outline of one of the objects hanging from the man's clothes. "This is Voodoo, the first of Dark Snake's warlords. He's a cruel man who aims to strike fear into the hearts of his enemies. In answer to your question, Rosie, they're voodoo dolls he ties onto his clothes. He makes one for everyone he kills and then he wears them to boast and show off his work."

Rosie gasped and said exasperatedly, "But there's loads."

Roy bowed his head and said, "Hundreds."

George was fixated on one doll in particular; it had pigtails and a little yellow dress. *That must be a child,* George thought to himself, repulsed. Further inspection of the man's trophies brought further similar dolls to his attention, then George noticed three that had been sewn together as if holding hands, *a family*, he guessed before reverting his vision from further anguish. His retreating eyes fell on Roy and found a tear rolling down his cheek. "Has he killed someone you know?"

Roy looked up with his eyes bloodshot. "My beautiful mother, Sara," he croaked.

It was in seeing Roy's pained visage that George realised Voodoo did not display the same bloodshot eyes from sadness. The Tombstone warlord seemed intimidating and angry, filled with rage and malcontent at those around him.

Roy composed himself and snorted the fluid escaping his nose back into his head before returning to his presentation with determination. "That son of a bitch will pay for what he's done but I'm not the only one he's hurt, nor is he the only one we need to stop." Roy revealed the next page, 'Butcher'. The picture showed a very large and hairy man. On top of his copper-coloured head sat a white turban with blood splattered on it. The whole bottom half of his face was dominated by a thick, black bushy beard which hid his mouth, smothering any chance of a smile. The rest of the clothing was no cleaner; hairy chest and arms stuck out from a vest stained with both blood and grime. Again, Roy provided further detail: "He carries a large cleaver that'll cut straight through the bone as well as a hook that he uses to dangle his victims helplessly by a skewered piece of flesh. Dark Snake used Gaia to combine him with a bear, the same way she combined herself with a snake. The attempt left him with excessive body hair as well as the height and strength of a fully grown grizzly. This monster is so deranged it's been rumoured he's eaten those he's killed in battle after picking up the taste for their flesh by licking it from his cleaver."

George glanced at the others to see if they shared the same fear and doubt he was and was relived in a way to see Rosie shaking and Cheikhou sweating profusely next to her.

Roy noticed the tension too. "Now Cheik, do you see the kind of monsters Dark Snake has working for her? The final picture will reveal who you wanted to track down on your own. I hope the information about the others will have already proved the foolishness and rashness of that decision."

Alex was the only one who seemed composed.

George couldn't believe how calm and collected he was. "Aren't you scared?" he asked.

Alex stretched and replied, "I'm a tough guy myself, nothing I can't handle."

George looked in disbelief and then let a little smile escape before laughing hysterically. "You really are something else."

Alex looked offended that George doubted him. "I never bite off more than I can chew. I can take him."

"There isn't much you *can't* chew, you fat bastard," Cheikhou added, also annoyed at Alex's bravery.

Roy shook his head as Alex attempted to lunge at Cheikhou whilst George and Rosie played as peacekeepers. So much relied on those in front of him and they weren't much older than kids. Taking a deep breath, he revealed the final picture.

"This is Amazon…" he began by speaking loudly to cut through the fight and refocus the group, "…the last of Dark Snake's warlords but, as we've already seen, by no means the least dangerous. You can see in the picture she's small, but don't let that fool you – she's an expert at jungle warfare and very good with a bow and arrow. I realise now, the only reason Barbara and I escaped was to lure us all away from the truck to steal the armour. Had we been struck and wounded we'd have remained in place making the robbery more difficult."

George looked at the image and decided that the woman was obviously from some tribe; she was sinewy, showing no signs of fat, but instead a hard muscular physique from a life heavily reliant on physical strength. The deduction also explained her expertise at jungle warfare as well as her weapon choice. There was, however, was something troubling him about her appearance. He didn't need to wonder long before Roy answered George's unasked question.

"Amazon shaves her head, leaving it bald. She refuses to grow her hair until all Dark Snake's enemies are dead."

""Sounds like she's dying as an egghead then," Cheikhou predicted with a wry smile. "Might even crack her open and make you an egg butty, Alex."

"Aww, it'd be nice to see you two finally getting along," Rosie teased.

"Oh, he's still unbearable but it's time I accept him as part of the team," Cheikhou allowed.

"Come on, he's not that bad. I think he's funny," Rosie whispered with a giggle.

"I'm going to hold you to that," Alex grinned to Cheikhou. He didn't hear what Rosie said.

George voiced the thought that he supposed everyone was thinking, bar perhaps Alex, "What're we supposed to do against them?"

Roy looked between their faces; they were eager to hear how they could stop such admirable foes.

"We're here!" Barbara called from the front, saving Roy from answering a question in which he knew not the answer.

George leaned forwards to look out the front window and saw the small plane waiting on the private runway with a pilot smoking next to their ride.

Barbara brought the truck to a gradual stop and Roy jumped straight out to meet the person standing next to the plane.

"Wait here," he ordered before he clamoured out the back. He breathed a sigh of relief at the timing of their arrival and whispered a prayer for Presley to return soon: *I hope I did the right thing telling them what they're up against; you always knew what to do.* Roy tried to walk over as coolly as he could to meet the pilot. Presley once told him that a leader can be spotted by the way he presents himself. Roy overthought it and was awkward with his hands, taking them in and out of his pockets, not to mention his green hair which had chosen its own style after the earlier skirmish.

"Name's Roy," he greeted with his hand outstretched.

"Jeremiah. Pleasure to meet you, sir," the pilot replied in a thick Southern American accent whilst shaking Roy's hand firmly. "I've been sent to ferry you guys across the Atlantic, correct?" Jeremiah was a small man, similar in size to Roy but had thick brown curls in lieu of Roy's green hair. The American also had tinted sunglasses and a pencil thin moustache decorating his face. He wore a jacket with the head of a bald eagle depicted on the back.

Roy took a while to answer the question as he surveyed the American but eventually came out with his reply. "Yeah, that's the idea but surely we aren't doing the distance in that," he said while pointing to the plane which didn't look any bigger up close.

"Whoa there, son," Jeremiah said, looking offended. "Lucy will take you wherever you need to go." He patted the plane but withdrew his hand quickly where the sun had heated the metal case. "If there is one thing you Brits are bad for, its underestimating us Americans." He smiled and revealed a mouth full of pristinely perfect straight white teeth. Roy swore he even saw them glint like in the adverts.

"I'll go get the others then," said Roy out loud whilst his internal monologue voiced what he wanted to say, *If there's one thing you Yanks are bad for it's over exaggerating!*

"How bad is *he*?" joked Barbara when Roy got back to the truck.

"He bleeds red, white and blue," moaned Roy.

The whole truck let out a long groan together.

Barbara drove a little closer so that they wouldn't have to transport Jedrok's weight further than they needed to. When they retrieved it from the rear of the vehicle, they placed it on the runway and shared the same thought as Roy did about the plane's capabilities to carry them such a long distance.

"It's not going to happen," judged George to Cheikhou next to him.

"Not with that attitude," Jeremiah added, making George jump with the sudden comment behind him. The curly-haired pilot trotted past George and opened the back of the plane with a button on the side of the vehicle. As the hatch opened revealing the inside of the vessel, they waited with bated breath. Gradually, the interior came into view.

"It's the same size," grumbled Rosie.

"Do you think I carry a sonic spanner?" Jeremiah retaliated, sensing everyone's disappointment that it wasn't bigger on the inside. He smiled his perfect smile in an arrogant way. "This, boys and girls, is property of the United States of America." When he said that he marched off into the cockpit and sat in the pilot's seat. He then reached for his tannoy and made an announcement. "Please step away from the plane, you're about to witness the superiority of the American race."

Full of doubt but deciding that they had better do what the patriot wanted, the group stepped back and waited for what was in store.

"A little further, please," came the order over the tannoy.

George looked at Cheikhou and shook his head as he waited for what Jeremiah had in store.

"OK, brace yourselves. All together now, 'USA, USA, USA'."

There was a deathly silence.

"That's the difference, you have no spirit," Jeremiah complained. Suddenly, the plane creaked and screeched into life. The wings extended and the body began expanding as the metal skeleton separated to reveal further metal underneath, enabling it to grow in size. The process went on for about five minutes until the whole plane had changed in shape and appearance. The vehicle that was left after the transformation was quadruple the size of the original one and on the back stretch was a large minotaur head painted onto the side.

"All aboard!" came Jeremiah's command from the huge plane.

Cheikhou turned to Roy and patted him on the shoulder. "I'm sure their secret base doesn't have an elevator hidden behind a minotaur painting which can only be accessed by turning the nose ring. They got nothing on us." Cheikhou laughed and went to help George and Alex move Jedrok into the storage compartment on the plane before finding a seat for the long journey. The interior was no longer underwhelming, there were plenty of very comfortable-looking black leather seats, a bar and a large TV.

"Wow!" Rosie exclaimed as she first stepped foot on the plane. Whilst taking in all the features she made a beeline straight to the bar and poured herself a drink. "I need this after the morning we've had."

Alex decided that was a good idea and went to join her.

Yuanli and Barbara helped the weakened Carlton to his seat and they were ready for take-off. There was a roar as the plane's engines kicked in properly, preparing for take-off.

Roy took his seat next to Jeremiah in the cockpit so he could talk over the current situation during the flight. Whilst watching the plane transform into one capable of taking them across the Atlantic, Roy had spoken to Yuanli and Barbara about waiting for Presley and Annabel. They had decided together that they could not wait as they didn't know how close they were or if they were even still alive. Roy prayed under his breath that they were both OK and begged forgiveness for leaving without them, hoping they would understand.

Jeremiah gave a warning to brace themselves as he began the run up in order to take flight.

Rosie was visibly nervous so Alex tried his best to calm her. He reached for her hand and took it in his. "You'll be alright," he promised.

"I've never flown before," Rosie confessed.

"I've flown thousands of times," Alex said, trying to put her mind at rest, however, his tone was more boastful than reassuring. "I once helped land a plane," he continued, "the pilot was ill and needed help so asked the passengers if there were any capable…"

Rosie smiled to herself and let Alex talk at her. She was so amused by Alex's elaborate story that she didn't even realise the plane had left the ground and was already halfway through its ascent.

Just after an hour into the flight everyone was enjoying themselves. Rosie was still at the bar being spoken to by Alex who had finished his story of landing a plane but had immediately moved onto another exaggerated anecdote. Cheikhou was asleep and George was trying to listen in to Barbara and Yuanli talking about the plan once they reached America.

When Roy was happy Jeremiah was up to date with what had

been happening in England, he left the cockpit and joined the others in the large passenger area.

"Can I have your attention, please?" he asked with an authority that demanded their focus.

Alex had to be hushed by Rosie and directed towards their makeshift leader.

It was decided that it would be best to let Carlton sleep, but the same decision was not made for Cheikhou who had been shaken awake by George.

"I just want to take this opportunity whilst we're safe in the sky to expand on some details," Roy began. "I appreciate the sacrifice you've all made in joining me in this mission despite your limited knowledge of where we're going or who the foe is."

George found it weird that he seemed to be talking to Yuanli and Barbara, too. *Surely they know more than we do*; however, they were nodding along just as oblivious as himself.

"I'm going to explain a brief history of Sanctum and why the items in Jedrok were created." Roy looked around the plane and saw everyone waiting eagerly.

Cheikhou got up to get himself some water, drinking some and splashing the rest on his face to wake himself from his weariness. "Don't want to miss this," he yawned.

Roy acknowledged Cheikhou's readiness and began the history:

"Horatio Petrov was easily the most powerful man in Sanctum. He was the keeper of Gaia and everyone treated him like a god for keeping their planet safe and stable. He was the latest in a long line of Petrovs who understood that the purpose of Gaia was not only to keep Sanctum safe but also to maintain homoeostasis on Earth. He didn't need to do much, he left Gaia in its rightful place in the heart of Dreadnoque, calling upon its power only in times of great need for one of the realms. Horatio was much loved by nearly all the people of Sanctum and no one loved him more than his wife, Stella. He met Stella in his youth whilst being shown around Sanctum by his father. During this tour in which Horatio was to be shown what he would one day inherit, he saw a young Stella in Chungwantanya playing in a pool of water. Horatio jumped in the water whilst his father

shouted at him to behave and not disrespect their family name. They splashed each other and messed around for as long as they could before Horatio was pulled from the pool and told to remember who he was and why he was there.

As he grew up he left Dreadnoque more often to visit Stella. This continued until one day no one could pull him from the water for he had grown so much in size and strength. Their relationship blossomed to a point where Horatio married her and brought Stella to Dreadnoque to rule alongside him.

Sanctum was a peaceful place then, suffering only isolated small pockets of rebel factions who resisted the Petrov rule and wanted to use Gaia to make Sanctum superior to Earth before ultimately invading and claiming the planet for themselves. Horatio's ancestors ensured these rebels would never achieve their goal by giving the leader of each realm a powerful item forged with the power of Gaia to maintain the peace. Just as ownership and protection of Gaia had been passed down to Horatio, the powerful items were passed down through the generations of the leaders of each respective realm.

Kalysta of the jungle realm Chungwantanya was given Ufakazi, a mask that enabled her to use the animals and loyal tribes of her forest to keep tabs on any threat to the peace. She used the power of the mask to see through the eyes of those faithful to her; the gift ensured she was always a step ahead of the rebel groups. Kalysta then set traps for and captured the rebels threatening peace.

Polyphemus, leader of the ocean realm Moanatenger, received what many believe to be the most powerful of the gifts, Stormsbane, a sword that Polyphemus wielded with such ferocity that it was rumoured even the dangerous and unpredictable weather at sea bowed down to him. No one dared cross him or rise up lest they feel his wrath.

Johnnie Lang was charged with controlling the dusty and arid Barren Valley. To do so, he was given a whip which he promptly named Freya after his favourite cow. Freya gave Johnnie the ability to bend any that the whip touched to his will. He didn't use the whip to create an army of slaves however, Johnnie had such a love for his cowboy lifestyle that he solely used Freya to ease the transport of his cattle from point A to B. He made himself the richest man in

Sanctum with his booming business and, as such, had eyes and ears everywhere. There wasn't a rebel meeting in his jurisdiction that he would not know about and put a stop to.

Finally, Horatio's best friend and leader of Liberterra, Henry Salvatore, received armour which was indestructible, rendering the wearer nigh on invincible. Equipped in the armour there wasn't a skirmish that would break out between the rebels and the loyalists that Salvatore wouldn't win. His sheer presence in the mythical armour sent the terrorist fighters running for the hills.

Nevertheless, despite lasting peace, the Petrovs created a final item when they finished crafting for their fellow rulers. They always knew that one day a force would come along that could rival the power of the leaders with their weapons. As a precaution the final creation was Jedrok, capable of locking the items away and removing them from the war, preventing them from ever falling into the wrong hands. When each weapon was originally handed out, the first leaders in each realm all agreed that they would lock their items in Jedrok if the need ever arose. Each time the items were handed down to the next generation the new leader had to make the same promise."

Roy finished the first part of his story and was happy to see everyone was still intrigued and eager to learn more.

George got up to get himself a drink from the bar, he was surprised to see that Alex and Rosie had moved to the chairs. He was focusing so much on Roy's story that he didn't notice them move. He had barely finished pouring himself his rum and coke when Cheikhou asked for a beer. Alex then asked for one in quick succession; not long after that request Rosie and Yuanli asked for water.

"Just bring me over a bottle of gin," cackled Barbara.

Refreshments sorted and everyone ready to continue, George asked what everyone was thinking. "So what went wrong?"

Roy looked at him and smiled. "The same thing that always goes wrong. A woman and man's lack of will."

"Horatio and Stella were comfortable in power and the leaders of the other realms had the rebels in check. The only slight issue was

that Gaia was having to exert more of its energy onto maintaining stability on Earth. This was due to a great increase in pollution and damage being done to the planet by the people on it. Every bit extra that Earth required took from Sanctum's ability to remain stable, as such the resistance to Horatio's rule had begun to grow. No one wanted to have to support a planet that was being killed by those that lived on it – a murmur of unrest began to spread through Sanctum.

In order to try to appease the people Horatio and Stella tried for a baby. They succeeded and named her Sonya. The birth of the next Petrov heir was a victory for Sanctum but, unfortunately, the joy it brought was short-lived. In the early years of Sonya's life, Earth continued to be abused by its people and Gaia was having to exert more energy into maintaining the planet's health. Horatio and Stella tried to bring up their daughter in the same way as the Petrovs had done for years, with journeys to the other realms under their protection. However, the trouble on Earth was proving the Earthlings' inferiority meaning rebel groups were growing in size and Sanctum began to lose stability, also. Visits were stopped completely when Sonya was only three after they were attacked on a tour of Moanatenger by a Kraken, a creature long dormant under the threat of Stormsbane. They only survived because of Captain Quint's expert seamanship and bravery. The captain sacrificed his leg that day in a duel with the Kraken to ensure the Petrov heir escaped unscathed. The assault showed that Sanctum was no longer at peace, horrors unknown for centuries were beginning to resurface.

Horatio decided that he needed to see what was happening on Earth with his own eyes and left the day after Sonya's fifth birthday. No one had crossed the portal between worlds for years, but Henry Salvatore knew what to do when Horatio turned up one day wanting to make the journey. The portal was under the biggest castle in Liberterra, on the opposite side of Sanctum to Dreadnoque. Horatio entrusted his wife and daughter's safety to his friend and embarked on his cross-world adventure. When he arrived on Earth he couldn't see much difference to his home world. The portal on Earth was located in Arizona and, as such, when he first emerged he likened our planet to Barren Valley in Sanctum. Nevertheless, after he left the immediate location of the portal and travelled deeper into our world, he was met with technology years in advance to anything they had in Sanctum. He wasn't impressed by our advancements, though, as immediately he could see the price for development. The planet was being torn apart for materials to build large structures towards the sky, putting unbearable pressure on the ground that provides our food and resources. The more he travelled the more he understood why Gaia was struggling to maintain decorum on our planet. We take but never give back, a one-way ticket to push the planet past its limits and into an abyss. By communicating with the people on our planet he learnt that we have become out of touch with nature and are unwilling to revert our ways, even if our current course is doomed. Out of hope and unsure of how to turn our fate around, Horatio had given up, he was ready to admit defeat and return home.

That was when he met Maria. Maria was unlike most people on Earth and understood our need for change. She convinced Horatio that Earth could be saved, and each day met Maria in order to learn how she was planning to turn the situation around. Maria told Horatio of the Earthlings' desire to move on to renewable energies, and find more sustainable ways to live. Every day for two years Horatio learnt from Maria and was fascinated by her enthusiasm and intelligence. They grew closer until one day they kissed and Horatio begged her to come on an adventure with him. Unknowing what he had in store for her she accepted the invite and Horatio took her back to Sanctum with him. Maria was amazed by life in Sanctum but her joy wasn't to last. Horatio couldn't let Stella find out about his relationship with Maria so he begged Henry Salvatore to hide her for him.

Horatio returned to his family and found that Stella had struggled in bringing up Sonya alone. Sonya was not able to travel to Sanctum like her father and all those that came before him and, as a result, had come to blame Earth and those that lived on it for her troubles. Together, Horatio and Stella were unable to sway their daughter from her opinion and the difficult family life meant Horatio wanted to escape to his secret love more often. Over the next ten years rumours began to spread about a paramour that Horatio's best friend, Henry, was hiding away for him. One morning, Horatio awoke to a letter from his wife explaining that she had to see if the rumours were true herself.

A year later, Stella returned to Dreadnoque and a lot of her luxurious hair had fallen out and she had large bruises round her eyes from excessive crying. Stella's arms were cut from self-harming and her speech was broken. The shell of a woman was met by her husband and daughter on the edge of Dreadnoque. It's rumoured that the only words she could whimper through her battered body were, 'The bitch is pregnant'. Then she pulled out a knife and slit her own throat.

Husband and daughter could only watch as the most important figure in their lives bled out in front of them.

In the wake of his wife's death, Horatio became weak and obsessed that Sanctum would soon fall. He convinced himself it was so likely that he made adjustments to Jedrok, preparing for the worst. The first change he made was that it would leave Sanctum and reappear on Earth, far away from the threat. Secondly, he linked each of the items belonging to the leaders in Sanctum to a respective artefact on Earth. The idea was that if Jedrok was closed then it could only be opened again by Sanctum's saviour with the collected artefacts. Salvatore's armour was linked to St George's armour he used when slaying the dragon. Kalysta's mask was linked to Moctezuma II's headdress, Johnnie Lang's whip was linked to Jesse James' pistol and finally, Polyphemus' sword was connected to Mary Read's sword. Horatio hoped that if the day ever came when Jedrok was closed then the weapons could be recovered and Sanctum could be rescued.

Sonya hated her father, rightfully blaming him for the ill that had befallen the family. Nevertheless, she hated Maria more. Sonya started communicating with the rebels and planned a secret operation to let them into Dreadnoque and take control of Gaia.

Not expecting inside help, Horatio was not prepared to stop the rebel assault when it came.

The rebels used the element of surprise and managed a successful invasion of Dreadnoque.

Horatio ran to the heart of his realm and saw his daughter holding Gaia where she had removed it from its rightful place in the mountainside. She announced her hate for her father and his concubine, Maria, and began the formation of Tombstone in order to put an end to both. She tried to use Gaia's power to overthrow her father and the powerful object took her personality and personified it with aggressive snakelike features, her teeth likewise, her eyes went from blue to green and a tattoo of a snake burnt into her back and abdomen, wrapping round her body. Sonya was killed and Dark Snake was born. Dark Snake then killed her father by ripping his throat out with her razor-like teeth and spitting it onto the floor in front of her.

When Horatio had finished breathing without a throat and his blood stopped spurting from his open neck, he became still.

Dark Snake had now watched both her parents die right in front of her and love was but a wound in her broken heart. Bereft of mercy, she struck quickly, killing all those in Dreadnoque still loyal to her father and sent rebels after those that escaped. Dark Snake then tried to solidify her power by inviting all the leaders from the other realms to pay homage to her; nevertheless, this was her first and biggest mistake.

The leaders came and saw her power. They knew then that they wouldn't be able to stop her when she wielded the power of Gaia, even with their weapons. Certain they couldn't win, they rushed to Jedrok and stashed their powerful items away.

Jedrok disappeared and Dark Snake was without the legendary possessions. She captured all the former leaders and sentenced them to death for their betrayal. Before each execution she asked them, "Any lasts words?"

Kalysta stared Dark Snake in the eyes and spat on her feet, "Earth and Sanctum will survive." Beheaded.

Polyphemus did the same and spat on her feet, "Earth and Sanctum will survive." Beheaded.

Johnnie Lang followed suit, spat on her feet, "Earth and Sanctum will survive." Beheaded.

Then Horatio's best friend, Salvatore, was the only one left; he didn't spit on her feet, instead he smiled and began laughing. "Maria has had her son. Horatio's heir will be your downfall. She's safely back on her planet and you'll never find her boy, he'll finish–" Beheaded.

Dark Snake became obsessed with finding Maria's child and killed any boy under the age of one she could find. Her brutality and use of Gaia turned the tide of war between the loyalists and the rebels she had named Tombstone. The loyalists became the rebels as Sanctum gradually fell to her dark rule. All looked lost in the years that followed as Dark Snake recruited war chiefs to her cause who would intimidate the battlefield: Amazon, Voodoo and Butcher. Sanctum was about to completely descend into darkness when a beacon of hope came from Barren Valley. Those loyal to preserving the Petrov mindset of peace on Sanctum and Earth were rallying behind a leader who was getting victories against Tombstone. That leader was Presley."

Everyone on the plane let out a shocked breath and murmured to each other.

"What was Presley doing in Sanctum?" George spewed as he thought out loud.

"Let me finish the story," said Roy who was smiling from ear to ear after his big reveal.

"Presley was born in Sanctum, as was I, however, unlike myself he is a descendant of a great line of leaders making him technically royalty. Presley used the alias Earth name of Presley Jones in order to avoid detection by potential Tombstone spies. In Sanctum he was Presley Lang, rightful heir to rule Barren Valley. The people of Sanctum rallied to Presley's victories and began fighting back. I, myself, was fighting in Liberterra, that's how and where I met Presley. I was brought up in Liberterra by my mother, Sara. She was a shield-maiden and fought in the battles against Tombstone. When I was old enough, I joined her in the conflict and tried to repel Tombstone's evil rule. I'll never forget the day I met Presley when he saved my life for the first time. My mother and I were part of a squad of warriors tasked with holding a strategic gulley. Despite our fierce resistance we were being pushed back by Butcher leading a horde of screamers and our defence was destined to fall. When all seemed lost and our unit was down to critical numbers, we heard a gunshot and Presley rode over the hill at the head of a group of Barren Valley

resistance fighters. Presley, using the power of his family's legendary weapon–"

Roy stopped himself abruptly by throwing a hand over his mouth, then he strangely continued as if nothing had happened.

"His reinforcements were able to turn the tide of the fight and Butcher had to retreat. It was a bittersweet moment because it was the day I met my hero but also the day we embarked on the quest that my mum wouldn't return from.

Presley was impressed with how my mother and I had fought and asked us to go with him to Moanatenger to try to push Tombstone back there. We went and succeeded but during the conflict was when Voodoo killed my mother. I was distraught and in no state to continue the fight. That was when Presley named our resistance group Minotaur and begged I set up a branch here on Earth to recruit help to stop Tombstone.

Presley came with me and we left them fighting in Sanctum. Upon our arrival on Earth, we met Maria who had received Jedrok when it was banished from Sanctum. Horatio must have known she planned to flee and arranged for Jedrok, in its sealed state, to go to her. She was waiting for one side or the other to come seeking it and fortunately we found her first. That's how I came into possession of it. She also left me her house, which I turned into my antiquities store and then she left, never to be seen again. I haven't returned to Sanctum since I left all those years ago but Jeremiah says that both sides are at a stalemate. The deadlock is why we are both now trying to bring the weapons in Jedrok back into the fight on our respective sides."

There was silence as everyone absorbed the story and the vast amount of history they had just heard. Abruptly, the peace was shattered by a blood-curdling shriek from Carlton. He was shaking in his seat and already frothing at the mouth.

"What's happening?" asked a worried Cheikhou who was first to his guardian's side.

Barbara ran to the cockpit to warn Jeremiah of the issue and

Yuanli pulled Carlton out of his seat in order to lay him comfortably on the floor.

Roy took over from Yuanli, mopping around Carlton's mouth, trying to remove the liquid from around his lips.

Cheikhou was being held back by George who was trying to convince his mate that there was nothing he would be able to do and to give their guardians space.

Roy looked him over and ripped Carlton's shirt off to expose the cuts dealt to him by Amazon. They were bleeding again and had a yellowish pus around them. Using all his knowledge he diagnosed that Carlton had been poisoned.

"My guess is that Amazon laced her blades with snapetella," Roy voiced to the group.

"What is that?" barked Cheikhou who was beginning to panic.

"A poisonous plant found in her homeland of Chungwantanya. The same little purple plant which the assassin at your paintballing day used to kill himself."

That sent Cheikhou into meltdown. His usual cool persona was out the window. No one that was there that day had forgotten how easily the small flower shut the minion of Tombstone's body down.

Roy tried to calm the situation but that was no easy task when you were worrying yourself. "The assassin chewed a petal which would result in instant death. Carlton's in deep trouble but won't die straight away as the dose is much smaller." Roy ran over to the bar and grabbed the strongest liquor he could find and got a glass of water before bringing them straight back.

"Is that to clean the wound?" Cheikhou asked, frantically glancing back and forth at the alcohol.

"No, this is for me." Roy swigged the bottle and immediately felt his nerves relax. He poured the glass of water onto the cuts on Carlton's body and then some of the liquor. The response was a deep groan and murmur as the alcohol stung the wounds. Roy then reached into his pocket and pulled out his lighter. Without hesitation he set fire to the alcohol trickling down Carlton's abdomen. The liquor set alight instantly and extinguished almost as fast. "That'll have burnt off the surface poison and prevented any further snapetella entering his system. There's now very little we can do without proper medical equipment. His best chance would be to sleep the rest of the flight so his body isn't as active. A dormant body will limit the efficiency at which the snapetella can travel around his system."

Carlton was shaking violently and was quite obviously not going to get any sleep.

Yuanli sensed this and stepped up. She approached Carlton and tried to put him to sleep. As she closed in, Carlton caught her with a flailing arm and knocked her down. Yuanli persevered, though, and dodged his swinging arms and legs a second time, managing to reach Carlton's neck to apply pressure. The flailing limbs ceased and Carlton lay peaceful, knocked out by Yuanli's assault on his pressure points.

"I hope you know what you're doing," she declared to Roy.

CHAPTER 16

Earth
England
South-east

Presley was baking hot in his protective motorbike gear which made him irritable when dealing with Annabel; she insisted on asking him questions that he could hardly hear over the sound of the bike and the wind rushing past their helmets. Deciding it was time for a rest and that he had better provide Annabel with at least the basics situation, he pulled over into the next village so they could purchase refreshments. The arrival of Presley's bike over the one-way stone bridge into the quaint village was like a stone dropping into a tranquil pond shattering the peace. Locals scowled from their fishing rods dipped in the beautiful river running through the hamlet. Gardeners grumbled as the bike roared past thatched houses bordered with fragrant bright gardens decorating them. Presley parked the bike in the car park of a riverside café and helped Annabel take her helmet off. When her blonde hair tumbled out of the hat it was slightly dark from sweat and it stuck to her forehead and neck.

"That was amazing," she exclaimed whilst taking in a large mouthful of the countryside air. "I love motorbikes".

Presley smiled and acknowledged that she enjoyed the ride; he hadn't lost as many teeth as she originally thought but there were some gaps.

"You need to clean yourself up," Annabel warned him, "you have dried blood all around your mouth."

"OK, I'll head to the toilet to sort myself out; you get the drinks," he ordered whilst passing her his wallet. The swelling in his mouth had gone down drastically and his speech was back to normal again.

As they entered the small café a little bell chimed to warn the owner of their arrival. A petite lady with sprouts of grey hair came over to greet them. She instinctively recoiled at the sight of Presley's beaten face but soon recovered with a smile and a warm welcome before showing them to their seats outside on a bench opposite the water. As soon as they were shown their places they each got up to perform the tasks they were originally planning on doing.

Presley walked to the toilet and emptied his bladder before beginning the clean-up of his face. When he reached the mirror, he saw that one of his incisors was out on the bottom of his mouth and two from the top. His lips were all cut as well, framed by a border of crusted red blood. He had a large bruise round his left eye and an equally large bruise on his right cheek. *That poor lady must have wondered who I was*, he realised as he began washing the blood from his face. Red water spiralled down the sink's drain by the time he was done. Before he left, he rinsed round the edge to clean it all, not wanting to leave it for the next person. A final look in the mirror to check he was presentable proved there was nothing he could do with the bruises but the blood had disappeared. He walked back outside and found Annabel gazing at the river, deep in thought. Next to her on the bench were two crystal clear glasses of water.

"Is that all you wanted?" Presley was surprised there was no food or a more exciting drink. Before Annabel had time to answer, a young man with a large spot on his nose brought a tray to the table.

"Your two full English breakfasts, a pint of beer and a *large* strawberry milkshake," he reeled off.

"Brilliant, and thanks," said Annabel as the boy left the table.

Even with her post-kidnap and bedraggled bike riding appearance she still drew the eye of the waiter.

"I only asked for a small," she giggled to Presley as she appreciated the upgraded milkshake.

They drank both glasses of water instantly in order to quench their thirsts and it didn't take long before they were tucking into their respective breakfasts.

Annabel was chewing on a tomato when she looked at Presley and repeated a question that was presumably the same as the one she inaudibly asked on the bike, "Who were them people?"

"Tombstone. They're an evil force led by a villainous traitor named Dark Snake that's hell-bent on destroying Earth. The damage and terror she spreads through her own world to achieve this seems of no mind to her." Presley was aware that the next question would be related to the fact he just broke the news that Earth wasn't the only habitable world and so he continued his explanation. "They come from a world called Sanctum on which is the source of this conflict, Gaia. A–"

"The theory that all organisms and their inorganic surroundings on Earth are closely integrated to form a single and self-regulating complex system, maintaining the conditions for life on the planet?" interrupted Annabel.

Presley nodded in-between swallowing a mouthful of breakfast, "Yes, that's its definition on Earth – beautifully put, by the way – but it's so much more in reality. Gaia is like the heart of both Earth and Sanctum, keeping both stable, however, it can only perform its purpose if it's left in its rightful place within the highest mountain in Dreadnoque. Unfortunately for us and the inhabitants of Sanctum, it's been removed…"

"…by Tombstone," confirmed Annabel, trying to keep up with all the new information. She wouldn't have believed him but for her experience the night before. After that she was willing to trust Presley. "Where's Dreadnoque then?"

"Dreadnoque is a realm in Sanctum, one of five, each with its own specific terrain and biome. Dreadnoque is mountainous and difficult to traverse, even before Dark Snake made it her home. Chungwantanya is a large jungle ruled by tribes and is home to a large biodiversity of plants and animals. Moanatenger splits the north and south of Sanctum in two and is the only way to cross. It's mainly ocean, dotted with islands; as such its people are seafaring. Barren Valley is a dust bowl, a large depression of unbearable heat and sand. It never used to be like that until they built the Tourniquet." Presley clenched his fists as he envied the free-flowing river beside him.

"That's four," Annabel said, whilst taking note of the sudden change in Presley's demeanour after mentioning the demise of Barren Valley.

Presley broke from his fixation on the river and saw Annabel waiting with wide eager eyes. "Finally, there's Liberterra. This realm is vital to life on Earth and Sanctum as it is home to the portal which allows transport between our two worlds."

Annabel fell back in her chair and breathed out in awe as she tried to puzzle out how any of what she was being told made sense. A fly enjoyed her breakfast whilst she was in a daze, imagining what all these fabled lands looked like.

"So, what're we to do about it all?" she asked, fearing the answer.

"We're going to Arizona to train and get ready for our journey. Then we're going to take the fight to them and restore Gaia to its rightful place before Earth falls apart. You must've seen the increase in natural disasters in the news?"

Annabel closed her eyes as she acknowledged the gravity of what she was being asked to do. "So, if we succeed in putting Gaia back then the disasters will stop? It seems like we should be punished in some way for our mistreatment of our planet; will we learn nothing if we achieve our mission?"

Presley noticed a contrail from a plane soaring above. "No. Work still must be done to reduce our impact on the planet. Gaia just prevents these disasters becoming apocalyptic. Sanctum suffers for our misuse of this planet as the scales of power required to keep both worlds stable become unbalanced."

Annabel sighed. "I was worried for a second that my years of education had been wasted. I've never been more relieved by the threat of soil erosion, greenhouse gases and overexploitation of our resources." Annabel noted the strange look Presley was giving her. "My whole career path was about to be thrown into jeopardy, it's good to know I still have future plans should I survive this ordeal."

Presley chuckled at that. "We need to reach the plane before the others leave." He was back on mission after their chat and was well aware that they were against the clock. "Eat up, we're leaving!"

Annabel pushed her plate away to signal she was no longer hungry and rose to depart.

"I have to watch my figure; my 'likes' have been down recently." Then her shoulders sunk and she added, "I don't suppose I'll be posting too much without my phone, anyway."

Presley put a hand on her shoulder. "Career driven, conscious of the world around you, not to mention the definition you gave me of

Gaia. All this proves there's more to you than what people see. When you realise that yourself, you'll be far happier." Then he motioned with his head over to the waiter, waving goodbye with a smile, "But for now, there's your validation; now let's go."

They got back on the bike and drove to the village petrol station to quickly refill the bike's tank before completing the last leg of their journey to the airstrip.

When they were nearing the location, they slowed up to look at smoke rising in the distance. "What could it be?" asked Annabel.

"I'm not sure, but I don't like the look of it!" Presley shouted over the roar of the engine. He revved the bike and accelerated towards the black smoke.

When they got to the bonfire they were overwhelmed with the stench of searing flesh.

"Oh my god, it's bodies!" screamed Annabel.

Presley was much calmer when he checked the heap and disposed of his biggest fear. "They're screamers. The group must have been attacked, but it looks like we won so don't worry."

Annabel decided it was all too much for her and ripped the helmet from her head. The headgear was removed just in time before she showered the floor in front of her with sick.

Presley hugged her close and told her it was going to be alright so he could quickly get her back on the bike. He knew they were very close to the airstrip now and didn't want to miss the flight.

"The fire is fresh, which means they're not far away. The plane will be just a little further up this road. We need to leave."

Just as Presley finished talking, they heard a rumble come from up the track.

Annabel went to grab her helmet, but Presley bellowed, "NO! There's no time. Jump on!"

Annabel was barely on the bike when Presley accelerated off towards the rumbling sound. He was taking the corners very fast and Annabel was struggling to hold on.

Presley winced as her tight grip put pressure on his weakened ribs, but he fought through the pain and continued driving. They reached the open just in time to see the plane increasing speed up the runway. Presley twisted his right hand and revved his engine, the tyres squealed on the spot and smoke and dirt flew into the air. The tension released and the bike was unleashed on the track beneath. The bike was going fast but the plane was faster. Presley zoomed off the end of the runway just as the plane lifted off the ground with a thunderous noise and rose out of their reach, disappearing into the midday sun. Presley swore as he swerved his bike to a halt and watched their transatlantic ride leave their view.

"Now what?" Annabel panted, still trying to regain her composure after the wild ride.

"Now for plan B," mumbled Presley.

Annabel looked at him expectantly.

"We swim!" he smiled.

CHAPTER 17

Earth
Wyoming
Site of the fire

Deacon was unsure whether he could keep his feet, the heat was unbearable in his full uniform with the raging fire burning around him. Sweat was trickling down his forehead and his blonde hair was stuck to his temple, darkened by the sweat that filled it. He was becoming claustrophobic in his helmet as it began to steam up in the heat and severity of the situation. Without thinking he ripped it off his head and threw it to the ground to try to get some air. He took a deep breath and inhaled a lungful of smoke. Deacon fell to his knees and began coughing; thick globules of dark saliva were coming from his mouth as the ash mixed between his cheeks. He could hear Mark shouting after him but ignored his colleague's pleas for him to return and instead strained his ears to listen for the bear cub. Now submerged in the burning forest, he had lost his bearings and no longer knew which direction the bear could be found in relation to his current position. Suddenly, a loud whimper brought Deacon back to reality; *it's this way*, he convinced himself. He left his helmet on the floor and stayed low to the ground to limit the amount of smoke he would breathe in. The limited visibility in the fogged up headgear would hamper his chances of finding his target.

"I'm coming for you, hang in there, Yogi Bear!" he yelled to the fiery oblivion in front of him. His eyes were beginning to sting which sent second thoughts through his head as to whether leaving his helmet was a good idea. Going back now wasn't an option though, with the bear in dire trouble, besides, he didn't know which direction he left it in anyway. Deacon rubbed his eyes and tried to refocus, but it only served to rub ash further into his sockets. Coughing again and spitting up the black fluid, he made his way deeper into the blaze, certain he would reach the bear cub soon. His heart leapt when he heard a loud groan to his left but sank twice as fast as a burning branch loosened itself from its tree and began hurtling towards him like a kamikaze bomber. Deacon dived out of the way and just narrowly avoided being squashed by the fiery assailant. His protective trousers and jacket absorbed the impact of his leap of faith so he could quickly recover and brush himself off. Looking around through his watery eyes, all he could see were burning trees and falling branches; all he could taste was smoke and his ears were ringing with the sound of a thousand bells. Shell-shocked but with desire burning in his heart as strongly as the vegetation around him, he pushed on through the heat. He was stumbling rather than walking now and kept having to pick himself back up from the floor. The fifth time he collapsed he couldn't rise again straight away. Deacon felt his eyes closing and for the first time took comfort in the warmth around him. He smiled as he let the forest embrace him in a deadly hug.

Drifting off into an endless sleep, he found himself getting annoyed at a constant screeching next to his ear. Deacon waved a hand towards the noise but there was nothing there, then something pulled on his ear and screeched again, right into his eardrum. The unwelcome wake-up call did the trick and he found himself face to face with a raccoon. He was taken aback and rolled away, but the small mammal followed and tugged on his arm. He got to one knee and let the raccoon climb up his limbs until it was sitting on his shoulder. Then the small animal nestled into his neck and held on.

"You want my help, little man?" Deacon asked feebly in his weakened state. The timid raccoon brought Deacon back to his senses and he stood back on two feet. He grimaced and remembered that others relied on him to keep them safe.

"I'll get you out, but first, where is Yogi?" he pleaded in his dreamlike daze. It might have been the toxins or the fact his brain was starved of oxygen, but he was sure the raccoon pointed towards the direction he must take. Trusting in what was most likely a hallucination he followed the raccoon's guidance, dodging and ducking burning timber all around him. His companion had given him strength and he knew that he had to survive in order to help both the raccoon and the bear cub get out alive. Miraculously, after swaying a matter of metres he found a cowering bear cub under a tree. A patch of fur on its right side had burnt off leaving a pink blistering raw section of skin highlighted by the obsidian black fluff surrounding the wound. The young animal was hurt which made the rescue more dangerous. The bear cub spotted Deacon and roared, however, he didn't back down. Unable to move very well due to its burn, the bear continued to show its power in other ways, baring its teeth and snarling. Then it saw the raccoon clinging to the fireman and stopped its aggressive behaviour. The bear seemed to realise in that moment that Deacon wasn't there to hurt it. "Come on, Yogi," he said delicately.

The cub slowly limped over to him and sniffed Deacon's hand. It gave him a look up and down whilst making its decision whether to trust the fireman. The bear was only small but it could still do some damage with its teeth and sharp claws and, as such, Deacon stood deadly still whilst the analysis was ongoing. The bear then placed its paws on Deacon's legs and looked up at him.

In his diminished state the bear made Deacon wobble but he kept his feet just. Another branch broke from a nearby tree and crashed to the ground sending tiny orange sparks skywards. The bear whimpered with its paws still on Deacon's legs and he took it for a sign he could continue with the rescue. He reached down and lifted the bear up with both arms; the effort was monumental in his unhealthy condition, but with what must have been by some divine intervention, he let out a roar of his own as he struggled to cope with the bear's weight.

The bear moaned as its burn brushed against Deacon's ash-stained uniform leaving a red smear of blood on the clothes.

Deacon knew he couldn't hold the bear for long and so he began a slow stumble towards the sound of Mark's voice. Every step felt like he was walking in deep mud, with each movement forward his legs bent a little more under the pressure. He could hear Mark clearly; he was so close to liberation from the wildfire's grasp when he buckled and anticipated he would fall to the ground. Making a split-second decision, he swiftly but gently lowered the cub and took the impact full on his knees, his back twinging as he crumbled into a pile on the floor. There was a burning wall of trees in front of him as he closed his eyes and passed out from exertion.

He was only out for a matter of seconds, however, before he was awakened by the cold kiss of water on his face, legs and arms. His whole body was soaked as Mark's hose broke through the fire's defences and brought Deacon back to his senses.

The bear was pulling at Deacon's leg trying to pull him away from the fire raging behind his head and the raccoon was standing next to the cub as if on guard. He somehow managed to regain balance with his feet and joined the animals he rescued to safety in the final couple of metres.

Mark was screaming at him but soon shut up when the bear growled and snarled a warning shot. Harriet, another of Deacon's squad, helped him to a waiting ambulance but was unable to rid Deacon of his newfound friends. The animals wanted to make sure their saviour was going to be OK. After an initial check the ambulance crew were not yet happy for Deacon to rejoin his squad and insisted he needed to come with them to the hospital for treatment. He hated that he had to leave his team to tackle the fire themselves but gave in when he convinced himself that the blaze would be dealt with in the coming hours, besides, the paramedics were not taking no for an answer. In the time Deacon's check was undertaken, a vet had seen to the bear; normally it would have had to be sedated but the vet was able to do what he needed to without the sedation as the bear was more concerned with what was happening to Deacon. Just before leaving for the hospital they had an unlikely visitor. A large black bear was coming towards them with two cubs at its side. "Normally a mum would never bring her cubs so close to humans," exclaimed the vet.

The burnt cub ran out to the larger bear and they growled at each other in unknown dialect. Then the two other cubs, presumably the burnt cub's siblings, ambled over to Deacon and each dropped a dead fish at his feet.

"I'm guessing that's 'thanks'" he laughed as they galloped back to their mother.

The burnt bear turned and roared at Deacon one final time before leaving with his family.

"Goodbye Yogi," he whisper-coughed. "Thanks for the fish." He tried to shout but it emerged as another weak cough. The paramedics were insistent they could wait no longer, they needed to get Deacon seen to. They sat him in the back of the emergency vehicle and closed the rear door before starting their transit to the hospital.

On the journey Deacon retold the story of how he, the bear and the raccoon all saved each other. The bemused looks on the paramedics' faces were only to be expected that day, they clearly didn't believe his version of what unfolded in the burning forest, most likely blaming the lack of oxygen in his brain caused by the smoke in his body. Deacon didn't need to be believed, though, he knew what happened and didn't underestimate nature's ability to come together in a crisis.

They were speeding along and were just cresting the top of the bridge to enter the city in which the hospital was located when there was a loud crack followed by a long groan of metal. Tyres squealed and car horns beeped furiously, then the whole ambulance shook and the bridge crumbled underneath them, collapsing onto the road below. The world went black and murmurs of pain could be heard all around.

CHAPTER 18

Sanctum
Barren Valley
Sixshot Tavern

"Tonight!" Jessica slammed down her tankard as if to reinforce her point.

The other people round her table, two women and one man, nodded their agreement. They were situated in a dark corner of the tavern, hiding their plans and discussions under the shroud of the shadows. The only light came from the end of the cigar in Jack's mouth, a glowing orange circle which grew lighter and fainter with each drag the man took of the tobacco. He was chewing the end that was between his cracked pink lips, the cigar sliding from left to right and his saliva was making a noise that cut straight through Holly.

"Stop chewing that infernal thing!" she growled whilst hitting his arm.

Jack responded by grasping the body of the cigar with two fingers and having one last long drag. He then proceeded to blow a mouthful of smoke into Holly's face.

She swore and coughed under the assault of the strong-smelling drug. She began swatting the air in front of her in trying to wave away the smoke, then she felt an iron grip grab hold of her hand.

Jack moved her arm out of the way and leaned in for a kiss but he was cut short by the feeling of a cold barrel of a gun against his chest.

"I don't think so," Holly smirked.

Jack drew away under the threat of the gun to his chest. He didn't think his partner would shoot him but with Holly's track record he wasn't taking any chances.

The fourth member of their table sat in silence, not by choice but by necessity. Her name was Simone and she let her guns do the talking. She stared at the two fools in front of her, flirting in their own dumb way. It wasn't the lovers that made her anger swell inside her, it was the memory of why she was now known as the Mute Marauder. Simone was part of a gang that stood up to the Tombstone debt collectors when they arrived for the first time to collect their tributes. Her and nine others didn't agree with the way Butcher was throwing around the women and children in their small town, demanding what he thought was owed to him. The resistance was swift when Dark Snake revealed her latest twisted creation. The monsters were called scorpios; they were mutilated beings that looked every part human but for the four foot-long scaly tails with venomous stingers at the tip. The horrors emerged from the ground as if the gates of hell had opened and was spilling its contents to wreak havoc on Sanctum. Simone's eyes still showed the disgust and terror of when she saw the sand around her move and the demons come forth. The assault was swift; many of the defenders of the small town were too shocked to react – five of their number fell to the venomous barbed scorpios before they managed to subdue one of Tombstone's number. Not to be outdone, Butcher had carved his way through a further four leaving Simone standing alone. She earned the scar on her right cheek that day, also. When Butcher asked if she was the only resistance fighter left in the town she dug deep and spat a large ball of phlegm at her tormentor's feet. Simone then kicked the half bear in the shin and ran to the raised platform in the centre of town.

"We shall not be subdued!" she had called to the onlooking townsfolk. "Whilst Presley Lang lives there is hope. He will return with the weapons of Sanctum's past. Stormsbane will again rule the seas and Ufakazi will return order to Chungwantanya. His homecoming will see him indestructible in Salvatore's legendary armour. We will resist. We will fight." Simone had choked back the tears in her devastation at the lack of response from those around her, too scared to resist.

"Presley isn't coming back. He's been gone for years," heckled one particular spectator.

The stuffing knocked out of her, Simone was subdued by some locals eager to prove themselves to Butcher, one of Dark Snake's most infamous war chiefs. The rough hands grasped at her, pulling strands of black hair from her head and their dirty fingernails drew blood from her skin. Butcher's heavy footsteps could be heard walking up the steps to the raised platform. Simone saw two huge feet in black boots stand before her, her head was jerked upwards by one of Butcher's paw-like hands.

"That tongue will get you in trouble," he warned in a low voice, "we don't want that."

It was only then that she saw what he was holding in his other hand, and glowing red – fresh from the coals were a pair of pliers. Simone's mouth was forced open by two of the blood crazed locals and Butcher plunged the hot metal into her mouth. The smell was revolting as the metal seared her soft flesh and blistered her cheeks. The burning claw grasped her tongue and retracted in one quick motion. Butcher was laughing as Simone's tongue momentarily continued to wiggle in the hold of the hot pliers. The fight in her that day died as she passed out through the pain.

When she woke the next morning, her inner furnace was burning hotter than ever. Butcher made a vital mistake in letting Simone live as he intended to send a message of warning, but instead created a hero for all Minotaur fighters to rally behind.

Years later she was ready to exact her revenge. Tonight she would raid Tourniquet, the dam that kept Barren Valley subjugated. With Holly, Jack and Jessica's help she would finally be appeased. The plan that had been in the works for so long was finalised that night in the tavern and she was determined to be the one that ensured its success.

Jessica rose to leave and Simone followed her example.

Holly and Jack were now kissing, signalling the end of their aggressive flirting techniques. When they realised the other two had got up they did the same.

The only other soul that knew of their plan was Maximus, the barkeep. He had been beaten more times in the past than would be worth remembering for suspected aiding and abetting of Minotaur fighters but without solid proof the Tombstone loyalists were unable to bring the bartender down. Maximus was well-loved and, as such, was protected; they couldn't just make him disappear like they had with numerous others.

Jessica was first to leave the tavern and step out into the cool night air. The temperatures in Barren Valley soared during the day but dropped right down during the night due to the lack of cloud cover able to retain heat in the environment. The sign to the taphouse was banging against the wall of the building; the establishment was called Sixshot and bore six bullet holes underneath the writing.

As Simone was leaving she turned to Maximus and gave him a nod who returned the gesture and signalled to the bottle of liquor waiting on the shelf – 'only to be opened when Barren Valley was free again' was the secret rule.

Jack was first to climb on his horse as he had hitched his nearest the tavern. It didn't take long for them all to be mounted up.

Simone's gelding was chestnut coloured with a luxurious silky mane running from the top of its head down the length of its neck. It was a present from Maximus years ago; he was the first to embrace Simone's wish to free Barren Valley and he wanted to reward her for her brave speech. Simone had kept the horse clean and maintained her in the following years and it kept her safe in return. Before she departed, she gave the tavern a final glance and imagined the first fine sip of the victory liquor she would experience upon her return. Then she kicked her horse into action and rode out of town.

The wind was flowing through Jessica's long blonde hair at the front of the posse as she galloped towards the Tourniquet. Jessica's thoughts were concentrated solely on the dam they were aiming to wrestle from the control of Lucius, the chief debt collector. Lucius was one of the willing locals that helped hold Simone down on the day she had her tongue ripped out. His good work earned him control over their town and the one further down the dusty road, as well as protection of the dam which had only just been constructed at the time of his promotion. He named the dam Tourniquet for its ability to withhold life from those at its mercy. Positioned on the River Esprit it stopped the flow of water through Barren Valley, a vital supply that helped support life in the harsh terrain and climate. Tombstone controlled those reliant on it and demanded payments to fund their war with Minotaur. When the tributes were made the citizens of Barren Valley received their water quota, but when payments were not made, or anyone stepped out of line the water was withheld from them and a drought would thus ensue. Tonight, the task was to seize control of the dam and claim back power over their realm. Jessica crested the top of the sand dune and saw the monstrous barrier in front of her holding back the river and, in the process, holding back life. The four Minotaur fighters lined up along the top of the dune and looked down at their target.

Jack's horse whinnied loudly in the quiet of the night and white breath could be seen coming from the gelding's nostrils.

"For freedom!" barked Holly and she spurred her mount into life, beginning the gallop down the hill. Jack was close behind not wanting his partner to go alone, Simone was third and Jessica was at the rear. They were gaining speed as they charged down the steep slope and carried the momentum onto the flat. All of a sudden there was a howl of pain from the back and Jessica was lying on the sand next to her horse, struggling to rise. The horse became silent and then the sand next to the dead palfrey began to move. Out of the yellow ground appeared a scorpio; before Jessica could react, she suffered the same fate as her horse and was injected with the creature's venom. The other three resistance fighters leapt from their horses and shooed them away – they didn't want to let their horses die in their risky attack on the dam. Standing shoulder to shoulder, they each drew their firearms and surveyed their surroundings. The very earth looked to be moving under their feet as scorpios rose from the sand all around them. Gunshots rang through the air as they fired at will, desperately trying to escape the scorpio ambush. The fire power of all three firing at the same time was enough to repel the first wave, but when the earth began to shift again their nerves began to show. Jack only just shot an enemy in time; its tail was set to lash out aggressively at his partner. Holly was not able to keep up with the speed they were coming, she couldn't reload in time. Fumbling with the ammunition in her hand, she tried to load the bullets in the chamber of her gun, she cursed under her breath and then began to panic – *click* – the gun was loaded and she could return to the fray. Holly arrived at the fight at just the right time; Jack was beginning to struggle and Holly blasted three scorpios away from him.

Simone was a woman possessed; she was using two guns – when one was firing she would be reloading one-handed with the other.

The beasts fell at her feet, she was an angel of death. The assault ceased, the sound of battle died and the final gunshots echoed over the terrain. In her frenzy, Simone failed to notice that she had been alone for the final minute of the fight. When the adrenaline wore off she spotted Jack and Holly huddled on the floor, arm in arm, where they had tried to comfort each other in their final moments. Now on her own, the task was next to impossible, but she gritted her teeth and stumbled towards the dam. The occasional scorpio attempted to emerge from the sand to ambush her but she was ready and the beasts died before even having the opportunity to fully rise. All the hurt and pain was running through Simone's thoughts as she remembered the day on the platform, the burning of the pliers. A tear fell to the sand and disappeared under her feet. Now a sole figure stood in her way about ten metres ahead. The man blocking her path approached with no concern for Simone's expert marksmanship.

"Fool," she muttered through tears. She unleashed a hail of bullets but the figure kept coming. The bullets that had hit him simply fell to the ground. She reloaded and fired again to no effect.

"Die!" she screamed, her eyes flowing tears like a river now. As the beast approached she noticed it was covered from shoulder to toe in armour, bone armour by the look of it. The abomination's rib cage had been moved to the outside of its body and wrapped round it like a protective coat.

"An armourdil," came a voice from behind her.

She turned and saw Lucius standing with a smirk on his weaselly face. He had horrible little beady eyes with short dirty brown hair and protruding small ears marked the edge of his petite head.

"Her latest creation to help us keep the peace... Its bones are moved to the outside and its rib cage is twisted round its whole torso. The casing is bullet-proof, as well. I'm told it's most painful."

Simone went to raise her gun to shoot the evil man but, whilst he was talking, the armourdil had reached her and he knocked her weapon from her hand. She tried to fight back but the monster was too protected by its armour. He smashed a fist into her face and knocked out a few teeth. Blood poured from her mouth, a body part that frequently still brought her pain after the pliers. Beaten and bloody, it didn't stop Simone rising a final time. She put her hands up to the armourdil and motioned for it to bring the fight, a final act of defiance. The armourdil didn't move, instead staring with dead, bloodshot eyes.

Then Simone felt a sharp pinch on her leg. "Coward," she managed to moan before the scorpio venom took its toll and she fell to the ground convulsing.

Maximus heard the door to his tavern creak and knew it could only be one person at this time. Smiling from ear to ear he clapped his hands and put two glasses on the bar. He then scooped up the celebratory bottle of liquor which heralded Barren Valley's freedom and placed it next to the glasses. He ducked under the bar to retrieve the flowers he had purchased at great expense that night as soon as Jessica and her gang left. Flowers were expensive at the best of times in Barren Valley due to the poor growing conditions and lack of water from the dam. Nevertheless, these cost twice as much as Maximus arrived at the florist's house well after closing, a normal customer wouldn't have been seen at all but Maximus used his reputation to gain access.

"Surprise!" he exclaimed, bursting out from behind the cover of the bar. What he saw made him drop the flowers; they separated and fell to the floor in a heap.

"What's wrong? Expecting someone else?" Lucius snarled. In his hand he held a head, decapitated from the rest of its body. Slowly, he placed Simone's severed skull on the bar next to the glasses and the liquor, watching all the time to see the turmoil on Maximus' face.

"We know you helped them. I would get out whilst you can," Lucius counselled the barkeep. "In the meantime, enjoy your celebrations." He left the head on the bar and strolled out of the door, not looking back.

Maximus broke down and felt the last of his hope drain from his body. "What've they done to you? My beautiful hero," he managed through his burning tears.

Simone was silent, just as she had been for years.

CHAPTER 19

Earth
Arizona
Private desert airstrip

A unit of American Minotaur workers met the plane as it landed. Jeremiah had radioed during the flight to warn the welcome comity of Carlton's state. As the plane bounced down the dusty runway it sent up gusts of sand with each collision with the surface. Having barely landed, the rear of the aircraft opened to allow the health staff on to the transport. They didn't take any notice of any other passengers, instead focusing solely on extracting the dying man. Two men loaded Carlton onto a stretcher and another two lifted it up and started walking away. Carlton was awake again and wheezing, clearly struggling to breathe. There was sweat dripping down his body and his cuts were looking more yellow than the physicians would have liked. The rest of the passengers stood in shock, silently praying for Carlton's recovery, all but Cheikhou who was questioning the doctors and demanding to be taken with him. Unfortunately for Cheikhou there was no space in the emergency vehicle for him and he had to make his peace while waiting with everyone else to find out his fate.

"We'll do the best we can," assured the last departing medic as he ducked out under the plane, a statement of reality, not false hope. After watching the ambulance-like vehicle disappear into the distance, Roy thought it time to proceed with their journey.

"Thanks Jeremiah. You got us here in good time. Your flying may have saved his life," Roy said while patting the pilot on the back. "We're all worried for Carlton," Roy addressed the rest of his team, "however, we're not helping anyone by staying here. We need to continue our journey and reach our rendezvous of the American Minotaur facility."

The team knew the sense in his words and they each pulled

themselves together – every time it was becoming more difficult. Carlton was gone and there was nothing any of them could do to help him. Moreover, Presley and Annabel had been missing for days; their team was gradually falling apart before the real fighting had even begun.

George's sense of loss was even greater with the strange disappearance of Jacob, but he couldn't let his morale get down. Looking outside, he noticed they were on a private airstrip, similar to the one on which they had departed for the USA, the only difference being that this one was surrounded by sand as opposed to grass. There were dunes all around and they seemed to be in the middle of a desert somewhere; his survey of their environment brought his eyes onto a sandstorm approaching on the horizon. The dust cloud reached them and revealed that it was not, in fact, a storm; instead it marked the arrival of two open-backed off-road Jeeps and a small truck. They turned up with a roar and were lost in a further cloud of dust when they screeched to a halt.

A lady with tinted sunglasses emerged from the dust screen. She strolled into vision wearing a baseball cap with 'Grand Canyon' written on it and a loose-fitting plain black tank top.

"Howzit guys!" she welcomed them in a South African accent. "Well, c'mon. Get in," she instructed, motioning to her vehicle that gradually appeared as the dust settled back to the ground.

Alex was first to leave the plane and he immediately felt the dry Arizona heat hit his face. His throat tightened with the lack of moisture in the air, and he coughed to try to ease his breathing.

Rosie tied her top in a knot so that it exposed her belly and then stepped into the warmth.

The rest followed one at a time, each bathing in the heat as they left the shade of the aircraft.

Rosie, Barbara and Yuanli climbed into the South African's Jeep and learnt their driver was called Toni.

Roy and Jeremiah received help unloading Jedrok and putting it on the truck at the front, then took their seats on the transport, leaving Cheikhou, Alex and George to enter the vehicle at the rear.

The driver quickly threw a bottle under the passenger seat as George got in, but it wasn't quick enough to avoid him seeing.

Cracking under the scowl he was being given for drink-driving, he put out his hand to introduce himself. "Yo lads, I'm Scott."

George was unsure whether he wanted this man transporting him – not only had he been drinking but his appearance was unsettling, also. Scott had a black mohican running down the centre of his scalp with fully shaved sides. His clothes were scruffy and through his left ear was a small hoop.

Alex was unfazed and shook the outstretched hand vigorously, eager to please.

"I'm Alex, this is Cheikhou and the ginger kid is George."

"Cheikhou – exotic name," Scott said as he looked in his rear-view mirror.

Cheikhou shrugged and looked out of the Jeep, unwilling to engage in idle chat.

Toni grabbed her steering wheel and turned to the girls in her car, "Let's show these fellas howta do it." Without further conversation she accelerated and left the others in her wake.

Rosie laughed as they sped off and waved to Scott's car, taunting them to race, "See ya!"

It wasn't long before George and his friends were back close to Toni, giving as good as they got. The passengers were shouting at each other and egging their drivers to go faster. Scott pulled past the girls' car and Alex gave a sarcastic wave to Rosie as they overtook them.

"Nice one," Alex acknowledged while patting Scott on the back and he applauded his driving to retake the lead. They had been in the lead for a while and Toni and the girls seemed to have fallen a fair distance behind, no longer visible through the dust spraying up from the back of the Jeep.

"Easy," Scott bragged to his boys as they weaved between the sand dunes.

George was watching the mounds of sand fly past, covering his face with his arm as they went to stop the particles going in his mouth. In George's eyes, the giant pile of fragmented rock currently next to them seemed to be vibrating. Leaning out to get a closer look he was certain that something was disturbing the dune. Abruptly he pulled his head back under the cover of the Jeep as a huge section of the top of the dune collapsed down its side. Toni jumping her vehicle from the top of the dune and flying through the air to land with a thud in front of Scott's car had caused the mini landslide.

Rosie blew a kiss to the guys now behind her and Barbara's uncontrollable cackle could be heard from the front.

"Told you it would work," Toni chuckled. She didn't relinquish her lead again until they came to the edge of the desert and joined a proper road. Once on the tarmac they had to abide by speed regulations and correct driving procedures. The more relaxed journey allowed the passengers to converse more easily.

Scott was talking about his favourite topic, alcohol. He was going round the Jeep asking what each of their favourite liquors were, even Cheikhou joined in after cheering up on the race across the desert. Once they all made their pick, Scott asked if any of them had any funny stories from when they were drunk.

Alex immediately nominated himself to tell what happened to him once.

"It was my eighteenth birthday and I'd been drinking most of the day after lunch at a pizza place. Me and my dad stayed in town and continued drinking until the early hours of the morning, getting absolutely wasted. I stumbled home and felt a bit peckish; I hadn't eaten since the pizza at lunch. I remember preparing my food but then I passed out on my bed. Waking up the next morning I reached for my phone the same as always but found only a slice of toast. In my drunken state I stumbled downstairs and looked for where I could've left my phone. Seeing the fridge reminded me of what I'd made myself to eat last night – cheese on toast – however, with the toast next to my bed I couldn't have finished it. Still unable to find my phone, I proceeded with my breakfast of a bowl of porridge. I measured the oats and the milk, went to put it in the microwave… and there I found my phone covered in melted cheese."

The story managed to get a laugh from everyone, even Cheikhou had a smile, despite his disdain for the storyteller.

Alex felt a warmth inside him as the group laughed with him opposed to at him for one of the first times. "I wish I knew you guys then. It was a bit lame going out with just my dad for my eighteenth."

"OK, me next." Cheikhou waved his arms to hush the laughter.

"First of all, I doubt I'd have gone even if I *did* know you, mate; secondly, this isn't a story of when I got drunk but it's still a good one. It's from when I was little and helping Carlton on his ranger duties in Africa. We were just getting ready to head out for the day when we received a distress call from one of the nearby ranger outposts. No time to waste, we quickly jumped in his truck and sped to the call for help. When we got there we saw four elephants rampaging around the facility and one of Carlton's colleagues was hiding behind a tree outside. The elephants had broken in during the night and ransacked the supplies tent. In doing so, they found litres upon litres of alcohol and didn't stop until they'd finished the whole lot. It took a further six rangers to arrive before we were able to shoo the intoxicated animals off. Me and Carlton named that particular story 'Trunk and disorderly'." Cheikhou laughed briefly before becoming very quiet and looking out of the Jeep.

"He'll be OK," George comforted his friend with a hand on his shoulder.

Cheikhou gave a nod to appreciate his mate's attempt to ease his concerns and politely removed his hand from his shoulder.

Not sensing the change in mood, Scott looked in his rear-view mirror and asked, "What about you, Ginge?"

George let the nickname slide and just told of when he and Jacob would always get drunk on tequilas because of his holidays to Mexico. The memory of Jacob had a similar effect on him as the memory of Carlton had for Cheikhou, though, and again the passengers became quiet.

"I was in Mexico recently," Scott piped up again. "It was tequila that did for me, also." That was all Scott said about that trip or at least all he was willing to tell. The driver pulled off the road again when there was no traffic around and followed Toni across the sandy terrain once more. It didn't take long for Scott to reignite the race for a final time for the last leg of their trip, but he was unable to overtake Toni with the girls teasing the slower boys. The off-road trip lasted for about thirty minutes before they pulled up outside what appeared to be a large ranch, hidden in the heart of the desert.

"Welcome to ya home for the coming months," Toni said to her passengers. "You'll have a lekker time," she promised.

"What's she saying?" Yuanli asked Rosie.

The look she received in return implied they were both none the wiser.

"Sorry. South African slang," Toni explained, apologising for her lingo, "'Lekker' means something's good."

"That's alright, then," Barbara said in a dismissive voice as she hurried to exit the Jeep. "Where's the shower? A woman of my girth doesn't do well in the heat."

"Wow, she moves fast for her size," Toni commented when Barbara closed the door.

George looked at his temporary home for the first time and saw a brown picket fence surrounding the perimeter of the base. There was a gap in the boundary where a large arch was situated for pedestrians and vehicles to enter and exit the compound. The arch was also brown in colour and on the top of the curve, 'Oasis' was scribed in large black letters. The truck carrying Roy, Jeremiah and Jedrok pulled up last, it had been slightly left behind by the racing Jeeps on the last leg of their journey. Roy wasted no time disembarking and strolling to the rear of the truck to begin the dismount of the monument.

"Help me get this inside," he ordered the onlookers.

Cheikhou, Alex, George and Jeremiah all rushed to aid in the task. The combined strength of them all made the transfer of Jedrok both easy and fast. Together they ferried their most prized possession under the archway and towards a large wooden building.

George tried to survey the location whilst hauling the weight, but every time he tried to look around he couldn't see properly past the object he was carrying. In the end he resigned to scouting the area when Jedrok was safely stored away. The large wooden building turned out to be a communal area. It was one big room with no separate compartments; there were tables towards one side next to a kitchen, then there was a games area with a range of entertainment from board games to pool tables to table tennis. The rest of the room was just a relaxed bar area with big settees and armchairs, most likely used for those late-night chats over a couple of drinks before bed. Jedrok was placed in the heart of the bar area; the logic behind it seemed to George that it was the most central area of the whole facility. The large wooden building was the hardest place to get to for any potential Tombstone attacks – they would first have to reach the middle of the base. In addition, with George's limited knowledge of the place, he still presumed that it was the easiest location to defend if the need arose. Jedrok was set down and the boys turned to see the rest of their group also in the building with them except Barbara and Toni.

According to Yuanli, Barbara had insisted that Toni take her to the nearest bathing area immediately. It wasn't long before the door to the large wooden building swung open again and a lady in the trademark red suit with a green minotaur logo walked in, flanked by four of her colleagues in matching attire.

"Good afternoon," the leading female began. "My name's Cindy. I hope you had a pleasant journey from England to the States. Soon we'll provide you with lunch as I am sure you're all very hungry. However, before we eat a few introductions are in order. I'm the owner of this ranch and, as such, will always be around if you have any grievances or concerns. As well as running the everyday activities around the ranch I'll also be training you in ranged weapon combat."

This was met with an excited chatter in her audience.

Cindy was a tall lady with long red hair that stretched down to the middle of her back. She had a youthful and angelic appearance that didn't suggest a master markswoman.

Cindy shifted her focus from the newcomers to Jeremiah. "Thank you for delivering them safely. You remember our conversation we had before you left?"

Jeremiah's eyes flickered over her colleagues beside her and then nodded without word.

Cindy seemed uneasy as she continued, "I'd be wary. Now go and see how bad it's got. Remember, you can't spread the truth if you're dead. Take care and good luck."

"Be wary. Good advice for us all at this time." Jeremiah darted his eyes across Cindy's colleagues a final time before saluting and marching out of the door.

Cindy returned her attention to her recruits. "Beside me, to my left and right, are the other people who will be instrumental in your training." Pointing at the man on her left she said, "This is Masood. You'll be seeing a lot of him as he's going to train you in both horse riding and close combat."

The group looked over at the man and saw he was of Indian descent with a bald head. The only hair on his whole face was a pencil thin moustache that ran between his nose and top lip. The most distinctive feature was the large scar stretching from just below his left eye down the length of his cheek, stopping at the chin.

He put his arms out and said only, "Welcome, guys."

Cindy turned and motioned further. "On my other side is Donna who'll be teaching you aquatic skills. Her task is no doubt the most difficult, seeing as we're located in the heart of a desert."

The audience laughed at Cindy's remark and took in Donna's small stature of dark skin and short black hair.

"There's a small reservoir on the far side of the ranch, an oasis that gives this ranch its name," Donna informed them to slightly put their minds at rest as to how she would undergo her training.

Cindy pointed to the final two men waiting at the end. "Last but by no means least is Harry and Lee. They'll do some climbing with you to prepare you all for your terminal destination and assault on Dreadnoque."

Lee was smaller than Harry and lurked slightly behind with his messy brown hair and droopy eyes. When George looked at Harry he did not feel as welcome as the others had made him. Harry had a stern face, grey hair and no sign of a smile.

"Climbing is a dangerous business. These aren't trees we'll be scaling, but rock faces hundreds of feet high. A fall would be fatal and, as such, ill-advised, so listen when spoken to and shut your mouth when I am talking!" Harry began to shout towards the end and seemed to direct his words at George who had turned to Cheikhou to voice his concerns about Harry's demeanour.

Cindy appeared to miss the aggressive behaviour or maybe she just knew that was what he was like. Either way, she continued, "Now we're all acquainted, it's time for food. When you've finished, I'll take you on a tour of the facility, ending at your rooms."

"Where's Carlton?" Cheikhou piped up in concern for his guardian.

"He's being take care of. We don't have the necessary equipment to save him here. He's been taken straight to Sanctum where he'll get the medicine he needs." Cindy gave Cheikhou a reassuring smile that was validated by Roy who nodded.

"Sanctum...Well, where's that? How long to get there? I thought it was under control of Tombstone. I need more answers," Cheikhou complained as he glanced at the others for support.

"I would like to know more about our destination," George agreed.

Roy looked to Cindy and they shared a nod. "Well, if you can hold off on food a little longer then we can talk and try to clear up some of your questions."

"I think I'm OK. I don't have any questions and I'm ready for f–" Alex felt Rosie's hand touch his arm and his words caught in his mouth.

"Cheik wants some answers," she whispered.

"I could probably go a little longer," Alex allowed, "if everyone else is struggling."

Rosie patted his arm and smiled. "If I'm still struggling after this I'll know who to go to, then."

Alex was breathing sharply without realising; he nodded with a gulp.

Roy bowed his head in thanks for Rosie subduing Alex, and began his talk. "Gaia," he announced, "is what this is all about. On Earth you're taught it basically means that when one natural cycle starts to go out of kilter, other cycles work to bring it back, continually optimising the conditions for life on Earth."

Rosie thought she understood. "So, if the atmosphere has too much carbon dioxide in it, as it does due to our excessive use of fossil fuels, then Earth will try to counter that by making conditions better for the growth of plants. When these plants grow they'll remove the excess carbon dioxide from the environment replacing it with oxygen which we can breathe."

"Not quite, b-but I can help you l-like you said, if you want?" Alex stammered.

"Exactly," grinned Roy. "In theory, that's what it is in its simplest form, however, Gaia is not just a theory, it's a powerful instrument of creation that manipulates climate and topography. For years it was kept safe in Dreadnoque and was able to perform its primary purpose of stabilising Earth and Sanctum. Furthermore, Tombstone has risen and has removed it from its rightful place. Now its powers have been put to perverse use to forge an army to first subjugate Sanctum and then leave that world to destroy life on this planet. The tampering of Gaia has set Earth on a countdown to self-destruction. The planet can't efficiently counteract the damage us humans are doing without Gaia's help so it's trying all it can to fight back. You must've noticed an increase in natural disasters in the past few years?" he asked.

The question was met with nodding and groans of understanding.

"The frequency and severity of these disasters has reached an all-time high with the drought and famine in Malaysia in its eighteenth month, the landslide in Nepal killing thousands and, most recently, the floods drowning much of Siberia."

"Hang on," Cheikhou intervened, "So you're telling us that our planet is somehow kept stable by an object called Gaia that's stored in this other world?"

"Stored on Sanctum – correct – which I believe was what you wanted more information about."

Cindy came in with a large map and unfurled it on the floor beneath them.

"This is Sanctum," explained Roy with a twinkle in his eye. The alien world was split up into five different terrain types. In the centre was a watery area labelled 'Moanatenger' that split the north and south land masses apart. To the south of Moanatenger was a green jungle terrain labelled 'Chungwantanya' and beside that furthest south was a rocky expanse, 'Dreadnoque'. To the north of the water was 'Barren Valley', coloured yellow to show vast swathes of desert and, finally, 'Liberterra', a lighter shade of green lacking the many trees depicted on the Chungwantanya section of the map.

"Here in Liberterra is where Carlton's been taken. They're better equipped to deal with his wounds than us – they'll have dressings for the snapetella and more understanding on stopping its spread."

"How do you get there from here, then?" George asked.

"The portal is not too far from here and emerges at the base of Magellan Castle, the last stronghold of Minotaur in Sanctum," Roy answered.

"That's handy," George allowed, with a chuckle.

"It's no coincidence," Roy scolded. "Many have lost their lives to hold that position."

Sensing the change in tone and being uppermost responsible for starting the conversation, Cheikhou stepped in. "OK, I understand better now and I'm sorry for demanding this when we're all hungry and tired. Let's see about fixing the first of them issues now– I'm ready to eat if we all are."

Roy acknowledged his outburst and apologised, also. "Sorry. If we're all happier now then by all means lead the way, Cheik."

Cheikhou walked with the others over to the tables.

They hadn't been seated for long before lunch arrived in the hands of the chefs dressed in their whites. Everyone had a burger and chips delivered to them or a vegetarian bean burger was served to those who didn't want the meat option. The chips were amazing; crispy on the outside so they crunched when bitten into, but fluffy as a pillow on the inside.

Alex had dived into his food as soon as it arrived, as a result he was the one who found out to his dismay that the scrumptious chips were also molten lava on the inside, sticking to and burning the roof of his mouth. Watching him burn himself for being greedy was funny enough but when he tried to disguise it by saying he was fine and then taking frequent sharp inhales and exhales of breath, it set the whole table laughing.

Barbara returned with Toni halfway through the meal. Feeling refreshed she took her seat and quickly ate her own portion. Despite turning up so much later than the others she still finished before Yuanli who then groaned, holding her tiny belly and asking Barbara if she wanted any more. The plus-sized lady happily accepted the chips but left the bean burger, foolishly assuming it wouldn't be as nice as its meaty counterpart. After letting the food go down and waiting for the plates to be cleared, it was time to begin the tour.

Cindy rose from her seat and signalled for the rest to follow. They exited the large wooden building and took a left. A short walk took them to a row of stables in which the horses were keeping out of the hot midday sun.

"This is the corral in which you will receive your first horse riding training. Once Masood is happy that you're ready, you'll be allowed to take the horses for a ride outside the ranch. It's very important, however, that you check with Masood before doing so, both so we know you've left the ranch but also to ensure the horses aren't taken out when it's too hot." Cindy motioned for them to follow once again. The facility was large but with so much packed into it the journeys between buildings and training areas were quick. Barely having only just left the stables, they reached a large open area with wooden soldiers dotted around and hay bales for seating.

"This is where Masood will take you for close combat training. Anyone found to have removed weapons from their storage outside of training will be dealt with severely." She gave a warning glance to the group and her angelic look disappeared into a lady that would not be messed with. Continuing on, they reached the reservoir; it was not as small as George thought it was going to be. The water source was twice the size of the stables and surrounding pens in which the horse riding would take place and would be plenty large enough to learn what they needed to know. Surrounding the reservoir was a small green halo of grass and trees, it was a beautiful area in stark contrast to the dry and mundane environment encompassing it. Unfortunately, the tour had to continue and they had to leave the small spot of vibrant life in the middle of all the surrounding sand. Their next destination was the ranged combat training area; the targets, bottles and locked weapons cabinet spoke for themselves. Finally, they reached a row of small wooden buildings that led all the way back to the archway they entered earlier.

"This is your accommodation," Cindy told them. "You'll be sharing with two others. In each shack there's just a bed each and clothing space." Pointing over to the largest of the accommodation buildings, she said, "That's the communal toilet and wash area. There's just the one building so both sexes will have to share. I hope that won't be of any concern."

Alex blushed at the thought of having to shower in a cubicle next to Rosie. "So we'll have to wash *and* dry, all in a small area behind a cubicle door?" Alex was beginning to panic; he didn't want to be naked where anyone could see him.

"I didn't say anything about doors," Cindy replied before turning her back and leaving. She smiled as she listened to Alex behind her.

"She's joking, right?" he was asking. "George, tell me she's joking!"

CHAPTER 20

Earth
Wyoming
Earthquake-struck city

Deacon's eyes fluttered open and immediately he was overcome with the ear-splitting screech of the ambulance siren. His head felt like it was being used as a drum, his temple throbbed as his brain attempted to burst through his forehead. A trickle of blood ran from his left nostril and he could taste the iron in his mouth as the wound oozed over his top lip. Overcome with pain, his eyes fell shut again to try to give his body some respite.

When he roused again the siren had died but his head was still pounding along to the tune of a marching band. He started slowly by wiggling his toes, then he moved up his body by bending his knees gently. Once below the waist was checked, he proceeded to flex his fingers and lift his arms. Happy his body was fully functional, with the exception of many aches and bruises, Deacon attempted to rise. He felt as if his torso was tied down with straps. No matter how hard he tried to get up he was pulled back down to the floor of the ambulance. After several failed attempts, he looked down in his dazed state and saw that the problem was that he was still belted into the stretcher. He shook his head for his stupidity, but the motion made his headache double in pressure. Groaning under the pain, Deacon undid his restraints and checked his surroundings. The ambulance appeared to be on its side, the medicinal cabinets had all spilt their contents across the base of the vehicle. Seeing some painkillers amongst the sprawled drugs he reached for a packet and popped two of the pills. Deacon was part of the population that could take tablets without water; never before had he been so happy for the trait. Almost immediately the medicine started to take effect and his head eased a little, enabling him to continue the analysis of his surroundings. The ambulance crew were still unconscious around the vehicle. After checking their pulses, Deacon was happy they would be OK. The emergency serviceman spirit in Deacon's soul pushed him on to escape the vehicle and see if anyone outside the ambulance required assistance. His ears were beginning to recover from the siren that had been echoing around his skull and the absence of the ringing enabled Deacon to hear the moans and pleas around him. After struggling to a vertical base, the fireman had to crouch in the upturned vehicle. Looking for an exit he tried the rear door but it was jammed. Gathering up his entire energy reserves he tried to kick the door open but it didn't budge. Taking a deep breath he tried again, this time the exit flew open and revealed the chaos outside. Cars were crushed everywhere; many had drivers leaning on the exteriors of their transports attempting to regain their composure and recover from the disaster. Unfortunately, many and more of the cars still had drivers in their seats, either dead or dying. One lady had collapsed on to her steering wheel and the horn was heralding her journey to meet her maker.

Deacon stumbled from vehicle to vehicle trying to see to as many wounded as he could but most he saw were already deceased or beyond his help. He had just closed the eyes of a small oriental man that lost his battle with life when he heard a child's screaming coming from a gold-coloured Chevrolet further up the road. Leaping over wreckages and trying to avoid the rubble from the bridge that had collapsed onto the road below, he managed to reach his destination. The first impression was not good: the large car was upside down and the windows were smashed, leaving glass scattered around the crash. Deacon hurried to crouch down and look in the front to check on the condition of the driver; what he saw was not good. A shard of glass was embedded in their head through their left eye, death on impact. Struggling to pull his gaze from the horrific sight he noticed the source of the wailing in the back. A little girl was sat in a booster seat, amazingly unharmed but desperate for attention from her unresponsive mother. Deacon rushed round to the back and forced the door open to help the child out of her seat and the car.

"It's OK, I've got you," Deacon whispered as he pulled her from the wreckage, trying desperately to calm the crying child. It was obvious that she just wanted her mother but it was down to Deacon to look after her now, down to him to convince her to leave her parent in the car.

"You have to trust me," he said in a calming voice. This wasn't the first time in his line of work that he had to extract a child from a scene that their parent wouldn't be walking away from. It took a while, but he managed to remove the girl from the car's vicinity and get her to follow him. During the conversation he had to gain the girl's faith; he learned that her name was Chloe and she was eight years old. Her and her mother were on their way to swimming, she was very good and was on the brink of being given the opportunity to try out for the local team that competes in tournaments around the state.

Chloe was old enough to understand who Deacon was when he explained he worked for the fire department and also mature enough to realise leaving her mother behind meant leaving her forever. She was gripping Deacon's hand tight, needing his support to pull her from the accident. She didn't know if she had the strength to walk away of her own accord.

Deacon couldn't respect the young girl more. He wouldn't expect anyone to be able to leave their parent behind, but the strength and bravery Chloe was showing was inspiring him to get them both out.

The collapsed bridge made their surroundings dark. They were buried under the rubble but with enough space to move around. A slither of light appeared to Deacon's left, then the slither became a hole that let the light pour through and show off the demolition around him. He covered Chloe's eyes to save her from the horrific sights around them and made his way to the light. The hole was getting bigger by the second as people were removing the rubble with their bare hands. Deacon passed Chloe through the hole to a man with his arms outstretched and then scrambled out himself. The city was in disarray, the damage immense.

Chloe grabbed back hold of Deacon's hand and looked up at him expectantly.

He tried to smile but the pain in his body made it come out as more of a grimace.

"There's been an earthquake," he told the little girl. "A big one," he added with a huff. They were surrounded by collapsed buildings and people running around frantically in panic.

"Stick with me and you'll be fine," he said in a reassuring voice. They began walking amongst the carnage and the majority of buildings in their immediate area had collapsed due to liquefaction. The structures were built on unstable ground; muddy and loose sediment had become like water when the quake hit and the loss of support meant the buildings just fell to the ground. There were no warnings that the quake was coming so many of the places would have been full of people either working or visiting the businesses. Fires raged all around them as electrical cables and power lines were snapped and sparked causing blazes. Deacon watched as a fire crew attempted to get water from a fire hydrant but were unsuccessful. The fault in the equipment most likely due to burst and ruptured water pipes. He would have helped the struggling crew but his priority was Chloe now – nothing else mattered to him as much as ensuring the safety of the little girl at his side. His plan was to reach a safe zone where they could try to locate the girl's family and return her to her father or another guardian. According to reports, unfortunately, the nearest meet-up was on the other side of the city in the richer area that was less affected. The more affluent area was safer – buildings were reinforced in the case of earthquakes with protection such as rubber shock absorbers and shatterproof glass. Walking hand in hand, Deacon tried to keep the young girl's mind off the situation and the danger by talking to her. He began by retelling his story of how he had put out the forest fire earlier that day with the help of the bear and the raccoon.

Children always enjoyed stories with animals and Chloe seemed no exception. "So you gave a real bear a 'bear-hug'," she pointed out with a chuckle.

Deacon smiled at the realisation, "I guess I did." He couldn't believe that it was still that same day – the fire seemed like weeks ago now. They were making quick progress through the damaged city; their conversation was making the journey fly by. Deacon was beginning to feel dizzy, he coughed but that wasn't enough to clear his airways – he coughed again more aggressively, this time having to let go of Chloe's hand in order to cover his mouth with both hands.

"Are you OK?" the girl asked, beginning to feel panicked.

Deacon fought back his illness and tried to hide his discomfort. Gazing down at Chloe he managed a wink. "Fine, kiddo!" He motioned her to continue walking and took back hold of her hand. The two arrived at the safe zone after about half an hour of strolling through the city. There were a lot of people gathered and the buzz around the place was overwhelming as families tried to reunite and check their loved ones were OK. The organisation was magnificent, the zone had been set up so different areas were sectioned off depending on surname. It was easy for Deacon to find the right area to take Chloe, they just had to go to the 'A–E' region for her surname, Bennet. The section was crowded so trying to find Chloe's father was a task but, after around fifteen minutes, she pulled Deacon's arm and dragged him to a tall man with glasses and grey hair. She let go of his arm and ran to her father. "Daddy! I'm here, over here!"

He turned just as she reached him and lifted her into the air, overjoyed to see her.

"Where's Mummy?" was his inevitable immediate question.

Chloe couldn't remain strong any longer. Now in the safety of her father's arms, she cried into his neck.

His daughter's sorrow answered his question. The grey-haired tall man didn't show any of the strength his daughter had shown. "Noooo... nooo…oh noo," he cried, and hugged his daughter tight.

"How did you get here?"

Eyes full of tears, Chloe removed her head from her father's neck and pointed at Deacon.

The six foot-plus blonde fireman was slowly making his way over.

Chloe's father lowered her to the ground to thank his daughter's saviour.

"Sorry about your wife," Deacon began, "there was nothing I could do."

"Thank you so much, sir," was Chloe's father's first response. "You're the man that saved my daughter. Let that be how you remember today; don't dwell on what you couldn't have fixed."

Removing his glasses to wipe his eyes, Chloe's father lunged forward and hugged Deacon tight whilst continuing to thank him. When he went to release the fireman, however, something was wrong.

Deacon had passed out and gone limp. Chloe's father laid his daughter's saviour on the floor and called for help.

A week later Chloe and her father were still standing over Deacon's lifeless body.

Beside them stood Pat, chewing her gums with her head bowed. A whimpering was coming from her side; she had insisted on bringing Bennie as the dog had loved spotting Deacon each morning on his way to work. The fireman had died later on in the day after saving Chloe. The decision to get her to safety was one that meant he couldn't seek the treatment he knew he required. A fireman all his life, he knew the dangers of acute respiratory failure. When the symptoms of dizziness and coughing began, he was sure the smoke in his lungs from saving the bear would be the death of him unless he reached a hospital. Nevertheless, he pushed on to ensure Chloe reached her family at his own detriment. He was now being lowered into the ground in a black box, the pastor was saying his holy words as Deacon's friends, family and workmates looked on, tears in their eyes. When the coffin reached the bottom of the hole in the ground it began to be covered with earth. The first layer came from handfuls of soil thrown in by those closest to him, the rest was shovelled in by undertakers. When the last of the soil was thrown onto the coffin, everyone turned to leave, all but Chloe and Bennie.

Chloe placed her doll on the grave and Bennie lifted his head high to howl a long, final goodbye to his friend.

CHAPTER 21

Earth
Somewhere in the Atlantic Ocean
A couple of thousand miles off the East Coast of the USA

Annabel was struggling. She had been in the water for a very long time now. Every time she came up for a breath she would be plunged back under the icy depths. Presley was coping much better, he was managing to keep his head out of the water and, as such, was not struggling at all with his breathing. Annabel burst out of the water once again and spat a mouthful of the liquid back into its source. Coughing, she tried to locate Presley. The water ran down her long eyelashes and into her blue eyes, the same crystal colour as the water she found herself in. Her ears were ringing after being under the water and having only just re-emerged, as a result she didn't hear Presley's shout to her left. Too late she saw the danger and, with no time to react, she could only watch through her blurry vision as the ball splashed to a halt in front of her.

"Good effort," said Presley, laughing, whilst applauding her attempts.

"You could've helped!" Annabel snapped, angry with her team-mates.

Now the water volleyball match had gone to a draw, the next point would win.

It was Presley, Annabel, Luke and Steve that made up the team which had reached the final. Presley's sheer size had come as a massive advantage, his height meant that he was easily able to return shots or even spike the ball quickly towards the opponents' watery court.

Luke and Steve were of limited help hence why Annabel was being run ragged during the previous point, attempting to return all their opponents' efforts. Instead, the two boys seemed more concerned with watching Annabel and admiring her every movement.

"Can you concentrate on the game for just this point? Please," Annabel rhetorically begged the duo.

"Anything for you," Luke drooled.

"Creep," Annabel whispered to herself.

The whistle was blown and the opposition served the ball into their side of the pool.

Luke kept to his word and returned the effort brilliantly, forcing the opponents immediately onto the back foot. Somehow, they kept it alive and the ball came back over Annabel's side of the pool.

She cupped her hands together and levered the ball in Presley's direction. This tactic had worked for most of the tournament: she would give the ball plenty of height in front of him and then he would smash it into the opponents' side of the pool. Time seemed to stand still as everyone watched the ball float through the air. The opponents moved to the back of their side of the pool in anticipation. Presley connected but didn't smash it like so many other times that day, instead he opted to lightly knock the ball into the forecourt of the oppositions' pool. They would never get to it; Annabel's team began to celebrate by high fiving each other. Unbelievably, mid-celebration, the ball came gliding back over the net – somehow they had reached the shot. Quick as a flash, Steve leapt backwards and kept the play alive. Luke used his head to get some extra height and headed the ball further into the air. He reeled backwards holding his aching skull after performing his heroics, but he kept his eyes open in order to see Presley lift Annabel into the air. It was like a scene from a movie, she was lifted from the pool by her hips and with the extra height she was able to easily pick her spot and scoop the ball over the net. Their opponents had no chance, the ball splashed into the water and the crowd went wild. Most of the ship had stopped what they were doing to watch the final of the tournament.

"The winner of the water volleyball tournament, ANNABEL'S ANGELS!" the entertainment staff boomed over the microphone. The two teams shook hands and complimented each other on a good game.

Annabel's team all high fived each other. She turned down Steve's offer for a celebratory hug, same with Luke. They each got the message when Presley loomed over her shoulder, a silent warning not to push their luck.

"Good game, lads," he said in his deep voice. "See you around," he finished as a means of dismissal. Annabel wrinkled up her face. "They were as slimy as the base of that pool," she said as she thanked Presley for his assistance. Together they returned to their deckchairs to relax after their victory.

"I can't believe I actually thought you were going to make me swim to America," Annabel giggled.

It was five days ago that Presley and Annabel were left stranded on the dusty airstrip, helplessly watching as Roy and the others flew over their heads in the private plane to America.

Presley set off immediately for the coast in order to gain transport over to the States by boat. After being continually questioned on the journey to the sea by Annabel as to why they couldn't just get a plane, Presley had to reveal to her that he was, in fact, from Sanctum and, as such, was unable to travel by conventional methods without a passport. That opened a whole can of questions that he faced and answered in turn; the only one he dodged was how he was planning to gain access to the boat. When they arrived at the docks it became time for Annabel to find out the answer to her mystery. Presley's bike roared to a halt. He switched off the engine and immediately they could hear the sea gulls crying as they flew through the sky. The air smelled salty and there was a cool breeze coming from the water. Presley sat surveying the cruise liner for a few good minutes in complete silence. Every time Annabel tried to speak he cut her off.

"Wait here!" he ordered. He rose from the bike and opened up the storage compartment.

Annabel feared he was getting his guns but instead he emerged with the whip she saw in the back the night he rescued her.

"What're you going to do with that?" Annabel asked, beginning to panic. She didn't want to see Presley get arrested for assaulting a sailor, forcefully trying to gain access to a ship.

He ignored her question and walked straight for the gangplank, tucking the whip into his trousers and covering it with his top as he went. She watched from afar as he spoke to the lady responsible for getting all the passengers on board. After a while she pointed further down the boat and Presley disappeared from view. Unwilling to miss where he was going next, Annabel made the decision to leave the bike and pursue him. Nobody would be able to steal the motorcycle, it was all locked up and Presley had the keys. Annabel bumped into oncoming pedestrians as she rushed to see where Presley was heading, apologising profusely with every other step. Finally, she caught sight of him again. He was currently talking to the man responsible for loading vehicles onto the ship. Annabel crept a little closer and hid behind a statue to get a closer look.

A little boy laughed as he passed her and pointed at where she was sitting.

Looking around she noticed she was level with the stone figure's genitalia. She shuffled to the right slightly and cursed the cruelness of children. The conversation appeared to be getting heated; Presley's plan was obviously not coming together as he had hoped. Shrugging his shoulders aggressively, he swivelled round to return to Annabel – at least that's what she thought he was doing. In hindsight, he was actually analysing his surroundings and checking the coast was clear. Extremely swiftly, Presley pulled the whip from the back of his trousers and struck the man on the arm.

Something made Annabel reach for her own arm when she saw the impact and rubbed it, a forgotten memory of a previous incident.

There was no scream of pain and, before the sailor realised what had happened, Presley had placed the whip back in its hiding place under his top. Stranger still, Presley then spoke to the man again as if nothing had happened. The sailor listened to what was said before laughing and putting his thumb up to the man that had just assaulted him.

Presley turned his back again, this time to definitely return to his bike and the waiting Annabel. She rushed back to the motorcycle and took her seat as if she had never left. She was running the events over in her head, debating whether to confront Presley on what he had just done. In the end she decided it was best if he thought she remained on the bike like he had suggested the whole time.

"I told you to wait here," were his first words.

Startled, Annabel was worried and her voice went squeaky. "I did," she lied.

"OK." Presley fixed her with a knowing look.

She shrivelled under the pressure and looked at her feet.

Without another word he popped the storage open and laid the whip back in its place. Then he mounted his bike and reignited the engine. "Hold on," he warned before accelerating off towards the ship.

They reached a small queue that had formed since Presley had spoken to the man loading the vehicles onto the boat. Whilst waiting for the cars to be boarded they sat in silence. Annabel was wondering what the man would say when he saw Presley again. They reached the front and her question was answered in the most bizarre way. The sailor welcomed Presley like an old friend and then turned to Annabel with arms outstretched to greet her.

"Oh my. Haven't you grown? Last time I saw you, you must've been up to about here," he said with his hand on his hip.

Annabel was about to tell the man she had never seen him before when Presley turned to her.

"You remember Eddie, don't you?" he winked to encourage Annabel to play along.

"Oh yeah. Yeah, of course I do," she replied, smiling foolishly at the man. "How's the wife?" she inquired, trying her best to play along.

"You mean 'husband'?" he corrected her, looking cross. Then his false anger was removed and he laughed. "Richard's fine. It's OK, I wouldn't have expected you to know, you were only little when I last saw you."

Visibly relieved that she hadn't ruined the whole charade, she decided to stop talking and let Presley deal with the situation. Moments later they were moving again and parking on the cruise ship.

"How did you get us tickets?" Annabel asked, hoping for an explanation about the whip.

Presley pretended not to have heard and instead changed the subject.

"The cruise leaves in two hours. We have time to head into town to get some clothes and necessities for the trip."

"OK, great!" Annabel screeched excitedly. The enthusiasm

was an act – for the first time in her life she cared not a dime about shopping – all that was on her mind was the object stored in the back of Presley's bike.

CHAPTER 22

Earth
Arizona
Oasis

"It's my dad's birthday today," George told Cheikhou as they were dressing for the day ahead.

"I bought him a book and a card and left them in my room. I hope he finds them," he sighed with sadness, remembering his family that he had to leave at home.

"He won't know who it's from," Alex piped up from the corner.

George couldn't believe he had to share a room with him. The boy was intolerable, always had something to say and always knew better than anyone else.

"He will when he reads the card that says 'Love from George'!" he spat back.

"They'll have wiped him. You know that. He won't have any clue who George is. They go in with a small device that flashes and, to avoid wiping themselves, they wear black sunglasses."

"Oh, do shut up!" George retorted, for he knew Minotaur had the power to wipe memories but not how Alex had described. They simply waved some sort of metal block across the victim's face; he remembered seeing it happen at RAS. Despite what Alex said, George could only pray that the present reached his father and that he would know who had bought it.

George thought back to the night before whilst he waited for the others to get ready, remembering fondly the first shower he'd had for what felt like an age. Every member of the team had showered in the communal bathroom by now, the girls went first and the boys went second. It was easy to negotiate a schedule that first evening, but it was inevitable that someone would walk in on another sooner or later. The thought of Alex walking in on Barbara brought a smile to

George's face and he allowed himself a small chuckle.

"Come on then, let's go!" Cheikhou announced when he was prepared.

The day marked the first in which they would be undergoing training. The clothes they were wearing were provided by Cindy. They were already on their respective beds when they reached their rooms on the opening day. Khaki trousers and plain black tank tops were designed to fit perfectly, thanks to Yuanli, who had taken their measurements at the end of their trial day at RAS, an event which seemed like an eternity ago now.

George and Cheikhou were halfway out the door heading to breakfast when Alex hollered at them, "Hang on a second!" His large size meant that he struggled to stretch over his belly to reach his feet and put on his footwear. Embarrassed, he finally got both socks and shoes on and rushed to the door, "Come on then, guys, you'll make us late!" he tutted as he bustled past them.

The boys were the last to reach the large wooden building for breakfast, they had to hurry to eat as they didn't have long before the training would begin. Despite being limited for time, Alex still managed to eat a bowl of oatmeal, two yogurts and a plate of waffles.

"The food's amazing," Alex tried to say through a mouthful.

The rest eating looked away disgusted, averting their gaze from the gunk swirling round his open mouth.

The door to the canteen rattled open as Masood entered holding a horse riding hat.

"Good morning," he announced. "I hope you're all well-fed. Today we'll do our first session with the horses."

Rosie was excited, she loved horse riding and had done it when she was younger.

Alex was not so happy, in fact, he looked like he wanted to be sick – whether that was the plate of waffles or the thought of the horse riding, no one was sure. Their chairs screeched against the floor when they pulled them out to leave, and again when they tucked them back under the table.

Rosie led the way with Yuanli and they were talking to Masood about what to expect and discussing previous experiences with horse riding.

When George left the air-conditioned food hall he already felt the overwhelming heat of the Arizona sun despite it only being the early hours of the morning. On the one hand, he took heart in the fact that, however much he was struggling in the soaring temperature, Alex would be struggling more.

Cheikhou, on the other hand, was feeling fine, he was used to the extreme heat from growing up in Africa. "If you boys are struggling now, then I'm worried," he laughed.

When they reached the stable Masood turned abruptly and threw his hands out to his sides. "Welcome to your first day of training. I hope you've eaten well and are ready for the day ahead."

"Some of us have eaten better than others," Cheikhou called out whilst motioning towards Alex.

Masood ignored the interruption as well as the push Alex gave to his mocker.

"We're going to start with basic horse care today; if your mount is not correctly looked after then it will be inefficient in the field. A motto of mine is that a pampered palfrey means a protected passenger." Masood then put his fingers in his mouth and whistled loudly to summon his horse. As the sound of hooves drew closer, he bent down and picked up a brush ready to use. The gelding that galloped round the corner was magnificent, it had a metallic chestnut coat with a deep black mane running down its neck. When it pulled up next to its owner the full size of the beast could be acknowledged as it towered over Masood.

"This is Lenny," he said as means of introduction. Then raising his brush, he got to work in showing his students how to prepare their horses. "OK, I'll show you on Lenny how I expect you to saddle your mounts. First, use a brush to remove any debris that could have built up on its back; if left on it can lead to pinching or irritation. You know what it's like trying to put a sock on a sandy foot. Always brush in the direction of hair growth, like this… yeah, good boy. This prevents discomfort for the horse. Next, we need to brush the saddle pad which sits directly onto the horse's back; again, any foreign debris will scratch the horse. The saddle pad is then placed on the horse, making sure to cover the withers."

"The what?" George asked, trying to keep up.

"The *weathers*; I know, it's hard with the accent. He wants us to cover it to protect it from the weather." Alex was as sure of himself as always.

"No, Alex; the *withers*. The ridge between the shoulder blades," Rosie corrected with a giggle.

"Thanks Rosie," Masood smiled at her. "Here," he pointed on Lenny to show the boys. "Once the saddle pad is in place, grab the saddle. Place the right-hand stirrup over the saddle horn and the girth over the seat of the saddle."

"Stirrup?" Cheikhou inquired.

"The ring that holds the foot of the rider," Rosie answered again.

"Girth?" wondered Alex.

"I'm fine with that one, although I'm not surprised you're not," Cheikhou piped up.

Eyes rolling, again Rosie provided the answer, "It's the band that goes round the horse's belly, essentially holding the saddle on the horse."

"Very good," Masood said, putting his thumb up to his star pupil. "Next, stand to the side of your horse and hoist the saddle onto its back. The saddle horn should be in line with the horse's withers, like so..." With an audible groan their teacher lifted the saddle onto his horse's back. "Then release the stirrup from the saddle horn and pull the girth down from the seat. Sling the girth under the horse's belly, just behind its front legs. Then feed the cinch strap, which is this bit here…" He lifted the strap to show the boys who inevitably had no idea what the cinch strap looked like, "…through the ring of the girth and then back up. Pull the strap to the left of the upper ring and then cross over to the right. Feed the strap behind the upper ring and then through to the front, tucking it under where it crossed itself. Finally, take up the slack in the cinch strap, pulling up from the bottom to fit the saddle snugly on the horse. EASY."

There was silence from those watching on. A fly buzzed around the heads of the students sounding like a helicopter in the confused quiet.

"It takes a while to get used to, but it isn't as hard as it seems," Masood assured, trying to pull back his audience.

"OK, let's go!" Rosie commanded, slapping her knee before

marching off to one of the pens.

Rather reluctantly the boys followed.

They each had their own horse in its part of the stable to tack up. The guardians were training too, so Yuanli, Roy and Barbara were also involved.

George entered through the half-door and came face to face with the horse he would be saddling. It was brown with caramel-coloured spots and the same caramel colour oozed down its neck in the form of a mane.

"Hello buddy," George greeted as he stroked his mount's nose. Then he reached for his brush and began the first steps. The loud snort from his gelding told him that he was brushing the wrong way; a quick change of direction and the problem was solved. Once he was happy that the horse was clean, he moved onto the saddle pad and cleaned that, also. Before long he had successfully saddled his horse. Smiling to himself, he sucked his finger which was bleeding after catching it in the cinch. Yuanli and Rosie had finished first and went round to help the others.

George had managed to do his himself, but Rosie was helping Barbara and Yuanli was aiding Cheikhou.

Suddenly, there was a wail from one of the pens.

George rushed to see the commotion and entered a crowded enclosure.

Laying on the floor holding his face was Alex.

Yuanli was trying to see to him whilst Rosie calmed the horse and ushered it out of the stable. With the gelding out of the way there was much more room to move around, and with the extra space George was able to position himself so he could see Alex's bleeding nose.

"What happened?" Yuanli asked whilst holding a bloody rag to her patient's nose.

"I was brushing it the way I was shown and then when I went round the back it kicked me in the face."

"You only needed to brush the area where the saddle was being placed, Alex. Plus, it's never a good idea to walk behind a horse." Yuanli had given Alex the rag to hold now, not wanting to get herself bloody.

"I bet he was telling the poor horse one of his infamous stories," Cheikhou whispered to George through a stifled laugh.

The look he received in reply showed George didn't doubt it.

"OK, back to your own horses. I want you to guide them outside to the riding area," Masood instructed, giving the order from the door. "Are you OK to continue, Alex?"

He could hardly see past the rag he was holding to his face, but he gave a determined nod and got to his feet to go outside. When they all regrouped in the corral Alex found that Rosie had saddled up his horse for him; she gave him the reins with a smile.

"It's OK, I'll help you learn."

Alex removed the rag from his face and smiled wide, unable to hide his excitement. "Thanks Rosie," he murmured through his wounded features.

Masood showed them how to mount their horses and then watched as the group followed his instructions.

Alex and Barbara struggled the most due to their sizes but eventually managed to get mounted up. Then Masood led them in a slow walk round the corral. They were trying to go round in a circle in a clockwise direction but it didn't take long before Alex was going counterclockwise and having to be retrieved by a laughing Rosie. For a while Rosie helped guide her friend round until he got the hang of it. She let go and began trotting off.

"Don't worry, you'll get better. I was awful when I started, too, but it comes after time," she called behind her.

No one was listening, however. Alex, who she thought was following close, was in fact being taken for a ride to the centre of the corral.

"Stupid beast," he moaned to his horse. "Take me back to her. Where're you going?" he pleaded. Alex leaving formation once again was the last straw for the morning half of training. They all retreated to the lunch hall and refreshed themselves. It was also the hottest part of the day and so Masood wanted his horses back under the shade. After the food they were ready for the next half of the day's training. They met back at the stables and Masood greeted them with the plan for the afternoon.

"Hope you all enjoyed this morning. I have a treat for you now.

We're going to go for a ride outside Oasis. You'll all be riding the same horse as this morning as it's important to build up a relationship with your mount."

Alex scoffed, "'Build a relationship'. I'd rather walk on broken glass."

"Alex, I've decided it would be best if your horse was attached to Rosie's as we can't have you riding off any old place when we're outside the Oasis grounds."

Alex discreetly punched the air beside him. "I think that's the best way to build up the required relationship."

They each had to saddle up again, Masood removing them during the lunch insisting that practice makes perfect. He may have had a point as George didn't hurt himself this time and Alex avoided being kicked in the face, albeit with a little help from Yuanli.

When they set off the heat was still unbearable, especially with their riding hats on which limited air flow to their heads. They rode in single file along a sandy path which led them between dunes and up and over some rocky outcrops.

Alex was grateful for being tethered to Rosie as it gave them a chance to talk during the journey and also stopped him trotting straight off a cliff.

Nearing the end of their gait, Rosie was allowed to free herself from Alex in order to go for a gallop with Yuanli.

As the two women raced off sending up plumes of dust, Barbara made her way over to Alex. "This heat is making me sweat like a pig in a sauna. I can feel a river running between my bosom."

Alex groaned as he tried and failed to not imagine what his guardian had just described.

Gagging, he said, "Pigs don't sweat much. They don't have many sweat glands." Desperate to escape Barbara, Alex found some hidden horsemanship in his time of need and managed to trot away at speed.

George was riding along with Roy talking about Annabel and Presley. They decided together that they were both fine and soon they would arrive at Oasis. Roy put George's mind at ease a bit when he explained that their journey would take longer as they missed the plane and would have to find a different way to cross the Atlantic.

One thing that was obvious from Roy talking about Presley was how much he respected him and needed him back. Roy had been telling George about stories of Presley's heroism in Sanctum and how he started Minotaur and the fight back against repression. He seemed desperate for his friend to return before they made their journey to Sanctum. Roy made it clear that their arrival would have much more impact if the mountain of a man was at their side.

"Wow, look at that!" George said in amazement, pointing at a large outcrop of rock throwing shadow over the bright desert.

"That's the sandstone butte that we'll be learning our climbing on with Harry," Roy said.

George went white as a sheet for he had a crippling fear of heights. Shaking his head to rid his mind of thoughts of plummeting to his death, he asked Roy to change the subject.

The sun had begun to disappear over the horizon when they returned back to Oasis. The horses were put back in their stables and the group went to shower and change before dinner.

George showered first and returned to his room to see what Cindy had arranged for them to wear that evening. An ironed black shirt was folded on the bed, beside it was a red jacket and a pair of black trousers. George put it all on and looked in the mirror. *That's sick*, he thought. He pulled down the jacket sides and rubbed a small green crest on the left breast. *The Minotaur logo*, he realised. Unable to help himself he gave a quick wink in the mirror. He heard the door open and turned to see Cheikhou enter. "Look how dapper I loo–" he was cut off by a shock change in Cheikhou's appearance.

"It's gone," Cheikhou said, confirming the obvious. In place of his signature afro, he now had a fully shaved head.

"The shine, mate. The sun is bright enough without your head gleaming at me, too," George laughed.

Cheikhou grinned but quickly grew serious again. "If that bitch has sworn to not grow her hair until all Dark Snake's enemies are dead, then I make the same vow. The afro will return, George, don't worry about that. Until then, may the shine from my head be a constant warning to this Amazon that she's on borrowed time."

"Amen to that, brother," George nodded in support. "Now let's see how good this suit makes you look." He gave Cheikhou his attire and waited for him to change.

Alex even looked respectable in his Minotaur uniform, which was testament to the design; it managed to make his fat look like muscle and, in turn, filled him with confidence.

"Come on, boys," Rosie called into their room, "it's supposed to be the women that take longer to change."

"Coming," came the muffled response through the closed door.

Alex burst through the entrance almost knocking Rosie off her feet and behind him were Cheikhou and George.

"I feel like I'm on holiday, changing before dinner," George told the others.

"Well, you're not," Roy said, having overheard him. "Don't lose sight of what you're here for and all that's at stake," he said not unkindly. Roy was standing with Yuanli and Barbara.

Yuanli, on the one hand, looked stunning in a tight black dress that showed off her smooth unblemished shoulders and fit physique. Barbara, on the other hand, didn't seem to have any 'nice' clothes per se, she was wearing a tracksuit and looked completely out of place.

"I didn't want the dress they provided me with. It showed off more of me than even *I* want to see." Everyone else was happy, though, with what Cindy had provided them with for their evening attire. Together they walked to the dinner hall.

Upon entering the large wooden building, George could immediately smell an array of herbs and spices: nutmeg, cinnamon, thyme, jasmine and basil were just a few of the aromas seducing his senses. The table was set in one long banquet-style layout and the food was already on display. Barbara couldn't contain her excitement. She ran down the length of the table and remarked on each and every dish.

Alex would most likely have done the same a week ago but, in his eagerness to impress Rosie, he held in his wonder. They sat in two lines facing each other and began to tuck in. After a short while Cindy arrived with Masood and the other men and women responsible for their future training. They all ate while discussing their endeavours. By the time they had finished everyone was full to the brim and satisfied completely.

Barbara was the last to finish; she was taking her time on a choice piece of steak and didn't shrink under the pressure of everyone watching her.

Alex, surprisingly, was one of the first to finish, his hunger for the delicacies on the table was surpassed greatly by his hunger for the one opposite him, Rosie. Instead of eating he was more concerned with talking to the girl and finding out as much as he could about her. The day was supposed to be centred around learning to horse ride, but for Alex, all he had learned was how much he actually cared for the girl that had been so nice to him since they met. It was a new experience for Alex but one he somewhat enjoyed – to listen to another person talk and relish in their stories and accomplishments. Sometimes he disagreed with something she said but he noticed the usual desire to interrupt was subdued.

The group retired from the banquet and walked across the large hall to relax onto the black settees and armchairs.

"Welcome to the cool side of the hall," came a voice from behind the bar. Then the mystery man rose from behind his cover, revealing himself, shaking a cocktail with a big grin on his face. It was Scott, he was wearing a shirt with orcas on it, unbuttoned to reveal his hairy chest.

"What can I get you, then? Let's get this party started."

Everyone placed their drinks orders and again the conversation got into full flow. When Scott finished his serving duties he walked over to Harry and Lee in the corner and spoke to them. For some reason they were distancing themselves from the rest of the conversations. Rosie was laughing at something Cheikhou had said and George was continuing to hear about Roy's war stories from Sanctum. Again, most, if not all the stories had a starring role for Presley, either saving someone's life or everyone's lives. Unable to hide his emotions after having a few too many rums, Roy finally broke down from the strong persona he had been putting on in his friend's place. Beginning to cry, he left in a hurry.

Yuanli cut off her conversation with Barbara and pursued Roy in order to console him.

Seeing the commotion, Scott made his way over to George and sat down in Roy's warm seat.

"What was that all about?" he questioned.

"He's missing Presley, the leader of our expedition. Roy's been filling in for him… very well, I hasten to add."

"Sounds like he needs another drink."

"A typical alcoholic's solution," laughed Harry as he and Lee passed on their way out.

"Ignore them," Scott pleaded. Now it was brought to his attention, George could hear the slur in the barman's voice.

"What were you three talking about over in that dark corner, then?" George inquired.

"Do you really want to know?" Scott leaned in close and motioned for George to do the same. "Closer," he whispered, then when they were just a hair's breadth apart, he burped in his ear.

"That's disgusting," George repelled in horror.

Scott laughed and apologised. "I can't tell you, I'm afraid. Secret Minotaur business." Then changing the subject, he began to question George about his trips to Mexico. What started as an improvised diversion tactic turned into a full-scale conversation about the Mexican cuisine, ancient ruins and, most importantly of all, the tequila testing.

"I once had one that was infused with ghost chilli, it almost blew my head off!" boomed George, a little louder than necessary. The alcohol had gone to his head and he was beginning to shout.

He and Scott had talked the night away, everyone else had gone to bed an hour previously.

"Wow, I want to try that one now. It makes my jalapeño-infused tequila sound amateur." Scott slapped George on the back. "You're a good man. We have much in common, however, have you ever had the Death Shot?" he raised his eyebrows for effect.

"No, and don't think I want to. Guessing you have and defied the name?"

"Of course, I have; let me set the scene."

"Oh, please don't," chuckled George.

"It was late and me and my five Mexican señoritas were stumbling our way home after winning big at the casino. We turned down an alley and were faced with a lone figure in a poncho and sombrero. 'Good evening señor' he said." The accent that Scott put on for the man in the alley was ridiculous and George fell on the floor in his merriment.

"Hey, stop laughing, it's serious." He continued with the story. "'Good evening señor. Drink this and you can live', and he offered me a tequila shot. Obviously, I accepted but there was a catch. Before handing me the shot he placed a live scorpion in the glass. The señoritas at my side were begging me not to take the challenge but, like the hero I am, I accepted. Without a moment's hesitation I drank the liquor and the scorpion fell into my mouth. The man in the alley laughed for he thought I was defeated, but then I outstretched my tongue and the scorpion walked to the tip. With a snip of its pincers it dropped to the ground and disappeared into the night. The strange man ran from the scene and I returned home victorious with my girls that adored me all the more for my bravery."

George was drunk but he could still smell a lie when he heard one. Nonetheless, for the sheer entertainment factor he let it slide.

"Well, at least the shot with the live scorpion was true. It may have come from a bar, though."

Scott laughed as he left the room and went to bed.

Shaking his head, George did the same.

CHAPTER 23

Earth
Texas
Interstate 10

Presley and Annabel docked in New Orleans during the early hours of the morning. As they departed on the back of Presley's trusty obsidian Harley-Davidson, they used the large minotaur-shaped headlight to illuminate the path forward. The great cruise liner was the largest ship in the harbour but, as they left the port, Presley slowed as he passed a smaller vessel unloading their cargo.

"What is it?" Annabel asked.

Presley was concentrating so hard that he hadn't heard Annabel's question. He watched as a small woman with a shaved head directed traffic and hurried the grunts to unload the cargo faster. The woman turned and looked towards Presley whom Annabel felt had seized up in front of her. He reached for his pistols and Annabel knew something was wrong.

"What is it? Who are they?" Annabel asked again.

Presley was brought back to the present and remembered Annabel was with him. He quickly replaced his weapons in their holsters and sped away from the group who were scrambling for their own weapons at the request of their petite leader.

"A problem for another day. I just hope that wasn't what I think they were unloading; if it was, we need to get to the others with all haste."

Driven by Presley's fright at the dock they had rushed to make as much ground as possible towards their destination. By midday they reached Texas which they had to pass through before reaching Arizona. Annabel had been sitting in silence for most of the journey, thinking about a horrific event on the cruise ship. Presley didn't know what she knew, and she hoped for her own safety that it stayed that way. The transatlantic journey was marred for Annabel by her obsession with the whip Presley had used to grant them access to the cruise liner. Every day she would wake and come up with a plan to lose Presley and make her way to the cargo hold in order to have a closer look at the item. Nevertheless, every day Presley did something she didn't expect and foiled her plans, that is until the penultimate day of their voyage. That morning she woke and formed a plan the same as every other day, unwilling to be put off by her previous failures. Luck was on her side this time, the meal the previous night had been seafood-based and Presley had more than enjoyed himself with the shrimp meal. It was only after his third bowl that his stomach began to ache and soon after he disappeared into the toilet. Annabel was yet to see her companion that morning and so she assumed he was still having issues with food poisoning. Seizing her opportunity, she rushed down to the cargo hold after a light breakfast, the salmon meal the previous evening having been both filling and correctly cooked. It took her a while to locate the beautiful bike but eventually she found it hidden between two all-terrain vehicles. When she reached the Harley her suspicions of foul play grew deeper. Still attached to the sides of the bike in their holsters were Presley's trusty firearms, Thanatos and Hades. Annabel assumed the security guard couldn't have failed to notice the illegal weaponry as they boarded a week ago, so why had he just ignored it? At the time she was still trying to figure out how they were gaining access in the first place as well as playing the role Presley asked her to perform so the firearms were far from her thoughts. Whatever Presley did with the whip completely rendered the guard useless at his job after being struck. Unable to wait any longer she moved over to the storage compartment and opened it up with the key she stole earlier on in the week. There it was, just lying beside the other objects in the storage space, thrown in as if it was any old thing. Slowly and rather apprehensively, she reached out and grasped the handle – expecting a shock or something she quickly pulled her hand away. Nevertheless, nothing out of the ordinary happened so she gripped it again and removed it from the lock box. Turning it in her hands she saw the word 'Freya' engraved in the mahogany handle.

"What're your secrets, Freya?" she asked the inanimate object.

"What're you doing down here?" came a voice.

Startled, Annabel swiftly pushed the whip behind her back and turned to see who had spotted her. She let out a large sigh of relief upon finding out that it wasn't Presley, it wasn't even a member of security. Instead, it was one of the fools she was playing water volleyball with the day previously – Luke, she suspected, though it might have been Steve.

"What're you hiding behind your back?" He was trying to get a look behind her but she kept rotating to block his view.

"None of your business. Go away!" she ordered, trying to shoo him off with one hand whilst still holding the whip hidden with the other. He wouldn't give in, though, and soon his real intentions became clear.

"Come here," he said, stepping forwards and reaching out to grab her.

"No!" Annabel spat, stumbling backwards whilst darting her head back and forth in search of help.

"I said, COME HERE!" he shouted as his fingernails dug into her outstretched arm. He pulled her closer and she tripped, dropping the whip in the process. "A whip, hey? You kinky slut."

When the rapist became distracted by the object Annabel was able to break her aggressor's grip and set herself free. She launched for the weapon and spun round to stop her approaching attacker. On the turn, she caught the man on the arm with the whip. He stopped dead still like he was frozen solid and it gave Annabel a chance to regain her composure.

"What do you think you're doing?" she screamed in his face.

"Whatever you want," he replied, monotonal.

"Leave me and jump off the ship, for all I care. Just get away from me!" she yelled.

The man that up until recently was driven on by his primal lust for her, abruptly turned and walked away.

Shaking, Annabel returned the whip to the bike storage and ran back upstairs to the main deck. She was met with a bumble of activity; something was causing a lot of commotion.

"What's happening?" she asked a passing lady.

"Some poor boy has thrown himself off the ship into the sea.

Why would someone so young even think about ending their own life?" She wept into her hands as she waddled away.

Annabel ran over to the edge where everyone was crowding and desperately scanned the sea.

"Where is he?" she gasped.

"He hasn't resurfaced since jumping. We think he's knocked himself out," a man answered.

Trembling once more, Annabel ran back to her room and returned the bike key to its rightful place. Presley woke when she did so and together they returned to the main deck to join the concerned travellers and wonder what could have driven the young man to jump. Annabel thought she knew, and a shiver ran down her back. Worse still, they never did find the body.

The bike ground to a halt and the bestial roar of the machine died away. The sudden stop in movement shook Annabel from her memory and she was returned to the present.

"Why we stopping?" she asked.

"This is the Alamo," explained Presley, "the site of a historic battle that coincides with our own mission and fate."

"Oh wow, I've heard of it but I thought it was a famous defeat that took place here." Annabel didn't see the link that Presley was referring to. "Are you implying that we're destined to lose this struggle?" she asked, a hint of panic entering her voice.

"You're correct, it was a defeat, however, the staunch defenders held out for thirteen days before being overthrown. Their fierce defence and bravery served to galvanise the rest of Texas against its Mexican dictatorship that was repressing it. Later that year, Texas won its independence from Mexico and during the decisive battle the soldiers were said to have been shouting 'Remember the Alamo'."

"So, you're saying that in order for us to win this war against Tombstone, we must first be faced with a heavy defeat?" Annabel was still unsure with what exactly Presley was suggesting.

"Dear girl, we've been faced with defeat after defeat in Sanctum ever since Dark Snake began her crusade against your planet. Not yet has Minotaur given up, however – we've still managed the odd victory to keep our hopes up, none more so than the unbreakable defence of Magellan Castle. Magellan is Sanctum's Alamo, but without the defeat, no matter what Tombstone threw at us, the castle has never fallen. A vital achievement, as under that castle is the portal to this world. So, you see, I've brought you here today to further your understanding of the war raging in Sanctum. Minotaur are losing, but if we rally behind our small successes and believe in a common goal, then together we can free Sanctum from its dictatorship and in the process protect this planet from its unknown threat."

Annabel was silent for a moment, both contemplating what she had been told but also paying respects to those who had lost their lives in the pursuit for freedom.

Once she finished reflecting, she grabbed Presley's right arm and looked up into his face, giving him a squeeze as she promised, "We won't let Sanctum fall. Let's go and regroup with the others. They need us."

They returned to the bike and set back off on their way towards Oasis. As Presley was driving along, Annabel sat behind him holding his waist, thinking about the fort they had just visited. To her, it was difficult to imagine this other world and the struggle Presley was referring to. Nevertheless, she liked to think that she knew Presley after the last few weeks of being with him, and at the fort he was not himself. Never before did she feel that her presence was really required in this whole journey, but minutes ago when she gripped his arm, she realised she was all that was keeping him going in that moment. The more she thought about it, the more she believed that the stop at the Texan fort was not for her benefit but his. Faced with unfavourable odds, he needed to reassure himself that there was a point to his trials and tribulations. The Alamo gave him hope that even from the darkest of places can come a light that will guide the way to the most unlikely of fortunes. Annabel hugged her driver tighter to show she was there for him and lifted her head up high; for the first time in a long time she seemed certain. Certain that she belonged and was not just caught up in something she shouldn't be.

"We're coming," she whispered into the howling wind.

CHAPTER 24

Sanctum
Liberterra
Trade route to Magellan Castle

"They're out there. I can sense it." Asmir narrowed his eyes to try to see through the surrounding fog.

"That's the worst part about it. We know they're there just lying in wait and there's nothing we can do about it." Alessia sniffed audibly to try to retract the fluid escaping her nose. They were standing in a large open expanse of grassland with gentle rolling hills around them, but the lack of visibility meant that it was hard to see the soldier next to you. Together, Asmir and Alessia had amassed fifty fighting warriors to go in search of whoever or whatever was interrupting supply routes in Liberterra. During the last few months Magellan Castle, the largest and best defended fort in the region, was having to cut its rations in order to compensate for the lack of deliveries. The convoys that made it to the castle told stories of assaults on the road as well as a thick suppressing fog making movement slow and cumbersome. The most interesting rumour, though, was of a monstrous figure watching from the shadows – whenever the fog cleared for a moment the menace was said to be visible for a moment before retreating back to cover. The descriptions varied, some said that it was a screamer seven foot tall, others believed it to be Butcher back from his mysterious absence and one traveller even described it as a divine saviour sent to guard those who needed protection on the road. Despite all the sightings by supply trains and merchants that arrived at Magellan Castle, Asmir and Alessia were still yet to see the phantom on the horizon during their current expedition. That wasn't particularly surprising given the thickness of the surrounding fog. The lack of visibility was causing distress in their ranks; they were being smothered into submission before any combat had even begun. The previous day saw one unnerved soldier lash out at an approaching friend who didn't make his presence known. The startled warrior pierced his comrade's armour and underlying skin with his spear. Realising his mistake, he shouted for help but, no matter how many gathered round, they could do nothing but watch as the life drained out of the gaping wound. Alessia had no choice but to command the murderer to return to the barracks, he would have been more of a hindrance than a help in his current state and the other men and women in their ranks demanded no less. Other than that incident their journey had been unhindered and without event, a fact that Asmir was grateful for but not entirely happy about. His mission was to search for and destroy the Tombstone force that was ambushing their supply routes. The longer it took to find them the longer it would be until he could return to his family and, as such, he wanted the fight over sooner rather than later.

"The cowards are most likely too scared to attack us with our current strength," Alessia said, looking to her fellow commander to gauge his thoughts.

"Are you suggesting that we split up?" Asmir didn't like the idea but felt deep down that Alessia might be right.

"I don't want to, but it might be our only option. The soldiers are growing restless and want this mission over so they can return to their loved ones." Alessia reached for her belt and unhooked her horn. "We use these. If one of us triggers the trap, then we blow the horn and the other will come to their aid."

Asmir looked at the instrument and racked his brains for another way. "Fine," he responded in his gruff voice. "Good luck."

"You too," she said softly, resting a hand on her friend's shoulder. Then her tone changed when addressing her soldiers to be more authoritative and decisive. "RIGHT, WARRIORS GEAR UP, WE'RE MOVING OUT!"

There was much hustle and bustle whilst Alessia's men and women prepared to leave. To their side, Asmir's warriors were doing the same under their commander's orders. The well organised squads were ready quickly – they had to be prepared for an attack at any time so many were already fully geared up.

Alessia took her soldiers off into the distance and soon the sound of their footsteps was consumed by the hungry mouth of the ever-present fog. The silence left when her squad had gone sent a chill up Asmir's spine. The wind suddenly picked up and began to gently whistle through the gaps between the closely grouped armoured warriors. Asmir gave the order and his soldiers moved out in formation; immediately the silence was broken by the rattling of chain mail and the thud of footsteps. As they marched, they ensured they could see the warrior in front so that they didn't get lost, it was easy to keep tabs on what was going on ahead that way. Nevertheless, with the entire concentration used to focus on the soldier ahead to ensure they stayed together, no one noticed as their number began to be depleted from behind. One by one, the soldiers at the rear of the formation were silently taken out by stealthy bandits. Their necks were cut from behind leaving them unable to call for help, and then they were lowered to the grass by their assailants to complete the soundless take down.

"I can't see anything further than your head!" the now rear most warrior called to the soldier in front.

When the woman turned to reply she saw a wide red cut on the speaker's throat. Behind him was a masked killer dressed in black flowing robes flanked by two others in similar attire.

"Bandits!" the female warrior yelled as she sliced diagonally down the masked man's body. Her blade cut through the assailant's neck and blood spurted out as he fell to the ground. Before the other bandits had time to retaliate, they were faced with armoured foes of their own. Chaos broke out. Tombstone soldiers, dressed more appropriately for battle than their assassin counterparts, came pouring over the neighbouring hills shouting obscenities as they ran.

Asmir's troops were thankful for the loud approach as it alerted them to the direction of their enemy through the fog. Steel met steel and battle broke out.

Asmir managed to slice his way through two overeager warriors with some expert swordsmanship, then he reached for his horn and gave it an almighty blow, *arhooooooo*, the instrument cut through the clamour. He hooked it over his neck and let it bounce against his chest as he dispatched a further three Tombstone soldiers. Gazing around he saw that the arrival of their enemy had coincided with the lifting of the fog; visibility was much clearer and the battle could be witnessed. His warriors were fighting well, but for every one of Tombstone that fell, another two arrived over the hill.

"Keep fighting!" he shouted to his warriors before giving the horn another blow, *arhoooooo.* Again, the device hit his chest as he quickly dropped it to deal with an approaching enemy. Asmir's arms were growing tired as the fight drew on and still Alessia had not arrived with reinforcements. He looked around and saw that his warriors were becoming slower with fatigue. A woman was too lethargic to counter an easily blockable advance and paid for it with her life; the bandit withdrew his dagger from her neck and snarled at Asmir. Taking an almighty breath, Asmir raised the horn to his lips for a final attempt to call to Alessia. The note never escaped the instrument, however, as blood seeped out of Asmir's mouth. He tried to blow anyway, but only blood spurted over the horn; choking on his own bodily fluids he collapsed to the ground and became still. The creature howled as it retracted its claw from Asmir's chest and joined its fellow monstrosities in routing the flagging Minotaur warriors. The battle was over with the arrival of Dark Snake's minions, their aggression and energy left the last remaining remnants of Asmir's force with not a chance. The slaughter that ensued was one that Sanctum had become all too accustomed to.

The bandits scavenged the dead and left quickly with their spoils, eager to reset their trap and leave the screamers to their meal.

The leathery translucent skin clung to the screamers' bones no matter how much they ate. Their claws ripped through armour and bone in order to reach the warm entrails of their kills. Their hairless heads, but for the occasional brown wisp, were buried in the stomachs of their fallen prey. A roar came from atop a neighbouring hill, but the screamers were too busy indulging to take any notice.

"Get away from them, you scum!" The man kicked one of the feasting screamers and the minion howled to alert the others. They charged the new foe but were repelled easily by the aggression and strength of their opponent. Swinging his large sword, he beheaded two and mortally wounded a third with a single movement. The dying screams and cries were a constant reminder as to how the creatures got their name. The man wasn't finished there, though, he continued his advance until the entire group of minions lay shrieking in their deaths. The battlefield grew soundless once again when he pulled his large sword out of the throat of the last enemy to put an end to its ear-splitting histrionics. He knelt over the dead monster and removed his knife from his boot. Then he got to work.

Alessia was huffing and puffing whilst trying to run in her armour. She had heard two horn blasts but ever since there was no signal from her fellow commander. Behind her the warriors were also struggling to keep up the pace. One of their number had stopped completely, the excessive exercise had led to throwing up, an action that is bad enough anyway without having to be carried out in a hot helmet.

"Almost there!" Alessia called to her soldiers to surge them on. "Our friends need us!" The commander crested the hill she had been running up. "They should be just do–" the shout turned to a whisper as she called up her deity, "by the Man in the moon." The position atop the hill gave Alessia a perfect view of the battlefield. There was but one survivor, although she knew not who they were.

"Who're you?" she shouted down into the depression.

The large figure saw her for the first time, slowly got to his feet and walked in the opposite direction.

"Stop that beast!" she panted to the warrior beside her.

The order was ignored as the warrior was just as out of breath as she was. They watched as the large figure disappeared over the horizon. Together, Alessia and her warriors walked the battlefield and made note of the dead. The first corpse she came across was Asmir's; next to his body was the horn covered in blood. She knelt down on the cool frost-covered ground and put a hand on her fallen friend's chest. "I'm sorry I wasn't fast enough," she croaked as a tear rolled down her cheek and her mouth grew taut.

His lifeless eyes gazed back in accusation that silently blamed his death on her.

"Hey, come look at this!" called one of the female warriors in her group.

Alessia closed the eyes of her fallen friend and walked over to see what her soldier had found.

The warrior was looking at a screamer that had been mutilated after its death. The leathery skin had been removed and the claws were gone, also. Upon further inspection all but a few of the screamers had been skinned and had their claws removed. Alessia walked over to where she saw the large figure rummaging earlier and sure enough there was a half-skinned screamer in the exact place.

"Who're you? And what're you doing?" she asked in the direction the beast had gone. One thing was certain. The rumoured watcher on the hills was real, as was the threat to the supply routes.

CHAPTER 25

Earth
Arizona
Oasis

The smell of bacon was wafting through the air as George and his friends made their way from their accommodation over to the breakfast hall. It had rained overnight and so the ground was a little wet. The cool air rising off the sand made the weather pleasant for once in contrast to the usual intolerable heat. George hadn't slept particularly well. He went to bed late by the time he had finished drinking with Scott, but then he opted to stay up and watch the lightning fork across the night sky afterwards. As he sat and gazed up at nature's display of strength, he remembered what his mother always used to tell him when he was scared in his youth. She would pull him close and fabricate stories of gods having mighty battles with their hammers. His fear would turn to excitement as every loud clap of thunder became a thrill and every streak of lightning sparkled in his young eyes.

"Wonder what we're doing today," remarked Cheikhou as they neared the entrance to the canteen.

"I hope we get to use a weapon today. That's when I come into my own," Alex commented, following close behind. "I once won a game of laser tag all by myself. My whole team had been eliminated and I was the only one left. They tried to rush me but lost two in their first advance."

"Nobody cares about your past stories of grandeur at kids' birthday parties," Cheikhou butted in.

"It wasn't a party, it was the regional championships with adults. I was voted 'Most promising prospect' two years running and also got the 'Player of the day' award a record five times, which is why it was clearly a mistake when you got the same award when we went paintballing."

"I chucked it at you after you didn't stop complaining, didn't I?" Cheikhou asked rhetorically.

"Rightly so," Alex finished before barging past Cheikhou to get the first choice of the breakfast on display.

George shook his head and laughed as Cheikhou mimicked Alex grabbing all the food and smashing it down his throat.

There was barely time for their opening meal to have gone down before Masood came crashing through the door in deep conversation with Cindy. They finished their talk and Masood approached the table.

"Close combat training today. Meet you over at the hay bales." Then once again he left the building.

Rosie, eager to learn, led the way to the training again like she did the previous day. When they arrived at the hay bales, they saw Masood in full flow practising on a straw dummy. He was wielding a short sword with elite skill, striking his target both fast and precisely. Upon seeing them arrive he gave the dummy a final combo before turning to welcome his students.

"Morning everyone, I see a lot of excited faces today. Swordsmanship is a great skill to possess and can be enjoyable to learn, so you're right to be eager. Before we begin, however, it's paramount that you all understand the risk of the weapons we'll be using. We've blunted weapons for you to practise but the danger is still there. I'm sure you have all noticed the feature I have on my face," he said while pointing to the scar. A few of them nodded. "I wish I could say that it was achieved in a mighty battle but that's not the case. It was caused by me and my friends messing around with weapons we thought we knew how to wield properly, but if we did in fact know then we would never have been messing around. These are not TOYS, they're WEAPONS designed to inflict pain and death."

"Cheery this morning," Cheikhou whispered to George, but he didn't hear, he was too entranced in Masood's lesson.

Masood pointed to the hay bales scattered around the practise area. "Take a seat," he told them as he approached the weapons shack and undid the lock. "I'm going to remove some weapons and show them to you in order to give you a basic understanding of the types of blades you could be faced with."

"No doubt Alex will already know them all," Cheikhou again whispered to George.

Masood emerged from the shack with a small blade and presented it to the class. "Anyone know what this is?"

"A dagger," Rosie blurted out as she leapt from her seat. Then she flushed red and sat back down. "Sorry, I didn't expect to know any."

"Correct; the smallest of the weapons I'll be displaying but by no means the least deadly. It has an average blade length of twenty-five centimetres but that makes it perfect for stealth and real hand-to-hand combat."

"Good work," Alex winked to Rosie.

"Sorry I beat you to it. You'll have to be quicker next time," Rosie replied, sticking her tongue out a little. The seconds following Rosie sat in silence wondering where the confidence to call out the answer had come from; her usual doubt and uncertainty had disappeared momentarily. *It was obvious,* she scolded herself: *'Celebrating a trivial achievement is akin to being proud when a panda correctly identifies bamboo'*. Her mother's words echoed round her head.

Masood spun the dagger round and dropped it, catching it in his other hand. "Cheik, come up here, please." He motioned for him to stand beside him.

Rather apprehensively, Cheikhou rose and walked over to the designated spot.

"OK, thanks. You're a big man and would no doubt easily overpower me in hand-to-hand combat. That's where the dagger can come in." He then put the dagger in his belt and turned to his volunteer. "Slowly come at me as if you were going to try to take me down."

Cheikhou delayed as he glanced at the dagger in his opponent's belt but then proceeded to do as he was told. Cautiously, he reached out to grab Masood but, quick as a flash, the dagger was out of Masood's belt and at Cheikhou's kidney.

"Again!" Masood ordered.

Cheikhou came once more with a different tactic this time but, again, was halted when the dagger was drawn fast and placed expertly at his throat.

"See? It's a quick draw option that offers both surprise and an advantage in close-quarter situations. Thank you." He motioned Cheikhou to sit back on a hay bale with the others whilst he disappeared back into the weapons shack. This time he emerged with two blades of similar length.

"These two are short swords," he told his audience. "Can anyone name the type of short sword in either of my hands, th–"

This time, Alex was not going to be beaten to the answer; he barely let Masood finish before he shouted, "Cutlass!"

"Yes, this one in my right hand is a cutlass. Well done. A short, slightly curved blade, usually about sixty centimetres in length. Commonly us–"

"At sea by sailors!" Alex finished for him.

"OK, you've made your point," Rosie tutted, rolling her eyes.

"Yes. Any guesses what this one's called?" he lifted his left hand to better show off the other short sword.

Alex shouted out multiple guesses but was wrong each time. Much to Cheikhou and George's amusement, each wrong answer turned him a brighter shade of pink as he grew more cross.

"Just tell us," said Cheikhou, laughing, "before Alex turns himself into an actual beef tomato."

"It's called a gladius, the Roman short sword, again, about sixty centimetres in length. These short swords are commonly used if the other hand is being taken up with a shield or, in the case of the cutlass, maybe a flintlock pistol." Masood walked back to the shack again and emerged, this time struggling with a large sword in both hands.

"FREEEEDOMMMM!" shouted George in a dodgy Scottish accent.

Everyone stared at him, utterly confused, as the reference blew straight over their heads.

"Come on… *Braveheart*," George confirmed, looked around. "No one? Unbelievable."

"I don't know what you're talking about but this is a claymore. Its weight requires two hands to hold and the blade is over a metre in length. It originated in the Scottish Highlands, so I don't see how your Irish accent had anything to do with it," Masood stated, perplexed.

"That was Sco–" George began to protest. "Oh, never mind."

"Oh yeah, baby!" bellowed Cheikhou. "That's my girl." He raced up to Masood and took the weapon. Cheikhou's superior strength allowed him to wield it with far more ease.

Masood was visibly relieved to have relinquished his hold of the weapon, "These broad swords or long swords are used when the warrior doesn't have a shield and can use both hands to wield it. As you can see, usually the stronger members of an army wield these size weapons."

In wake of such a presumptuous statement, the whole gathering decided they would need to have a go at lifting the weapon. On the one hand, Alex managed OK and Rosie struggled to do it, but George, on the other hand, couldn't lift the end of the blade from the ground for longer than a few seconds. Even with Cheikhou goading him that he was weaker than a girl, it was an impossible task.

"She's had years of experience at gymnastics to build her muscles," he feebly retorted. The excuse merited him no sympathy.

Cheikhou flexed his muscles and tensed. "I didn't get these by doing some cartwheels and Hula Hooping."

"A terrible example of gymnastics," Rosie giggled, both at Cheikhou's naïvety but also at the sight of his physique which was making her blush.

"Who wants to practise using some of these blades, then?" Masood asked in an attempt to put an end to the frivolities.

The answer was a resounding "Yes".

They started by using the blunted short swords and following Masood's lead in striking technique and movement of the feet. Then they each practised what they had learnt on their own straw soldier. Rosie showed the most promise; with her small stature and speed she was able to piece together some vicious combos.

Cheikhou grew bored fast and kept asking when he was allowed to use his 'baby' again, the name he had given the claymore.

Alex was puffing almost instantaneously with the exertion of swinging the sword and moving between his targets. He kept panting that his prowess was in ranged combat where he didn't have to move so much.

George spent a lot of his time watching Roy batter his emotions out onto the straw victim. Before the end he was excused to limit the damage to the equipment.

Yuanli had the impossible task of helping Barbara. She was far too clumsy and showed no ability whatsoever. When she wasn't dropping her sword, she was swinging wildly at the target and putting no real precision into her strikes.

After lunch they returned and undertook some one-on-one training.

Alex and Cheikhou were grouped together due to their abilities, leaving George to go with Rosie. Collectively, on the one side of the coin, George and Rosie helped each other learn and corrected each other's stance. They were gently practising and not putting any vigour behind their strikes.

Alex and Cheikhou, on the other side, were going for it. It was never a good idea putting the two of them together in an exercise such as this; however, when George tried telling Masood he just put it down to him wanting to go with his friend Cheikhou. The one sensible action that Masood *did* take was not allowing Cheikhou to have his claymore for this exercise – other than that, Masood was now learning the error of his ways. For every clash of blades the two shared there had already been four full force hits to their opponent's body. It was supposed to be a nonaggressive sparring in which you just tapped your opponent if you broke their defences. Nevertheless, Cheikhou was whacking lumps out of Alex and Alex likewise. They were being asked to calm down and ease off, but their battle-crazed minds couldn't hear the pleas of the others.

Alex showed none of the fatigue displayed whilst combatting the stationary straw man; it appeared that his desire to beat Cheikhou was what was pushing him on.

Cheikhou blocked an approach to his left side and forced Alex back when their swords clashed together. The weight of Alex's body threw him off balance and gave Cheikhou an opening. Exploiting it, he came forward and whacked Alex on the leg which brought him to one knee. Before he could drive home his advantage, though, Alex was back on his feet and somehow back on the offensive. A clever feint to the right by Alex removed Cheikhou's ability to stop a brutal blow to his left arm. It was at this point that Masood and Roy pulled Cheikhou away whilst George, Barbara and Yuanli dragged Alex back in order to stop the fighting.

"I think that's enough for today," Masood said in a hurry. "I'll clear up, you just go prepare for dinner." He needed to separate the boys from their weapons before one ended up killing the other. Reluctantly, they threw their swords to the floor which sent up a puff of dust where the sand was disturbed.

On the journey back to their accommodation the strangest thing happened. Cheikhou slowed his usual fast walk to fall back to Alex's pace and amble with him.

"You hit me with some good shots," he wheezed. "Guessing you can't feel my shots through all this?" he asked, rubbing his belly.

Alex groaned, "Ahh, no, I felt 'em. You hit pretty hard, you know. This is better for floatation than protection," he said, shaking and watching his stomach wobble.

Cheikhou roared with laughter and they walked together in silence.

"What happened there?" George looked to Rosie with his eyebrows raised.

"Maybe they've finally beaten some respect into each other," she suggested before separating off towards her room.

That night Alex didn't eat as much as usual; his body was aching too much from the sparring with Cheikhou. None of the food was wasted though because Barbara stepped up to the plate, quite literally.

"I've never seen someone put away that much beef," Rosie said in amazement as they made the short trip to Scott's bar across the hall.

When the group arrived, the bartender had to leave his conversation with Harry and Lee in order to serve the drinks.

"What're you three up to?" Yuanli joked as she received her water. Being teetotal was a big part of how she managed to remain so youthful in her advancing age.

"We were just reminiscing on our recent holiday together," Scott replied, showing he was unwilling to continue the conversation by quickly serving the next customer in line.

Yuanli went to join the two men in their dark corner of the room to find out more about their holiday.

George collected his beer and went to sit with his friends who were relaxing in a circle of armchairs.

"...you'll see tomorrow," Alex finished as George slumped into his seat.

"What is this?" George asked, having missed the start of the conversation.

"Alex thinks that he'll be the one teaching Cindy before the ranged combat lesson's finished tomorrow." Cheikhou's eyes gave George an indication of what he thought of that statement.

"He was very good at paintballing, in all fairness," Rosie added.

"Don't encourage him," pleaded Cheikhou.

"You're just jealous. You admitted *I* was the best when you corrected their mistake by giving me the 'Player of the day' medal. I showed ability with a gun that hasn't been seen since Rambo was last on the big screen."

Any respect that Cheikhou had gained for Alex throughout the day was lost after that statement and they engaged in one of their arguments that much better represented their usual relationship. After a while, Cheikhou gave up trying to reason with Alex and let him continue an anecdote about Bruce Willis personally congratulating him on winning a youths' shooting tournament.

George was saved from having to listen any further however, when Scott summoned him to follow and pulled him away from the rest of the group.

"Hey, mate. Good day?" Scott inquired whilst looking around erratically.

"Yeah," George replied slowly as he took in Scott's strange behaviour and noticed a bead of sweat running down his forehead. "Are you OK, man?"

"Yeah, yeah; all good, bud," he replied before becoming silent.

"Soooo, what do ya want?" George asked, suspicious of what was happening.

"Just wanted to chat like we did last night. It was fun, wasn't it? Two friends just talking."

"Yeah, it was goo-ood," George admitted, but cautiously again, still unsure of what was happening. "Look, are you sure you're OK, dude?"

Scott slapped his arm. "Why do you keep asking me that? How

about we have some tequila shots? I got this one the other week on my holiday I was telling you about; I want you to try it." He led George to the bar and then disappeared behind the counter before emerging with a grin and a bottle.

"Salted caramel flavour," he said, licking his lips. Without delay, Scott found two shot glasses and poured them both a taste. They knocked them back at the same time and shared an approving nod. Scott poured another and another until George had completely forgotten the strange behaviour the bartender had shown earlier.

"I'm happy we met," George slurred. "Finally, someone with good taste in alcohol," he announced, clashing his glass with Scott's and downing its contents.

"Me, too." Scott winked and slapped George on the shoulder again. "As my friend, you have my back, don't you?" Scott asked, rubbing his glass and looking at the ground.

"Of course," George promised, half in speech and half in spit due to his intoxicated state. "Why, what's up?" The question seemed familiar to George but he was too far gone to make note of the recognition.

"I made a mistake," he admitted to George. "You know, I'm not a bad man." Scott began to cry.

"Of course. Don't worry! What've you done?" George embraced his friend as he drunkenly sobbed into his chest.

Scott didn't answer, instead he exited the comforting hug and sniffed fiercely. "I shouldn't have said anything. I'll see you tomorrow," he said, then quickly departed the room.

Before George could give chase, he passed out with his head on the bar and fell into a drunken sleep.

CHAPTER 26

Earth
New Mexico
Interstate 10

The heat of the day had escaped, disappearing into the black night sky decorated with tiny illuminations of planets and stars.

Annabel pulled her cardigan tight to her body as she gazed up at the brightest of the stars. "It's amazing how beautiful the sky is without the impact of light pollution." They had pulled over to the side of the long desert highway in order to appreciate the beauty of the world around them.

"The sky's always like this in Sanctum," Presley assured her with a smile. "The technology on this planet that's gradually led to its doom isn't present in my homeland. We live simple and basic lives but, in return, have kept our relationship with our world. We care for our environment and in return it provides for us. On Earth they destroy vast swathes of forest and nature and label it 'progress' whereas in Sanctum it'd be branded a disaster. Trees release the oxygen we need to breathe and hold together the ground on which we walk and grow food. Here you'll take down the tree and complain when the air is polluted and when landslides destroy crops and homes. The careful protection of Gaia in the past by the Petrovs has meant that however much you harm your planet it was always able to recover. Now with Dark Snake using Gaia to fulfil her own personal goals, it's no longer possible for it to maintain life on Earth. I fear that if we don't stop Dark Snake soon then the people of Earth will continue to march headlong into a catastrophe that they've created for themselves."

"Even if we succeed in our goal of ending Dark Snake's tyranny, that won't be enough. Me and my friends must return to Earth and force change so that we are no longer harming our planet. It can't go on and must stop if we're to have any chance of preserving our futures." Annabel found the beautiful picture painted above more depressing than before the talk and felt a tear roll down her cheek as she looked away.

"Come on. We're both tired and in need of rest. Let's find somewhere to stay the night and finish our journey tomorrow." Presley put his strong arm around the small fragile body beside him and gave it a squeeze before guiding her back to the bike. Once they were both mounted again Presley turned the key in the ignition and the silence of the quiet desert highway was broken. The large minotaur headlight lit their way and they set off once more. It wasn't long until they arrived at a small biker bar that had accommodation available. Outside was a mix of motorbikes of different sizes and colours, although in the evening they all looked grey and black. The bikers had abandoned their vehicles anywhere outside, taking no notice of the designated spaces available. Unlike them, Presley parked in a proper spot in order to respect the owner's wishes. The board outside was supposed to read 'Bike mad', but the illuminated lights on the sign's words were failing and the sign actually flashed 'Bad', 'Bad', 'Bad'.

"That's a good omen," Annabel said apprehensively whilst pointing Presley towards the faulty electronics.

The only reply she got was a wry smile as he led the way into the building.

The cacophony of laughter, shouting and general noise died immediately as they entered the bar. Everyone stopped what they were doing and turned to look at the newcomers. The majority were men wearing sleeveless jackets that exposed their tattoo-covered arms. There was the odd woman sat on the lap of their man; one with greasy black hair near the front was whispering into her fella's ear.

Presley ignored the eyes on him and confidently walked towards the bar with an unnerved Annabel very close in tow.

"Good evening," he said to the lady behind the bar. "Two rooms for the night please, and two beers."

The barmaid parted her lips to reply and revealed a mouth showing more gum than teeth. "There's no rooms available," she whistled through the few teeth. "You'll 'ave ta go somewhere else."

Annabel turned to leave but Presley caught her arm gently. Without taking his eyes from the barmaid, he stated, "We'll still have those beers though, please. It's been a long day riding."

She gave him a vile look and spat, "We're out of beer!"

"I'll have two of whatever they're drinking, then," he asked, motioning with his head towards the bikers in the bar.

All of a sudden there was a shout from behind him, "Look, pal, you ain't welcome."

Presley turned to see who was being so unwelcoming and spotted a bald man with a nose ring making his way over to the bar. On his arm was a tattoo of a helmet pierced with a sword alongside the words 'Death' and 'Duty'. A quick analysis of the room revealed that they all sported identical tattoos.

"Is that because I'm not part of your club?" Presley mocked with an upturned lip. "That seems unfair."

The biker's stale breath wafted into Presley's face as he stood on his toes and looked up to the mountain of a man in order to retain eye contact. "Last chance," he growled, whilst reaching into his pocket and pulling out a flick knife. A quick flick of the wrist and the blade was revealed and pointed towards Presley's stomach.

"Come on, let's go!" Annabel pleaded whilst trying to pull Presley along.

George's guardian wouldn't budge, his feet were firmly planted on the ground.

"I'm thirsty and I'm sure as hell not going to let some follicle-challenged walking artwork with small man syndrome stop me quenching that thirst." His eyes narrowed, almost begging the biker to react. There were a few seconds' silence as Presley's words sunk in and the tension in the room built to a pinnacle.

"The only difference between you and me is that I have my friends."

Then all hell broke loose. Chairs screeched along the floor as the bikers rose to back up their friend and the man with the knife lunged at Presley.

It took Presley seconds to disarm his foe and crack his arm. By the time his backup arrived he was rolling on the floor desperately clutching his right arm. The sheer size of Presley enabled him to fight off the first few opponents with ease, but soon the numbers game caught up and he began receiving punches left and right.

Annabel tried to run away as soon as the fighting had begun but was blocked by the lady with the greasy black hair. "Where d'ya think ya goin', bitch?" she snarled.

Annabel screamed as she was pulled to the floor by her hair and kicked in the stomach. Coughing, she managed to look up and spit in the face of the woman assaulting her. The biker chick reeled and let go of Annabel's hair, enabling her to get back to her feet. Then the adrenaline of the moment made her reach out and grab a bottle from the table. She smashed it over the greasy-haired woman's head and watched as she fell to the floor. Everything around Annabel appeared to be in slow motion and become quiet; she stared in a daze at the woman on the floor reaching for her head, the sticky alcohol that was in the bottle congealing with the red blood pooling round her skull. The dirty fingers of the biker girl ran through her bloodstained hair and tried to put pressure on the wound as she lay moaning on the floor. Annabel snapped out of her trance and ran out of the door without looking back.

Presley noticed his companion flee but didn't feel any animosity towards her; after all, *he* had started the fight. He headbutted an overweight man with a brown bushy beard to make a path to the bar and then turned to defend himself, once again. The attacks became sluggish as they took note of the fighting prowess and sheer size Presley brought to the brawl, but there was still the odd biker who tried their luck. Once one of the larger members of the biker gang had fallen, it provided Presley a moment's respite in which to reach over the bar and get himself a beer. He twisted the cap off with ease to pour the contents into his mouth, then he threw the bottle to the side and put his hands out, motioning the bikers to come closer. "Come on, then!" he bellowed.

The unexpected surge of opponents took Presley by surprise and he became overwhelmed. The kicks and punches were beginning to hurt as they reopened wounds made by Butcher in the fight at the mansion. Presley fell to one knee and used his muscular arms to protect his face in a strong guard stance. He was unable to mount any attack of his own, now; his main focus was trying to protect himself the best he could, which at the moment was not very successful. The beat down continued until Presley was forced onto both knees; *maybe this wasn't my best idea,* he thought to himself. The punches abruptly seized and the bald man that had begun the trouble made his way through the mob with the greasy-haired woman at his side. She was covered in blood, but the wound had stopped bleeding and she seemed like she would pull through.

"The little bitch that was with ya tried to kill my Sharon!" he growled, whilst still holding his right arm and wincing. "For that, I'm gunna kill ya!" he promised, with a malicious grin. Groaning as he released hold on his injured right arm, he pulled out his flick-knife once more. Slowly he approached Presley and looked down at him. "Who's the little man now?" He didn't wait for an answer before plunging the knife towards his victim. The blade was destined for the heart, but Presley threw his right arm across his chest and felt the cool steel penetrate his forearm.

Presley roared in anguish like a bear caught in a trap.

"Now who's in pain?" the bald biker taunted. "Whose arm hurts now? Now who's in pain?" he repeatedly shouted into his face. The biker pulled back his left arm ready to stab him again when suddenly the door burst open and gunshots rang through the bar.

Annabel had retrieved Hades and Thanatos from the bike and returned to save her companion. She fired again, closing her eyes as she aimed the pistols at the ceiling. She shook with the recoil and one of the lights flickered out after being struck with a bullet.

Quick as a flash, Presley got to his feet and bowled over anyone that was in his way, which included the man who had just stabbed him. He ran to the door and pushed Annabel outside. "Well done. We need to get moving."

Together they ran to their bike which Presley was amazed to see Annabel had started. "Brilliant stuff!" he complimented her.

"Your arm…" Annabel reminded him as a warning that perhaps he wouldn't be able to drive.

He ignored her and jumped on anyway.

She followed his lead and they quickly accelerated off away from the bar.

"We need to put some distance between us and them!" Presley

yelled over the sound of the engine.

"It's OK!" she yelled back. "I slashed their tyres!" she giggled into his ear.

"Incredible!" Presley shouted.

"Let's just get to the others!" Annabel added, still shouting over the noise of the bike and still shaking from the adrenaline of the fight. "I've had enough of our joint adventures for the time being."

Presley nodded in agreement, accepting the all-night ride that would follow the decision. "I got my beer, anyway," he said, sitting tall.

CHAPTER 27

Earth
Arizona
Oasis

A percussion band with one hundred cymbals and twice as many drums woke George after his drinks with Scott the night before, or at least that's how he felt. Groaning and moaning, he kept his eyes closed and rubbed his head. He tried to move but his legs had seized up, having fallen asleep still seated on the bar stool. Pushing up with his arms, he managed to elevate himself enough to get his backside off the seat, however, as soon as he tried to put his weight onto his legs they crumbled under him and he fell into a heap on the floor, hitting his head on the bar in the process.

An hour later he had regained consciousness and the band's crashing sounds returned to his temple. Light was beginning to filter through the windows of the large wooden community building and the smell of breakfast prompted his nasal senses to kick in. Before attempting to shift himself once more and ending up in a pile, he tried to wiggle his toes and shake his legs to ensure they would be able to take his weight. Confident that they were up to the task, he cautiously brought himself to a standing position and leaned on the bar. Using a knuckle on his right hand, he wiped his eyes to try to force them into action. When he was happy they were ready for the day, he opened them and looked around. The bar was a mess, sticky with spilt alcohol and empty bottles. Scott would have to clear that up when he emerged from his room later. George pivoted round ready to go to his accommodation to change but was forced back into a stool in shock at who he saw. After frantically rubbing his eyes to make sure he wasn't imagining it, he reopened them and stared again, *Phew*, he thought, *I'm more drunk still than I realised.* Smiling, he began to stagger towards the door.

"Always *keen* to run away from your problems, aren't you, Mr Keen?"

George stopped in his tracks; his eyes hadn't deceived him after all. The use of his surname to mock him usually infuriated him, however, on this occasion it brought the broadest smile to his face. Hangover forgotten in a heartbeat, he swivelled round with outstanding agility and threw himself in the direction of the voice.

"Arhhh, watch the arm, lad. It's a little tender," Presley warned, embracing George with his left arm, almost crushing him in the anaconda-like grip. The tight hug was a result of both missing George and also an attempt to keep him away from the stab wound in his right arm that Yuanli had stitched up for him upon his arrival.

George began to weep as all the worry and fear he had harboured for his guardian in the past few weeks ebbed out and came to the forefront of his emotions. "I thought you were dead," George sobbed into Presley's large chest.

The large man winced and moved George slightly away from his aching body. "Mind the ribs, as well, it's not been an easy couple of weeks. *Dead?* Never! It'll take a lot more than they've thrown at me to take me down!" Presley thundered in his deep authoritative voice. He pulled himself over a bar stool and sat back as George embarked on a long monologue of every event that had unfolded since the two last met. In his excitement, it was sometimes hard to discern what George was rambling on about, but it didn't matter too much as Presley had already been debriefed properly when he was being bandaged up by Yuanli.

George was about to collapse from oxygen deprivation, having not come up for air for some time, when suddenly his eyes bulged and he shouted, "ANNABEL! Is she with you?"

It was now Presley's turn to detail the highlights of his past few weeks and for George to sit back and listen.

"Annabel's Angels. Oh dear, what next – Presley's Priests?" George joked.

"All of that action and you focus on the water volleyball team name. Did you miss the part about us taking on an entire bar of angry bikers?" Presley seemed genuinely offended.

Chuckling to himself, George got up and slapped his guardian on his arm, taking care to make sure it was the left one. "It's great to see you. I need to go and freshen up though, before I see Annabel." George left the hall and let the door slam behind him. On his walk back to his room he thought about all that Presley had told him. It seemed like Annabel had really held her own on their adventures; *Jacob would've been proud,* he couldn't help but think. Nearing his accommodation, he was swiftly stopped in his tracks when a girl came running out of the communal washroom screaming, "Sorry! I'm so sorry. Sorry!"

Equally horrifying shrieks could be heard coming from the wash block.

George gazed in awe at the girl apologising profusely. It was a familiar face, still pretty but somewhat worn. The weeks that had passed had clearly taken their toll on Annabel. She was wearing quite tatty clothes and her face was tainted with specks of dirt and mud. George could see immediately that the girl he grew up with was gone, replaced by a more mature woman who now understood that life isn't all about looks. The door to the showers burst open and Alex ran across the sand covering as much of his large body as he could with one of the towels provided. Water was dripping from his arms and legs which explained to George what he had just witnessed unfolding. He burst out laughing and ruined his reunion with his returning friend.

Annabel turned around and saw him creasing up with merriment. It was as if they had never been apart as she stormed up to him and yelled, "It isn't funny!"

"Bet you're scarred for life!" George retorted, choking on his laughter.

"Actually, he had more to offer than *you* probably ever would," Annabel replied as means of a comeback, but then she shook her head and saw the funny side of the incident. Within moments of the two being back together they were laughing and acting as if nothing was amiss.

Cheikhou emerged from his accommodation showing off his booming laugh; he had just received the story from Alex who was retelling his ordeal.

"Bet you're glad you arrived in time for that," he teased Annabel before heading to the washroom himself.

George fist bumped his friend as he passed her and offered to show Annabel around Oasis once they were both washed and dressed. The two of them were late for breakfast by the time George had finished the tour but still arrived early enough to get a bite to eat before the day's training began. The conversation at first was more of a lecture as Annabel was informed of all the information she had missed since the night she was kidnapped. She had been told brief parts of their mission by Presley on their journey but the talk at breakfast filled in the gaps in her understanding. As soon as Annabel had caught up, everyone was desperate to talk to both her and Presley to hear what happened on their journey; that is, all but Alex who sat in silence, still shocked from the incident earlier.

"Don't worry, these things happen," Rosie assured him, attempting to cheer him up and play down the incident.

"I was *completely* naked! She walked in whilst I was scrubbing my..." he shivered and stopped talking as he remembered.

"So? It's a communal *wash*room; the rest of us all just get on with it. Stop being so body shy."

"It's OK for *you*, no one has a problem with seeing you naked. Imagine their horror walking in on *me*. It's like seeing Porky Pig bathing – 'De di de, that's all, folks!'" Alex chanted, impersonating the stuttering cartoon pig.

Rosie giggled at the spot-on impersonation. "I didn't think you got embarrassed?" she said as if asking a question. "You always seem so confident. It's something I really envy from you," Rosie admitted, looking at the floor and letting her hair cover her face.

Alex noticed Rosie retracting into herself. "'Seem so confident'? I might talk the talk, but… OK, yes, I can walk the walk, too, but you're amazing. There's loads that you can do almost as well as me, if not better. I mean, look at the horse riding…"

Rosie nodded and smiled at the memory of Alex's struggles with the horse.

"See? You were a close second that day, weren't you?" Alex grinned.

Rosie hit his arm prompting a groan of pain. "Oh, sorry, that's where Cheik hit you with the sword, isn't it?" She began to rub it better with a soft touch.

Alex stared like a deer in headlights as his breathing grew laboured at Rosie's touch. He pulled away and rubbed the wound himself. "I-it's OK, it f-feels fine," Alex stammered in his fluster.

Rosie made note of the repellent signs from her touch and sighed, "Well, you have nothing to worry about, anyway. I'm sure Annabel didn't mind."

The care showed by Rosie made his earlier troubles disappear instantly, however, now he faced a new fear, one he hadn't experienced before. In search of distraction to allow himself time to gather his thoughts, he reached for a couple more boiled eggs.

Before he could eat them, though, Cindy walked in and announced that the ranged combat training would start in five minutes and that they must all start to make their way to the designated area.

Together they walked to the targets, listening to Alex boast about how this was his time to shine. Rosie managed to quieten him when she tapped him on the shoulder and handed him a boiled egg she had sneaked out earlier after seeing how disappointed he was when having to leave his breakfast early.

"Fanksh," he said through a mouthful.

The group wasn't waiting for long before Cindy arrived with the guardians, ready to start.

"Where has Cheik's man gone?" Annabel whispered as they approached.

George shot a quick look at his friend to make sure he wasn't listening. "Carlton got poisoned. He's receiving medical attention in Sanctum."

Annabel gasped in horror but managed to do it quietly enough so that only Rosie heard and Cheikhou didn't realise what they were talking about.

"Morning," Cindy welcomed them. She looked so young and angelic no matter the amount of stress or sleep deprivation she was going through. "Pretty straightforward, really. Over the coming months we'll be practising with an array of ranged weapons, from throwing axes to guns. Today we'll be practising with tomahawks, a type of throwing axe."

This revelation was met with joy and excitement from all but Alex who realised that his boastfulness and overconfidence would now count for naught with the introduction of tomahawks in place of guns. He swallowed loudly as Cheikhou turned to him and boomed, "Come on then, big boy, show us how it's done!"

There was no way out for Alex at this point, it was put up or shut up and he wasn't used to having to do the latter. Alex took a deep breath and a few steps forward until he was in line with Cindy.

She handed him his projectile and told him to watch to see the correct technique. Cindy demonstrated slowly. "First, put one foot in front of the other; you want the opposite foot to the arm you're throwing with, at the front. Like so."

Alex mirrored her stance as they were both right-handed and then waited for the next instruction. "OK, good. Now, when you bring your arm forward to throw you want to release the tomahawk when it's roughly level with your ear. Aim. Pull back. Then let it slide." Cindy released the weapon and it spun straight into the face of a waiting straw man. "You only want the tomahawk to rotate one time in the air for maximum power and accuracy."

The group clapped at the perfect throw and then waited eagerly for Alex to have a go. It seemed like an eternity as Alex kept adjusting his feet and practising bringing his arm forward to see where he would release the weapon. Clouds were forming over the nearby rock outcrops, they were black and full of promise of an afternoon downpour. The opaque blanket covered the sun briefly which immediately made the temperature drop.

Rosie crossed her arms to try to retain warmth, her fingers already knotted wishing Alex good luck on his throw.

Cheikhou was about to call out when Alex followed through with his swinging arm and the tomahawk began its flight. Everyone was silent as it spun through the air. It narrowly completed a full rotation before wedging into the straw target's chest.

Rosie couldn't contain her excitement as she squealed with joy.

Alex turned slowly with a wide grin on his face, nodding his head, and with arms outstretched, he cockily said, "My yard."

As the day wore on and the rain began to fall it became apparent that Alex had beginner's luck on his initial throw; he couldn't replicate his accuracy and his tomahawks kept hitting nonlethal areas such as the leg or arm.

Annabel was hopeless, failing to hit a single target. Her arm was too weak to get any real force into her throws, either.

Cheikhou was very similar to Alex in that he couldn't hit lethal areas, however, they differed on the fact that his throws had enough power to knock the straw men over and even go straight through their weakly constructed arms.

George moaned as his arms became sore after a short while of throwing, he was once again shown up by the superior fitness of Rosie who continually hit her targets without complaining of aching at all.

"How're you so good at everything?" George moaned.

He went unanswered for a while whilst Rosie lined up her throw, not wishing to jinx her good luck; however, when the tomahawk landed in the gut of the target she answered him. "Mainly concentration. However, recently I've discovered that a little self-belief goes a long way, too. You probably need more of both."

The session concluded when Barbara accidentally released her tomahawk backwards as she was winding her arm up. The projectile narrowly missed Presley who was strolling over to join their group.

"Not so happy I'm back?" he joked as he luckily saw the funny side and was untouched.

Even so, she was apologising the whole journey back to their warm accommodations. No one was worried about sharing the communal washroom that night as they were all desperate to change out of their soaked clothes and into their dry evening attire.

Rosie was happy to have Annabel back, she loved both Barbara and Yuanli, but having someone her own age to share her room with was more appealing. She was still getting changed when she noticed Annabel sitting on the bed waiting. "You ready? No make-up or anything?"

Annabel jumped up and looked in the mirror. "Why, do you think I need it?"

Rosie quickly backtracked, "No, no; it's just I thought you were more…"

Annabel waited with raised eyebrows and outstretched neck. "Well? More what?" Then she smiled, seeing the stress in Rosie's face. "No, you're right. I used to love the stuff. It's just over the past few weeks I've come to... not rely so heavily on it, and I've felt good."

Rosie tucked some of Annabel's hair behind her ear. "You look great – natural and still beautiful."

Annabel smiled then frowned. "On the topic of make-up, I thought you went without? I can't remember you wearing it before."

The light pink blusher on Rosie's face was illuminated with a real blush. "I thought I'd try something different. I always think you look amazing, and boys can't take their eyes off you, so I wanted to try it out. Now you've gone natural."

Annabel noticed her friend clutch her arm and bend her knees. "First off, you're actually one of my main inspirations for wanting to go natural so don't ever feel *you* should be more like *me*."

Rosie waved away Annabel's compliment. "I wish I saw what others did in me."

Annabel shook her head in disappointment. "About time you do, sis, but *secondly*, who's this boy you want looking at you, then?" she laughed as Rosie smiled at the thought of her crush.

"Oh, it's nothing, I didn't mean it like that," Rosie lied.

Annabel stared at her friend until she cracked under the glare.

"It's nothing. I don't think he likes me that way, anyway," Rosie said, sat on the bed with her shoulders slumped. Her lip started quivering and her eyes brimmed with tears.

Annabel rushed into the toilet to grab a tissue and sprinted back to the bed. "No, girl, we don't do that. Tears and make-up are a no go. Tell me who you think's stupid enough to not want you."

Rosie took the tissue and dabbed her eyes, removing some make-up in the process. "I rubbed his arm and he pulled away. He was repulsed by my touch."

Annabel clasped her friend's hand. "I doubt that very much."

Rosie nodded. "He started breathing funny and got all weird – I was only apologising for hitting his hurt arm. Then he wanted to just eat and not talk; I mean, I know Alex likes his food, but–"

Annabel was laughing which stopped Rosie in her tracks.

"It's not funny," Rosie said in disbelief her friend could be so cruel.

"Girl. He was nervous. *You* made him nervous. He likes you,"

Annabel said, chuckling once more.

Rosie composed herself and asked, "You think?"

Annabel smiled and pulled her friend back into the bathroom. "I know so. The guy lacks friends. He probably isn't used to anyone being nice to him, but I promise you, someone as hot as you? Forget it, he's probably putting make-up on for *you*." Then she handed her back the mascara to replace that which she'd removed. "Come on, let's see how flustered you can make him."

The aromas were intoxicating that night as they entered the canteen. A strong smell of garlic was most prominent but there were also hints of tomato and pungent cheeses. It seemed the chefs were putting on a special celebratory meal in honour of Presley and Annabel's safe arrival.

Annabel made a special point of getting seated before Rosie arrived. When her friend walked in, she analysed Alex's reaction to see if her theory was correct.

Rosie sat down and tucked her chair in. "Well?" she asked.

Annabel shook her head. "It's bad."

Rosie deflated from the tall confident figure that glided in.

"The potato on his fork fell out his gaping mouth. Now he's trying to cover the stain." Annabel tried to cover her laugh with a hand.

Rosie regained her previous majesty as she looked over and stifled her own excited giggle.

When the food had been devoured they once again retired to Scott's bar to unwind for the day.

George was licking his lips, still savouring the flavour of his meal on the journey to get his drinks, when Roy grabbed his arm and pulled him away from his friends.

"What're you doing?" George protested quietly, not wanting to draw too much attention.

Roy released the arm and apologised for the kidnapping, "Sorry, I just needed to speak to you before you enjoyed your night too much." They shared a look that confirmed he meant 'got too drunk', by what he had just said.

"What is it?" George was intrigued now.

"It's about Scott. You seem to have a good relationship with him. Correct?"

We both enjoy our drink, George thought. "We have shared interests," he replied.

"OK. That's great. I hear he went to Mexico recently. I need you to find out what for."

"It was a holiday. He spent most of his time tequila testing and recovering," George laughed.

"That's what he's telling people, but we don't think that's the truth of it," Roy admitted, looking concerned.

"We? What's going on?" George was becoming confused.

"Yuanli's been talking to Scott and his cronies, Harry and Lee, about what they did on their holiday exactly, however, they're avoiding her and keep changing the story. Don't push too hard but, over the coming months, see if you can gradually earn his trust and find out what they *really* did."

"I thought he went alone," George said. "He didn't mention Harry or Lee." Then a memory came to him of the night before. Scott was apologising for something but never said what. George didn't want to worsen Scott's current status though, so he decided to keep the strange encounter to himself before he knew more. "OK. I'll see what I can do," George agreed as means of dismissal.

Roy nodded, saying, "Anything you find out tell me or Yuanli," before dismissing him to rejoin his friends.

George had only just reached the bar when his arm was once again tugged. Huffing, he turned and saw Annabel looking slightly distressed.

"I need you to come with me," she pleaded.

He was about to argue his case to at least be allowed to get a drink first, but after years of friendship with Annabel he knew this face to be serious. Wordlessly, he left the bar and followed her out of the large wooden building. The rain had ceased and the star-spangled sky promised a beautiful evening.

"What is it?" George inquired, still slightly annoyed he was yet to get a drink.

"It's about Presley. I think he's hiding something," Annabel whispered.

George's thirst disappeared as he swallowed what Annabel had just revealed.

CHAPTER 28

Earth
Arizona
Oasis

"I don't like the idea of going through his stuff. What if we're caught?" George had agreed to go with Annabel at first but with each step he took he regretted the decision a little more.

"Don't worry. Everyone's having a good time at Scott's bar. Presley won't be back for hours, he has so much catching up to do with the other guardians. Trust me."

George looked into those beautiful crystal blue eyes and, as hard as he tried, he couldn't say no.

"OK, OK. We best be quick, though," George said, caving in and giving Annabel a light push to keep moving.

"Where're we going?" George whispered when they turned away from the accommodation and towards the exit.

As means of a response, Annabel put her finger to her lips and motioned for him to keep following in silence. A short walk later she stopped next to Presley's obsidian motorcycle and tried to open the storage compartment. It made a clunking noise when the lock denied her entry.

"He isn't going to have left his bike unlocked, is he? Come on. We're going to get caught," George warned, turning to walk away.

Annabel coughed to regain his attention and jangled a set of keys in his face.

"Please tell me those aren't... Oh God." He could only watch on as she opened the storage with the stolen keys. The mischievous smile on her face disappeared almost instantaneously as the opened compartment revealed an empty void.

"It's not here," she moaned in disbelief.

"That's because you're imagining things. Of course he isn't

hiding anything. He's the leader of Minotaur. He's bound to do things you don't understand. Let's return to the group and pretend we never left." George thought he had persuaded her as she locked the bike's storage back up and began to amble back towards the large wooden building. Nevertheless, it was evident she had a different destination in mind when she took a sudden turn and began to walk towards the accommodation huts.

"No. I'm drawing the line. There's no chance I'm raiding the apartment of the scariest man I know." To emphasise his point, he stomped his left leg down and crossed his arms in resistance.

"Look under the bed," Annabel ordered as she placed the bike keys back on their hook.

"I can't believe I'm rummaging around Presley's room," George admitted, shaking his head in disbelief. The search under the bed revealed only dust, stray hairs and one very scary-looking spider. George scrambled back quickly due to a quick bout of arachnophobia brought on by the eight hairy legs and countless eyes staring back at him. He was going to protest his case to Annabel once more, but when he turned to make his objection he saw how desperately Annabel was searching and convinced himself she wouldn't be so worried if nothing was amiss. In the past few weeks, she had spent a great deal of time with his guardian and perhaps knew more about Presley than even George knew. Most of his life he thought the mountain of a man was just a football coach bully, it was only recently that he found out about the massive double life he was leading. A sudden belief in Annabel's cause led him to ask a question that he should have asked from the beginning. "What exactly are we looking for?"

"A whip," she replied quickly, concentrating on her search.

"A whip? Why would you think that means he's hiding something?" George asked, confused. Annabel stopped her frantic searching and her shoulders slumped. When she turned to face her friend she had tears pouring down her face.

George lunged forward and embraced Annabel in a tight hug. "Hey. What's wrong? What happened?"

Through tears, Annabel began telling the strange story of how the whip seemed to grant them access to the cruise ship and the sharp pain she felt when she saw it being used. Then she moved on to the reason for her relentless tears. She believed that she somehow forced a young man to commit suicide with the whip.

"I'm a murderer, George. I forced him to take his own life. He had to do what I told him when I held the whip, it's the only explanation. I had my suspicions, but I used it anyway knowing the possible consequences," she wailed.

"Incredible," George breathed, completely out of context with the situation.

Annabel looked up at him and slapped his face. "How dare you!" she screamed as she slapped him again.

"No. You don't understand. It's Freya. It *has* to be," he said in amazement.

"What're you on about? Did you hear what I said? I'm a murderer." Annabel had stopped crying now, she was growing angrier with her friend who was so blatantly ignoring her confession.

"Presley has Freya. His father never gave it up. It's one of the weapons that's supposed to be in Jedrok."

Annabel thought back to the breakfast when she was bombarded with information about their mission. She remembered when the legendary weapon of Johnnie Lang was mentioned but the sheer volume of information meant she didn't make the link to Presley's whip. This, added with the fact that Presley was from Sanctum, clicked into place to mean only one thing. Johnnie passed his weapon down to his warrior son, Presley, and put a fake in Jedrok when he was called to Dreadnoque.

"What're you doing in here?" came a deep authoritative voice from the doorway.

It was Presley; they had been caught.

George was intending to make up an excuse but Annabel was done with the secrets.

"We know you have Freya and we know you used it on us!" Annabel shouted without fear of consequence.

"Wait, what?" George looked at his friend with eyebrows raised, he was completely confused now.

"You truly are brilliant, Annabel. You've amazed me over the past weeks. Come with me to the others, I have a confession to make," Presley said calmly.

Surprised they were not in major trouble, George began to stumble awestruck towards the door.

"Second drawer down next to the bed," Presley instructed George.

He looked where his guardian indicated and found the whip. He passed it to Presley and they walked together back to the group.

The door to the large wooden building slammed shut and the chatter over towards the bar and on the settees died down as everyone looked at the newcomers.

"Can I have your attention, please?" Presley boomed. It was an unnecessary request as everyone was already looking over at the large man wielding a whip. "I've been keeping a terrible secret from you all. A secret that has bound all your fates to this near hopeless mission."

No one seemed to understand what was happening which made George happier in his confusion. Annabel was the exception; she was standing with a smile on her face that George used to see when she solved a problem in maths class before anyone else or understood a piece of poetry the other students were struggling to get to grips with.

"I have in my hand Freya, the enchanted weapon of my father, Johnnie Lang. As you all know it gives the wielder the ability to control any that they strike with it. It was supposed to be in Jedrok with the other weapons infused with Gaia's power." He proceeded to use the whip to point towards the rock in the centre of the room.

"How's this bad?" Alex shouted out. "We have one of the powerful weapons. Who cares you kept it a secret from us?"

Annabel took this as her cue to step forward and explain Presley's betrayal. "Who here has thought about turning back?"

No one put their hand up.

"Who here wishes that they never had to leave their safe, previous life?"

No answer.

"Finally, what are our chances of success in this mission? Very low, is the answer. We're all most likely going to die, but we keep going – why?"

No one could answer.

"It's because we have no choice. Presley used that whip on us and sealed our fates to that of the mission. We can't turn back if we wish to. He's bewitched us to the mission until we're parted from our duty by our deaths."

"It's true," Presley admitted, ashamed. "When you chose your doors back at Roy's Antiquities Store I was waiting on the other side to bind you to your choice with Freya. Yuanli and Barbs, you two were put through the same process with poor Carlton who's already paid for my act by nearly dying. The only ones of us here of our own free will are Roy and I along with everyone you have met here in the States."

There was a silence as the admission settled across the room.

"We need you, however, it has to be your choice." Presley then systematically went round the room and struck everyone he had enchanted with the whip once more, not hard but a light tap, enough to break the spell. No longer bound to the whip they were free to do as they wished.

"No. He hasn't made us do anything," George piped up. "All he's done is give us the bravery and single-mindedness to achieve what we had already agreed to do. We committed to the cause when we chose our doors in the final task. *Semitasalvatoris*, 'The path of the Saviour' is the route we all picked. *We* agreed to this."

"*Semita salvatoris*, baby!" Cheikhou cried out in support of George and Presley.

"*Semita salvatoris!*" Alex bellowed, not wanting to be outdone by Cheikhou's bravery.

Rosie grabbed Alex's hand and rose to her feet. "*Semita salvatoris*."

Yuanli and Barbara were inspired by those they were guardians for and repeated the phrase themselves. Soon the whole building was aligned in chanting, "*Semita salvatoris*, *Semita salvatoris*, *Semita salvatoris*," rhythmically.

"We are with you by our own choice," George confirmed to Presley with a pat on the shoulder.

"The question is, are you with us?" he asked Annabel.

She was not so sure; she missed Jacob and wanted to go back to him.

"I wouldn't have made it here without you," Presley admitted. "You gave these people their freedom back. Help us give the people of Sanctum theirs."

She was undone by the love and unity of the group in the room. She had a new family now and she would be damned if she let them down. The nod of her head was met with a great cheer from everyone.

"Free drinks all round!" announced Scott, unfazed by the fact that the drinks were always free.

Harry and Lee shook their heads and muttered angrily to each other before departing the building quickly. Their Tombstone contacts must be informed that Presley was in possession of one of the weapons supposedly stored in Jedrok.

CHAPTER 29

Earth
Arizona
The petrified forest

Yuanli gazed in awe at the orange inferno slowly rising over the horizon. The spectacular sight of the sun bringing the first light into what had been a very dark and cold night was just what she needed in order to stay awake. Even wrapped in her black jacket, Yuanli was unable to remain warm. Cindy had not provided clothing back at Oasis suitable for the inexplicable plummet in temperature recently, it was cold like Arizona hadn't seen for years. Dark heavy bags underlined Yuanli's aching eyes, it had been a long night's ride whilst the rest of her group slept snug in their beds. The evening's shenanigans had ended with everyone being brought closer together; it was a make-or-break moment for the small Minotaur contingent, but George's speech ensured the group was aligned more than ever. Whilst Scott was pouring the drinks and the joy in the room was palpable, it didn't escape Roy or Yuanli's attention that Harry and Lee were very swift to leave and took no part in the merriment. It was Yuanli's idea, supported by Roy, that she should follow them and report back what she saw. Rosie's guardian didn't, however, expect to be riding through the night on one of Masood's horses in pursuit of the two suspicious characters. Nevertheless, the task required her to do so which is what had brought her to watching the sun mark the start of a new day. Yuanli was keeping a healthy distance from the duo in order to remain hidden – if she was spotted then the whole plan would dissolve. Immediately following their exit from the large wooden building at the heart of Oasis, they rushed to the stables and each acquired themselves a horse for their journey. Peculiarly, their mounts were already tacked up as if their trip had been preplanned. The time it took Yuanli to then prepare her horse for the pursuit allowed for the gap required to remain unseen. Unsure on how long she would be riding, she set off tracking her targets. The duo rode without rest through the desert and onto a small road. Every time Yuanli thought they were coming to a halt it turned out they were just checking co-ordinates and changing direction slightly. Yuanli was beginning to rock in her saddle as sleep came for her when the sun breached the horizon and forced her back awake. Squinting to protect her eyes from the morning rays, she saw Harry follow Lee off the road and onto a rough unbeaten track. In the darkness of night it had been easier for Yuanli to remain hidden, nevertheless, now that day was breaking her job would become twice as hard, which is why she was leaving a little extra space. With the gap between them now more to Yuanli's liking, she patted her horse to encourage it to slowly continue the chase stalking from shadow to shadow. On the final stretch down the dusty road, she needed to cover her eyes as the full strength of the sun poured over the horizon.

"Where're you going?" she rhetorically asked the unsuspecting couple ahead of her as she turned her mount down the same unbeaten path they had taken. As she continued her journey, she noticed what looked like logs just randomly lying in the middle of the desert as she rode. The introduction of the logs coincided with further grass breaking up the previously sandy ground. After ten minutes of riding off-road she was surrounded by patches of grassland as opposed to an endless desert.

Harry and Lee stopped next to a large pile of logs and dismounted.

Lee looked around to ensure they weren't being followed and only just missed Yuanli as she hid herself behind an outcrop of rock.

She jumped from her horse and tethered it to a leafless tree out of sight. Leaving her mount behind, she continued on foot, ducking and diving between boulders and large logs. She was just out of audible range and was looking for a place to get closer when a third rider arrived and began talking to Harry and Lee. Yuanli knew she needed to get closer to hear what was being said but was also very wary of the risk of being caught. Nonetheless, she convinced herself that the conversation was too important to miss so she took a chance and rolled in the direction of a lone log between her and her targets.

The roll was timed to perfection and she avoided detection whilst managing to reach an audible range. When she leant against the log, she realised that the bark was not in fact bark at all. It felt like stone, not wood. The hard piece of timber was polar to what she expected; in place of the soft and bouncy bark she felt a smooth and shiny surface. *Petrified wood*, she thought to herself. She recalled seeing how it had formed on a documentary once, the organic remains are forced out of the wood and replaced with minerals via a process of mineralization. As fascinating as her surroundings were, she had to concentrate on the mission and try to figure out what Harry and Lee were up to. Yuanli peeped over the petrified wood and looked at the third rider for the first time properly. *Odd choice of clothing*, she supposed as she analysed the jet-black trench coat. Straining, she just about made out what was being said.

"The whip? You're sure?" the new arrival asked. He briefly gazed in Yuanli's direction but soon returned his glare to the duo he came to meet.

Harry was restless and clearly uneasy in the presence of their current company, "Yes, Pres–"

"Speak up! We're alone, are we not?" the man barked.

"Presley has it," Harry repeated, louder this time.

Thanks, Yuanli thought, *you might not be as alone as you think, though.*

"You need to strike. Some of the guardians are becoming suspicious," Lee demanded in a moment of bravery.

The man in the trench coat rotated with speed and grabbed Lee by the throat.

Yuanli saw his face for the first time. He wore a wolf mask with unkempt, filthy red hair sprouting from the scalp and running down his upper back.

Blood-red beads stared into Lee's watering eyes as he choked his victim. "Butcher and Amazon are on their way. Be patient. The attack will come soon when all's in place." He threw Lee back down and watched in displeasure as his victim coughed and sputtered to try to regain his breath.

Yuanli had to look away from the violence, the scene was too distressing to watch, even in the knowledge that Lee was aligned with Tombstone.

"Who are you?" Harry shouted at the third rider whilst helping his friend to his feet. "How do we know we can trust you?"

The masked man evaded the first question and elected instead to answer the second. "Without me you would've failed the theft in Mexico. Question me again and I'll personally ensure Butcher finds out about your disobedience."

Harry decided against doubting the authority of the third rider again, remaining silent instead.

"The attack on Oasis will come soon. You must be ready. In the meantime, deal with these suspicious guardians; we can't have your cover blown!" the masked man ordered. "Be ready!" he growled a final time before riding off into the rising sun.

"Asshole!" Lee spat at the retreating figure whilst still wheezing.

"Come on, we need to get back," Harry instructed, helping his friend back to his horse.

Yuanli took this as her cue to leave and slowly sneaked back to her horse. When she reached her mount, she realised that Harry and Lee would be passing her in order to return back. With nowhere to hide, she began to panic as she heard their voices grow closer.

"Scott will come through," Harry said in answer to a question Yuanli hadn't heard. "He likes his drink and the boy does, too; that's all it is. It could've been a perfect friendship in different circumstances." They both laughed at a joke unknown to her. Their voices were very close now, they were just the other side of the outcrop of rock she was hiding behind.

She slowly began riding round the rock counterclockwise so she would come out behind them again and remain unseen. Miraculously it worked, and they passed her continuing to chat.

As the duo and their words faded into the distance, the final remark she heard was, "…As good as dead."

The betrayal was beyond doubt now, Yuanli had to get back and warn the others. Oasis was corrupted – three of their number were loyal to Tombstone and had their minds set on Earth's downfall. In the importance of the moment and with the buzzing of activity in her head, Yuanli didn't hear the warning hisses. She urged her horse forward and the gelding reared up, throwing her from the seat.

Now level with the ground she could see the snake with its fangs buried deep in the horse's rear leg. The distinctive diamond-shaped markings on the body and the large head were all dead giveaways that the snake in question was a western diamondback rattlesnake.

Yuanli knew that the serpent had the most effective venom delivery system of all snakes, and her horse would be in trouble if it didn't receive medical attention. The tail was rattling aggressively as the snake released its grip and formed its defensive shape ready to strike again. Yuanli grabbed her gelding by its reins and pulled it away from the danger. The injured horse was not easy to control but Yuanli managed to calm it enough for it to trust she was trying to help it. The only way to arrive back to Oasis in time for no one to know she had gone would be to ride the horse in its weakened state, most likely killing it in its efforts. Yuanli stood next to her gelding and patted it on its nose. "I can't make you do that," she said out loud as she made the decision. Then she grabbed the reins and began the slow and gruelling long walk back to base.

After six hours of walking, Yuanli sat down to rest. The sun was at its peak in the sky; for a normal day in Arizona it would have been fatal to undertake such a long walk exposed to the elements. The usual sweltering heat wasn't present, however, the sun was shining in all its glory but the heat was absent. Yuanli actually found herself hugging her jacket closer to her body to try to retain some warmth. Her horse was struggling as the venom pumped round its body but, in the circumstances, it was managing unbelievably well. It seemed to understand the importance of reaching Oasis so Yuanli could tell the others of the impending danger.

"It's not right," Yuanli told her horse, "it shouldn't be this cold. We're running out of time to stop the complete breakdown of Earth's stability."

The horse's response was an exhausted neigh.

Yuanli fumbled with the water in her hands as her weakened body struggled to undo the lid to expose the liquid within. Finally, the cap popped off and she trickled the cold drink down her throat. Her temperature dropped further as she shivered, but the coolness also served to keep her awake. Knowing it was no good just sitting by the side of the road with a dying horse, she rose back to her feet and egged her gelding to follow her once more. Yuanli stumbled forward one foot at a time to reach Oasis. The horse trotted along behind with its head bowed, a limp in its right rear leg. It didn't take long after setting off once more for the horse to fall for the first time, the venom affecting the horse further, the longer it stayed in the body. Reluctantly, it regained its footing and tried to surge on ahead; despairingly, the toxins brought it back down within ten minutes. Yuanli knelt by her horse and stroked its mane to try to comfort it; it would be unable to make it back, it wouldn't make it even halfway. Hope seemed lost as a tear began to trickle down Yuanli's left cheek.

The sand around her began to shift, warning of a truck approaching on the horizon. It was the first vehicle she had seen on the deserted road; Yuanli was convinced it was her fatigued body playing tricks on her. She rubbed her eyes and opened them again, but the truck kept advancing. Given life by the new hope, she jumped to her feet and waved her arms. The truck pulled up next to her and the passenger door flew open immediately.

Out jumped Masood with an animal care kit under his arm. "What's happened?" he inquired as he rushed straight to his horse, ignoring Yuanli's poor appearance.

"Western diamondback bite," she replied downheartedly.

Quick as a flash, Masood opened his veterinary bag and began treatment. There was a second bang as the driver door closed and Roy emerged round the front of the truck.

"Yuanli, what were you thinking?" The shocked tone seemed genuine but she knew Roy was acting.

"I'm sorry," she whimpered as if caught doing something she shouldn't have.

"I told you to check with me before taking my horses!" Masood yelled in his distress. "What are you doing all the way out here, anyway?"

Roy gave a slight shake to his head to indicate to Yuanli to keep the truth hidden.

The delay in answer only served to anger Masood further. "WELL?" he barked.

"I wanted to go on an evening ride, I'm so sorry." The tears came easy in her tired and fragile state.

"I'll talk to her," Roy assured the worried Masood. He motioned for Yuanli to join him behind the truck.

"Yes, do. She should have known better." The worry for his horse was bringing out a side of Masood that none had seen before.

Yuanli rose with her head downcast and slowly trudged to Roy, apologising to Masood as she passed him.

The riding teacher ignored her and continued to see to his horse.

Once they were out of audible range behind the noisily vibrating truck, Roy consoled Yuanli.

"Are you OK?" he asked her with his hand on her shoulder. It was a stupid question, and he knew it. She was exhausted, felt like a failure, and blamed herself for the horse's pain. "There's nothing you could've done," he tried to console her. "We aren't here legally so you couldn't ask for help in case the emergency services showed up and you couldn't have seen the snake coming. I had to be harsh as Harry and Lee made it back with their horses before we woke. What did you find out, anyway?"

"Oasis is infiltrated. There are three," Yuanli began to tell Roy, but she was cut short as Masood appeared round their side.

"We need to get back. He isn't in a good way but with the treatment I have given him he just needs to rest back at Oasis." Masood carefully led the horse to the back of the truck and told the others to sit in the front whilst he cared for his horse. The return journey gave Roy and Yuanli the chance to catch up with what she found out; with traitors in their midst their very lives could be at risk. When the truck began to move and Roy turned to speak to her, however, he found Yuanli snoring softly in the chair beside him. Her vital information would have to wait as her exhaustion took her into a deep sleep.

CHAPTER 30

Sanctum
Moanatenger
Grumpy Kraken gambling den

"You're a liar unna cheat!" Lucius Silverton erupted from his seat and knocked the cards off the rotten wooden table. A bit of spittle rested on his salt-and-pepper beard under his large hooked nose. Grey scraggly hair that showed his age and experience aligned his tiring face.

"It's sleighta hand. Takes skill un' practise ta learn," the winning captain smiled in his victory.

"You'll be sleighta two 'ands before I pay out ova dat robbery," Silverton promised with a snarl. Drawing his sword in one swift movement, he sliced the cheek of the cheating captain and blood spattered over the old shrivelled cards they were previously playing with.

Knowing better than to retaliate, the wounded trickster stumbled backwards with a hand trying to stop the stem of blood.

"I'm takin' me crew outta dis dump. You'll neva take arr coin again!" he bellowed towards the balcony where the owner of the establishment was looking on.

"Arrhh, good riddance, ya lazy hornswoggler!" Silverton shouted after him with a throaty laugh. His numerous crew that filled the gambling den laughed with him to try to curry favour with their captain. Silverton's bosun picked up his mandolin and continued playing the tune he was entertaining the building with prior to the outburst:

...Once the Kraken had destroyed the ship, and taken its pleasure,
The poor Cap'n floated on debris screaming, 'Arhh, bring back me treasure'...

Silverton looked up at the owner of the gambling den and saw he was making his way down to the lower level. Lucius need not fear repercussions from losing the proprietor some custom for he was the one that allowed the building to remain open. Silverton was the ringleader of the small band of captains who were fighting back against Tombstone's subjugation of their watery realm. For these captains, the open water of Moanatenger always signified freedom and an ability to roam where you pleased, they would not allow Dark Snake and her fleet of captains to take that from them.

The owner's heavy footsteps were thundering down the wooden steps one at a time, the sheer size of the man meant that the infrastructure moaned and groaned as he put his weight on it.

"Lucius, d'ya 'ave ta scare off me money?" he began with a rife smile, the man's cheeks wobbling as he spoke. The money the gambling den had brought him was spent mainly on luxurious food imported from other realms or seafood that was tough to acquire with most of the water controlled by Tombstone. Skip Barkley was as wide as he was tall and in much worse physical condition to Silverton despite his far younger age. Black messy hair crowned his head in place of Lucius' grey colour.

"Ya don't want 'is sort in 'ere," Silverton promised him. "Once one starts ta fiddle da system, it'll become known ta all dat da Grumpy Kraken's da place ta go for easy coin."

"Ya neva complain when ya hoodwink yar opponent?" Barkley retorted.

"Ea-sy," Lucius warned, signalling to not push the matter any further. "Ya hear dat Quint survived his battle with Glob Karver?"

"Da man's wi'out an arm unna leg now, yet still as twice the seamanship of any of us put togetha." Skip was fascinated by the captain's prowess. Whilst the two were talking a third captain walked up to them without them seeing his approach.

Silverton wrinkled his nose and turned to face the newcomer. "Av a showa Joe!" he ordered.

"Yeah, come on Fish-lips," Barkley agreed, "ya stink!"

The third captain was named 'Fish-lips Joe' for his big rubbery lips. Joe was unhygienic, had greasy brown hair and was always filthy. No one would ordinarily want to be within a hundred leagues of the man, yet desperate times called for desperate measures. These were indeed desperate times and they needed all the help they could get. Even his ship was named *Grim* for its revolting appearance and conditions onboard. The vessel always reeked of body odour and faeces.

"I'm clean. I washed this morning," Joe blubbered through his oversized lips. Ironically, despite his careless physical appearance, he was one of the better educated of the seamen and spoke with care. It was something he learned from Quint – just because one acts and lives like a savage, doesn't mean you have to sound like one.

"In da future, don't wash inna cesspit!" Silverton ordered him, half joking and half certain that that was indeed where he had cleansed himself.

"What were you talking about?" Joe asked, ignoring Silverton's remark.

Another fight had broken out on the far side of the den whilst they were talking. It appeared to be between some of Fish-lips' crew and Barkley's; even Joe's crew were disgusting, embracing the filth of their captain and ship.

"It's too loud in 'ere. Let's take arr business outside," Lucius suggested. Being the leader, they all followed his suggestion and the three captains found themselves outside the building and in the cool night air. The smell of the water lapping at the shore just in front of them filled their nostrils and Joe's odour disappeared into the outside air.

"Dat's what we're fightin' for," Silverton told his allies as they gazed out at the open water.

"What's our next move?" Joe asked.

"Quint's waitin' on da next island ova. 'e's just returned from 'is transport mission for Chungwantanya," Skip informed the others.

"Dhere's a rumour in da taverns dat Butcha un Amazon are on Earth tryna find Jedrok ta finish us off," Lucius said solemnly.

"I 'eard dat Presley's close ta returning with it for Minotaur ta use," Barkley countered.

"Either way, we can't stop now. We must continue the fight, especially in two of Dark Snake's war chiefs' absences." Joe tried to bring the conversation back to their next move.

"Voodoo ain't exactly restin' whilst they're gone. I 'eard 'e wiped outta 'ole village in Chungwantanya recently," Barkley said, shaking his head in sorrow.

"Even more reason for us to act," Joe reasoned.

"Quiet," Silverton whispered quickly. Narrowing his eyes, he strained to hear a slight rustling coming from the beach in front of them. "'ere dat?" he asked his fellow captains.

As they listened the rustling noise grew louder. They drew their swords and stood back to back.

Out of the darkness came a small army of Dark Snake's minions.

"Pincerniks," Joe said, drawing in breath in awe of how many were appearing around them.

The humanoid monsters were mostly human-looking with the exception of claw-like hands and a tough shell on their backs, more monstrosities created by Dark Snake's wicked use of Gaia.

"'elp!" Skip screamed to his crew inside the Grumpy Kraken, but the fighting, laughter, gambling and merriment were too loud for the captains to be heard. They were alone.

Lucius lunged forwards and plunged his sword into one of the monsters. It fell with a thud and another pincernik walked over its corpse.

"FIGHT!" Silverton bellowed. "FIGHT NOW OR DIE!"

The three captains broke formation and set to work trying to set themselves free.

Skip was not very good at hand-to-hand combat due to his ungainly weight, his skill was in navigating his ship. His attacks were slow and it didn't take long for one of the pincerniks to catch his sword in its claw and jerk his weapon from his hand. Unarmed, Barkley had no choice but to flee the scene. He stumbled backwards and ran as fast as his heavy frame would carry him towards the gambling den. A pincernik barred his way but the captain was like a locomotive at the speed he was going with his obesity. Easily knocking the monster to the floor, he disappeared into the building.

"Coward!" Joe screamed, unaware that his friend had been disarmed. Whilst he was fending off two pincerniks at his front, a third was sneaking up behind him. The flanking pincernik opened and closed its claws before reaching out to sever Joe's head from his neck.

A gunshot rang through the air which made Joe swivel round to be face to face with the pincernik behind him. It fell forward where Silverton had shot the beast, saving his ally's life. Unfortunately, the creature landed on Joe and brought him to the ground, burying him briefly under its corpse. Silverton was alone and desperately outnumbered. He fought the best he could, felling the enemies with the same ease that a lumberjack fells trees. Nevertheless, their number soon became too much for him and he sank to his knees in defeat. A pincernik was about to finish him off when his crew came rushing past him and engaged the remaining enemies.

It was a rout once Barkley arrived with the captain's respective crews. The numbers drastically shifted in their favour and the pirates put the remaining pincerniks to the sword. Whilst his crew enjoyed the sport of hunting the minions of Dark Snake, Silverton got to his feet and went to Joe's aid.

"Ya OK?" he asked after removing the heavy pincernik from across Joe's chest.

"I'm fine. I owe you an apology," he stated in the direction of Skip.

Barkley waved his comment away. "Ya weren't ta know I were unarmed. Was for da best in da end," he laughed.

"We need ta leave!" Lucius bellowed for all to hear.

"But me den!" Skip tried to protest.

"If dey know we're 'ere den none of us arr safe. Karver un' 'is cronies arr most likely on dheir way if they aren't 'ere already," Silverton reaffirmed his point.

With no time to waste they returned to their ships and got to work on setting sail before they could be hunted by the superior strength of their enemy.

Joe and his crew quickly boarded *Grim* and took no time at all in preparing to leave.

Barkley next door was pushed on even more by the foul stench drifting across from Joe's vessel. His crew held their breath as long as they could whilst rigging their ship to leave. Barkley's ship was named *Walrus* after its captain's large size, a name suggested by Silverton during the years of peace gone by.

Lucius had the most efficient crew, so it was him that set sail first in his ship, *Reaper*, and watched as the others set sail also. The name of his ship was actually suggested by Butcher when he tried to recruit Silverton to Tombstone. Although hating the man that provided the idea, he couldn't help but love the name.

"May de man in da moon watch over ya," Silverton whispered into the sea breeze, trusting it to carry his message to his fellow captains. He finished watching *Grim* set sail through his spyglass and then motioned to find Skip's *Walrus*. His eye zoomed over leagues of ocean and then a shadowy figure on the horizon, until his gaze fell on Barkley. Cursing, he realised he had spotted something before finding Barkley – he focused on the shadowy figure and a ship came into view.

"*Devil's Charm*," he exhaled as all the air left his body. He felt winded as the largest ship to sail Moanatenger came into focus. Its captain, Exie Burns, had never lost a battle and never left any alive. It was rumoured that any surviving men were executed instantaneously, and women were given the choice of joining the all-female crew or face death. Removing the spyglass from his face he could only watch helplessly as unrelenting cannon fire ripped through *Walrus* and shredded the vessel along with its crew. Silverton ordered the retreat whilst listening to the screams of Barkley and his men carry across the water behind him.

CHAPTER 31

Earth
Arizona.
Oasis

George woke up to the sound of Alex and Cheikhou having another of their signature arguments.

"No, you didn't!" Cheikhou repeated whilst shaking his head.

"I have a medal that proves it," insisted Alex, who was visibly distressed.

"What's this?" murmured George, rubbing his eyes and stretching.

"I was just telling Cheikhou here that I once–"

"He says he was the world champion Hawaiian surfer in twenty fourteen. He entered the competition whilst on holiday," Cheikhou said while shaking his head. "More like you watched *Surf's Up* on the plane."

George laughed at that comment. "What brought this up, anyway?"

"The area where *I won my medal* has been incinerated with molten lava. A freak eruption that just didn't stop."

Cheikhou turned up the radio where they got the news:

"The large shield volcano, Mauna Loa, devastated a large part of Hawaii last night, completely covering the so-called Big Island in molten rock. Lava erupted from its vent in previously unseen quantities. In nineteen eighty-four the lava flow stopped just short of the Hilo, a settlement on the island. Unfortunately, this time the lava didn't stop and wiped out the town along with the rest of the island. It's being called the worst disaster in recent history as the Big Island has been buried under molten rock leaving, some say, none alive. I'm joined by Lola Sedouk, a volcanologist at Yellowstone National Park, to explain the disaster. Good morning Lola."

"Well, in the context it isn't really but good morning to you, too."

"What can you tell us about last night's eruption?"

"Mauna Loa is what we call a shield volcano, so-called for its gently sloping sides in comparison to composite volcanoes which have steep sides, such as Mount St Helens. Shield volcanoes are not normally considered as dangerous because the molten rock within tends to ooze out of the vent as opposed to explode, like we saw with St Helens in nineteen eighty. However, the lava that is *ejected from shield volcanoes is low in viscosity which means it will flow much faster than the thicker substance from composite volcanoes. This is where the issue has arisen last night. The sheer speed and surprise of the eruption left insufficient time for evacuation leading, regrettably, to the death tolls we have been hearing of in the aftermath."*

"Is this related to the seemingly more frequent and aggressive natural disasters we've been seeing recently?"

"Scientists such as myself are unsure of what's brought on this sudden spike in disasters at the present. Nevertheless, rest assured we are working tirelessly to ensure we aren't caught off-guard again like last night."

"One listener has messaged the show to ask about what they call a 'supervolcano'. Surely they have made that one up?"

"Unfortunately not. There's such a thing as a supervolcano and, worse still, we're forty thousand years overdue for an eruption of the one under my place of work, Yellowstone National Park. They're large depressions in the earth called calderas. Underneath these calderas are magma chambers that hold the molten rock emitted during eruptions. As we haven't had a supervolcanic eruption in the time we've been studying volcanoes we're unsure exactly what one will entail. To give a basic understanding, however, the large-scale eruption of Mount St Helens – where the north face of the volcano was blown off during the eruption – ejected one cubic kilometre of pyroclastic material. Yellowstone is predicted to eject one thousand times that. The crater left after the St Helens eruption is about one to two miles wide whereas Yellowstone's caldera is about thirty by forty miles wide. I beg anyone listening to avoid Yellowstone completely. It isn't safe; evacuate now, it's going–"

The radio presenter suddenly cut off the scientist who had begun to go off script, then they returned attempting to make light of what the listeners had just heard.

"Thanks for that, Lola; safe to say you've ruined a lot of our listeners' days with that. I, for one, will struggle to enjoy my bologna sausage sandwich at lunch with the threat of a cataclysmic eruption over my head. Now, hopefully with happier news, it's Tom with the sport."

"Christ!" George exclaimed, breathing out heavily as the information sank in. Realising it was more than the news that was making him uncomfortable, he looked down and noticed his top was inside out – his thoughts were with the victims of the disaster. After correcting his error, he opened the accommodation's door and ambled over to the communal washroom. He was the first to leave his room; he liked being in the washroom early each morning before it got too busy so he could take his time with his morning routine. Once refreshed he began to return to Cheikhou and Alex in his room but was distracted by the sight of two riders heading towards the stables. Curiosity got the better of him and he pursued the horses as quietly as he could. He found a rock to hide behind and watched as Harry and Lee dismounted and returned their horses to their respective pens. They were very careful to make it look as if the horses had never been removed in the first place. Looking a little longer he realised that a third mount was missing. *Where have you been?* he wondered to himself. He ducked down and quietened his breathing as the duo made their way back past him to their accommodations. They were often hard to find during the day so no one would raise any questions if they didn't emerge for the rest of the day having caught up with lost sleep. George decided that the strange night ride and missing horse were worth reporting to Roy or Presley, it just so happened that Roy emerged from his accommodation as George returned to the sleeping blocks.

"Roy!" George shouted to get his attention. "Over here!"

The small green-haired man twisted and turned as he struggled to locate the source of the call.

"Over here!" George shouted once more before being located by the guardian.

"What is it, boy?" he asked with sleep in his eyes.

"There's a horse missing from the stables. I saw two people returning so I followed. It was Harry and Lee, they've been somewhere."

Roy's eyes shot open and immediately seemed more awake, the news was troubling. He tried to play it cool and dismissed George. "OK, thanks for telling me. I'll deal with it." Shaking his head and murmuring to himself, Roy walked off in the direction of Masood's apartment.

George hoped he had done enough and went back to tell Alex and Cheikhou what he saw.

Roy, Masood and Yuanli were absent at breakfast, along with Scott, Lee and Harry who were never present in the morning. News had spread about the disaster in Hawaii and, as a result, the missing people were not the main topic of conversation, in fact their absence was barely noted. Cindy entered the hall with Presley deep in conversation, they seemed concerned about something. Cindy stopped at the long breakfast table and coughed to get everyone's attention. "We're running out of time," she began. "Earth's deteriorating at an unprecedented rate and we need to get you guys to Sanctum sooner rather than later. As such, we have less time than originally planned," Cindy explained to everyone. "Today you'll go with Donna to do your aquatic training and tomorrow you'll do your mountain training and learn how to climb treacherous landscapes. We then hope to have repeat sessions over the coming weeks in order for you to improve your skills. This is opposed to you learning over a period of months, thus you'll not have anywhere near as long as we originally hoped. Sorry for forcing this upon you, however, circumstances require it. Good day." Cindy turned abruptly and left with Presley at her heels.

George led the way with Donna towards the reservoir to start the aquatic training. He was much taller than the dark-skinned lady and they looked like a strange pairing to Annabel as she saw Donna's small frame topped with her short black hair bob up and down beside her friend ahead.

It was Alex's turn to encourage Rosie. A near-death experience on a boat when she was little had led to a lifelong fear of water.

"You'll be fine," he winked whilst grasping her hand. "I won't let you drown. I promise," then he gave her hand a squeeze to reinforce that he was there for her.

"What's going on there, then?" Annabel asked Cheikhou with a smile on her face. She hoped Cheikhou might spill if Alex had said anything about her friend behind closed doors.

"Rosie's been helping Alex keep up with the rest of us. He knew he was out of his depth from when a horse kicked him in the face on the first day," he chuckled to himself. "I think she feels sorry for him," Cheikhou finished.

"I think she feels more than sorry for him," Annabel giggled whilst watching her friend with Alex.

"How'd you mean?" Cheikhou asked, confused. "Wait. You don't mean to tell me... No... no. Don't be silly," he added, laughing off the suggestion.

"Well? Has he said anything about her to you? You know, in 'private lad chat'?" Annabel probed.

Cheikhou boomed his usual laugh. "We don't engage in pillow talk, 'Bell. Even if we did, I'd convince him not to get hurt. A boy like him? A girl like her?" Cheikhou scoffed.

"Sounds like someone's jealous." Annabel walked away smiling to herself.

Cheikhou looked back at the flirting duo and shook his head. "Nah, man. There's no way," he mumbled.

The wind was picking up as they journeyed over to the reservoir. When they reached the water they saw ripples skating across the surface as the wind ruffled it. The trees were rattling as their leaves fell in the autumnal gale. It was a weird feeling when George set foot on the grassy halo surrounding the water. It was easier terrain to walk on than the soft sand he had been traversing recently. He sat down and felt the wetness of the morning dew on the short green blades. Brushing his hand through it he looked at all the moisture collecting in his palm.

"Wow, look at that," Annabel exclaimed when she first laid eyes on the boat they would be practising on. It was a black wooden galley with a red band of paint circling the hull. It had a striped sail and a cannon protruding from a section of the red paint. There was a rotten-looking brown plank leading from the ground to the deck of the boat. Despite its fragile appearance, Annabel ran straight up the wood and onto the ship. The others followed more carefully, a little more concerned about the state of the plank they were using to board.

Rosie was petrified of falling in the water, so Alex held her hand and walked backwards to ease her onto the boat.

Barbara stopped short of the plank and gave it a long look. "Are you sure it'll take my weight?" she yelled up at Donna.

"Just take it slow, you'll be fine," she promised.

Barbara stepped onto the wood and the plank creaked under the pressure. The second step merited an even louder groan. *Screw this,* Barbara said to herself before running the rest of the way. The plank bowed but held her weight.

"Wow, you moved fast there," Donna joked as she helped Barbara enter the boat.

"Yeah, people often say that," Barbara puffed, out of breath.

On the deck of the boat the wind was even noisier, and Donna struggled to be heard. "OK. Welcome to aquatic training. First of all, what do we know about boats?"

Alex was his usual eager self, ready to show off. "The stern is the front of the boat and the bow is the rear. Starboard is the left side of the boat, and the port side is the right. I know because I used to sail all the time." He winked at Cheikhou to provoke him.

Just as he was about to retaliate, Donna dealt Alex a blow. "The exact opposite, actually – the complete opposite of everything you just said," she scoffed in such a way that Cheikhou knew Alex would be hurting. "The bow is the front, the stern is the back, starboard is the right and port side is the left. Dare I ask if anyone knows anything else about boats?"

Alex was about to pipe up again, but his recent bruising made him keep quiet.

Instead, Annabel offered an answer. She recalled a long list of knots that she had learnt in the Scouts and how they would be used on the boat. She surprised herself at how much she remembered and wondered why she ever quit; it seemed 'uncool' at the time but the memories she had were always joyful. By the time she was done

Donna was very impressed.

"Do you want to run this class?" she joked, pretending to hand the ropes she had for demonstrations over to Annabel.

She didn't run the class but was instead very helpful in showing the others how to tie the knots and easy ways to undo them.

On the safety of the deck with the water out of sight, Rosie was calm enough to thrive in the knot tying and, before long, she was again the one helping Alex and not requiring help herself.

George shivered as his cold numb fingers struggled with the intricacies of the knots. The rough rope was hurting his fingers and before long he gave up and shoved his hands under his arms to keep warm. The uncharacteristically cold weather was continuing, and everyone was beginning to get fed up. They thought they had left the cold behind in England when they came to Arizona.

Cheikhou was upset that he had to wait until next time to learn how to fire the cannon when he asked, nevertheless, as recompense Donna promised him that she would still have a surprise before the day was out. The wind was blowing the cold water up onto the boat which only served to make them chillier. Rumour spread of Donna's surprise though, which kept their dwindling morale high enough to continue. They opted to keep training through lunch so they could finish earlier. None of them could face warming up only to have to return to the cold ship.

"Come on, what's the surprise? I'm freezing and need something to keep me going. The suspense is killing me," Alex moaned.

"OK," Donna gave in. "You've all worked hard in horrible conditions today. Let's bring this to a close." The excitement in the group was palpable, they were finally getting their reward for triumphing through a tough day.

"As you all know after today, working on the water can be very cold, at times debilitating and joy-sapping. You may be thinking, 'Argh, I hate boats', but remember, your boat is all that keeps you from worse conditions of being in *there*," Donna enforced, pointing to the cold water that was crashing against the side of their vessel violently in the strong wind. "In some circumstances, your ship may be too damaged to continue or overrun with enemy. In this situation your only choice is to abandon ship. Your surprise is to learn how much you actually love being on boats, as now you each have to jump in the water to complete your day of training. Alex, as you just brought it up, you can go first." Donna cackled in her malice.

Before Alex had time to protest, Cheikhou had grabbed him by the arms and lifted him as if he was a doll. He flung him over the side and Cheikhou collapsed laughing onto the deck. There was a loud splash and a faint muffled rant coming from a displeased Alex, now rushing to the shore. One by one they each took the plunge and returned to the washroom soaking wet. There was no time to wait for each other to finish, they were drenched and very cold – all humility vanished as they piled into the shower block together. They tried to keep their eyes to themselves but Alex couldn't help gazing at Rosie in the shower opposite once or twice and George said a silent apology to Jacob as he took in Annabel's naked figure. The girls were just as bad though, both taking sneaky glances at Cheikhou's muscular figure. Alex's heart sank as he noticed Rosie's eyes devouring their treat. Once everyone was dry and dressed they enjoyed a warm hearty meal to heat their insides.

Yuanli, Masood and Roy had now returned for dinner along with Harry and Lee.

Scott was behind the bar ready to serve everyone when they were ready.

The table was strangely quiet.

Alex was ignoring Rosie's attempts to talk, still enraged with her for looking at Cheikhou in the shower.

Yuanli seemed tired, barely managing to spoon her soup into her mouth.

Roy was whispering something to Presley.

Masood was seething about something. Rumour had it that Yuanli had got lost on a night ride that she hadn't run past the horse master first. The depressing atmosphere continued into the evening drinks; many simply retired to bed whereas the ones that stayed up sat in silence.

Harry and Lee were the only ones that appeared upbeat for once. Their normal scowls were replaced with grins whilst they played a drinking game with Scott at the bar.

George decided he was just going to bed. He pulled himself

out of the hole in the settee he had made and got to his feet. Just as he turned to leave, though, Scott grabbed his arm. "Follow me," he whispered, whilst looking back anxiously.

"Where're we going?" George inquired as he was pulled along.

Scott elected not to answer until he reached the outside of his accommodation. "Listen to me, mate. They're coming and they know it's here."

"Who's coming? What are you on about?" George didn't need this drama after the day he had had.

"Look, I'm trusting in you as I have no one else to turn to. I've made a mistake."

George remembered Scott acting similarly before and then acting as if nothing had ever happened.

"Me, Harry and Lee are helping Tombstone. *Were* helping. *Are* helping. They're still. I'm not. You have to trust me."

George stepped back. Roy was right, there was something off about Scott and his friends.

"Mexico – you stole the mask for them, didn't you? It's here, isn't it? Now they're coming to open Jedrok with all the artefacts in one place." George was starting to worry.

"You're right, but I'm with you now and we need to stop them," Scott was pleading.

"How do I know I can trust you?" George looked deep into Scott's eyes, trying to see the good.

Scott opened the door to his room and showed George inside, "Harry and Lee aren't coming anytime soon. I kept pouring them drinks in fake celebration; they won't be able to walk by now."

"What were you celebrating? Earth's downfall? The deaths in Hawaii? The betrayal?" George was so furious that his face was red, bursting with rage.

"They were celebrating exactly that. I was just pretending. Look, I'm taking you to the…" 'Artefact' he was going to say, but when he turned the light on he saw that the headdress was in the hands of Yuanli who must have broken into the room.

"Get away from him!" Yuanli screeched at George.

He knew that if he stepped away from Scott now, it would likely seal the troubled man's fate. Trusting his gut instinct, he decided to believe Scott was with them and shook his head in defiance. Arms crossed, George stayed by the traitor and tried to plead his case. "He's with us. He's had a change of heart."

Scott, meanwhile, was overcome with emotion. He had taken a seat on his bed and was weeping into his hands. "It's too late. They're on their way," he sniffed to George and Yuanli.

"You don't have a right to be upset!" Yuanli spat at the sobbing villain. "You've been found out and are now just trying to join us again in fear for your life."

The door opened once more and the room fell silent, as time appeared to stand still. Surely Harry and Lee couldn't have reached them in their paralytic state. The ominous sound of approaching footsteps was replaced with the large figure of Presley. "What's the problem, Yuanli? Oh," he said, shocked by the congregation. Closing the door behind him he stepped into the room and tried to understand the situation. The tension was not helped by the limited space in the crowded dorm.

George spoke first. "Scott's realised his mistake in helping Tombstone. He was taking me here tonight to show me the mask."

Yuanli hissed to show her displeasure and looked at Scott. "I heard your cronies talking last night when I followed them." Then, with sadness in her eyes, she moved her gaze to George and softened her voice. "They were saying Scott would come through. That he could have been friends with you in different circumstances. The last I heard was Harry saying, 'As good as dead'. Scott was only earning your trust in order to kill you."

After this revelation George took a step away from his supposed drinking buddy. With a scowl on his face he croaked, "Tell me it isn't true."

Scott was in too much of a state to answer, but Presley wouldn't let him avert the question.

In a flash, he grabbed Scott by the collar and lifted him off the bed with superhuman strength. "Answer him," he warned.

Scott could only manage a cowardly nod.

"You were going to do it tonight, weren't you?" Yuanli probed with aggression back in her voice.

"NO, NO…" Scott choked as he struggled to breathe, suffocating under the pressure his collar was asserting against his neck.

Presley lowered him back to the bed and Scott coughed fervently, trying to recover his breath.

"That was the original plan but I changed after seeing you guys." He coughed again as the last of the air returned to his lungs. "There was no hope before your arrival, so I joined Harry and Lee in line with Tombstone. They showed me... so many already believed... the messengers... It doesn't matter. After a few days of you being here, I saw there was hope and, with a new vision of salvation, I realised we could still stop the tide of evil. I was taking George here tonight to show him the mask. I promise."

"I say we expose him to the rest of the group as the cowardly traitor he is," Yuanli suggested maliciously.

"NO!" Presley and George burst out in unison.

"No?" they asked each other in shock that they were aligned.

"I think he's telling the truth. He's been trying to tell me for days now but never quite built up the courage," George said in his defence.

"I think we need to keep a close eye on him for the time being, however, I agree we should keep his part in the betrayal a secret. Whilst Harry and Lee think he's still aligned with them, Scott can inform us on their next moves. Equally, we don't want to spark a panic by revealing we have traitors in our midst. We have the last artefact. We know Tombstone are on the way to open Jedrok with the artefacts they've already collected. We have all the information and now Scott can be our trump card." Presley sounded more certain than he looked.

"I'll prove my worth. I promise," Scott nodded, seeing that mercy for his actions was looking more likely.

Yuanli wasn't happy but the others were satisfied with the outcome, none more so than Scott.

"We now hold all the cards. We need to be ready. In the meantime, word of this exchange doesn't leave this room. Agreed?" Presley asked.

"Agreed," they echoed together.

CHAPTER 31

Earth
Arizona
Oasis

"It's with deep regret that we wake you for a second consecutive morning with horrific news of another devastating natural disaster on our beloved planet. It's my job to inform you that a huge tsunami struck the coast of Papua New Guinea during the night. An earthquake measuring just under ten on the Richter scale sent a thirty metre-high wave crashing across the country. The Pacific early warning system put in place to limit the impact of these disasters by giving time to prepare was ineffective as the record-breaking quake broke the instruments. The original death tolls fluctuate around the two hundred thousand mark. The disaster has also left hundreds of thousands missing, millions without running water and many of the cars, homes and buildings in towns and cities have been swept away. Much of the immediate response has involved evacuating survivors as well as providing thousands of blankets and bottles of fresh water. The Australian Army have been sending troops over throughout the night to provide much needed aid. After providing you with this unnerving and terrible news I'm left asking, 'What have we done to provoke these deadly disasters? Is America safe? Or could we be next..?'"

Barbara turned the radio off to save herself from the menacing morning news. "We need to get Gaia back where it belongs before we all end up doomed." Expecting a response, she turned to see Yuanli sitting on the edge of her bed staring at herself in the mirror. "Yuanli... Hello, is anyone in there?"

The Asian turned with a blank look on her face, she seemed pale and unwell. Without answering her friend, she rose from the bed and walked out of the door.

Barbara hurried to put her shoes on and went after her. "Is everything OK?" she called.

"No. Like you said, we need Gaia back. The world is falling apart and our delaying is costing lives. It's time we take the fight to Tombstone and go to Sanctum."

"We have to complete our training or we won't be able to do any good, though," Barbara retorted. Yuanli just grunted and entered the breakfast hall.

There was a strange atmosphere, no one seemed to be discussing the disaster like the day before. Instead, the group were sitting in a silent memorial for the victims of recent events.

Yuanli took her seat quietly and joined the remembrance to show her respects.

The peace was shattered like broken glass when Harry and Lee arrived laughing to each other about some inside joke.

"Who died?" Lee barked at the room whilst Harry roared with laughter.

"Did you not hear the news?" Barbara inquired.

"Don't like it. Too depressing," Lee answered.

"I know what'll cheer you all up. Let's go do some mountain climbing," Harry suggested.

Yuanli went to confront the insensitive morons but Presley put his large hand on her left knee to stop her.

"Sounds good," Presley smiled.

The weather was worse than the day before, there was rain in the air and the temperature was at an all-time low. They walked together out of Oasis and towards the large rock formation that George had seen whilst riding on the first day of training. A rumble echoed across the sky as the dark clouds shrouded the peak of their destination. A light drizzle began to fall which became a full-on downpour by the time they reached the base of the butte.

"Are you sure it's safe in this weather?" Annabel asked, voicing her concern to Harry.

"You won't be able to choose when you come across an obstacle such as this in Sanctum, so there's no point only tackling it when you feel like it here. If everyone just shuts up and listens then we can keep you safe." Harry struggled to be heard over the thunder and heavy rain. After going over the basics and showing them how to climb safely, everyone was drenched from standing in the downpour.

"We don't even have equipment?" Rosie asked, astonished.

"Equipment breaks. You need to be able to do it yourselves," Harry answered with no emotion.

George began to shiver as his clothes soaked through. Despite being deathly scared of heights he was glad when the group was split in two to begin their climbing, just so he could warm up.

Harry was taking half up one side and Lee was taking half up the other.

George was with Barbara, Alex, Presley and Annabel in Harry's group, which left Cheikhou, Yuanli, Roy and Rosie in Lee's group.

Water was dripping off Yuanli's nose as she began the climb, her hands struggled to get a grip on the slippery wet rocks. "This isn't safe in these conditions!" she shouted to Lee. Her warning was ignored though, as Lee continued climbing on ahead. Grumbling under her breath, she followed as carefully as she could. "Go steady and take your time," she urged those still on the ground. The higher Yuanli climbed the more her fingers ached and grew colder. Looking down she saw Cheikhou behind her, looking more concerned than she had ever seen him. When gazing up, however, she noticed Lee had disappeared into the fog. The harder she tried to make out the leader's outline the more the bladelike rain cut into her streaming eyes. Shaking her head, she continued the climb and pulsed her fingers to try to regain the feeling in them.

Miraculously, all reached the first ledge safely in her group.

Rosie was the first to shove her hands under her arms to try to warm them back up and soon everyone else followed suit.

They were about to embark on their next leg up the rock when there was a yell from their right. Someone was in trouble and required urgent assistance. Before long the shout could be heard again.

Lee went to help but Yuanli held him back. "They need you with them." She motioned at the cold and tired faces on the ledge alongside her. "I'll go. I'm a good climber and will be able to help if anyone needs medical attention."

Lee saw the sense in that and let her go in his place.

Yuanli wasted no time before setting off in the direction of the pleas for help. Contrary to her initial belief, the weather could in fact be worse on the other side. The further round the rock she travelled the wetter and more treacherous it seemed to become. *This is madness*, she told herself. It didn't take her long to reach the other group and witness the situation unfolding. Luckily, her friends were safely on a ledge which immediately put her mind at ease. Unfortunately, it was Harry that had gotten into trouble.

George was pointing to show Yuanli what the issue was and, following his finger, she saw that the supposed professional rock climber was dangling by a few fingers about thirty feet above the others. Cursing under her breath and fighting the urge to just leave him, she put her own life in danger to rescue someone she desperately detested.

"I'm coming!" she called up to try to calm him.

"Hurry up. I'm falling!" he replied without a note of thanks.

Gritting her teeth, Yuanli put one hand above the other to try to reach him. When nearing the stranded man she felt her foot slip on the moist rock and her body dropped half an inch before she regained her footing. Below, a loud gasp of horror could be heard from the onlookers.

"Come on. You're bloody useless!" Harry called down at her.

The comment was almost the last straw, but she knew she had to set an example to those below her, those who both literally and metaphorically were looking up to her. She roared herself onwards determinedly with a growl that echoed off the cold rock. The final push brought her level with Harry.

"Hold on, I'll go a bit higher and pull you up to that ledge."

"Get on with it!" he spat in panic.

Once again, Yuanli had to swallow the cruel remark and continue with her objective. She reached the ledge and laid down on the rock. Shuffling forwards, she peeped over the edge and saw the dangerous drop.

Annabel had her head in George's chest, unable to watch.

Bravely, Yuanli leant over the precipice and reached her hand down to Harry. He pulled himself up the best he could and threw his hand at Yuanli but their fingertips only scraped one another. He tried once more and clasped her hand, but the clammy skin just slipped straight out of any grip. Yuanli felt herself get pulled forward and her chest was now over the edge. Her unbelievable balance kept her in place and she managed to restabilise herself before calling down, "One more time. You can do it!"

"It's your fault, you let go of my hand!" Harry maliciously replied. Then he threw his body upwards and grabbed her outstretched limb. Holding tight, he didn't lose the connection this time and moments later he was pulled to safety and lying next to an out of breath Yuanli.

"Don't say 'thank you' then," she panted.

"Why would I?" Harry began. She remembered fully why she detested him at that moment. He rose to his feet in order to tower over her. "Are you really dumb enough to believe that I needed help?" He let out a hateful laugh. "I'm a professional rock climber." He chortled again at his own genius.

Yuanli sat in disbelief at whatever was happening. She went to speak but couldn't find any words. "I needed you separated from the group and this was the only way to do it. You shouldn't have followed us the other night. Now you know too much."

Yuanli pivoted herself to shout down to the others for help, but she was grabbed from behind and felt a cold, damp hand clamp her mouth shut. She tried biting his palm but however hard she gnawed he kept his hold airtight firmly over her mouth. She could taste his warm and metallic blood seep into her mouth where she had broken the skin.

"It's a shame. Such a waste for someone so pretty," Harry whispered into her ear as he smelled her hair and licked her neck.

She wriggled to attempt to worm her way free, but his other arm was strong enough to contain her. Ordinarily, her expertise in martial arts would be sufficient to fight off a jerk like Harry but her lack of sleep combined with the hard and gruelling climb left no energy in her tank. Yuanli went limp as the fight left her. She wouldn't give him the satisfaction of seeing her tears, so she kept her face hard and cold. The sharp rain continued to blast into her features, like the injections of a thousand small needles. Yuanli gagged when she felt Harry's warm breath at her neck.

He brought himself in line with her right ear and whispered,

"For Dark Snake. For Tombstone." Then he gave her a fierce shove and sent Yuanli tumbling over the edge.

Alex stopped telling George how he would have been able to save Harry in half the time as he watched Rosie's guardian hit the side of a rock above and plummet past their position. Time stood still as Annabel's scream pierced their ears.

George cautiously walked to the edge and gazed down at the ground. He saw the guardian's twisted and deformed body in a heap at the base of the rock. George felt a burning sensation in his throat and then, unable to stop himself, he spewed up his breakfast over the edge.

Annabel shuffled in shock over to the edge but George held her back and saved her the sight. Presley tried to calm those in his group and told them to make their way back down the rock face. He went first and moved Yuanli's crumpled body from view of her arriving friends.

"Barbs, take everyone back to Oasis. Tell Cindy what's happened. I'm going to wait for Harry and the other group," Presley ordered.

Barbara was unable to hold back her tears after watching her friend have such a horrific death, but she nodded and took on her role.

"Oh, and tell Cindy not to let Scott out of her sight," Presley added with a small glance at George.

George took the look to mean that he was charged with that particular detail and then used his eyes to answer Presley inaudibly to show he understood.

Everyone from Harry's group was in the large wooden building at Scott's bar deep in conversation when the door opened and Presley entered holding a badly beaten Harry by the scruff of the neck. Once the mountain of a man was through the door, Lee's group entered with Roy and Cheikhou at the back, holding a less badly hurt but still bruised Lee.

Cheikhou threw Lee next to his crony on the floor at Presley's feet and ambled over to George.

"We didn't know until we hit the ground. Lee tried to make a break for it but my right hand had something to say about that,"

Cheikhou smirked at his good work.

"That explains the bruises, but what happened to Harry?" George asked whilst revelling in the messed up appearance of the man responsible for Yuanli's death.

"Presley had some time on his hands whilst waiting for us to return," Cheikhou replied.

Harry had a badly broken nose, a deep cut beneath his right eye and what appeared to be a dislocated jaw. The villain had been beaten within an inch of his life, but Presley knew just when to stop.

"On the ground before you two are traitors to the cause, loyal to Tombstone," Presley began in his booming voice. "They've been conspiring to help Dark Snake complete her goal of bringing death and destruction to Earth. It's recently come to my attention that together they schemed to steal one of the artefacts required to open Jedrok. They succeeded and have in their possession the Aztec headdress here ready for an imminent attack by Butcher and his kind to try to take Jedrok from us."

Scott swallowed hard expecting to be ousted any second, but Presley continued without mentioning his name. "They've been updating the Tombstone warlords of our movements and, as such, knew we would be here with Jedrok. Yuanli risked her life to follow them and uncover the plot, now she's paid for her courageousness in the worst way possible."

Masood, now understanding why his horse had been taken the day before, sat in regret for how he had treated her in their final exchanges.

Presley proceeded to finish his small speech. "We'll now go and bury Yuanli and show her the respect she deserves. An inspiration to us all, she'll be a shining light in our war against the tide of evil."

Whilst Cheikhou, Alex and Presley dug the hole for the burial, the others gathered weapons ready to fend off the impending assault by Tombstone. Once everyone was armed they returned to the burial site and handed the men who dug the grave their weapons.

Cheikhou was given the large claymore sword by Masood.

Alex was given a small firearm from the practise range by Cindy. "Time to put all that talk into action," she said.

Annabel brought Presley Hades and Thanatos from his bike

along with Freya.

Ready to defend against any threats, they could finally put Yuanli to rest. Standing over the grave, the group said their final goodbyes to the lady who had helped them all so much in the past.

Rosie began with a long heartfelt speech dedicated to her guardian. At its conclusion her crying frame had to be consoled by Alex who was trying to stay strong for his friend. In the emotion of the moment, she turned and planted a kiss on Alex's mouth. It was a bittersweet moment as their love finally blossomed under the terrible circumstance.

Annabel shot a look at Cheikhou and saw him smiling for his friend. *They're both all talk*, she thought to herself.

Masood then apologised to the mound of earth for the way he had treated her when finding his wounded horse. The venom was out of the mount's system now and it had made a full recovery. Everyone had something to say and it was always good. Even the rain had stopped to pay its respects to the fallen hero. The moon was shining bright in the night sky, a thin beam of light illuminating the makeshift gravestone they had erected.

The final person to step forward was Scott. With his head bowed low he gently admitted his crimes. "It was Yuanli that discovered I was in line with Harry and Lee."

His admission caused a stir, but Presley spoke up and told them to hear him out.

Scott gave a small nod to show his appreciation and continued. "Her compassion convinced me that I was wrong to align myself with such evil people. Now I'll do all I can to help you in your liberation of Sanctum and rid both this world and theirs of evil. All this I'll do in Yuanli's name and a shameful hope I can do her proud."

A slow clap echoed behind them. "How very heartfelt. It's a shame you'll never make it to Sanctum." The statement was given by a deep voice full of malice and threat.

George turned to see a large man in a turban and bloodstained clothes. To his left was Amazon and to his right a man in a demonic wolf mask. Behind them was a group of screamers. Tombstone had arrived. The battle for Jedrok and an advantage in the war was about to commence.

CHAPTER 32

Earth
Arizona
Oasis

The two opposing forces stood in complete silence waiting for the other to make the first move. Sweat trickled down the back of Harry's neck despite the cold temperature. He knew with the arrival of Tombstone that he may be saved from whatever fate Presley had in store for him. He could feel Cheikhou's hand on his shoulder holding him down. If he was able to loosen the grip then perhaps he could join his allies with their small army of screamers. One glance at Lee told him that his friend had the same idea.

Without warning, Lee threw his left arm back and caught Alex in the genitals. Whilst the young man collapsed to the ground in pain, the traitor made a break for the Tombstone battle line. Being held in place by fear of the menacing Tombstone force, no one was able to stop him. Harry saw how powerless the Minotaur team was compared to the threat of their rival and decided there was nothing they could do to stop him. He went to rise but Cheikhou forced him back to the floor. "No you don't," he warned.

"Let him go," Butcher demanded in a voice that brokered no argument. Showing signs of his previous meeting with Presley and Annabel, he had a bandage round one arm and appeared to be placing most of his weight on one leg.

Cheikhou wouldn't give in, though, he stared the war chief down and held his ground, forcing Harry to the floor once more when he tried to leave.

"Do as he says," Presley ordered.

Cheikhou couldn't believe what he was hearing. "He murdered Yuanli; he can't get away."

"DO IT!" Presley shouted.

Cheikhou obliged with a growl and kicked Harry forwards towards his friends.

In his weakened state the shove was enough to make Harry spit out a mouthful of congealed bloody saliva onto the floor. After struggling to his feet, he ambled over to his accommodation and returned shortly after with the headdress he had stolen.

"This is yours," he managed through his battered features as he handed the final artefact over to Butcher.

The warlord took it without thanks.

Harry turned to face Cheikhou and with a victorious grin he cockily erected his middle finger to further enrage his earlier captor.

Cheikhou was about to run and rip Harry's head from his shoulders when something unexpected happened.

Butcher brought his long cleaver down through the top of Harry's head, splitting his cranium in two. The blade continued down to the chin before being yanked back out again, flinging blood and brain outwards.

Harry crumbled to the floor and his head smashed against the sand, a pinkish liquid oozing from the top of what was once his head.

Lee had no time to run before the man in the wolf mask grabbed him from behind and threw him to the waiting screamers. The near naked abominations set about their work like a shoal of piranhas, cutting and slicing his flesh from the bone. His horrific shrieks and blood-curdling pleas for mercy made Annabel collapse in fear.

"Good job, Redfang!" Butcher patted the man wearing the wolf mask on his back. The force of the large bearlike paw made the dry red hair on the mask swing with the impact.

Scott began to weep. Despite their traitorous natures, Harry and Lee had been his friends for as long as he could remember and seeing them come to such disturbing ends in quick succession took all the fight from him.

Butcher licked the gore from his cleaver and laughed at the pathetic resistance force Minotaur had gathered to liberate Sanctum and save Earth.

Scott was beside himself.

Annabel was shaking with fear.

Rosie was mourning her dead guardian with Alex at her side.

George was struggling to hold back the vomit in his throat.

"Enough!" Presley roared. "Take your evil back to whence you came!"

Butcher couldn't believe Presley was still trying to fight. His makeshift army was in bits and he stood alone.

"How'd you plan to stop us by yourself?" Amazon asked, shrieking with laughter.

The screamers behind squealed at the prospect of more fresh blood to feast upon.

"He's not alone." Roy stood by his friend.

"Not whilst I'm breathing," Barbara panted heavily as she shifted her bulk in line with Roy.

"I'm itching for a piece of you." Cheikhou pointed to Amazon and rolled his sleeves up before taking his place next to Presley.

"We'll kill you all and take Jedrok by force. We're Tombstone," Butcher declared, "and where we walk is Tombstone," he finished with a step forward.

The screamers howled and raced ahead of the warlords to do their master's bidding.

"Come with me," Butcher signalled to Amazon and Redfang, "we need to find Jedrok."

Presley felled as many of the approaching screamers as he could with his pistols, but the thin frame and erratic movement of the beasts made them hard to hit. Only three of the fiends had fallen when Cheikhou disembowelled the first, to reach their position with his claymore. The guns Presley was armed with were useless at such short range and the sheer number of screamers soon began to overwhelm their position. Presley holstered his trusty sidearms and brought Freya out in a wide arch around him, knocking over several screamers in the process. He bellowed a command and sent the stinging tongue of his weapon towards an unsuspecting minion. Having been struck by the magical whip, it took note of its wielder's command and lunged at the monster beside it, beginning a tussle of teeth and claw.

Barbara was showing a completely different level of skill to what she displayed when training with the swords. Whether it was the risk to her life or trying to do Yuanli proud, she had become a warrior queen. Her weight failed to slow her at all as she shifted her large frame from side to side as gracefully as a ballerina. Her sword rose and fell swiftly, spelling the end for any screamers that dared venture her way.

Donna, the aquatic teacher, was not faring so well and tried to flee but was bitten on the leg. She fell to the ground and then succumbed to the hungry mouths around her.

George saw Butcher and his fellow leaders leave their minions in order to find Jedrok. He grabbed Annabel and tried to shake her out of her fear coma. "I need you to help me, Annabel. They're going after the weapons."

She looked at him with a blank expression and saw his lips moving but was unable to hear what he was saying. A gunshot from Alex's firearm snapped her out of her daze and she agreed to go with George. Rosie and Masood threw themselves into the fight with the screamers to try to even the numbers, but when Barbara noticed George and Annabel going after the warlords she left the fray to protect them, once again giving the enemy an advantage. The gap she left meant Cheikhou's left side was exposed and almost instantly the weakness was exploited by a screamer. Whilst Cheikhou was trying to pull his claymore from the corpse of his latest victim he was unable to intercept the beast running towards him. It leapt through the air with its razor-sharp claws aimed at his unprotected face. Cheikhou gave up on the sword and raised his hands to try to deflect the blow. A gunshot made him wince and a thud marked the screamer, dropping mid-jump and crashing to the ground. Cheikhou turned to see his saviour and Alex winked at him before going to help Rosie who was starting to struggle.

"He isn't going to let that go," Cheikhou moaned to himself before he finally unwedged his weapon.

George and Annabel kept a safe distance from Butcher and his friends whilst they searched for Jedrok. They knew that to reveal themselves would be suicide.

After checking all the accommodation's rooms, the warlords turned their sights to the large wooden building that sat at the heart of Oasis. Their pace quickened as they closed in on Jedrok's location.

When Redfang reached the door he was met with Cindy holding

a gun. As she went to raise her arm an arrow whistled past the wolf mask and planted itself in her chest. The gun dropped from her hand as the strength left her body. The sound of approaching footsteps was the last she heard before Amazon overtook Redfang and claimed her kill. Without missing a step, she drew her blades and sliced Cindy's neck in passing. The leader of Oasis fell to the ground and gently closed her eyes to accept her fate.

Annabel once again buried her head in George's neck as she tried to avert her gaze from the dying woman.

"It's up to us now, Annabel, we have to be brave," he whispered with a rub of her blonde hair.

"I'm scared," she wept. "I don't want to face them. I can't do it." She shook her head in defiance.

George stepped out from the building he was hiding behind and began to walk towards the door the war chiefs had just entered.

"Come back!" Annabel screamed. "George, they'll kill you!"

He kept walking, trying his best to block out the pleas of his friend. He reached the door and stopped. If he looked back at Annabel he would struggle to continue, so with a deep breath he entered the building.

The battle with the screamers was beginning to appear ill-fated. The lack of experience in the Minotaur team was showing. Only Presley and Roy were used to such a fight and the others were succumbing to fatigue.

Cheikhou's arm began to spasm after he had overexerted himself and he dropped his weapon.

Alex shouted, "I'm out of ammunition!" as he threw his gun to the floor and pulled out a short sword to protect himself.

Rosie screeched in pain as her arm was gashed open by one of the razor-like claws of her enemy throwing itself at her, desperate for fresh flesh.

Cheikhou was unable to control his pulsating arm. The harder he tried to control the muscle contractions the worse it became and he collapsed to the ground in agony. A howl to his left alerted him of an approaching screamer. He turned and saw the fiend staring straight at him. The beast had big black eyes without a glimmer of white, a representation of the evil within suppressing any light. It slowly began to hop towards Cheikhou all the while keeping its dead eyes fixed on its prey.

"Piss off!" he shouted at the approaching horror. Still, it kept coming. "OK. You want some of this..? Come on, then." He struggled to rise but the pain shot through his arm and he fell to the floor again. Cheikhou was preparing to fight his last fight when he heard the sound of hooves. All of a sudden, a horse galloped past him and knocked the screamer to the floor – the impact was enough to ensure the monster didn't rise again.

Masood roared from his mount and urged the horse back into the fray. It gave the struggling Minotaur warriors a boost as the horse crashed through the screamers. The confidence didn't last long, however. The gelding stumbled and Masood was thrown from his seat. In a heartbeat the animal was set upon and ripped apart by the screamers, the blood-curdling screech of the dying horse sent Masood over the edge. He ran with his short sword to try to save his mount, but it was a hopeless attempt. He skewered one of the fiends but was not quick enough to block the gnashing teeth to his right from sinking into his neck and ending his resistance.

Having just witnessed Masood's terrifying death, Alex grabbed Cheikhou's arms and pulled him back from the battle, screaming that he was unfit to continue in his current state.

"Retreat!" Presley boomed. "Fall back!" he shouted as he decapitated another screamer.

They were about to do so when, finally, some luck came their way. A horn sounded at the entrance to Oasis, *arhooooooo* was the first blow. The second longer, *arhooooooooooo.*

The screamers ceased their pursuit of the beaten Oasis defenders and turned to face the new threat. Presley squinted to try to see through the darkness; nevertheless, it wasn't his eyes that alerted him of their saviour first, it was his ears. The roar of the battle-crazed men and women cut through the night and grew louder as they approached. Their footsteps were muffled by the sand on which they ran but, eventually, a small group of warriors emerged from the night. At their front was a lady dressed in armour and to her left, leaning on a wobbly cane, was a deathlike Carlton.

"For Sanctum," the woman yelled as her small force crashed

into the screamers, taking the fiends with unexpected vigour.

George watched as Butcher took a big bag from his back and carefully put it on the floor. Such is the size of the half bear humanoid that George didn't spot the bag at first and thought it was just part of the large man's figure.

Amazon quickly began taking items from the bag and slotted them into the moulds in the unguarded monument. Firstly, she placed the pistol which once belonged to Jesse James, the first artefact they acquired when arriving on Earth. Secondly, she slotted into position the headdress that belonged to Moctezuma II that Harry and his fellow traitors stole. George could only watch as Amazon continued the ritual. Thirdly, she placed St George's armour that she stole when she severely wounded Carlton. Finally out of the bag emerged Mary Reed's sword that George vaguely remembered hearing was stolen before he even knew of Sanctum's existence or any of the madness he had witnessed since opening his letter from RAS. The large wooden building was supposed to be the most secure location in the compound. That hadn't halted Tombstone's attempt to walk straight up to it and begin the process of retrieving the weapons.

George waited for a good time, sneaked further into the room and hid behind one of the sofas. He had just ducked in time when a horn sounded outside which made Redfang look back.

"Leave it!" Butcher ordered. "We need to finish up here."

Redfang nodded and scanned the room to ensure it was empty. With a snort he returned his gaze to what Amazon was doing.

"After so long, Dark Snake will finally have what she's been waiting for," Butcher proclaimed.

"Armed with these weapons of lore we'll be unstoppable in our mission," Amazon agreed.

All the moulds were filled apart from the one awaiting Mary Reed's sword.

Butcher handed Amazon the final artefact and watched as she placed it in its hole. Jedrok began to shine as all the pieces clicked into place. The Earth artefacts melted into the monument, one by one their moulds disappeared. When the final artefact was gone the shimmering ceased and the sound of a lock breaking rang out through the hall.

"It's time!" Butcher announced. Just as he stepped forward to open the door there was a shout from the entrance to the building.

"Stop! I can't let you do that!" Annabel yelled, whilst holding a handgun in two hands. Her arms were shaking which meant that any potential shot would be inaccurate with the vibrating barrel.

"Here to shoot me again, you little roach?" Butcher barked angrily.

Amazon proceeded to draw her bow but Redfang stopped her. "No," he growled, "this one's mine."

George popped up from his cover and tried to help his friend. "Leave her alone."

Redfang paid the request no mind and continued marching towards the girl with his long black coat tailing behind him.

Annabel tried to shoot but her aim was off and the bullet hit a bottle behind Scott's bar.

Redfang kept walking towards his target.

When Annabel went to pull the trigger for the second time, Redfang was on her. He slapped the gun from her hand and sent it skidding across the floor.

"Help me!" she screamed at George, but he was paralysed with fear. "Please... help me."

George could only watch as his friend was lifted from the ground and hoisted over Redfang's shoulder to take her back towards Jedrok.

"What're you doing?" Butcher demanded of his accomplice.

"I like her, she comes with us," Redfang growled.

"Dark Snake said 'no survivors'," Amazon reminded them.

"SHE COMES WITH US!" Redfang affirmed whilst putting a hand on his weapon, a long, curved dagger inlaid with a silver pack of wolves hunting a deer.

"Is that a threat?" Amazon moved to square up to Redfang.

Butcher stepped between the two and, in doing so, stopped the argument in its tracks. Neither of them were going to argue with him. After breaking up the disagreement with his size alone, he turned to Redfang and gave a warning about his new pet. "If she tries anything, I'll rip her insides out of her mouth myself." Then he moved his attention to Jedrok and wrapped his paw-like hand round the door.

Grunting, he pulled the door open and revealed its contents.

"There'll be no stopping us now," he chuckled whilst gazing at the legendary weapons.

Redfang put Annabel down but kept hold of her with one hand whilst he gazed at the mythical objects.

George was still unable to move; he had completely departed from any bravery he once possessed. At the most unfortunate time he was learning that wanting to be a hero was very different to actually being one. None of the books or films he desperately wished to be part of informed him of the organ-twisting fear that came with facing evil. Too afraid to act, he could only watch as a tear of helplessness fell feebly from his eye. The more Annabel screamed for him to help, the deeper the paralysis rooted itself in his body. Outside there was cheering but inside the situation was dire.

Butcher reached into Jedrok and withdrew his arm with his hand clasped firmly around Stormsbane, the famous sword from Moanatenger. He pointed the blade to the sky as he raised his arm in victory and smiled an ugly smile. The joy disappeared as quickly as it had come, however – when the sword began to glow in his hand Butcher dropped it in pain. "Hot!" he spat. The inside of the monument was radiating the sheerest light while all the legendary items became red-hot.

"What's happening?" Amazon panicked. It wasn't long before she got her answer.

Horatio Petrov's voice boomed from the vault:

The weapons you seek are not yours to be had.
In order to claim them you must prove you're not bad.
The power you'd have is too much to bear.
Return to Sanctum and you will find them there.
First you must be worthy, possess an old owner's trait.
Until you can show your true intentions, the weapons shall wait.

Then the weapons vanished and a portal opened up within Jedrok.

Butcher felt himself getting dragged in and, unable to hold his ground, he disappeared into the vortex.

Amazon was sucked through next.

Redfang was desperately holding onto Annabel who was trying to cling onto the sofa.

George finally snapped out of his trance with the intimidating Butcher no longer in the room. He leapt into action to try to grab Annabel, but her grip left the sofa and she stumbled back in Redfang's arms. The villainous masked man was about to drag Annabel into the vortex with him when Barbara came sprinting into the room.

"You can't take her away again," she panted as she ran to Annabel's aid.

"Wow, she's fast for her size," was all that Redfang managed before Barbara crashed into him and sent Annabel flying to the floor. The collision took both Barbara and Redfang through the portal which closed seconds after they disappeared.

"Barbara!" Annabel cried whilst hitting the monument. She withdrew her hand quickly as the rock was hot despite its traditional lack of conduction.

"I think we should run," George told her.

"Why didn't you help me?" Annabel was furious with the cowardice of her friend.

Without answer, George grabbed her by the arm and pulled her behind him. "It's going to blow!" he yelled as they ran out of the building. They only just escaped in time before Jedrok exploded and sent the whole building up in flames.

Annabel rose to her feet without thanks and stormed away from her friend to check if Rosie was OK. She found her with Alex, nursing each other's wounds. They were shaken but both relatively unharmed bar a few deep cuts and bruises.

Presley stood over George on the floor and asked what happened.

Still trembling from the confrontation with the war chiefs and the explosion ringing in his ears, George explained the whole thing.

Presley's eyes lit up at the news of Horatio's message; previously he had been left bamboozled as to why the legendary whip he was wielding in battle had suddenly disappeared. Then he fell to one knee when he heard of Barbara's sacrifice to save Annabel.

George asked what happened outside and inquired about the horn.

Presley informed him how Carlton arrived with Alessia from

Liberterra along with a small group of warriors. "The battle would've been lost without their intervention." He accepted with relief and frustration that his own efforts would have been futile.

"Where's Carlton now?" George asked, excited to see the guardian he had sorely missed.

"He's with Cheik," Presley answered, saddened. "George, it doesn't look good," he warned, before pointing in the direction the two were in. "I suspect he came as only a guide to Oasis. There was no strength left in him after the poison."

A lump formed in George's throat. Expecting the worst, he went to find his friend. When he reached the scene he found Carlton was in worse shape than when he had last seen him.

Cheikhou was trying to hold back his tears over his dying guardian and friend.

"You're going to be OK," Cheikhou told him.

From what George could see, that was a lie.

"He was protecting me," Cheikhou told George. "My bloody arm failed me and I couldn't lift my sword. I was helpless and Carlton protected me. I let you down, man," Cheikhou whispered to Carlton.

The mortally wounded guardian blinked his bloodshot eyes. Tears were falling down his cheeks. "I'm s-so proud o-of you, C-cheik," he managed through fits of coughs.

George guessed one of his lungs was punctured before noticing the blood leaking out beneath him.

"You're b-brave, strong, c-clever and p-passionate, Cheik. You're like a s-son to me and I l-l-love y-you." Carlton coughed and spat out some blood.

"Don't speak like that. You're going to be fine. Don't start with these final speeches," Cheikhou pleaded.

The shake of Carlton's head broke Cheikhou's heart. He was clearly suffering just to prolong his life for his protégé. "F-felix," he managed to say through a weakened voice. "F-felix," he repeated with a grimace.

"No, come on, man. No, you're not going to…"

Carlton stopped Cheikhou from speaking with a shaky hand on his arm. "Please... Fe-lix," he begged.

"What's he saying?" George asked. "Felix?"

"It was the name of a lion on the reserve back in Africa." Cheikhou could no longer hold back the tears as he struggled to pick up his sword with his weak arm. "One day we found him on the side of the road, his paws removed by trophy hunters and bullet wounds all along his back. He was bleeding to death." Cheikhou managed to raise his weapon having been given strength by his memory with Carlton. "Felix was the king of the Savannah and didn't deserve to die suffering, so we humanely helped him find peace. We ended it before the hyenas could rip him to shreds and the vultures could peck out his eyes." Cheikhou's tears were dropping onto his guardian's body before he plunged the claymore into his friend's heart.

"Thank you-u," Carlton exhaled as his final breath.

They buried Carlton next to Yuanli so the two friends could rest together and make the journey to the afterlife hand in hand. Two brave souls had left their group, but the mission must continue.

"We leave for Sanctum tonight," Presley ordered after the burial. He told everyone the fate that befell Barbara along with what George had informed him about the message left by Horatio.

Under the darkness of night as well as their loss, they set off for the portal to Sanctum, hoping they could stop the same darkness engulfing the people there, too.

They were only a short drive from the location but there was still time enough for Alex and Cheikhou to patch up their differences for good.

Alex reached into his pocket and pulled out the 'Player of the day' medal from paintballing that seemed like an eternity ago.

"This is yours," he said as he pressed it into Cheikhou's hands.

"No," Cheikhou said, shaking his head, "I've been a dick to you. Granted, you've been a complete asshole this whole time, but you proved your merit back there. You saved me, remember."

"I wasn't going to mention that," Alex laughed.

"Yeah, right!" Cheikhou managed a smile despite his mourning. He threw the medal back to Alex.

The Jeeps pulled up at the bottom of a sandy hill dotted sparsely with small green shrubs. The morning light was beginning to illuminate their surroundings, but the sky remained black with clouds. Atop the hill was a small building that they all made their way towards.

"'Meteor crater'," George read out when they arrived outside.

Annabel ignored him and began to talk to Rosie.

Roy input the door code and they walked inside. It was like a museum with boards explaining different aspects of meteors and the site they were at. In the centre of the room was a large black rock labelled 'Meteor fragment'.

"I tried to get that for my antiquities store," Roy told Cheikhou, "but they wouldn't part with it."

"WOW!" Alex suddenly exclaimed whilst looking out the window.

George joined him at the glass and saw the breathtaking view of the largest hole in the ground he had ever seen.

"Wouldn't want to fall in there," George commented, squirming at the thought. "Where's the portal, then?"

Roy simply pointed.

George gulped audibly and Cheikhou's booming laugh echoed around the building.

George was kissing the ground at the base of the crater when he finally reached it, and he wasn't the only one to be grateful the descent down the treacherous rocky sides was over. Even Alex who loved heights had jelly-like legs by the time he reached the bottom.

Roy marched over to the six foot manikin of an astronaut placed at the bottom of the crater for tourists to see the scale of the hole. The spaceman looked like an ant from the rim but was now much taller than Roy, even with his spiky green hair. Next to the astronaut was sited an American flag planted in the ground. Roy pushed the flag downwards and there was a small rumble. Next thing George knew, a section of the ground parted to reveal a portal very similar to the one that Butcher and his cronies disappeared into. The main difference was that it appeared much brighter on the other side as opposed to the dark and mysterious location Tombstone returned to.

"Well, they don't have a secret elevator," Cheikhou said to Roy. "I still think our British branch was cooler."

Roy laughed, remembering their exchange after watching the plane transform back in England.

Alessia's soldiers that survived the fight with the screamers jumped into the vortex which they had come from earlier in the night.

"We'll go on ahead and prepare for your arrival," Alessia nodded before following her warriors.

Presley stood aside the portal. "We've finished our journey on Earth. Your training has been cut short, but with time running out and the weapons in unknown locations, we must now go to Sanctum and liberate its people. We've already seen the breakdown of life beginning on this planet with Gaia removed from its rightful place. It's now up to us few to save the fate of everyone. There'll be no turning back once you enter the portal, so only do so if you think yourself capable of continuing. Good luck and thank you," Presley finished before leaping through the portal.

"Him and his speeches," Roy muttered as he followed suit.

"For Carlton!" Cheikhou shouted before taking the plunge.

"Yuanli will not have died for nothing," Rosie said determinedly.

"Wait for me!" Alex yelled, chasing his love into the portal.

"I'm not staying with you," Annabel told George.

"I hear they have great alcohol in Barren Valley," Scott said smiling before jumping in.

George was left alone standing in the middle of a meteor crater in a foreign country. He hoped his parents would have been proud of him if they had been able to remember who he was. George looked up as he felt something hit his head, then another cold stone rebounded off his shoulders. Soon he was getting pelted with hailstones in the middle of the desert. Gaia needed to be put back in its rightful place, Earth was falling apart.

"Here goes nothing," he said to himself.

EPILOGUE

Earth
Wyoming
State swimming competitions

"What an incredible finish. Phillip Farmer, with a narrow victory in the boys' under twelve race, coming from behind to take the gold. Up next is the girls' under twelve race commencing in three minutes' time."

Chloe stopped listening to the commentator over the speaker and looked up at her father. Her short blonde hair that normally hung to her shoulders was tucked into a moss green swimming cap.

"I can't do this," she whimpered.

"It's just nerves," her father said smiling down to her. Crouching so he was on her level, he looked into her green eyes and held her shoulders. "You're the best swimmer I know. No matter what happens, you'll always be my inspiration. So, just go out there and try your best. Most importantly, enjoy it." A tear trickled down her father's face as his pride in his daughter was mixed with the sadness of looking into those bright green eyes that her mother had given her. "She would've been so proud of you," he sobbed.

"Dad… Don't, you'll start me off. I'm about to compete," Chloe said, hugging her father tight.

"*Can the swimmers please take their positions on the start line.*"

Chloe let go of her father and bravely marched over to the edge of the pool. Looking left and right, she saw that she was the youngest to be racing. Most of the other girls were nearer the upper limit of twelve. Chloe knew that with her father's support and her mother by her side always, she could overcome any challenge. Gazing out across the swimming lanes, the lengths looked like they stretched for miles; she felt like a goldfish challenged with swimming the Atlantic Ocean. Chloe took a deep breath and all sound faded to silence as she awaited the gunshot. *BANG!*

"And we're off. This should be an interesting race with returning champion Pippa Salmon in the far left lane. Beside her and already falling behind, is Laura Jarvis, a regular to the race that's yet to win any prestige. In the middle lane is newcomer Chloe Bennet who's managing to hold her own despite being the youngest to have ever competed in the state championship. As we can see, though, she'll have to be fast to catch Pippa who's already taking a convincing lead. Next to Chloe is Tia Delaney and in the far right is Harriet Knewell. The technique being shown by Pippa is sublime. The way she cuts through water really pays homage to her surname. Again, though, I have to compliment Chloe on her unbelievable ability to not only keep up with those older than her but be beating most of them as well. Pippa is the first to turn around for the return leg but there's Chloe just behind. This is looking like a two-horse race at this rate with Harriet in third, only just turning round now. Back to the leaders, I can't believe what I'm seeing here. It appears that Chloe is making up ground on the reigning champion. It's going to be tight... My God, look at that burst of speed. She's a girl possessed. She's going to do it. It's Chloe. Chloe in the lead and WOW, she's taken the gold. Nice touch from Pippa who, as soon as she reached the end, turned to congratulate her young rival. Humble in defeat, Pippa really is an ambassador for any young girls looking to get into the sport. Oh, but look how much it means to Chloe in the middle lane. Tears pouring down her face. Her father's pulled her from the pool. Beautiful."

"You did it! You did it!" Chloe's father kept shouting into her ear.

Chloe was in a shell-shocked state. The sounds of cheering and the commentator were blurry as she hugged her father.

"You need to go to the podium; go get your medal." Chloe was pushed away by her father who immediately turned to tell all those around him that she was his daughter.

Chloe took her place on the podium and was presented with her medal by Michael Phelps, the special guest for the day. Chloe was starstruck as one of her idols congratulated her on her success and then moved on to hand out the silver and bronze medals that went to Pippa and Tia respectively. A small man with a weak hairline and big glasses waddled over to Chloe atop the podium.

"What have you got to say about your shock win?" he asked in a nasally voice with a microphone outstretched.

"I wouldn't have been able to do it without my father's constant help and unbelievable strength in the wake of my mother's recent death. I owe a lot to you, however, I want to dedicate this win to a hero who should have still been here today. A man who put others before himself and paid for it in the end with his life. I dedicate this win to Deacon, a proud former member of the firefighters here in Wyoming, the man who saved my life."

"Spoken like a woman beyond your years," the small man said, congratulating her a final time.

Applause rang out from the crowd which began by Pat who had brought Bennie with her to see Chloe perform. The owners of Bennie had been struggling to give him the care he needed so they recently decided to give the golden retriever to the elderly lady with which it had formed such a bond. They now went everywhere together.

Pat walked over to the young girl with Bennie to congratulate her on her achievement. "Gary!" she called in her feeble voice, trying to get Chloe's father's attention. "Gary!" she repeated, a little louder. Her weak voice wasn't strong enough to be heard over the commentator talking about the next race and the general bumble of activity.

Bennie noticed his owner struggling and started to woof so Gary would hear. The hound's aid worked and, moments later, the tall, grey-haired man was hugging Pat and stroking Bennie.

"Well done," the elderly lady grinned to Chloe, "Deacon would've been very pr–" She was cut short by the sound of an almighty explosion. Less than a second later the ground shook uncontrollably. The water in the pool was displaced and the commentator fell from his seat up high. Screams and shouts erupted around the pool, only to be drowned out by a further three explosions making huge ground tremors.

Gary hugged Chloe tight to him and put a hand on Pat's shoulder who was trying to calm Bennie down and stop him howling.

"Have mercy on us all," Gary whispered to himself as he looked left and spotted a great thick cloud of smoke enveloping the sky before blocking out the sun and plunging Wyoming into darkness.

ABOUT THE AUTHOR

Damien Ellis is a self-published author from Colchester, England. While he currently works as a baker, his focus has shifted from 'proving' bread to proving himself in the self-publishing industry. Throughout his education, he displayed a profound interest in environmental studies, through which he discovered both the intricate beauty of the planet and the diverse flora and fauna that inhabit it. The challenges posed by climate change and habitat destruction are particularly close to Damien's heart. He leverages his books to raise awareness, skillfully bringing these issues to the forefront within fictional settings that are both enlightening and captivating. During his leisure time, Damien is not only an avid board gamer but also finds enjoyment in watching professional wrestling.

Printed in Great Britain
by Amazon

28204922R10179